THE LUMBERMILL

LAYA V. SMITH

Black Rose Writing | Texas

ISBN: 978-1-68433-528-2
PUBLISHED BY BLACK ROSE WRITING
www.blackrosewriting.com

Printed in the United States of America
Suggested Retail Price (SRP) $20.95

The Lumbermill is printed in Chaparral Pro

*As a planet-friendly publisher, Black Rose Writing does its best to eliminate unnecessary waste to reduce paper usage and energy costs, while never compromising the reading experience. As a result, the final word count vs. page count may not meet common expectations.

For George, who never let me give up.

THE LUMBERMILL

"I tread with care in matters of life and death. If it is given me to save a life, all thanks. But it may also be within my power to take a life; this awesome responsibility must be faced with great humbleness and awareness of my own frailty. Above all, I must not play at God."

~Hippocratic Oath

CHAPTER ONE

Greater Los Angeles, 1954

The body of a woman lay sprawled in the road. Augy's hands shook on the steering wheel. White knuckles. The smell of burnt rubber. A single smoky headlight bored into the darkness.

He slammed his shoulder against the rusted door of the old 1941 Ford pickup and scrambled out of the cab. The woman's eyes were closed, limbs splayed. Motionless. He knelt at her side and touched her matted, wet hair with trembling fingers.

Blood. A thousand nightmares flooded his mind. Not his usual companions—sinister visions of the distant past. These were horrible premonitions of a future behind bars, a hated pariah of society.

A murderer.

"Come on. Wake up." He slapped her face lightly. "What's the matter with you darting into the road in the middle of the night? Didn't you see my headlights? For crying out loud…"

He should've seen her in time to swerve. He'd driven the abandoned road through the mountain pass so many times that white-line fever was the norm. Thick forest surrounded the road, and there wasn't a house for miles. It was past midnight, a dim moon hiding behind gray clouds in the black sky. But none of that was an excuse. He should've seen her.

"Please wake up," he said, frightened by the tremor in his own voice. He reached his hand towards her neck to check her pulse.

She moaned, and a wave of relief crashed over him.

"Oh, thank Christ." He yanked a handkerchief out of his pocket and folded it over to make a bandage for her head. "Stay with me. I'm gonna get you help. You're gonna be okay."

He had to get her to a hospital, but there was nowhere nearby to call an ambulance. He'd have to drive her into the city.

The unmistakable crack of gunfire split the night, echoing down the canyon. Augy froze, his eyes scanning the darkness.

A man stumbled onto the road, cloaked in shadow but for the shine of gunmetal. He fed another round into his bolt-action rifle and leveled the barrel. "Step away from the girl."

The voice was deep and gravelly. A southern accent.

"It was an accident." Augy stood and put up his hands. "We need to get her to a hospital."

Without warning, the man fired. The Ford's passenger window cracked.

"What the hell are you doing?" Augy ducked around the side of the truck as another blast cut the night.

It crossed his mind to dive into the cab and drive away, but a painful twinge in his gut stopped him. He peeked over the hood of the truck. The woman moaned in pain, writhing on the ground. The man reloaded his rifle and stepped into the headlights. He was profoundly ugly, as if a preschooler had molded his face out of clay. The woman pushed up on her hands and knees, but the man dropped his heavy boot on her back, knocking her into the asphalt.

Had she been running from this maniac?

Augy yanked the Colt Government out of his jacket pocket. "All right, handsome," he called, unlocking the thumb safety. "You've got three seconds to drop the gun and step away from the woman before I use your nuts for target practice... One."

Augy took a slow deep breath and rolled his shoulders. "Two."

He glanced over the hood. The man brought the rifle sight to eye-level.

"Fuck this." Augy leaned around the side of the car and fired.

Blood exploded from the man's hip. He didn't go down, but growled and limped towards the forest for cover. Augy shoved the gun in his pocket and raced into the road. He snatched up the woman and threw her over one shoulder. Another shot rang out. Pain exploded in his thigh like he'd been hit by a stray fastball. His knee buckled and he fell against the driver's side door. He yanked it open, pushed the woman inside and climbed in after her.

A shot slammed into the back windshield, cracking it down the middle. Augy threw the truck in gear, slammed his foot on the gas pedal, and sped off into the night.

When they rounded a bend, Augy patted the spot where he'd been shot. There was no blood on his pants, no harsh bite of a bullet hole. But the shot had hit him dead-on.

"What the hell?"

Beside him, the woman moaned in pain. He flicked on the dome-light and looked her up and down. Long black hair hung in limp strings around her shoulders. She wore black dress pants and a ripped white blouse. Thin cuts laced her skin as if she'd fallen into a rose bush. Her bare feet were bloody.

They hit a bump. Augy braced himself against the wheel, but the woman was thrown forward. Her forehead hit the dash, splattering droplets of blood across the cracked leather. As if suddenly snapped out of a deep sleep, she whipped a knife out of her pocket, lunged across the seat, and pressed it to his throat.

"Who you are?" she hissed.

"Settle down." He tightened the muscles in his back and throat, trying to keep himself from being bounced around by the truck's lousy shocks.

"Tell me now or I cut your throat." Her accent sounded Russian.

"Talk about ungrateful." He reached in front of her and shifted gears. "I just got shot trying to get you away from that psychopath."

She snorted. "You hit me with car!"

"You ran into the road out of nowhere!" Augy paused and took a slow, deep breath. "Why don't you put the knife down, huh? If I hit a pothole, this could get messy."

"Who you work for?"

"I don't feel very conversational with a knife to my throat."

"You work for her?"

"Her who?"

Her face relaxed, thoughts working behind her eyes. Golden. Gorgeous. She lowered the knife.

She was in her mid-thirties. But for a few crows' feet, her features were sculpted as if from marble—thick black eyebrows, a hard cleft chin, pouty lips with a sharp cupid's bow. Half-moons of old makeup darkened her under-eyes as blood dripped down one side of her face.

"We need to get you to the hospital," said Augy. He pushed in the cigarette lighter and grabbed his pack from off the dashboard.

"No hospital." The woman threatened the blade again, but he could tell she was dizzy as she tried to slow her breathing.

"You left a lot of blood back there on that road," he said.

"Shut up."

"You're leaving a lot on my seats."

"Shut up, I said. Drive."

"Where?"

"Away. Do not stop."

She leaned back against the headrest. Her hands were shaking, her skin sickly pale. It wouldn't have taken much to overcome her, even without the gun in his pocket, but her eyes were already drooping. There was no point.

She curled up in the seat, knees hugged against her chest. It had been years since he'd seen somebody pass out in a fetal position. She looked phenomenally uncomfortable, but even in sleep, she had an instinct to protect her torso.

How could he have hit her? The embarrassment of it was almost worse than the guilt. He had been a fighter pilot. Quick reflexes were half his resume.

It was his sister's fault, he decided. Her and her incessant badgering, her smug moralizing. She'd gotten into his head. When she'd invited him over that night she hadn't warned him he was walking into a suburban nightmare of a dinner party. Or worse, that she was trying to set him up with one of her damn church friends.

It was his punishment for daring to ask for another favor.

The cigarette between his lips was growing moist. He lit it and ripped off his raincoat. Underneath was a collarless shirt with yellow stains at the pits. The only shirt he owned anymore.

If his sister ever found out he was homeless, she'd insist he move in with her, but spending even twenty minutes with Mary's husband—sensible, well-diversified, irrepressibly smug Harry Stern—was like submitting to dental torture. Harry had made plenty of money off the war in stocks, bonds, and all manner of financial this and that, of which Augy had at best a superficial understanding. He knew '50 was a bull market because Harry had bought a Cadillac. Harry bought two more Cadillacs in '52 and one more last year. Truth was, the only thing Harry loved more than buying Cadillacs was talking about buying Cadillacs. And Augy had wrecked one of Harry's Cadillacs.

Swallowing his pride to ask to borrow this piece of shit old Ford had nearly destroyed him. Augy had promised he wouldn't let anything happen to it, that he would bring it back in shipshape. Now, half the windows were cracked, and the cab was covered in blood.

Mary was either going to disown him or lecture him to death. He couldn't decide which would be worse.

His gaze shifted back to the injured woman. The makeshift bloody bandage on her head had started to dry out. Augy took it as a sign she'd stopped bleeding. Her clothes were torn to shreds. She was shivering.

He laid his coat over her and pulled to the side of the road to pry the blade out of her hand—a combat knife with a leather-wrapped grip and seven-inch-long serrated blade. He was about to pull back onto the road when he noticed a mark on her shoulder under tangled black hair. When he pushed it aside, he saw inch-high letters and numbers burned into her skin: *Property of Countess London, 13851677.*

He read it again and again. Memorized it.

Getting back on the road, he made a beeline for Irvine, the nearest suburb. He came upon a police station and decided to pull in, especially since he had no idea where the nearest hospital was. Augy parked in the lot and stepped out into the cool night.

Before going into the sheriff's office, he circled the truck to examine the crack in the back windshield. The size of the slugs that man had fired should've obliterated it, but the bullet had lodged itself in the laminated glass. He used the woman's knife to pry it out, which made an odd squeaking sound.

"Cork?" He rolled it between his fingers. No wonder the shot hadn't broken his skin, though he felt sure it had left a bruise the size of a dinner plate. "What the hell?"

Augy took the bullet with him and limped into the sheriff's office. The desk was empty. A silver bell beckoned.

A moment later, a bristly old cowboy type emerged from the back, pulling a tan Stetson over his pock-marked bald head. Red lines covered his face. He yawned. "Evening, sir. Is there a problem?"

"Sorry to wake you, Sheriff." Augy cocked an eyebrow. "There's a woman outside needs an ambulance, and I need to report an assault."

"Assault? What happened?"

"What part of I need an ambulance...?" Augy shook his head. "Ambulance now, interview later."

Leaving the sheriff to make the call, he went outside to check on the woman. The moment he stepped into the lot, he knew what had happened.

How could he have been stupid enough to leave the keys in the ignition?

CHAPTER TWO

"You sure it said *Countess London*?" asked Officer Robby Moretti, shoveling rice into his mouth with chopsticks.

"I'll never forget it." Augy moved noodles around on his plate. He always got noodles at Chinese restaurants. After spending three years living off nothing but rice, pickles, and seaweed, even watching somebody eat rice made him sick, but he'd never tell Moretti that.

"Well, there's no countesses in Los Angeles," said Moretti.

"It's an alias, genius."

"I sent out some feelers, but I wouldn't expect much."

"How can somebody who brands people with hot irons not be on the police's radar?"

"It's a big city, getting bigger all the time. And if this girl was Russian, she's probably part of some criminal organization. West Hollywood is crawling with them nowadays."

"I work West Hollywood all the time, Moretti." Augy sneered. "Granted there's no shortage of pimping, gambling, and human suffering, but what self-respecting Russian sadist would brand a girl in English, huh?"

Moretti shrugged. He had beefy cheeks, big brown eyes with long feminine lashes, and a dimple in his chin like someone had stabbed him with a ballpoint pen. "You're driving yourself nuts with this, Smalls. You've done everything you could be expected to do and then some. You're gonna have to let it go. You're never getting that truck back."

"You think I give two shits about the truck? The woman, she was scared. Like she'd just broke out of the joint or something. And that man had cork bullets in his gun. What the hell would those be for?"

"Crowd control. They're technically non-lethal, but they'd leave one hell of a welt."

"You're telling me." Augy rubbed the huge purple bruise on his thigh.

Moretti shook his head. "How'd Mary take the loss?"

"She disinvited me to her daughter's birthday party."

"What do you care?"

"You don't get it." Augy stewed but didn't say anything more.

"She'll get over it. She always does." Finishing off his root beer, the five-foot-six baby-faced cop belched. "I've got to get back on my beat." He placed his coffee-cream fedora on the front half of his head and tipped it over one eye. Augy wanted to snort derisively, but he lacked the energy to belittle his ever-so-fashionable friend today. Moretti dropped a five on the table, enough to cover the entire bill and then some. Augy stared at it, but before he had a chance to argue, Moretti said, "I owe you for the shoe rental last time we went bowling."

"That cost what? A dime?" Augy took two dollars and forty cents from his pocket and stood to press them into Moretti's hand. "Now we're even."

Moretti sighed. He tapped Augy on the shoulder before sauntering out of the restaurant. Augy sat back down to finish his beer and watch brightly colored fish swim in the big saltwater aquarium. He noticed Moretti had left his cigarettes on the table, and though he was suspicious his old friend had done it on purpose, he took them. He'd buy him a new pack next time he saw him.

Augy closed the manila folder in front of him. *Countess London* was printed on the label. He didn't bother the cost of stationery for the types of jobs he was doing now, so this was the only case file he had. He'd called around Cohen Dale and another neighboring town, but nobody knew anything about the woman or the good-looking gunman. He kept records of the interviews anyway in case something jumped out at him later. To this, he added the few scraps of useless paper Moretti had provided. He would've put the file in his old leather bag, but the Russian woman with the branded shoulder had stolen that along with the truck. So, he shoved it up under his arm.

He'd lost his agency almost a year ago and had been homeless for months, but the night Mary's truck got stolen was the final straw. He'd avoided sleeping under an overpass with the rest of the bums only by borrowing cars from his sister and parking in an abandoned lot at night. Getting Mary to loan him the Ford after what had happened to the Cadillac had taken wheeling and dealing worthy of P. T. Barnum. Augy had nothing left.

After he'd filed reports about the gunfight and the woman and the grand theft auto with the Irvine police, the sheriff offered him a lift home. It took everything Augy had not to laugh in his face.

In the end, Augy accepted. He had the sheriff drive him to West Hollywood and drop him off in front of his old office on Sunset Boulevard, not far from Little Armenia. A foreclosed sign hung on the door; the windows boarded up. The mantel out front still read: *Small Detective Agency*.

"You sure this is the place?" the weather-beaten cowboy had asked, twitching his mustache in contempt.

Augy tapped the roof of the car like a cab and the cruiser drove off. He jogged up the front steps. When he'd come by a few months earlier, a steel hatch had been installed to hold the door closed. Now, the only evidence of it was splintered wood. He touched the knob, and the door creaked open.

All the furniture was gone: the davenport at which his chubby hardnosed secretary had once sat, the stiff-backed waiting room chairs. The wiring had been stripped from the walls, some waxed floorboards ripped up. The frosted glass window in the door to his office proper was cracked, but the etching was still clear: *August Small, PI*.

From the smell, he guessed vagrants had been sleeping there. It made him want to cry, but all the same, he figured if any stinky old tramp was going to squat in Detective Small's office, it was going to be Detective Small himself. He jammed the door shut with a loose floorboard and hunkered down for the night.

The next morning, he took the foreclosed sign off the door, flipped it over and wrote on the back: *Gone Out of Business Special! All detective services 50 cents per day! No job too small for Small!* Since then he'd found a missing doll for a little girl, caught two school-aged bicycle thieves, and helped a woman collect chickens that had flown the coop—which hadn't involved any detective work at all, just old-fashioned elbow grease. No honest work was beneath him.

After accounting for five bucks in tips, and then subtracting the cost of the jacket he'd been forced to buy to replace the one the woman stole, and further subtracting the meal he'd just treated himself to, Augy had three dollars and eighty-five cents left. His rates had dropped more than a thousand percent in less than a year, but he was still in business. Somewhere far in the distance, Augy discerned a faint glimmer of hope.

He jogged back to the office, his energy renewed by lo mein. Over the last few days, he'd been driving himself crazy remembering the woman he'd hit. Even more than he regretted leaving the keys in the ignition, Augy regretted not having asked her name. It was inexcusably sloppy, never mind some psycho had been shooting at him. Something about her had thrown him off: an implacable fragrance, a familiar feeling. He couldn't stop thinking about it.

Augy turned the corner onto his street, headed for his unofficial office, but froze in place when he noticed the figure sitting on the stoop. Her legs were wrapped in white stockings, feet in tall black heels. She was wearing a knee-length blue skirt, a matching jacket draped across her lap. Her black hair was curled and pinned up under a blue and white hat decorated with feathers. Parked across the street in perfect condition was the Ford. In fact, it had a fresh coat of paint and the back windshield had been replaced.

She didn't notice him right away, so he took a step back into the shadows to watch her. Legs crossed, elbow on her knee, chin rested in her hand, and a cigarette between her fingers held a few inches from her lips. She stretched her neck to suck on it. Almost a minute he watched her, but she never moved from that position. No twitch, no itch, no nervous habit. The city around her moved, but she didn't blink.

Augy sniffed his armpit. A bit pungent, but not too bad, given he hadn't showered in two days. Four or five times a week he went to the YMCA to work out, and more importantly, to shower and wash his clothes. He smelled a far cry from morning dew on freshly mowed grass, but at least he'd staved off the reek of moldy yak piss that seemed to follow a lot of guys in his situation.

He turned the corner and started down the sidewalk towards her. "You've got nerve coming here. I'll give you that."

Expressionless, she unfolded her limbs to stand. She was tall; with the aid of high heels, she could meet his eyes straight, which wasn't something six-foot-three Augy was used to. It made him nervous and oddly titillated. "I have new car."

"So glad I could help you out in your time of need there, miss."

"I see your picture in the papers. You are famous detective, Augustinius Small?"

"Call me Augy."

"You are the man I need."

He tried not to smirk. "Is that why you held a knife to my throat and ran off with my sister's... *er*... why you stole my truck? You're lucky I don't call the cops."

"You will not."

"Don't dare me."

She pushed out her bottom lip, challenging. Augy rolled his eyes. "All right, Miss... what did you say your name was?"

"Yekaterina. You call me Katya."

"Last name?"

"My husband is Tyler."

Augy whipped out his notebook. "Yekaterina? Is that with a Y, or...?"

"Detective, will you not hear what I have to say?"

"I'm all ears," said Augy, wiggling the oversized saucers on either side of his face.

"We go in your office?"

"No offense, gorgeous, but I don't exactly trust you around my belongings." Augy lit another cigarette. Out of sheer instinct, he offered her one. She looked into his eyes before accepting.

"Walk with me?" she asked.

Augy searched for a reason not to, but nothing came. Together they strolled down the sidewalk. Most girls sounded like Shetland ponies when they wore stilettos like hers, but Katya barely tapped the pavement.

"Tell me about Hollisters' case," she said.

"That's what you wanna talk about?"

"I know them, before." She stared at the concrete as they walked. "My boss. They work for her."

"This wouldn't be Countess London, now would it?"

Her lips flexed. "How you find out Hollisters?"

Augy shrugged. He'd been asked that question a thousand times. "I wish I could say I did something brilliant, but it wasn't hard."

"Some papers say you frame them."

"That's right. Me, the DA, and all the kids they killed."

"For what you do, you lose your home, your business. You are the victim now."

Augy shifted. "How do you know that?"

"In my circles, everyone knows."

Augy had never figured out who was pulling the strings behind the scenes to make his life a living hell. Both the Hollisters had been given the electric chair. He figured they must've had connections to organized crime, though he'd never been able to prove it.

He often wondered why he was still alive and if they'd ever put an actual hit out on him. Or were they trying to drive him to do it himself? He thanked god he'd remained their only target, that they hadn't gone after his sister or his ex-wife.

"What happen to DA?" asked Katya.

Augy blinked, dragging himself out of a ravine of self-pity. "He's dead."

"How?"

"It was a car accident. He'd been drinking."

Katya looked up at him with the glint of a challenge in her eye. "Tell me how you catch Hollisters."

"To tell you the truth, it's one of the least impressive cases I've ever worked."

She lifted her eyebrows and waited.

He shrugged. "It was in the papers."

She didn't move. Not even a twitch. She looked like she could've waited for him for the next hundred years.

Augy took a long drag of smoke and sighed it out. "A girl called Betty Roberts showed up at my office. Mousey little thing. Eighteen years old. She was in tears. Told me about this baby she'd had, out of wedlock of course, and this sweet old couple she was paying to look after it. It'd been about a year, but she'd never once been allowed to visit the baby. Earlier that day when she showed up unannounced to try to see her son, she found the Hollisters had moved. The house was abandoned."

"Did she go to police?"

"Sure, but she was a poor black girl, so they wouldn't even let her file a report," Augy replied. "But I advertise down in Bronzeville where she lived, so she found me, and I followed her to the place. Empty. Had been a month at least. Didn't find any evidence of it having been a nursery. No drawings on the walls, no stains on the carpet, no dead patches in the lawn. Now, maybe Mrs. Hollister was one hell of a housekeeper, but there were supposed to have been thirty under-fives in a house with three bedrooms. The whole thing stank, so I took it on.

"I hunted down a number of girls who'd left their kids there," Augy continued. "They all had the same story. Poor girls, illegitimate babies, exorbitant payments, no visitation. And I started to think the worst. I convinced a friend of mine in the K9 unit to bring his basset down for a sniff. Dog found the body in about forty-five seconds. It was an infant. Female. Three months old. It'd been buried down in the basement under the stairs for about a year.

"That put the cops on the case. They figured the evil bastards had smothered the babies the same day they took them in, then went on collecting cash from the mothers." Frowning, he rolled a shoulder. "That's what they eventually confessed to."

Katya pursed her lips. "You do not believe it."

"We only ever found one body. If that's what was going down, what happened to the rest?"

"What you think happened?"

"Doesn't matter. They're dead."

Her lips were still pursed, gaze fixed on the ground. "Is true you hunt down Hollisters, not police?"

"What—are you writing a book?"

"Tell me how you find them."

He took a long drag of his cigarette and furrowed his eyebrows. "It was the dog."

Again, she didn't move, staring at him with those golden eyes and this *are-you-seriously-going-to-make-me-ask-you-again* sort of expression.

"This old bloodhound was always hanging around the crime scene. Fat, stubby little thing. Friendly as all hell. Anyway, I decided to follow him around a bit, and he led me right to them. They were five miles away, trying to set up the same operation."

Augy smiled. He'd given the dog to his nephew as a Christmas present that year. It had rubbed his brother-in-law red to have that sausage of a dog slobbering all over his loafers and digging up his rosebushes.

"I see sign on your office," said Katya. "You cost fifty cents a day, yes?"

He narrowed his eyes. "Why?"

Katya reached into the blue woven handbag hanging from her wrist and took out a bigger wad of money than Augy had ever seen, even in the good days. "I want to hire you," she said and shoved the entire stack into Augy's breast pocket. It barely fit. Based on weight and bulk, he guessed there had to be at least $5,000.

His jaw was already slack by the time Augy thought to drop it. Cold sweat formed on his palms.

"I have you for years now," she said, smiling.

"Where did you get this?" he demanded, yanking the bills out of his pocket.

"Why?"

"I can't accept stolen money."

"All money is stolen." She dismissed him with a wave. "Would not you like to know what happen to other babies?"

Augy opened his mouth and closed it. "How would you know that?"

She arched one dark eyebrow.

The money was hot in his hand. Lace on sweat, singing a seductive song only he could hear. He shook his head. "Mrs. Tyler..."

"Katya."

"Katya, if you really do have the sort of information you say you do, you've gotta go to the police."

"No police."

"I don't have the resources..."

"*No police.* You help me, or no one."

He looked at the money one last time, then held it out to her. "I can't work for you. I won't."

"The Hollisters are dead, but there are more. Many more like them. Like the ones who ruin your business. But you will not help me? Why? Because I pull knife on you? Because I take car? Because my money is stolen?"

"All that, plus you refuse to involve the police."

She laughed and poked him in the chest. Her finger was rock hard, sharp nails painted deep red. "The papers say you are hero, but all I see is coward!"

"You better watch what you say to me, lady."

"Why?" She poked again. "What you do? What coward do?"

"Ow. Quit poking me!"

"I poke you if I want!" She poked him again, then snorted and stepped back. "You are not worth my time." Scoffing, she snatched her money out of his hand. "More will die because you not help me. Women. Children. You will die too, I think."

"What are you talking about?"

Katya pressed her lips together, looking him up and down like a boxer sizing up his opponent. "I am at Hyatt on Sunset Boulevard. If you want work for me, come tomorrow night."

She took a step away and lit a cigarette. She snapped closed the lighter, looked over her shoulder and said, "Hollister was no their real name. They were Klein. Come from Germany after the war."

That detail of the case had never been leaked to the media. He scrutinized her eyes, but they gave nothing away.

"I see you soon," she said.

He watched in silence as she sauntered away. His heart twittered in his chest, breath short. It wasn't until she turned a corner and disappeared from sight, he realized how much he'd been enjoying her perfume. He'd never smelled anything like it. It was like she sweated vanilla.

Augy walked the two blocks back to his office, climbed inside the truck and fired up the engine. The interior had been detailed, the clutch oiled. "Mary's gonna be happy to see you," he said and pulled onto the road.

"No chance I'll work for that woman," he said, shaking his head. "Not a chance."

CHAPTER THREE

Ever since he'd hit Katya, Augy had wanted to return to the scene of the crime, but getting up to an isolated mountain road is difficult when you've got no car and even less cash. The prospect of finally learning the truth of what had happened to the Hollisters' fosters was intoxicating, let alone that sweaty wad of money she'd offered. But he didn't trust Katya as far as he could spit, so before he signed up for her team, he needed more information.

First, he needed to show Mary the truck. Given what great condition it was in, he was confident he could convince her to let him hold onto it. But as Augy pulled up to her house and saw all the shiny cars parked along the street, he had a horrible realization. Today was Monday, the sixth of the month: baby Carol's birthday party. Technically, he wasn't invited anymore, which had been both a relief and an injury. He hated disappointing his sister. He hated it almost as much as the things he had to do to keep from disappointing her.

Augy had a hard time dealing with Mary's flock of Presbyterian housewives on the best of days—not to mention Harry's kettle of chicken hawks—and with everything Katya had said swirling around in his brain, the scenario seemed comical.

His nephew Murphy sat splay-legged on the lawn; his obese canine companion flopped at his side. Augy whistled and tapped the side of the truck to get the boy's attention. Murphy's gaze lifted, his tongue peeking out one corner of his lips.

"How's it hanging, Murph?" asked Augy.

"I found a potato, so I put it on the radio."

"Atta boy." Sighing, Augy readjusted his hat to block out heavy orange sunbeams. The rays of the six o'clock sun were hotter than a ten-cent pistol.

"I need you to tell your mother something for me, all right? Tell her I found the truck and I'll call her later tonight."

Murphy didn't respond. Barely even twitched.

"Say it back to me, son. Uncle Augy found the truck and…"

The door to the house opened. Tennessee Waltz thrummed so loud the grass quivered to the tune. A river of men filtered out, his brother-in-law its headwaters.

Cursing, Augy tucked his chin and put the car in gear. He was about to bolt away when Harry called after him. "Is that you, Augs? Get over here you good-for-nothing, wise-guy, son of a bitch!"

Augy sucked a breath between his teeth. Harry was in a better mood than usual. With the heavy trudge of a man being led to the block, Augy stepped out of the truck and approached the gathering of men in smart suits with bushy mustaches. Augy had never been the sort for a mustache or a smart suit, even when he could've afforded them.

"Well, I'll be goddamned," said Harry. His bright red skin sweated with alcohol as he looked the truck up and down. "You found it."

Augy gave a thumbs up and showed his prototypical shit-eating grin. "Course I did."

"Is this the brother-in-law you've been telling me about?" said one of Harry's buddies, this one with a giant head, a golden mustache, and a shiny pocket watch chain. He clapped a meaty hand onto Augy's shoulder. "Harry tells me you're a detective. Is that right, big ears?"

Augy rolled out from under the oppressive, hot fingers. "That's right, fathead."

The man laughed. Augy lit a cigarette and tightened his jaw. Harry slung his arm over Augy's shoulders and led him away from the group. Why were finance guys always so handsy? It's like they all imagined themselves as all-star baseball players, slapping each other's butts for good luck.

Augy didn't care for baseball. Or finance. Or being touched, at least not by Harry.

"Listen, Augs. I'm glad you're here," said Harry. "I've been meaning to talk to you. Over these last few months, what with the Caddy, and the Ford, and the wife talking my ear off about the this and the that you've been doing, I've been about ready to strangle you."

"I'm sorry about the Cadillac, Harry. But I swear I will pay you back. And I found the Ford."

"You did good, kid."

"Kid?"

"But my question is why you gotta be borrowing our cars in the first place?"

"You know this. Mine got stolen, and the insurance…"

"You don't have to lie, Augs. I know what *really* happened to your car, and it's water under the bridge."

Augy narrowed his eyes. "What are you talking about?"

"I think it's swell you managed to scrape by with your *detective agency* for so long, but in the new economy I don't think there's going to be much of a market for that kind of thing."

"Uh-huh."

"Nobody cares about crime anymore. A land of rules and laws—that's all in the past. The future is gonna be a wild place, a dog-eat-dog economy, and in the end, only the big dogs are gonna survive."

"Uh-huh."

Harry chuckled and chewed on his stinky cigar. "There might be a place for a guy like you—an observant guy. A curious guy. A guy who doesn't mind getting a little dirty. You might have a place in the economy of the future, but only if you act now."

"Are you trying to sell me a bridge in Brooklyn?"

"Funny. No. What I'm saying is, you're almost forty and it's about time you got yourself a real job."

"Thirty-four is not almost forty. Where did you learn math?"

"I know somebody—my broker, Charlie. As a matter of fact, you two just met…"

"Fathead?"

"You're a real card, Augs." Harry chuckled again, throatier. "He's been looking for a man with your sort of qualifications to help him *scope out the market* if you know what I mean. I told him you'd be interested."

"Why in god's name would you do that?"

Harry wrinkled his nose. "I gotta say, Augs, I expected you to be a bit more appreciative."

"I bet you did." Augy shrugged off Harry's hand.

"Now don't rattle your cage. It's a great opportunity. You could be making six figures by the end of the year. Honest."

"Spying on businesses to help your fat friend time his shark attacks? I'd rather shine shoes." Disgusted, Augy marched away.

Stunned Harry called after him, "If that's the way you're going to be when I try to help you, don't come crying to my wife the next time you need a handout!"

"Go to hell, Harry." Augy slammed the gate and marched into the road. He'd been hoping to keep the truck, but now Augy had no intention of ever asking Mary and her husband for a favor ever again. He'd walk back to the city to avoid having to listen to Harry chuckle or smell his filthy cigar.

It was better to not owe nobody nothing. Besides, there was five grand waiting for him at a Hyatt on Sunset Boulevard.

It was about seven o'clock, the sunlight and heat still thick in the dry air, when he reached the top of a small hill and saw tire tracks where the Ford had spun out that night. He found a splash of Katya's dried blood on the pavement, brown and flakey.

Augy stepped off the road into the bushes and tried to determine from where she'd emerged. A blanket of trees stretched in both directions, with no discernable paths through. He found no footprint impressions in the leaf-packed forest floor but read evidence of movement in the breakage pattern of the delicate underbrush. He found a strip of white fabric tinged with blood on a thorny bush. Katya's shirt, her blood. He followed the trail.

The sun sagged below the horizon. Crickets, bats, frogs, and other chirping creatures commenced their chorus. No matter what he did now, he'd be walking most of the night. In the dark. Picking his way through a jungle.

Forest. California doesn't have jungles. But for a moment there, he could've sworn he'd felt the oppressive humidity, smelled the sickly vapors, heard the mud squishing under his boots.

He looked down at his loafers on the hard, dry earth. He was six thousand miles and eight years from that place. He'd keep going.

He came to a trickle of a river. For a moment, clean footprints became visible in the dried mud—bare feet followed by hiking boots—but soon he lost the trail on the edge of the water.

Augy sat on a mossy rock with a subdued harrumph. Hours of diligent tracking only to find a dead end. It was common enough in his line of work, but he never ceased to greet it with exhaustion.

The wind whistled through dense branches. The river giggled and talked back. Augy lit a cigarette. His last cigarette.

He crushed the pack and tossed it into the stream.

A scream sounded like the sudden blast of a trumpet. Far-off and echoey. A young girl—terrified, in pain. It froze the blood in Augy's veins. He waited, unmoving. The crickets and frogs quieted, too. The scream came again, but shorter. Choked.

He checked the .45 in his pocket. It was still there, its standard seven-round magazine fully loaded. Standing, he turned upstream towards the scream. He tried to follow the bank, but the spiny brush was overgrown, leaving him no choice but to take off his shoes and roll up his trousers to trudge over the slippery stones of the riverbed.

Now, he was in the jungle. He smelled smoke on the air, but he couldn't trust his senses. Not when it was so dark.

Silence crept in. Augy worried he'd lose his way, but after ten minutes another scream broke the night, weaker and yet longer than before. He thought he heard begging and sobbing, and then the sound of harsh voices. Women's voices.

When the night fell silent again, this time for good, Augy followed from memory.

He came upon a waterfall surrounded by thorny bushes and cactus-like grasses. Augy thought he wouldn't be able to continue any farther when a spotlight of a full moon rose and bathed him in glowing silver light. A few feet off, a pile of boulders cut a clean path up the steep incline. He put his shoes on and scaled them.

The unmistakable stench of rotting meat reached his nostrils, carried on a burst of warm wind. He closed his eyes to steady his nerves, fighting memories that had no business surfacing. He couldn't afford to time travel now.

Augy took the .45 out of his pocket and clicked off the safety, then pointed his feet towards the smell. It wasn't long before he found it. In fact, he nearly stumbled into it.

A sinkhole was hidden between enormous sandstone boulders. Down at the bottom, white and blue skin glowed in the moonlight. The red of blood showed dull gray on the bodies of no less than a dozen people. Even from his vantage point high on the rocks above, Augy saw the bodies had been burned, mutilated, dissected and dismembered. They were in various stages of decomposition, though none was older than a few weeks. Augy had to turn away when he realized half the bodies were of women, and the rest were kids.

He choked on vomit but kept it down. His bones shook in his skin. Wrinkling his nose to keep out the stink, he heard a moan from inside the pit. He froze and held his breath.

No movement, no sound. The corpses were frozen in a nightmarish tableau.

A girl's strangled call, as faint as a whisper.

"Hello?" said Augy. Hearing the fear in his own voice frightened him more.

Something in the pit moved. He scanned the trees, but the shadows gave nothing away. He shoved the gun in his belt where he'd be able to quickly draw it if necessary, then climbed down the steep boulders, slick as they were with blood. "Keep talking," he stage-whispered. "Keep moving. I'll find you."

When his foot contacted a corpse, a chill of disgust took him. He heard the voice again. Far across the pit, he saw a single finger twitch. Whoever was alive was trapped under the dead.

Augy slogged through the pool of corpses, saturating himself in their blood, gore, and filth. He slipped and fell face-first into the naked body of a girl who was missing her eyes and arms. Convulsions overtook him and he vomited. But he wiped his mouth and kept going.

When he reached the twitching finger, he flung aside a body—the chest cavity gaping open, the heart missing. Underneath, a girl shined with thick blood. She was missing all her fingers but one. Her face was rendered inhuman by numerous slashes, but her eyes were open. Blinking. A deep fresh cut split her lips vertically. She was naked.

Augy took off his raincoat. The girl whimpered as he wrapped her up, then gathered her into his arms. Step by slow excruciating step, he clambered out of the sinkhole. She slung one arm around his neck and held tight—tighter than he would've thought she'd be able with those fingerless hands.

Carrying her like a baby, Augy rushed down the hill to the river. He kept looking over his shoulder, anxious that whoever had deposited those bodies would still be close by. The heavy gun in his belt was small comfort. But the night was silent. Dead.

As he staggered downriver, the moon slipped behind a cloud. The girl's skin was tender and moist with blood. He quickened his pace.

His only option was to head for Cohen Dale. Light as she was—sixty pounds at most—he worried about his ability to safely carry her all that way. If he'd been able to throw her over his shoulder in a fireman's carry, it would've been easy. But she was so hurt.

She fell unconscious as he passed the woodcut sign that read: *Welcome to Cohen Dale.* His arms and fingers ached. His feet were covered in blisters. His legs burning.

He ran to the first building he saw, straight up to the door, and used his foot to knock hard for a minute straight until an old man in long underwear answered, a shotgun in his hands.

"What in Hell's blazes do you want?" he cried, but as he took in what he was seeing, the man's expression changed from anger to horror.

"I need a doctor," said Augy.

The red-faced old man lowered his gun. "Ain't got a telephone."

"I need to set her down. Please."

"You can't bring her in here." He wrinkled his nose. "You'd best hurry along to Doc Larkin's place as quick as them scrawny legs'll carry you. Turn left round the end of the block and follow to the end of the street. The white house with the gnomes."

Augy was speechless. A rant like no other brewed in his stomach. It was about to erupt out his throat like a volcano when the man slammed the door in his face. Augy made a note of the house number—896—then rushed around the block to the white house with the gnomes.

"Open the door!" he screamed as he bounded up the stairs. "This girl is dying! I need a doctor! Wake up! Wake up!"

Within a minute, a woman opened the door, dressed in a nightgown and cap. In her hand was a lantern, glowing low. Her long gray hair was braided over one shoulder. Thick glasses rested high on a tapered nose. "My God!" she cried, her voice raspy with sleepiness. "Bring her in!"

Augy rushed through the door. The woman directed him to a table where he laid down the trembling, blood-coated body.

"Go into the kitchen and start some water boiling," ordered the doctor. "Then bring me the box of gauze in the hall closet. And wash your hands!"

For the next two hours, he acted as the doctor's nurse as she dressed the girl's wounds. Dr. Larkin explained the wounds as she found them. All the fingers but one had been plucked out with pliers or something of the like. She'd been stabbed thirty-eight times with a short thin blade, perhaps an X-Acto knife. The wounds were so shallow they hadn't caused any damage to her organs. Her face had been maimed in a crisscross pattern, likely by the same blade. Most disturbingly of all, on her shoulder in the exact place where it had been on Katya was the branding: *Property of Countess London, 14121119.*

When the work was at an end, the wounds dressed, and the girl miraculously stabilized and sedated, Augy retreated to the porch and smoked one of the doctor's cigarettes with blood-stained fingers. Even during his stint in the Pacific, Augy had never been so caked in human suffering. He was rendered speechless, immobile. All he could do was smoke.

Dr. Larkin soon joined him and offered him a cup of coffee.

"In all my years, I've never seen anything like this. That girl has been systematically tortured. She can't be more than fourteen. I can also tell she's gone in for at least one cleaning."

"You mean an abortion?"

The doctor sighed and nodded. "You look awful, son. Do you have someplace you're staying in town?"

Augy shook his head. "I've gotta get back to LA."

"Nonsense. You'll stay here. But I'm going to have to insist you have a shower."

CHAPTER FOUR

Once he was alone in the shower, Augy collapsed into the bottom of the powder-blue fiberglass tub. He pulled at his hair and rocked back and forth in the hot water, as even hotter tears streamed down his face. His chest was full of lead. He fought for every breath. It was bright in the bathroom, but his eyelids were glued together, isolating him in darkness again. Back in the sinkhole. Back in the mine. Back, back, back.

In the mine, he'd been one of only six Americans. There were a dozen Canadians, and the rest were Australian. All pilots. All under thirty. They were split into two groups and each took twelve-hour shifts in the mine. Augy always had the day shift, which meant he spent three years without seeing the sun. Sometimes in summer, he'd catch a spray of pink sunrise as the guards led them to the shaft, but it never rose. Not until he reached Tokyo, and then the light was blinding.

About half the POWs died, mostly from starvation. Each day they were given the same meal: two cups of rice, some pickles, and a quarter cup of stewed seaweed. And on that, they were expected to perform twelve hours of back-breaking labor thirteen out of every fourteen days. Anyone who didn't work didn't eat. No Red Cross supplies ever got through. No letters. No packages from home. By the end of six months, Augy had lost forty pounds, and he hadn't had an ounce to spare. Every prisoner looked the same, or worse. Decaying skeletons wrapped in skin. His breath tasted of death, his body eating itself from the inside.

Augy never missed a day of work. No matter how sick he felt. No matter what happened to the others. No matter how the guards beat him.

"Just keep working," he told himself. "If you stop working, you'll never get out of this.

"If you stop working, they win."

He stood and washed the blood off his skin. No matter how much blood soaked through, it always washed away. It didn't mean all that much, really.

Once he was clean, Augy dressed in the long johns, jacket, shirt, and collar Dr. Larkin provided—relics of an old boyfriend who was almost as tall and skinny as Augy. With clean skin and hair, and a fresh shave for the first time in months, Augy strapped on his beaten old shoes, shoved his fully loaded M1911 in the back of his pants, patted the cigarettes in his breast pocket, and headed out onto the streets of Cohen Dale. It was still a little before sunrise. Dr. Larkin had fallen asleep in the chair beside the girl's bed. He left a note for Dr. Larkin thanking her for her kindness, apologizing for stealing her cigarettes, and promising to come back to check on the girl. He took an extra piece of her stationery and scribbled out a second note, which he took with him.

He arrived at the house in a matter of minutes. Number 896.

Augy cracked his knuckles and kicked the door until he heard the lock clicking.

"What in tarnation is it now?" the man swore. He still had the shotgun in hand. When he saw Augy, he started to lift the gun.

Augy grabbed the gun by the barrel and twisted it out of his grasp. Augy snatched him by the arm and pulled him in tight. The shoulder wrenched out of its socket with a ferocious pop. The man screamed in pain. Augy dropped him to the ground.

"Looks like you need a doctor," he said. "I understand it's down the road. The white house with the gnomes."

He picked up the shotgun and pulled out the slide, then dropped the useless weapon next to the groaning man.

A few minutes later, he was at his sister's house. Lil' Smokey loped to the gate to greet him, wobbling with excitement. Poor obese critter was out of breath in point-five seconds.

"Calm down, you stupid dog," Augy whispered. He cracked open the gate and snuck inside, pausing to pet the dog to shut him up. He tip-toed around the side of the house to the back door which Mary never locked in spite of how many times Augy warned her about the sort of people that might come sneaking around at night.

He crept across the kitchen to where the family keys hung on hooks in a neat row from a goose-shaped wooden holder. He slipped off the keys to the Ford and as quickly as he'd come, he was gone.

On the front porch, Augy saw the milkman had already come. No doubt Harry would consider grabbing the milk in the morning to be Mary's job, so Augy shoved the note he had written explaining why he stole her truck into the basket. Given they'd had a party that night, he hoped they'd both be saturated in too much alcohol to notice the engine turning over.

He sped all the way back to LA, and then through the city streets to the Hyatt on Sunset Boulevard. Parking the car out front, Augy stumbled into the lobby. He approached the desk, but someone clicked their tongue at him, and he whipped round to see Katya sitting on one of the sea-foam couches drinking a cup of coffee.

Katya stood to meet him. Her eyes poured up and down his body. She drew his brows together. "What happened?"

Looking at her severe expression, Augy lost his words. She took him by the hand and led him to the sofa. "Your skin is white like snow. What happened to you?"

"Why didn't you tell me about the bodies?" said Augy.

Darkening, she scooted into the couch and tucked her legs underneath her. "I know you would go to police."

"Of course I would've gone to the police." He realized he was still holding onto her hand, so he let go.

She narrowed her eyes and shook her head. "You can't. You will only make it worse."

Without asking, he took one of the cigarettes from her silver case on the table and lit it. "I found a girl."

"Alive?" Her voice trembled. He couldn't tell if it was from horror or disbelief.

He nodded.

"You save her?"

He couldn't bring himself to say yes. "I got her out."

Katya bit her bottom lip. "You climb in there? For stranger?"

Augy cleared his throat. Silence swelled between them and Augy looked at his knees. "That night I hit you with my car... Had that man taken you out there to kill you?"

Frowning, Katya met his eyes. She reached into his shirt pocket and took one of his cigarettes. "We cannot talk here. Come." Gathering up her purse, she made a quick line for the door, nimble in her six-inch heels. She chatted with the valet and moments later he pulled up a shiny car and handed Katya the keys. Augy opened the driver's side door for her and then got into the passenger seat. She pulled on a pair of big circular sunglasses and tied a pink and purple floral scarf over her hair before starting up the engine and peeling out onto the street.

They said nothing for a long time. She guided the car onto I-15. He watched crispy sagebrush and manicured palms be replaced by lush green acacia and cedars. The chilled morning air rushed over him, washing the heat from his brain. Slowly, he became aware he was sitting in a cherry 1931 Duesenberg Model J—choice leather interior, cobalt blue paint, chrome shiny as a mirror.

"Where did you get this car?" he asked.

She took the exit that led towards Cohen Dale. "Why you ask so much questions?"

"I'm a detective." He smirked. "If you want my help, you're gonna have to start being honest with me."

"I steal car from man. I shoot him in head, and I take his car and money."

"You shot a man?"

Katya furled her upper lip. "He was killer."

"Why won't you go to the cops?"

"Police is useless."

"They do everything they can to try to protect people like you. If you told them what you know…"

"They help you? They save your business?"

Augy looked away. "That is beside the point."

"Some police are part of it. Impossible to know which," Katya snarled. "And people even more high than them. You see book there?" She gestured to her purse with her chin, from which protruded a small, leather-bound black address book. Augy picked it up and flipped through the pages. Her handwriting was so awful it took him a minute to realize it was the Cyrillic alphabet.

"What is this?" he asked.

"People who need to die."

"*This* is what you want my help with? A hit list?"

"You find them, I kill them."

"No, no." He slapped the book down between them. "I thought you wanted my help getting at this Countess London person…"

"Not enough. We must kill them all."

Augy sighed and rubbed his temples. "I won't be a party to murder, and I don't care how much money you offer me, or how just your cause may or may not be…"

Katya came to an intersection and rolled the car to a stop. Even with her eyes obscured by dark glasses, he could see in her lips and eyebrows the wheels in her brain were turning. "So I kidnap you. Force you to help."

"Listen, Katya… It is Katya, isn't it?" Augy smirked, even though he'd memorized not only her name but every word she'd ever said to him and every contour of her face. "It won't be as easy to hold me under lock and key as you seem to think."

"Easy or no, is what I will do."

"Sorry, gorgeous, but the moment I decide to leave, you're not going to be able to stop me."

Katya snorted. "Bet your life?"

Augy saw the truck in time to shout, "Look out!"

The sound was unbearable: the crunch of metal, Katya's screams. The car did a flip. Augy was thrown. Smacking the earth knocked the wind out of him.

He blinked at the crystal blue sky above. Smoke filled his nostrils.

Augy rolled onto his hands and knees in the dry grass. He coughed out some blood. The truck that had hit them was still on the road, undamaged. Black, gray and rust-colored, it was a light industrial truck. It had made mincemeat of the Duesenberg.

"Katya!" He scrambled forward, ignoring the pain racing through his limbs and the blood in his eyes. Fire whooshed to life on the car's smoking engine. Underneath the upside-down car, she was trapped behind the windows. She pressed her fingers against the glass and screamed again. Her face glistened with blood.

"Hang on! I'll get you out!" Augy yanked the pistol out of his pocket. "Get back!"

She scooted away from the window. He smacked the butt of the gun into the glass. It cracked after the second hit and shattered after the fourth. Augy flattened the sharp edges, and Katya scrambled out of the car, wincing on broken glass.

They helped each other stand. Blood dripped over one of her eyes—the same head wound open again. He was about to ask her if she was okay, but she'd gone pale staring at the truck still on the road. Augy followed her gaze.

Three men stepped out, all thick-necked and tall, undistinguished in cheap-looking suits. Two gripped pistols; the third lofted up a Tommy gun.

Katya yanked Augy behind the burning car before the first shot fired. The gorilla unloaded half a magazine, pummeling the corpse of the car and setting off sparks.

"More friends of yours?" asked Augy.

Katya patted her pockets and cursed. "I lose my gun. Shoot them!"

"Katya…" one of the men called in a grating, sing-song voice. "You know this is pointless. Why don't you come out of there? Frank wanted you to know, he's not mad."

Katya shouted something back in Russian, dripping venom. Augy caught a glimpse of a necktie between twists of the metal car frame. He took a long slow breath and leveled his pistol. Narrowing his eyes, he counted back from twenty-one by threes. By the time he reached zero, he couldn't smell smoke, feel fire, or hear bullets. There was just wind and his target. He squeezed the trigger.

Blood squirted from the chest, and the suit went down. The machine gun clattered on the asphalt.

The two remaining men took shelter behind their truck. Augy picked up what was left of the car's busted side-view mirror and used it to peer around the edge of the car. He waited until he saw one of the men stick his head out to fire. Augy darted out from behind the car and fired three shots. Two went wide. The third struck the man in the neck. A spurt of red. The man clawed at the wound. Augy took him down with a final shot to the gut.

Silence. The cackle of the engine fire. His own hot breaths. Through the mirror, Augy watched the third man climb back into the truck. He revved the engine.

Augy shoved Katya out of the way. The truck smashed into the remains of the car. Steal folded over him, imprisoning him. It crunched down on his bones and Augy screamed in pain. Skin ripped on sharp edges. His senses blurred in white-hot, screeching agony, and then, mercifully, he blacked out.

CHAPTER FIVE

Muffled sounds. The dry smack of his own awful breath. Light against his eyelids. A familiar voice: "Dr. Larkin, come quick! He's waking up! August, can you hear me?"

"Mom?" groaned Augy.

"No, August. It's me." Her fingers touched his cheeks. Mary's features came into focus: paper white skin, plump cheeks, short black curls. Those hazel eyes that always regarded him with an equal mix of pity and incredulity.

Light poured through a wood-framed window. Dust in the air sketched out sunbeams. He lay under a floral afghan, surrounded by flaking damask wallpaper. This was no hospital room, yet he was hooked up to an IV. A whirring machine at his bedside pumped oxygen through tubes into his nostrils. Every breath hurt. Memories of the car crash and the gunfight pooled in the pits of his mind, blurred by dreams and exhaustion. Looking down at the IV, he realized drugs were involved too.

"Where am I?" he asked.

"We're at Dr. Larkin's house," said Mary, clasping his hand in hers. "You've been out for three days."

"Three days?" he balked.

"Make room, dear," said Dr. Larkin, shoving Mary away to be nearer Augy's bedside. Putting on her stethoscope, she said, "How are you feeling, son?"

"Like hell warmed over." He tried to sit up, but the pain held him back like restraints. He had no strength in his core muscles. Every bone had turned to mush.

"Don't even think about it." The Doctor frowned in that parental way doctors do. She handed him a glass of water, which he sucked down in three gulps. "You have four fractured ribs and all the toes on your right foot are broken. You're lucky that's all that happened."

"Yeah. I feel lucky."

"What were you doing in that car?" Mary demanded. "What is it with you and cars?"

"Give me a cigarette," he said, sighing with exasperation. Mary frowned hard, but reached into her pocket and passed him a full pack of Encores: his brand. She must've bought it specially.

The smoke only made his terrible breath taste worse. He searched for more water, but the glass was empty.

"The police found you on the side of the road and managed to pry you out. You were at the hospital in Anaheim for a few days, but once you were stable they let me bring you back here so I could keep a closer eye on you."

She watched him like she was waiting for something. A thank you, maybe. He couldn't be sure. "Can I have more water?"

Mary took the empty glass. "Robby and Yeltz are here." She turned and shouted down the hall. "Guys! He's awake!"

The doctor took off her glasses and let them hang on a beaded chain around her neck. "They mustn't overexcite him."

"Fat chance," said Augy.

Moretti appeared in the doorway, followed by his partner, John Yeltz. Yeltz was an old bastard marshal from way back when who refused to retire no matter how many meetings he passed out during or how many times he broke wind in court. He was redheaded with pin-prick freckles, a long white mustache and an overbite that would make a horse giggle.

The pair shuffled over to the bed, staring down at Augy with thinly veiled panic and worry.

"Smalls?" said Moretti, kneeling down next to him. His skin was pale. Dark circles clung to his under-eyes. "You awake, buddy?"

"God, Moretti," sneered Augy. "You look awful."

Moretti laughed, but it sounded like sympathy.

"How you feeling, kid?" asked Yeltz, taking off his hat to kneel beside Moretti.

"Peachy." Augy scoffed. How it hurt his throat to scoff!

"We saw there was shots fired," said Moretti. "We found two bodies at the scene."

"I killed them."

"You what?" Mary balked.

"I didn't have any choice," said Augy, looking between all their faces. "They rammed our car off the road and then started firing on us."

Yeltz stroked his mustache in thought. "As soon as you're up to it, we're gonna need you to come down to the station and give a statement on that."

"Wait a minute," said Moretti, tipping his fedora. "Who exactly is *us*?"

Augy groaned and tried to sit up. "Katya and me. I take it she's gone missing? The man must've gotten her."

"That woman?" Moretti lifted an eyebrow. "You saw her again?"

"She was taking me to... I'm not sure where she was taking me. She'd enlisted my help, wanted to hire me. I was trying to convince her to go to the police."

"Smalls, you need to tell us everything you know. That car you was in..." Moretti stopped himself. "Will you ladies excuse us?"

"I'm not going anywhere," countered Mary, crossing her arms.

"Give us a break, Mary," said Moretti. "This is official business."

Mary's expression hardened.

"Will somebody get me a cup of coffee?" said Augy. "My mouth tastes like I licked a monkey's ass."

The doctor smirked. "Five minutes. He needs his rest."

"All right, Doctor." Moretti rose and followed Dr. Larkin and Mary to the door, shutting it behind them.

"That car you was in," Moretti continued, "had been stolen from a man called Ethan Elmsly two days ago. Somebody shot him in the back of the head at point-blank range with birdshot. You never saw such a fucking mess!"

"It was Katya. She thinks he was some kind of sadistic killer, and I'd bet dollars to donuts she's right. She also seems to think all the cops in this city are owned by this Countess London woman."

"Never heard of her," said Moretti.

Yeltz nodded. "This bird's off her rocker."

"No, she's not." Augy sighed and chewed the inside of his bottom lip. "You follow the road here about five miles till you see the skid marks, and head south through the forest. Follow the river to the waterfall and you'll come to a sinkhole full of bodies."

"Bodies?" echoed Moretti.

"A dozen if there was one. I've never seen anything like it."

"When did you find this?"

"Last night… I mean, I guess it was a few nights ago, now."

"You'd better have a damn good reason why you didn't call us," Yeltz warned.

"I needed to talk to Katya first. Trust me, she's a stone you can't squeeze blood from. If you tried to haul her in for questioning, she'd go mute. And I knew she knew about the bodies."

They glowered down at him like a pair of gargoyles.

"Can't you give me the benefit of the doubt, for Christ's sake?" Augy snapped. "Have I steered you wrong before?"

Moretti softened a little. "So, who's this guy you think took her?"

"Search me. But we need to find her. God knows what might be happening to her if she's still alive."

"We don't have many leads," said Yeltz.

"Her last name's Tyler, and I think her husband might be called Frank."

Moretti and Yeltz looked at each other. The baby-faced Italian motioned with his chin, and the old cowboy stood and left the room.

"We found Katya's purse in the wreckage," said Moretti, turning back to Augy, "but there wasn't much in it."

Yeltz came back carrying a pair of white gloves and a paper bag, inside of which was Katya's woven purse. The strap was ripped and the navy blue surface spackled with brown stains.

Augy groaned as he sat upright. The dull throb in his ribs fought to steal his breath.

"You need to relax." Moretti grabbed a pillow and shoved it behind Augy's shoulders.

Augy put on one of the gloves and opened the bag. He pulled out a tube of dark lipstick and a roll of cash with a rubber band around it. That was supposed to be his cash. Now, it was evidence.

He picked up her silver cigarette case and ran his thumb over the initials E. E. printed on it.

"Ethan Elmsly," Augy mouthed. He opened the case. Inside were twelve long white cigarettes. One was half burnt with dark red lipstick stains around the end. Tucked underneath the silver spring was a black book of matches.

"The notebook," said Augy, furrowing his brow. "Where is it?"

Yeltz wrinkled his nose. "What the hell is it?"

Augy bit his lip. For all the times he'd castigated Katya for her refusal to go to the police, he hesitated to tell them now what she was up to. They'd been T-boned before she'd had a chance to explain. When he found her—if he found her—he still owed her that chance.

"You getting it translated?" he asked.

Moretti nodded and sat down on the edge of the bed.

"So, what about this Ethan Elmsly?" Augy continued. "Did you talk to his widow?"

"Not personally," said Moretti. "How'd you know he had a widow?"

"Most dead guys do. I need to talk to her. How soon can you get her down here?" He didn't even give Moretti a chance to answer before his mind shifted gears and he shouted, "Doc! Get back in here!"

Shouting sent his ribs trembling like piano strings.

Dr. Larkin rushed inside, donning her glasses like armor. "What's the matter? Are you all right?"

"How's that girl? Has she woken up?"

She took off her glasses. "Her sleep has been fitful, so I've been keeping her sedated, which I'm thinking I'll have to do with you if you don't calm down." She shook a disapproving finger. "No shouting."

Mary appeared in the doorway. "All right, that's enough. Robby, it's time for you all to go."

Moretti grunted. "Mary, we're on the verge of something big here."

She clenched her teeth and put her hands on her hips. "He needs to relax."

"This is no time for your mother hen routine," said Augy.

"You need to relax!" snapped Mary.

"No shouting!" hissed the doctor, giving Mary, Augy, and Moretti dirty looks: a mother standing over her unruly children. "Now, Mr. Small, I'm going to have to insist everyone leave so you can get some rest."

"I don't need rest. I need to find Katya," Augy snarled and swung his legs over the side of the bed. One foot was in a cast. His chest was wrapped in tape to keep his ribs from shifting. The morphine was wearing off. Sharp twinges of pain shot through him with every movement, but Augy scooted to the edge of the bed anyway.

"You're not doing a damn thing for anyone if you don't let yourself heal a little." With a pointed finger, Dr. Larkin barked, "Now, shut up and lie back or

I'll pump you so full of barbiturates you won't wake up for a week! Everybody out!"

"Yes, ma'am," said Moretti, then turned for the door without another word. Yeltz was close behind him.

"I wanna talk to the Elmsly widow," Augy called after. "Get her here pronto."

"Will do, Smalls."

"And I want a look at that journal."

"You got it." Moretti pointed his finger at him like a gun, then disappeared beyond the door frame.

Dr. Larkin grabbed Mary by the arm. "I said *everybody* out."

"That's not fair!" whined Mary. "What did I do?"

She pushed Mary out the door and then closed it in her face.

Augy struggled to his feet, but a rush of blood to the head made him reach for support. The doctor grabbed his arm. "Jesus H. Christ, are you ever a stubborn bastard!"

Augy snorted. He waited for his eyes to focus on her face, but it was a white blob. "You saw what they did to that girl. If anybody should understand why I need to catch these sons-of-bitches, and quick, it oughta be you. I've already lost three days."

"You're going to lose more than that if don't calm down, soldier." With an iron grip, she forced him to sit.

He took a few deep breaths, waiting for the blood to flow away from his eyes. "Listen, Doc. I respect the hell out of you, but you gotta make some concessions here. Ain't you got nothing in that bag of tricks could help a guy back to his feet?"

Staring into his eyes, she took a deep breath and blew out her cheeks. "Pfft. Let me give you a wheelchair at least."

"Much obliged."

With evident distress, Dr. Larkin left the room.

Augy used one of the bedposts to stand. Blood rushed to his head, and he swayed. The pain was such he thought he might vomit, but he held it back. With determination as his only crutch, Augy grasped the wall and edged himself to the doorway. He remembered two maxims he'd learned in the air force: *pain lets you know you're still living* and *anybody who isn't afraid is an idiot.*

Keeping close to the wall, he limped to the bathroom. After an epic struggle with fly buttons, Augy managed to relieve himself.

He was stumbling back to his room when he noticed a face watching him through a crack in the door at the end of the hall. When she noticed him notice her, she started and disappeared.

Augy limped to the door. He braced his shoulder against the jamb and tapped on the frame.

He waited, but there was no answer. Grasping the handle, he pushed in the door. "Hello?"

She was on the bed, pressed into the corner. Her knees were hugged to her chest and her hands wrapped around them. Thin beams of light peered through the drawn blinds to illuminate her face. The wounds had been sutured, but they were still raw. The cut cleaving her lips was the worst. Two similar cuts ran diagonally across her forehead and over one eye. She had a diamond face, clear complexion, and a round snub nose. Her eyes were striking: almond-shaped, monolid and upturned at each end so they formed a V across her face. They sparkled with intelligence and suspicion. She was dressed in a clean white nightgown, her short black hair in a low ponytail. Her body was emaciated, limbs so long and thin they were awkward to behold. She hadn't grown into them yet.

She stared at him for a long moment, blinking.

"Do you speak English?" he asked.

She didn't respond.

Though he didn't put a lot of faith in the idea, the girl looked East Asian under all her scars. He only knew one other language, so he took a stab in the dark. "*Nihongo-o wakarimashita?*"

The girl nodded.

"Do you remember me?" he continued in Japanese. "I'm the one who... who found you."

She glanced into his eyes. There was something so powerful about the way she looked at him—overwhelming, unrefined emotion. It was chilling.

"My name's Augy. Can I come in?"

She nodded. Working double time to hide his pain, Augy took three steps to a wicker chair near the bed and collapsed into it. "What's your name?"

The girl shrugged and looked away.

"Can you talk?"

She nodded but still said nothing.

"You just don't want to."

She shook her head.

"That's okay." He took the pack of cigarettes from his breast pocket and tapped one out. Putting it between his lips, he noticed a familiar expression in the girl's eyes.

"Would you like one?" he asked.

She hesitated before nodding.

He was about to hand it to her when he remembered she only had one finger, her hands wrapped in thick bandages. Augy did a quick inventory of the room and noticed a ruler, some scotch tape, and a box of paper clips sitting on a little desk. Holding the cigarette between his lips and squinting to keep the smoke out of his eyes, he bent the paper clip into a round, spring-like shape, taped it to the end of the ruler, and then affixed the smoke to the clip. He handed it to her and she was able to grasp the ruler between her two stubs and smoke out of the end. She took a drag and looked the rig up and down. It was miles from a smile, but her face changed in such a way as if to say 'thank you.'

They smoked in silence for a while. The two of them looked like they belonged in hospice, but both were too stubborn. He chewed his bottom lip. "Have you ever met Countess London? Is she a real person?"

In a trice her skin was white and she turned away, shielding her face behind her knee.

"It's okay, angel. Don't be afraid," he said, no matter how absurd the suggestion might seem. He couldn't think of anything more useful to say than, "You're safe now."

A single eye peered out from behind her knee. The pupil widened a little.

Augy smiled softly. "Do you think you could at least tell me your name? Otherwise, I'm gonna have to make one up."

She shook her head.

Augy grabbed some stationery off the table beside him and wrote down all the basic hiragana syllables. After he'd finished, he showed it to her and asked again, "What's your name?"

Scooting closer, she used the cigarette to point to three in succession. Augy sounded it out, "Su...mi...ka."

The girl nodded.

"Sumika. That's pretty." Grunting, he began the arduous task of standing. "All right, Sumika. I've gotta hit the pavement, but we'll talk again when I get back."

Noticing the anxiousness on her face, he said, "The doc's a good lady. A bit pushy with the drugs and she's got a foul mouth, but she's good. If you need anything, she'll get it for you. And I'm gonna make sure there's cops here to look after you round the clock, okay? Don't worry. Nobody knows you're here."

She nodded, folding over her cigarette. Augy watched her another moment, then stumbled out the door.

The more he learned about her, the more difficult it was for Augy to accept Countess London was a real person. He'd dealt with some despicable excuses for humanity in his time, from Japanese inquisitors to American murderers, not the least of which were the steely-eyed Hollisters, but never someone who could be so cruel to a child. It was inhuman. If he hadn't seen the girl with his own eyes, he wouldn't have believed it. Not to mention the state of the pile of corpses he'd found her in.

There was no time for healing, wheelchairs, or any of that nonsense. For the first time since waking, his head felt clear. And he realized finding Katya was just the beginning of his worries.

CHAPTER SIX

"Have a seat, Mrs. Elmsly," said Augy.

She was pushing sixty, with a long waddle on her neck and a green tweed hat pulled over coarse gray hair. She gripped the wooden handles of her bag with both hands. "What's this all about, Detective? Have you found the person who murdered my husband?"

"I need to ask you a few questions."

She suppressed a sob and wiped her nose with a lace handkerchief. Her cheeks were raw with tears. "I've already told the police everything. Ethan was a wonderful, caring man and a devoted husband. What else do you need to know? What do you people want from me?"

"How'd you two meet?"

She sniffed. "Why should that matter?"

Augy shrugged. "You're gonna have to let me decide what matters, Mrs. Elmsly."

"It was a few years ago. I was at the greengrocer and saw this handsome man examining the cantaloupes. He asked me how to tell if one was any good. I ended up taking him around the store showing him the proper way to pick out all his fruits and vegetables. The poor man had lost his wife only a few months before and hadn't had a decent meal since, so I went back to his place and cooked him dinner. We were married two months later."

"And you were fifteen years older than Mr. Elmsly?"

"Thirteen," she corrected, bristling. "What does that have to do with anything?"

Augy took a long breath and cracked his knuckles. He'd read the transcript of the interview she'd given to the investigating officer on her husband's murder, and it was clear she was in denial. Nothing a little Augy Small charm couldn't shed light on.

"Didn't you find it odd an attractive forty-five-year-old man was interested in an old bag of bones like you?" he asked.

"I beg your pardon?"

"Honestly ma'am, when the two of you were first getting together, did it never occur to you he might be able to get a hold of fresher cantaloupes?"

Her lips curled and her eyes darted back and forth. Augy could see her deciding whether to storm out or smack him first. "Not all men are fanatically obsessed with youth, Detective."

"This is Los Angeles, Mrs. Elmsly." Augy allowed himself a boastful smile. "Are you independently wealthy by any chance?"

She didn't answer.

"When a good-looking, healthy guy like your husband shacks up with an old bird like you, chances are there's money involved..." Augy trailed off and watched her reaction.

"No, I'm not wealthy," she conceded.

"You've got a fair amount of life insurance though, don't you?"

"I beg your pardon?"

"Nine policies that all name Mr. Elmsly as your sole beneficiary."

"Nine policies?" she exclaimed.

"You were unaware your husband had taken out these policies?"

"There must be some kind of mistake."

Augy grabbed a folder off the table. Moretti had brought the contents over that afternoon along with Mrs. Elmsly, which had given Augy enough time to shower and talk Doc Larkin into giving him another dose of morphine before the interview.

"Let's see. I got a $4,000 policy from Legal and General..." He dropped the file in her lap. "Here's one for $6,000 from Miller and Son." He slapped it down on top of the first. "This one's got double indemnity if you were to die in the next six months."

"These look like his signature, but this can't be right. I never..." Mrs. Elmsly's shaking hands flipped through the documents. "What are you trying to say?"

"Maybe this wonderful, caring man who'd just lost his wife was nothing more than a common black widow."

"A black widow?" she stammered.

"Black widower, I guess. Your late husband had been married six times. Did he tell you?"

"I knew he'd been married before, but *six times*? That can't be right."

"Betty Windsor, Sally Anne Hawkins, Frances Smith..." he added a few headshots to the pile of papers on Mrs. Elmsly's lap. "All but his first wife were at least ten years older than him, all were married to him less than three years, and all of them died of the same mysterious illness only after Mr. Elmsly had taken out several policies on their lives. Sound familiar?" Augy winked. That had to do the trick.

"Why are you telling me these... these lies!" Standing, she threw the papers in contempt. They spread like confetti across the room. "What does any of this have to do with my husband's murder?"

With all the grace of a rusty crane, Augy bent to collect the papers. "The woman who killed Ethan Elmsly was aware of his crimes and took it upon herself to punish him."

"A *woman* killed my husband."

"Mrs. Elmsly, I don't think you're grasping what I'm telling you. Your husband was a mass murderer. He'd picked you as his next victim."

"I've never been so insulted in all my life! With the tragedy I've suffered, how dare you bring me here to slur my late husband's good name? You ought to be ashamed of yourself!"

Augy scratched his forehead with his thumbnail. "Mrs. Elmsly, the woman who killed your husband is still at large. Regardless of whether you believe me about who your husband was, believe I want to find his killer. An investigation has been launched into your husband's crimes, and I fully expect mountains of evidence will surface proving he was guilty of everything I've suggested and worse. What I need from you is names. I need to get in contact with Mr. Elmsly's friends, his relatives, his business associates... anyone who might've known him better than you did."

"Nobody knew him better than me. You're all wrong about him, Detective."

Augy furrowed his brow and rubbed his temples. Doubt glowed behind Mrs. Elmsly's eyes now, but misplaced loyalty was still blinding her. It was time to shift his approach. "Mrs. Elmsly, your husband had connections to other persons who may have been involved in several similar crimes. Now, the police have his address book, but what I need to know is who his closest friends were… his brother… his other woman. I need to know who he told his secrets to, and we both know damn well it wasn't you."

She sneered and looked down, strangling the handles of her bag. The wood creaked under the pressure.

"Do you know who that person was, Mrs. Elmsly?" asked Augy, lowering his voice. "Did he ever let you meet that person?"

Her lips wrinkled, nose twitching in anger. Even her toes clenched in her sandals. She didn't say anything.

"Mrs. Elmsly?" Augy cocked an eyebrow. "Mrs. Elmsly, there are a lot of individuals… some of them children… who might be in danger as we speak, and the sooner you help me, the sooner I might be able to help them."

Snorting steam, she stomped towards the door. Taking the doorknob in her fist, she said, "Lily Wong."

He smiled. Tension melted out of his shoulders only to be replaced by dull pain. "Thank you for your cooperation, Mrs. Elmsly."

"Go to hell, Detective." She marched out of the room, slamming the door behind her.

A moment later, the door opened again and in strolled Moretti, pushing out his bottom lip. "Another woman caught under your spell, eh Smalls?"

Augy grunted and took out a cigarette.

Moretti ran his fingers underneath his hat before taking it off. "I hate to bring this up right now, but a Reginald Winston has brought assault charges against you."

"Who?"

"Guy lives down the road. Says you broke his arm."

Augy rolled his eyes. "I dislocated his shoulder."

"Why?"

"Because he's a son of a bitch who needs a lesson in being a decent human being."

"Christ almighty…" Moretti grabbed the bridge of his nose.

"Can't you take care of it for me?"

"Take care of it?"

"Yeah, you know. Make it disappear."

Moretti scoffed. "I'm not the goddamn Wizard of Oz!"

"Actually, the Wizard of Oz isn't a real wizard. He's just some old dude from Nebraska, so I don't know how much help he'd be."

"I thought he was from Kansas."

"In the books, he's from Omaha."

Moretti rubbed his temples. "I swear to god, you are the biggest egghead to ever live."

Augy flinched at the insult, then swallowed his irritation and put on an easy smile. He'd spent much of his life fighting against the label. His father, who was a professor of philosophy at Stanford University, had decided even before his son was born that he would be a professional egghead. From the time Augy was a little boy, he'd had books piled on him: The Republic, Nicomachean Ethics, Being and Nothingness, A Critique of Pure Reason, Beyond Good and Evil, and on and on, thicker and thicker. Augy tried to read them, but they invariably turned his brain into cheese that had been left out in the sun. Stinky and slimy and no good to anyone.

Not that he disliked reading, just that his tastes tended towards mysteries and thrillers. He had to hide such books from his father or they would be confiscated. Augy stashed Dashiell Hammett novels the way most boys stashed girly magazines.

"That pedestrian rubbish will rot your brain, Augustinius," Mr. Small always said. Maybe he was right.

"Honestly, Moretti," said Augy, running a thumb over the stubble on his cheek, "don't we have slightly more pressing concerns right now than the hometown of the Wizard of Oz? Did you find the sinkhole?"

Moretti's sigh was like air being let out of a tire. "I've had guys out there for almost twelve hours looking for this sinkhole of yours and they still haven't found a trace..."

"It was there four days ago. I pulled a girl out of it."

"I never said you didn't. What I'm saying is we can't find it."

"They must've filled it in. I'll come down and show you where to dig."

"You may have to, or risk losing your credibility."

"What credibility?" Augy chewed on his cheek. "Lily Wong."

"Who's that?"

"A friend of Ethan Elmsly who might be able to help."

Augy searched for a lighter, and Moretti pulled a matchbook from his trouser pocket and tossed it over.

Augy lit his smoke and rolled the matchbook over in his hands. It was the one from Katya's purse. A logo of a lone mountain was emblazoned in white on a black background. Augy didn't recognize it and there was no writing. He put it in his pocket.

"Any luck with Frank Tyler?" he asked.

"Francis Tyler," said Moretti, "owner and president of Holzklotz Medical Supply. Wife Yekaterina Ivanovna. Two children."

"Did you say, children?"

"Yeah, two." Moretti read off the file in his hand. "Eight-year-old girl, Clytemnestra, and a four-year-old boy, Sisyphus."

"Poor little bastards." Augustinius Erasmus Small shook his head at the nerve of some parents. No doubt his sister, Mary Wollstonecraft, would've agreed. "Have you sent officers to pick up Tyler?"

"For what?"

"To interrogate him."

"He hasn't committed any crime."

"His wife killed a man and now she's missing. You don't think it's worth questioning him?"

"You don't get it, Smalls. This guy's kind of a big deal."

"Meaning?"

"He's a millionaire for a start."

"I'll do it my goddamn self." Augy snorted. "Listen, we need to get a couple officers stationed here to keep an eye on that girl I found."

"We're gonna move her to a hospital."

Augy shook his head. "She'll be more comfortable here where there's less people, I think. I don't want to make a spectacle of her."

"She looks that bad?"

Augy rolled his shoulders and suppressed a chill.

Before they headed out, Augy asked for his gun back.

Moretti tightened the skin on his neck. "No can do, Smalls. You shot two people. You ain't never seeing that gun again. You're lucky you ain't locked up."

"Give me yours, then. You're a lousy shot anyway."

Again that tight skin.

"Don't be a dick, Moretti." Augy thrust out his hand expectantly.

"I really don't think…"

"Look at me! Look what those sons-of-bitches did to me! And you want me to go out there unarmed?"

"I don't want you to go out there at all!"

"Well, here I go. So, what you gonna do?"

After tremendous grumbling, Moretti relinquished a Browning HP 9 mm with a full thirteen-round magazine—a toy compared to the .45.

"Thank you." Augy shoved it in his belt.

"Promise you won't use it," begged Moretti. Augy didn't respond.

Yeltz met them in the car outside, but Moretti sent him back in to watch after Sumika. They were about to pull out onto the street when Moretti hit the brakes. Augy lifted his head to see Mary standing at the end of the driveway, arms folded and foot tapping.

"Where do you think you're going?" she called, her eyes fixated on Moretti, "and more importantly, where do you think you're taking my baby brother?"

"Get out of the way, Mary." Augy tapped his fingers on the side of the car.

"Answer the question, Robby."

Augy was about to tell his sister what a pain in the neck she was for perhaps the fifty thousandth time, but Moretti cut him off. "This is official business."

"August is in no condition to be conducting business of any kind."

"I'm fine."

"You're not fine. You nearly died. You may be stubborn as a mule and twice as thick, but if you think I'm gonna let you go out there to get yourself run over again, you've got another thing coming." She stomped over to the backseat, yanked open the door and climbed inside.

"Mary, we don't have time for this," Augy snarled.

She buckled the seat belt. "If you expect to go out there and fight crime in your condition, somebody needs to look out for you." She laid her purse on her lap and folded her hands on top. "Now, where are we going?"

CHAPTER SEVEN

They parked on the circular drive of sparkling quartzite flagstones. The Tyler house was a castle. Three stories high and fashioned from thousands of enormous square rocks. The garden was equally impressive, split by a waterfall and populated by lush green plants that had no business growing in Southern California.

Augy flicked his cigarette out the window, spoiling the perfection of the drive. "Let's go."

"I told you, Smalls, I can't do anything without a warrant," said Moretti, his generally smooth voice harsh and nervous. "I'm outta my jurisdiction here."

"Careful, Moretti. Your liver is showing."

Moretti sucked in a loud breath. "What if we bust in and she's not there?"

"Who said anything about busting in?" smirked Augy. "Use the doorbell, you animal."

"According to you, this is one of the guys who left a sinkhole full of dead bodies out in the woods. I don't even want to interview him without backup."

"I'm your backup, moron."

"You?" Moretti snorted. "Detective Gimpy McHobbles?"

Augy's nerves twitched as he gazed up at the house. Katya could be inside at that moment, being tortured—worse, she might already be dead—and all his so-called best friend could talk about were search warrants.

"You know what? Screw you and your jurisdiction." Augy popped open the door.

"August, you can't..." Mary snapped in her most matronly voice.

"You are physically incapable of performing a daring rescue right now," said Moretti.

"I'll try for a cowardly one then."

"Please, Robby," said Mary. "He's gonna get himself killed."

Moretti clenched a fist. "I'll get a warrant and then me and two dozen cops will come back and rip this place apart."

"Ain't got time for that."

"I'll do it myself," said Mary. She was about to slide out of the car when Moretti wheeled back and grabbed her arm. Her startled hazel eyes met his baby blues, and the two stared at each other for an excruciatingly long time. Then again, Mary and Moretti spent a lot of time staring at each other, even if they thought nobody noticed.

"Let go of my arm, Robby," she warned.

"Goddamn it! All right!" Moretti turned back in his seat and pouted like a six-year-old. Then he put on his hat and tilted it just so. "I'll go ask a couple questions, but that's all you're getting out of me."

"That's the ticket." Augy resumed his struggle to exit the car.

"Sit your ass down," snarled Moretti, giving Augy a stiff glare. He slipped out of the car and slammed the door behind him.

Watching Moretti march away, Augy smiled in the mirror at his sister. "You shouldn't have done that, Mary."

Mary stared after Moretti until he'd disappeared around a hedge. "If he gets himself killed, I will never forgive you."

"That's fair." Augy rubbed his chin. "I'm gonna go limp around. See what I can see."

"You're joking."

Augy opened the car door and swung his legs out. Mary reached over the seat and yanked the door closed on his shin.

"Ow! What's a matter with you?"

"What part of you can't walk...?"

"I can walk fine."

A gunshot broke the air. Birds fled the trees. Augy ducked, which ignited pain in his vertebrae like a spark to a string of firecrackers.

"Robby..." Mary whispered.

"Stay in the car."

For perhaps the first time in her life, Mary didn't argue. Augy took out his pistol and slipped out. Around the back of the house, he heard faint voices.

Augy crept towards the noise coming from the back garden, which was surrounded by a six-foot-high cobblestone wall. It took him several minutes to navigate to a surprisingly unlocked gate. The garden was well-manicured, a symmetrical labyrinth of red, yellow, and white roses. The hedges were short enough to see over. In the distance sprawled a field of Kentucky blue, and there he saw two men. They were both in suits and riding boots, one decidedly more expensive than the other, who had a slack shotgun cradled in one arm. At his ankles was an anxious spaniel.

"Excellent shot, Mr. Tyler." As the goon bent to retrieve the duck, Augy recognized the man who'd shot at him that night on the road. Though seeing him in the sun, he realized the unsightly angles of his face had been sculpted by fire or acid.

Frank Tyler, on the other hand, was handsome enough to be in catalogs, with clear blue eyes and a helmet of yellow hair held in place by half a gallon of pomade. His heavy square chin was clean-shaven. He hovered between thirty-five and forty.

"I'll have it for dinner," said Tyler, his voice a cool baritone.

A woman in a maid's uniform rushed onto the green. "Please excuse, Mr. Tyler," she said in a heavy Chinese accent. "There is police at door."

Frank Tyler laughed. "Tell that stupid pig it's only a duck."

"I tell. But he is ask for Mrs. Tyler."

Frowning, Tyler pushed the shotgun onto his man, then took off his gloves. "Well, don't leave him standing on the stoop, you cow. Show him in."

The maid nodded and ran for the house so quickly you'd think something was chasing her. Mr. Tyler sauntered after, goon close behind.

Something wet touched Augy's hand. He looked down at the brown and white spaniel. Its tail wagged as it licked him all over.

Dogs loved Augy. Even stalwart guard dogs had been known to abandon their posts to get a sniff of him. However flattering, they did have a knack for interrupting his attempts at espionage.

"Go away, you idiot," he hissed.

A loud whistle cut the air. The dog gave Augy one last lick, then bounded off.

Augy shoved his gun in his belt. He turned to head back to the car, but another whistle stole his attention. This one was much fainter.

"Hey there!" came a voice in a loud whisper. Augy looked around in a circle. "Up here!"

Peering down from the highest window of the tall house was a girl with a mop of curly black hair. He guessed she was about seven.

"What you doing down there?" she asked.

Augy double-checked Mr. Tyler was gone and ambled closer. "What are you doing up there?"

"I'm always up here."

"You wouldn't be Clytemnestra by any chance?"

The girl cringed. "Call me Clemmie. What's your name?"

"You can call me Augy."

She smiled, blue eyes like crystals in the sunlight. "You shouldn't be down there. If my dad sees you, you'll get in big trouble."

"Listen…" Augy looked over his shoulders again. "Is your mother home?"

A sad look overcame her. "We're not allowed to see Mama no more."

"When's the last time you saw her?"

"Long time ago," she said, biting her lips. "Before Dad locked us up here."

Looking at Clemmie sent pain through his chest like hoarfrost growing on his internal organs. All he saw was little Sumika and the cuts on her face.

"Your little brother with you?" he asked.

"Uh-huh." She turned and called to somebody inside. A moment later, another face joined her in the window. It was round with a deep blush in the cheeks and those same brilliant blue eyes. "Say hi to the funny man, Sissy."

"No," said the boy.

Clemmie rubbed her nose. "You should go. Dad'll be real sore if he finds you. He'll probably shoot you."

Augy's eyes darted from window to window, searching for any movement. "Why'd your dad lock you up there?"

"He said, well…" She was quiet for a second. "He said Mama was bad and we're not allowed to go outside till she's good again."

Clemmie's head snapped back. "Someone's here. I won't tell on you."

She disappeared behind the shutters. Augy scanned the grounds. An ash tree grew near the window, it's thick limbs as close to mother nature's ladder as you could get. Under normal circumstances, it would've been easy to scale, but with his foot and ribs, it seemed almost insurmountable. Still, a horror show was playing in his mind. The kids were being punished for what their mother had done. What more might Frank Tyler do to his own children to stop his wife from being *bad*?

When he closed his eyes he saw Sumika and the thirty-eight stab wounds in her chest and stomach. Those tiny wounds that hadn't been meant to kill, at least not quickly. And those words—*Property of Countess London*—written in twisted scorched flesh. On Sumika. On Katya. Would he find the same mark on Clemmie? On her little brother?

He looked back at the tree. It was going to smart like a son of a bitch, but he couldn't leave without those kids.

Sucking in a deep breath, Augy pulled himself onto the lowest branch. His ribs begged for mercy. Every instinct told him to scream, let go, fall on the ground and roll back and forth like an injured dog. But this wasn't the first time he'd had to press on in spite of broken bones. He gritted his teeth hard and climbed slowly, one hand and one foot at a time. One branch grew close enough to the window to scrape the shutters. Augy edged out along it and peeked inside.

Whoever had distracted Clemmie was gone now. She and her brother, who looked about four, sat on the floor eating what might've been called porridge, but was more properly called gruel. The dusty attic was furnished with two cots, a table, and a few battered toys. The ceiling of the triangular room was so low he would've struggled to kneel under it.

"Psst," he called.

Clemmie looked up and furrowed her brow. Under her curls, she had wide circular eyes, a button nose, and her mother's strong jaw and dark eyebrows. She had a scratch on one cheek and a faded shiner under one eye. Her ragged clothes hung like cobwebs over a rail-thin frame.

She pushed open the wooden shutter and smiled at him. "What are you doing now?"

The boy peered around his sister, saw Augy, and hid. "Tell him to go away, Clemmie."

"I warned you," said Clemmie, shaking her head. "You're gonna get shot."

"I… uh…" He looked down at the ground, rolling his tongue from cheek to cheek. "You two kids need to come with me."

Clemmie shifted on her bare, dirty feet. "I don't know you."

"I'm a friend of your mother's."

"Mama?" The boy poked his face out from under the bed. He was so cute it was hard to look at him—like somebody had taken a kitten and turned it into a real boy. "Where's Mama?"

"I was with her a few days ago," said Augy.

The boy's wide eyes widened even more. "Really?"

Clemmie folded her arms. "Mama said not to trust strangers."

Augy wrapped one arm around the branch and offered his hand. "Come with me now and I promise I'll get you to your mom."

It might've been a lie, but he said it anyway. And he felt vindicated when Clemmie reached for his hand.

The sound of angry voices flooded the air. He craned his neck to see Moretti being shoved out the front door. Marching towards the car, Moretti shouted, "I'll be back, Mr. Tyler. And next time, I'll have a warrant."

"I'll have you taken off the force!" shouted Tyler. "I know the mayor!"

"And I know the police chief." Moretti got into the car and slammed the door. Mr. Tyler stomped back into the house. Augy had turned back to Clemmie when a shot cracked the air. Mr. Tyler reappeared on the drive with a pump-action shotgun. He pumped the gun and fired again. Both windows on the driver's side of the cruiser shattered. Moretti fired up the engine and peeled away. Augy strained to see Mary ducked down in the backseat, her hands tight over the back of her neck. Tyler fired again but missed. He tried for another, but the gun was empty. Spitting, he stomped back inside.

There goes my ride, thought Augy, watching the car disappear around the bend. Now, what the hell am I gonna do?

CHAPTER EIGHT

The truck hit a bump and Augy groaned in pain. He thought fondly of Dr. Larkin and her long syringes filled with morphine. He wanted to go back for a top-up, but the cops were there. It was not lost on Augy he'd technically kidnapped these two kids. From a millionaire who knew the mayor, no less.

Getting the kids out of the attic was easy. They took to the tree like spider monkeys, but their feet were more timid once they touched the ground. Augy's getaway car had sped off without him, so he had no choice but to lead the kids onto the highway and try to hitch a ride. A passing chicken farmer had answered his prayers.

Four big blue eyes stared up at him in the bed of the truck. The boy clung to a stuffed rabbit that looked like it'd seen better days back when Garfield was president. Clemmie picked at a scab on her knee. A few minutes ago she'd asked where they were going, but Augy had yet to answer.

He wouldn't ask Mary and Harry for another favor. Besides, her place would be no more hidden from the cops than Dr. Larkin's. He'd already gotten Moretti into a jamb when he bullied him into going to question Tyler. There ended his list of friends.

There was only one person left, and he didn't want to ask her.

Augy and the kids climbed out when the truck stopped at Inglewood. With a final thank you to the farmer, Augy led the kids vaguely downtown.

"So...?" said Clemmie, long and lyrical.

Augy grunted and lit a cigarette. "So, what?"

"What now?"

"When do we get to see Mama?" asked the boy, bouncing from foot to foot. His little body was a swarm of anxiety.

"What's the matter with you?" Augy demanded. "You gotta pee?"

"No."

"Cause if you piss your pants, I ain't cleaning it up."

The boy's shoulders slumped and he wiped his nose. His chubby cheeks puffed as his bottom lip wobbled.

Guilt settled on Augy's shoulders like an overweight condor. "Sorry, kid. Wait, what was your name again?"

"Sisyphus," Clemmie answered for him. "But everybody calls him Sissy."

"I can't call you that."

"Why not?" he asked.

"I just… can't. Ain't you got a nickname or something?"

He scrunched his face in thought. "Mama calls me Zychik."

"It means 'bunny rabbit'," said Clemmie. Her brother stuck out his tongue.

"Well, it sounds like a tough bunny rabbit to me," said Augy. "A kind of Siberian warrior bunny. Do you mind if I call you Zychik?"

The boy nibbled his lips as he thought, then nodded.

"I'm hungry," said Clemmie.

"Me, too," said Zychik.

The mere mention of food made Augy's neglected stomach grumble. He searched his pockets and found a bit of lint.

"My feet hurt."

"Me, too."

"For crying out loud."

They kept walking. Every minute Clemmie had a new question or complaint, and Zychik was quick to echo everything she said. Hunger was a recurring theme. Augy started to question what he'd been thinking taking these kids.

They passed a church with dozens of cars in the parking lot and people in nice hats milling about. The smell of barbeque snaked down his nostrils and squeezed his empty guts.

He led the kids to the shade of a tree at the corner of the grounds. "You two stay here. I'll be right back."

"You're leaving?" Clemmie put her hands on her hips, stuck out her chin, and suddenly looked just like her mother.

"I said I'll be right back," said Augy. "Don't move, okay?"

Zychik folded into his chest. "I'm scared."

"Don't be scared. Stay close to your sister. I won't be ten minutes."

Augy straightened. He tried to hide his limp as he marched around to the back of the church. The clothes he'd gotten off Dr. Larkin didn't fit well, but at least they were clean and respectable. Nobody noticed him hobble over to the buffet table where the potlatch was laid out. He grabbed a plate and piled it up with everything in sight. Once it was full, he set it down on a nearby table and grabbed a second.

He was spooning up peach cobbler when a woman came to his side and touched his arm. She had much broader shoulders than Augy, though she was about a foot shorter. On her hat was the largest, pinkest flower he'd ever seen.

His stomach dropped. He turned with a feeble explanation in his throat.

"You must be Mr. Blaire," she said, offering a pleasant smile.

"That's exactly who I am."

"I'm Matilda Tidwell. I was so sorry to hear about all your troubles."

"Thank you."

"How did you ever survive it?"

"Well, you know… Actually, I'm not fond of discussing it."

"I understand, of course." She reached into her purse and took out a pocketbook, which was decorated in hundreds of pea-sized plastic pearls. "I meant to give this to you last week when they held the drive, but I was down in the mouth, you see."

She pulled out two twenty-dollar bills and offered them to Augy. "I hope this helps. I can't imagine anything worse than what you've been through."

Augy stared at the bills. He hated taking charity. He hated taking it from his sister, from his friends, and especially from churches. Not to mention he'd be stealing this particular charity.

He discreetly shoved a hushpuppy in his mouth. Barbeque was one thing, but forty bucks? And what had this poor Mr. Blaire bastard been through that Matilda Tidwell was so anxious to give him so much money?

Augy shook his head. "I couldn't."

"Please, I insist. It's the least I can do."

His insides burned. Out front were two hungry, dirty kids for whom he was responsible now. Forty bucks would get them food for days, a couple of pairs of shoes, a decent place to sleep, showers.

His hand darted for the money. "Thank you. I swear once I get on my feet I will pay you back."

"I would never hear of it," she said. "As the good book says, 'Give that which is within you as charity, and then all things are clean for you'."

"Well, okay. But I'm gonna pay you back anyway."

She touched his arm. "If you insist, Mr. Blaire. God bless you."

"Thanks. I mean, you too."

She walked away. Before anybody else had the opportunity to talk to him, he grabbed his plates and limped back to the kids, careful not to spill any baked beans over the side. He was grateful to Mrs. Tidwell, and not just for the money. After what he'd seen over the last few weeks he was starting to think it was too bad the nuclear holocaust hadn't happened yet.

The kids inhaled their food. Clemmie was a beast. But their poor stomachs were a lot smaller than their eyes. Zychik only had half a rib and a handful of soggy fries before he leaned back against the tree moaning like it was Thanksgiving. Augy scraped up the leftovers, but he'd always had a bird's appetite. Half the food got left behind for the squirrels and raccoons.

Augy only made them walk far enough to find a payphone, then he called a cab to take them to a motel. Once little Zychik was asleep with his bunny and Clemmie was in the shower singing like a diva, Augy swallowed his pride and made the call.

He knew the number by heart.

"Hello?" she answered, her voice like a cool breeze on burnt flesh.

He sighed. "Hey, Rutabaga."

"Augy?" There came a crackling sound as she shoved her hand over the receiver, presumably to make her way into another room. "I told you not to call here."

"Keep your shirt on. There's something important I need to ask you."

"What would you have done if Bill answered?"

"Put him on the line. Always a pleasure to talk to the human pocket protector."

"What do you want, Augy?" She groaned. "Mary told me you've been going through a tough time, but I hope you're not looking to rehash the past because I am not—"

"This has nothing to do with you and me."

"Why else would you call?"

"Will you climb down off your high horse for five goddamn seconds and listen to me?"

"Could you curb the language, please? What sort of man uses that kind of language?"

Augy chuckled. "All men use that kind of language."

"Not to a lady."

"For Christ's sake. You used to use that kind of language!"

"I grew up, Augy. Maybe if you did the same we wouldn't be in this situation."

"You say growing up, I say giving up. Tomayto, tomahto."

"That is total baloney!"

"You want to talk about us, Edith? Cause I'll talk about us if that's what you wanna talk about..."

"I did not give up on you," she said, her voice rising. "I tried everything with you, but you were impossible to be around. I tried to get you help, to get you out of the house to socialize..."

He snickered. "Here's me, teetering on the edge of sanity, and your solution was a bunch of fucking cocktail parties."

"That is horseshit!" Her voice cracked. She cleared her throat. "I did everything for you. I begged you to get help."

"To go to a monkey house, you mean..."

"An army hospital..."

"As if I'm the only guy came back from the Pacific a little neurotic."

"A little neurotic? You tried to kill me!"

He pushed a hand against his forehead. "I did not try to kill you."

"What do you call it when I wake up in the middle of the night and you're on top of me with a pistol?"

Augy pulled the phone away from his ear and pressed it against his neck. Clemmie stepped out of the bathroom sopping wet in a massively oversized hotel robe. She watched him with a wrinkled nose.

"Listen, Edith, I'm glad you left the house when you did." Augy paused as the truth of his own words rang through his brain. "If you'd have stayed, I might've hurt you. Not on purpose. Never on purpose. God, you know I would never wanna hurt you, right? Please God, tell me you know that."

She was quiet for so long he thought they got disconnected.

"Edie?"

"I know that." Her voice was gentler, sadder. "Are you okay, Augy?"

"I need a favor. You're the only one I can trust with this."

"What is it?"

He sighed, eyes scanning Clemmie as she crawled into bed next to her little brother. "There's these kids…"

CHAPTER NINE

"I don't wanna go stay with some lady," said Clemmie, sticking out her bottom lip.

Augy straightened his collar as he rang the doorbell. "I'm sorry, kid, but I can't take you with me. It can get dangerous out there and…"

"I'm not scared of danger. We wanna come with you."

"Yeah," echoed Zychik, though his little voice quavered.

"I can't allow it," said Augy. "I have to make sure you kids are safe."

The door opened and on the other side stood Augy's replacement. He wasn't short or tall, fat or thin, ugly or good looking. There wasn't anything great about him: he had an okay job, could afford an okay house, was of decent intelligence and possessed an average sense of humor. Of course, that meant there wasn't anything terrible about him, either. He certainly wasn't a neurotic sleepwalker without two pennies to rub together, like certain out-of-work detectives.

Augy hated him. He hated his yellow glasses and striped shirt. He hated his boomerang mouth which never smiled or sneered. He hated his pockets of baby fat and his huge chin. But more than anything, he hated somebody so mediocre was married to his extraordinary wife.

"What are you doing here?" said Bill in that flat voice of his.

Though it made him sick, Augy smiled. "Hi, Bill. You're looking… Bill."

"Hmm." Bill narrowed his eyes at the kids.

"Edie here?"

"She's in the kitchen." Bill stepped aside and let them pass, but he followed close behind. The kids clung to Augy's hands as they strode down the dull green hall. He followed the sound of a chopping knife.

She was as beautiful as ever. Of course, she was. Red hair braided down her back, skin that glowed even in the dullest light. She wore a yellow dress with white roses, cinched tight at her waist to make that perfect hourglass. His hands fit in those curves like they were made for them. Her eyes and nose competed for control of her face, with chin and lips falling far behind. When she looked up at him with those blue-green eyes he still dreamt about swimming in, he forgot everything. He looked down at the linoleum.

"Augy?" She dropped her knife and rushed over. "What happened to you?"

"I'm fine." He flinched when her hand touched his cheek.

"You look like you were talking when you should've been listening," she said.

"You're hilarious."

"But it was a fight?"

"Yeah. You should see the other truck."

"Jesus, Augy." Her eyes burned like warm embers on his face, but he watched her hands. Pink nails on slim fingers, rubbing together nervously. When he met her eyes, he couldn't not smile. She smiled back.

"How you been doing, Rutabaga?" he said.

Bill cleared his throat. "What exactly is this all about?"

Augy turned to Bill with a sneer. "Ain't you got lawn work to do or something?"

"Augy." Edith's little mouth tightened, then she addressed Bill, "I didn't get a chance to talk to you last night, honey, but I told Augy we'd babysit."

"Babysit?" muttered Bill.

Augy plunked down at the kitchen table. "Coffee?"

"Are you offering yourself coffee?" she snorted.

"I think somebody ought to."

Edith pulled down the Nescafé. "What can I get your little friends?"

"Couple chocolate milks?" asked Augy, looking at the kids.

Clemmie nodded and drew nearer, her little brother so close behind he stepped on the back of her shoe.

"Knock it off, Sissy," she said.

When Edith bent down in front of Clemmie and Zychik, Augy glanced down the front of her dress. His heart almost never beat in his ears anymore, but he heard it.

"I got some jacks in the living room," said Edith, her voice as soft as the inside of a new sweatshirt. "Would you two like to play while the grownups talk?"

Clemmie eyed Augy. When he nodded, she shrugged and led her little brother into the living room. Bill loomed in the doorway puffing his pipe till Edith said, "Bill, would you show the kids where the jacks are?"

Bill looked constipated, but he drifted after the kids into the living room. Edith settled in across from Augy at the table.

"Jacks, huh?" he said, sipping his grimy coffee. "So, that's how you and Billy boy pass those long winter evenings."

"They're my nephew's, smart ass. And you already know that." She rubbed the back of her neck. "I don't understand. Who are those kids?"

"It's complicated."

"Why can't you take them to your sister's?"

"Also complicated."

"I don't know nothing about kids, Augy."

He waved her off with a grunt. "What's to know? Feed them, wash them, let them listen to the radio. My nephew's big on dirt."

"I'm serious."

He sighed and leaned his elbows on the table. "I know this is a big ask, but take a look at those kids, eh? Their lives are garbage. Their father's a psychopath and their mother's missing."

"So, why not tell the cops? And don't you say it's complicated."

"It's... been a bit of a snafu."

"Cut the gas."

He took her pack off the table and lit a cigarette. Menthol. He wrinkled his nose in disgust but kept smoking. "I need to find their mother."

"And what if someone finds out they're here? What am I supposed to tell people?"

"What do you want, a script?"

She kept looking from the living room to him, drumming her fingers.

He laid his hand on hers. "I owe you a million."

"You owe me more than that." Her eyes swept up to meet his. Everything in him wanted to lean across the table and kiss her.

"Do you remember our trip to Key West?" he asked breathily.

She shook her head but smiled anyway.

"There was a table, a lot like this one."

"Don't." She pulled her hand away and pressed her fingers into her eyes as if blocking an image. Augy licked his lip and sat back.

"All right," she said. "How long do you think it'll take to find their mother?"

"Give me a week."

"And if you don't find her?"

"Put them up for adoption. What do I care?" Augy stood and rolled his shoulders. He glanced through the doorway into the living room at Clemmie and Zychik, settled on the carpet and fighting over the big red ball. Augy sighed. "I'm gonna be sincere for ten seconds, all right?"

Edith lifted her eyebrows. "Sounds refreshing."

"Clemmie's a spitfire, and that little boy is so goddamn cute I wanna squeeze him till his head pops off."

Edith laughed and shook her head.

"I will find their mother and I will be back for them. You can bet the farm."

She watched his eyes for a few seconds. "I believe you."

Augy headed into the living room. He plopped down between the kids as Zychik fumbled the ball. Augy grabbed it, bounced it up and snatched a jack. "Okay, you're all set here."

"Can we please come with you?" said Clemmie. The quaver in her voice was more than mere frustration.

"You see that lady over there." He pointed at Edith who was hovering in the doorway of the kitchen. "She's my best girl, and she's a hell of a lot of fun. At least, she used to be."

Edith smirked and looked away.

"Isn't she married to that guy?" asked Clemmie, pointing at Bill.

"Nobody's perfect." He winked at Edith.

"When do we get to see Mama?" Zychik demanded, clenching impatient fists.

"The sooner I go, the sooner I can bring her back."

"Well, go away then."

Laughing, Augy set down the ball and the three jacks he'd collected. "You two be good."

He stood and put out his cigarette in the ashtray next to Bill's lime green armchair. "All right, stud muffin. I'm gonna get out of your hair."

Bill groaned. "Goodbye, August."

Edith followed him outside onto the stoop. Closing the door all but an inch behind her, she held on to the handle.

The neighborhood was green and pink, square lawns and square windows. One of those planned communities popping up everywhere these days, luring people out of the cities with promises of sunshine and symmetrical white-bread perfection. Even the squirrels seemed cookie-cutter. Something told Augy he ought to hate the place, but he had to admit it had a certain charm. Thirty years in LA had left him with a sheen of sticky smoke all over his soul. A bit of sunshine and daisies were refreshing, even though it was a mirage.

"Next time you talk to Mary," said Augy, "let her know I'm not dead, all right?"

Edith raised her eyebrows and nodded. "Where's your car?"

He shrugged.

She pressed her lips together. "You ain't got a car?"

"I'm at the mercy of destiny, baby."

"Can I call you a cab?"

"I prefer Augy."

"Moron."

"Beautiful." He was still thinking about that table in Key West as he plodded down the concrete steps. The way she'd looked in her black gingham bikini. The way she'd looked without it. Part of him wanted to turn around and ask her how sex was with old back and sides McGee. He wanted to ask if Bill kept his tube socks and undershirt on. He seemed the sort to make love to a woman through the fly of his tighty-whities.

No, thought Augy. It was best to leave and not say anything more. Besides, if he had to look at Edith's little bee-stung mouth much longer, he'd have to do something about that perfect lipstick of hers. Something told him she hadn't been kissed properly since marrying that walking, talking sweater vest.

He felt her eyes follow him as he limped down the street. He was a few houses down the block before the screen door banged closed. He turned back. The round top mailbox in front of their house proudly declared "The Kowalskis" in white cursive. The red flag was up. Augy walked over and snapped it off. If he'd had a car, he would've run it over.

CHAPTER TEN

Trying to preserve what little money he had, Augy hitched his way from Whittier back to the city. This time he was picked up by a pink-skinned farmer dragging a horse trailer. The man invited Augy to sit in the cab and sing for his supper, probably because he spent most of his time with horses, who are by and large poor conversationalists.

He'd left the Ford parked outside the Hyatt on Sunset Boulevard, and hadn't revealed its whereabouts to his sister. It would've been towed by now. His profession gave him occasion to become acquainted with most of the impound lots in the city, as well as the people who ran them. So he made his way to Compton from where the farmer dropped him off in East LA.

The fenced-in lot was half-impound, half-junkyard. He circled around the back of a few aluminum buildings to the private home of the owner.

Ben sat out front on a pile of scrap metal throwing a tennis ball for his three dogs. He wasn't wearing a shirt, displaying the mosaic of Navy tattoos that covered his arms and chest. Like Augy, he'd served in the Pacific, first as a mess attendant, then as a cook, and finally on a gun crew on the USS Sunfish. Submarines gave Augy the shivers. He wasn't sure he could've handled what those human sardines suffered through day after day. He would've rather been stuck in a flooded foxhole taking mortar fire, or climbing coral beaches being shot at by submachine guns than listen to the ocean crush the walls around him, crammed in with eighty other sweaty guys, with less than a cubic foot of personal space, surfacing only at night, temperatures soaring to over one hundred degrees, breathing the same foul air until there was so little oxygen, you couldn't even light a cigarette. Other than the mine, Augy could hardly fathom a more loathsome corner of hell. And guys signed up to be on submarines. After Pearl, the line for the Navy had been the longest of all.

Girls liked the uniforms; that's all it was.

The dogs noticed him. They barked excitedly and raced to see who would get to bury their nose in his crotch first. These were no spaniels or hound dogs. These were junkyard mutts—half rottweiler, half velociraptor. Augy was knocked to the flat of his back and drenched in their happy slobber.

"Get off me, you miserable ankle-biting bastards!"

Ben laughed as he approached. "Get a load of this lanky motherfucker." He whistled and the dogs pulled back, then he gave Augy a hand to his feet. "Who smashed your face?"

"Car crash."

"Yeah? Heap end up here?"

"Don't know. It was a cherry Duesenberg Model J."

"I got it." Ben had a couple of rotten teeth, but somehow still managed to pull off a charming smile. "Ain't cherry no more. You was in that?"

Augy nodded.

"In that case, you're looking pretty good."

"I'd like a peek at the car."

"No problem. Why don't you come inside and wipe that shit off your face first."

Augy grunted in agreement. "Goddamn dogs."

Ben laughed again as he yanked open the door to his bungalow. "Ain't a bitch alive don't love you. Why is that?"

"Search me," said Augy, as he followed inside.

The house was about three-quarters of a Sears catalog Lynn model. The kit had shipped missing a roof and with a number of irregular beams, so it ended up at the junkyard. When Augy first met Ben, he and his brother had been slapping the house together. Augy was enlisted to hold up trusses and hammer a few nails, in exchange for examining a car he needed to get at for a case. The makeshift tin roof was by no means attractive, but it worked to keep the rain and wind out. Afterward, they'd shared a pizza and enough beers to become friends.

The interior of the house was littered with bric-a-brac Ben was fixing up to sell. Furniture, engines, electronics—anything that would fetch a price. Augy dodged through the clutter to the little bathroom where he cleaned off the dogs' adoration.

He hadn't checked himself in a mirror since the crash. Till now he'd been focused on his ribs and foot, but there were stitches in his forehead and big bruises on his neck. He'd always had a face for radio, but this was a new low.

When he came out, Ben had two cold beers in hand. "I'm glad you're here," he said. "There's something I've been wanting to show you."

Augy lifted his eyebrows, taking the beer with an inaudible thank you.

Ben produced a camera. Even before he had it in hand, Augy knew it was a Contax S by the Dresden-based company Zeiss Ikon. The camera was state of the art at the time of its release in 1949, being one of the first to have fixed eye-level pentaprism SLRs. Its gears were famous for their shabby construction, but otherwise, it was a respectable piece of machinery.

Augy brought the viewfinder to his eye and smiled. "Don't tell me this ended up at the dump?"

Ben shrugged. "Its insides just needed some tender loving care. It's shipshape now."

"How much you want for it?"

"Take it. I like to have you law-types owing me favors."

"About that…" Augy groaned as he sat down on a threadbare Lay-Z-Boy and threw up his legs. The dogs' loving assault had taken a bit out of him. "If any cops come by, do you think you could forget I was here?"

Ben sat down on the coffee table—a scrap-metal do-it-yourself masterpiece. "That don't sound good."

"It's a temporary situation."

"It's that case of yours… the what-do-you-call-ems?"

"Hollisters." Augy sucked on his beer. "Yeah, well."

"Ain't they the ones tanked your business?"

Augy shifted. Immediately after the Hollisters' case, his client list had dwindled. No amount of newspapers hailing him as a hero helped. In fact, they probably made things worse. Thugs parked outside his office all hours, keeping potential clients away. Then one night, his car was stolen. The police investigated. Nothing.

"I didn't think they'd sent nobody after you," said Ben, "like they was fucking with you from far back."

"That's a damn fact." Augy lifted his beer.

"So, what's changed?"

Augy hesitated. He still didn't know how the Hollisters were connected to Countess London, or if they even were. Katya had said so, but they'd been T-boned before she had a chance to explain.

Ben snorted. "Those motherfuckers are trying to drive you to put a pistol in your mouth."

Augy sighed and nodded. "Motherfuckers."

Ben laughed so hard he spat out his beer. Motherfucker wasn't a word most white people used, especially not someone as shockingly Caucasian as Augy.

"Don't worry, I don't much talk to cops anyhow." Ben wiped the corners of his mouth with his shirttail. "I tell you what. I finally got that Caddy of yours fixed up to sell."

He meant Harry's Caddy. "No shit?"

"Well, I mean, it ain't never gonna be the same after what you did to it."

"What I did?" Augy laughed. After he'd lost his business, and shortly after that his home, he'd moved into the Cadillac. The only work he could find at that point was cheap and dirty snoop jobs for wives who thought their husbands were having affairs with bullet-bra wielding secretaries, or husbands who were convinced their wives were getting diddled by imaginary milkmen. But it turned sour fast.

He was in his car taking pictures of a married man and his teenaged lover when the man noticed him and flew into a rage. He attacked the car with a baseball bat. By the time Augy tackled him down, the car was unsalvageable. The man was arrested, slapped with a small fine, and set free. Judges didn't like Augy. Moretti had once told him he had a face that made him look like he spent all his time eating shit and telling lies. Not a great look.

Now, he wondered if he'd been set up to be attacked by that unrelenting psychopath.

"Well, I'm glad somebody got something out of it." Augy groaned like an old door as he rose to his feet. "Let's get a look at the Duesenberg."

He followed Ben out to the auto yard. Other than the cobalt paint and a few twists of chrome, the car was unrecognizable.

The cops had already searched everything. They had Katya's purse, her hit list, her cigarette case. His money. Chances were there was nothing more to find, but Augy got down on his knees and poked through the wreckage anyway. The search turned up a tire gauge, a tube of bright red lipstick, a few cigarette butts, and a small paper sack full of garbage. He poured out the garbage and found a Styrofoam cup, a few used paper napkins, and a wrapper from a pillow mint. The logo on the wrapper looked like a mountain with the words "White Dragon" printed underneath.

He rummaged through his pockets until he found Katya's matchbook. The logos matched.

Augy stood and lit a cigarette. "Ever heard of White Dragon?"

"Sounds like something in Chinatown," answered Ben, helping himself to Augy's last smoke without asking.

"Chinatown." Augy shook his head. It was probably a coincidence—someplace Ethan Elmsly frequented. Katya probably found the matches in his car. Still, he didn't have much to go on. He had to trust Moretti had the Tyler house covered. Whether or not the helmet-headed son of a bitch knew the mayor, firing shotgun shells into a police car would end with his house being searched.

The unwelcomed thought ran through him once again Katya may already be dead. He hoped that wasn't the case, but even if it were, it didn't change anything. He'd already killed two men and kidnapped two children. And Sumika was still mutilated. There was no going back. Katya had suggested there was a network of people who deserved to die—people like Ethan Elmsly. Like the Hollisters. Like whoever it was had put all those dead girls in that sinkhole.

Countess London. The name still didn't make any sense, but every time he closed his eyes he saw it written in scorched flesh. He was going to find out who or what she was, or die trying.

CHAPTER ELEVEN

The Ford wasn't at the lot, but for a signature, Ben let Augy borrow a 1951 Studebaker that smoked like the Hollywood Hills in July. It rattled when it moved and popped when it stopped, and the driver's side door and the front panel didn't match the rest.

Augy had a case once—a double murder in fact—that led him into San Francisco's Chinatown with its gambling, prostitution, hidden passageways, and exotic drugs. Up there, murder and extortion went uninvestigated. Outsiders were only welcome if they had money to spend. A white guy could get himself a girl for the night, a sack full of sunshine and a bowl of chop suey, but once he'd finished he'd better agitate the gravel in a jiffy. And don't expect a damn fortune cookie.

By comparison, LA's Chinatown was Disneyland. In fact, it was a planned community built in the late thirties by Paramount Studios so they'd have somewhere to film their Chinatown scenes without having to go to the real Chinatown. LA's Chinatown had a lower crime rate than neighboring districts because, in many ways, it was a posh area, filled with restaurants, markets, and night clubs. They were all Chinese owned, but they were the sort of businesses that paid their taxes and didn't hide bodies in their dumpsters. They were frequented almost exclusively by whites from Hollywood and Malibu.

So Augy wasn't trepidatious when he parked the Studebaker and approached a building with the words "White Dragon" glowing on the sign. But when he saw a line of people out front waiting to get in, all dressed to the nines, a depressed sigh emanated from the recesses of his soul. He'd been praying for a takeaway restaurant; what he got was a trendy dinner club. The kind of place he'd have a hard time getting into on a good day, let alone in an ill-fitting suit with cuts and bruises all over his face making him look like something out of a horror movie that ended with a bunch of torch-wielding peasants storming a castle.

He adjusted his fedora and headed straight to the front of the line. He wasn't about to waste what little money he had on bribing doormen. If he couldn't talk his way in, he wasn't getting in.

"Pardon me, kitten," he said to the young woman at the front of the line, then in surreptitious tones, he addressed the tuxedo-clad doorman. "I'm here about Ethan Elmsly."

The doorman furrowed his brow in a tell-tale way.

"He was my cousin," Augy continued. "I don't know if you've all heard, but he cashed in his chips a few days ago."

"Yes, of course, we've heard," said the doorman in a monotone that said he didn't give a hoot.

Augy decided to take a wild stab. The name Mrs. Elmsly had given him for her husband's confidant had been nagging at him. He thought he may have finally figured where a guy called Elmsly might've met a dame called Wong. "He gave me a final message for his friend, Lily Wong. She works here, right?"

"Miss Lily is performing tonight," said the doorman.

"Is it all right if I go in and watch her show, then talk to her after?"

"What did you say your name was, sir?"

"John. John Elmsly."

The doorman scanned his list, but Augy put a hand on the host podium. "I won't be on there. This kind of place ain't my scene. I'm too old. Too married. You know what I'm saying?" He spread his hands wide in what he hoped seemed like an honest appeal. "I'm just trying to do right by my cousin."

The doorman tilted his head back so Augy could see right up his nose. "You may go in, but I must insist you rent a coat and tie as yours is, shall we say...?"

"Oh, I know. Thanks a million, Kemosabe. It's downright decent of you."

"That will be ten dollars."

"Ten?" Augy suppressed the urge to whistle. After the cab ride and the motel last night, plus breakfast for the kids this morning, he had $31.45 left of the forty Matilda Tidwell had so kindly donated. His fingers stiffened as he reached into his pocket and passed over a twenty.

"Oh, thank you, sir," said the doorman and stuffed the bill in his jacket.

Augy opened his mouth to argue, but it was too late. With clenched fists, he stormed over to the coat check where a four-foot-ten Chinese man with an English mustache and nothing to say fitted him with a bowtie and black sports coat with thin velvet lapels. Augy was forced to check his fedora, so he spat in his hands and slicked back his unruly hair, then used his thumb to try to get a spot off his leather lace-ups. If he'd known he were headed to a dinner club, he would've stopped and had them shined.

He tried to stand up straight and not limp as he headed through the second set of doors into an elegant dining room. The curtains were closed on the stage and the band was playing. Augy got the attention of a cigarette girl— a plain thing wearing a beautiful silk dress with a high collar that was tight all the way down her thighs. He put a quarter in her tray and grabbed a pack of Encore filters. Moretti and Harry always gave him guff for smoking filters, saying they were for ladies, but Augy didn't care. Just because he was a man didn't mean he liked having tobacco in his teeth.

The cigarette girl lingered a moment, squinching her tiny nose. He never knew what to say to cigarette girls. They had to deal with so many pick-ups, come-ons, and ass-slaps, it seemed rude even to make small talk.

He realized she was waiting for a tip.

"Son of a bitch," he whispered and reached into his pocket for another quarter.

She smiled and bowed a little. "Thank you, mister."

Augy found an empty table near the back, ordered water, and lit a cigarette. He wanted a G and T, but contemplating how much one might cost in a joint like this gave him a stomachache. He felt like a mouse in sunglasses trying to hide in a cats-only club. The people here had money. Ethan Elmsly had driven a Model J for Christ's sake. That was the same car Al Capone and Greta Garbo drove. Clark Gable, for crying out loud. These people had money, and at least a few of them smelled he didn't.

On the other hand, the women frequenting the club were something to see. He was trying to decide which one he wanted to pretend he wasn't staring at until the curtain was drawn and Miss Lily and the Tam-Tam girls were announced.

He'd seen a lot of showgirls—more than his fair share in his line of work— but Miss Lily was something special. She wore a turquoise dress with a neckline that plunged almost to her navel and long black gloves. She was lousy with jewels. Her lips were so red it was threatening, like a lioness fresh from the kill. Her long black hair hung down to her waist even though it was done up with sticks in a high-top ponytail. Augy loved long hair. Not many women let it get past their shoulders nowadays, and curled it even shorter with chemicals and heat.

Edith had long hair. So did Katya.

Miss Lily took her spot behind the microphone, and the scantily-clad Tam-Tam girls set up behind her. The band played the unmistakable introduction to *Quizas, Quizas, Quizas*. Miss Lily sang:

"You won't admit you love me
And so, how am I ever to know?
You always tell me
Ho nang, ho nang, ho nang."

The crowd laughed at the Chinese, and Miss Lily winked. Her tiny infantilized voice cut into Augy's skin like nails. Being raised by a suffragette, he'd seen behind the curtain of the sexy baby doll routine and it wasn't pretty. A lot of showgirls used that grating childlike voice. That Marilyn Monroe *I'm-so-small-and-helpless-don't-you-just-wanna-stick-it-in-me* bull. Nothing ruined a good-looking woman quicker.

When Miss Lily and the Tam-Tam girls finished their set, the crowd gave a standing ovation. They put on a good enough show, but Augy would've grumbled to stand to applaud the Sermon on the Mount, so he kept his seat and finished his cigarette. He waited a few minutes, then made his way backstage. A bouncer gave him a hard time, but he told him the same sob story he'd told the doorman, and soon he was led to the greenroom.

Augy had learned long ago that filtering lies through the truth was the best way to go about things, even if the story ended up more convoluted than if he'd told a fresh lie. Twisting what people thought they knew confused them, made them question themselves, and left enough space in their minds for a rat to wriggle through. A little bit of wisdom from Satan himself, that was.

Augy knocked and waited. A call came, but it was as Chinese as everything else. He hoped the words meant *come in*, because that's what he did, closing the door behind him.

Lily Wong sat at a tiny dressing table, illuminated by rows of spherical bulbs. She was still in her turquoise dress, still every bit as beautiful. When she glanced at him in the mirror, she sucked in a breath. Obviously, she was expecting someone with a different face.

"How'd you get back here, huh?" Her voice was husky and world-wise, a far cry from the grating baby doll shrill. "Sorry, baby. I don't do autographs."

"That's just as well. I ain't got a pen."

"Then what do you want?"

"I'm here to talk about Ethan Elmsly. I understand he was a friend of yours."

"You can't expect me to keep track of all the fellas wanna buy me things." Lily Wong turned back to her vanity and pulled out one teardrop diamond earring, but her eyes stayed on Augy through the mirror. "What do you care anyway?"

He lit a cigarette and took a few steps closer, then settled on an ottoman at her back. "Mr. Elmsly was murdered."

"Am I being accused of something?"

"Of course not."

"Then what are you asking me for, baby?"

Augy cracked a knuckle. "Miss Wong…"

"Call me Lily."

"Lily." He smirked. He couldn't help it. "Mr. Elmsly is suspected to have been involved in a crime syndicate."

"Most of 'em are." She snorted. "Well, I ain't involved in no syndicate. And I don't know nothing about who killed him."

"I already know who killed him."

"You do?" She turned in her seat to face him, peering with cat eyes over her pointy shoulder. "Who?"

He tented his fingers. "I might be willing to share that information, darling. If you could be a little more helpful."

"You a cop?"

"I'm a private investigator." He saw the way her nose wrinkled and added, "I guarantee anything you tell me I'll take to my grave, if that's what you want."

"Now, I am confused." When she crossed her legs the fabric of her dress fell away, revealing black lace garters. "How'd you know Mr. Elmsly?"

"I didn't."

Lily pressed her lips together. "What you say your name was, baby?"

It occurred to him to lie, but what would be the point? These people already knew his name, his profession. It would be easier for everyone if he owned himself. "My name's August Small. You can call me Augy."

"Augy Small?" She lifted an eyebrow. "Now, that wouldn't be Augustinius Small?"

"Not if I can help it."

"As in Augustinius Small what sent the Hollisters to the chair?"

He grinned. For all the hell it had caused him, he never ceased to be proud to have been the one who ended the lives of those two monsters. But now that he understood the network they'd been a part of, the types of people who'd been hurt by their deaths, and that his name was already famous among this spiderweb of sadists—well, Augy was downright honored.

Lily bit her bottom lip and looked askance at the door of her dressing room. In a low voice, she said, "We shouldn't talk here."

"Oh?"

"Give me a few minutes. I'll meet you in the ally out back."

Augy nodded and left without a word. The patrons had taken to the dancefloor, so he skimmed the outer wall to get out. He returned the clothes and was thankful to get back his fedora and seven dollars, minus the cleaning fee. He'd worn the jacket less than an hour. It felt like robbery, but when he tried to complain the man pretended not to speak English. Augy grumbled as he stepped back out onto the street.

He grabbed his camera out of the car, then circumnavigated the building towards the narrow alley. Lamplight reflected off the side of a large dumpster; otherwise, he couldn't see a thing. He paused, turned his back on traffic, and pressed it against the lamppost. Hardly a bulletproof bunker, but better than nothing.

He almost never had real flashbacks anymore—those waking nightmares that came on without warning and highjacked him: brain, body, and soul. That filled him with smells, sounds, and physical sensations, as much as visions and emotions. When reality washed away, sending him reeling back through time. To the unending blackness. To the white lights and rubber gloves. The screams and the blood.

When he blacked out, he never knew what might happen. That was the most terrifying part of it—knowing that at any moment he might slip out of his own mind and wake up having done something horrible.

He had no more control over it than he did the weather. He bit down hard, the muscles tightening in his face. His eyes began to ache, bulging as he searched the darkness.

The memory was already pulsing against the back of his eyes, his wife's frantic screams tearing into his ears.

He glanced over both his shoulders and lit another cigarette. "Get it together, Small."

One moment he was watching Japanese guards beat three men to death with the butts of their guns. Kicking and cursing. Blood everywhere. The men begging in a language he didn't understand. Then, Augy snapped. He shoved his way out of line, tackled one of the soldiers, and wrestled away his gun. Straddling the guard's chest, Augy leveled the pistol and pulled the trigger. Blood spattered, warm and metallic on his tongue.

He saw Edith shaking under him. Begging. Thank god the pistol wasn't loaded.

Augy jerked his head and opened his eyes. He hadn't realized he'd closed them.

The black alley stretched in front of him like a train tunnel. For all he knew, Lily Wong had gone to grab some thugs with semi-automatics to blow his brains out the moment he slunk in to meet her. He fingered the gun tucked in his belt—the Browning 9mm Moretti had given him. It was too light to be of much comfort.

"Nobody lives forever." He flicked his cigarette and watched the ember pinwheel into the darkness. He cocked the gun.

CHAPTER TWELVE

A door opened in the alley, bathing the moist bricks in ruddy light. He didn't recognize her at first, in her black pencil skirt and batwing jacket, with her beautiful hair pinned up under a pillbox hat.

He tipped his hat vaguely in her direction.

When she saw him, she shook out her shoulders, lit a cigarette in a cocktail length holder, and approached. She passed him without a word, but the way she widened her eyes spoke volumes. He waited until she'd gone about half a block, then followed.

They walked like that up to College Street, then along Bunker Hill Avenue, away from Chinatown's central plaza into the residential area. She kept looking back and forth as if forcing herself not to look back at him. Augy wasn't shy to glance over his shoulder. Nobody was there.

The streetlamps were spaced farther apart here than in the business district, extending the darkness. Four and six-plexes lined the road behind bushy palm trees. Lily Wong stopped at one such building—a white box with dark tile shingles. He came to her side but said nothing as she pulled her keys out of a little black clutch, and they both slipped into her apartment.

"So, who's following us?" he asked, as she bolted the door with no less than four locks.

"You saw someone?" Her voice was on the edge of panic.

"No, but you seem to be expecting somebody."

She sighed with relief. "Nobody they don't know comes home with me, you dig?"

She strode past him into her kitchenette and started fixing drinks. The apartment was all one room—a bed in one corner, a dresser in another. A half-open door leading to a bathroom. It was illuminated by one dim overhead light, buzzing gently. Candles dotted the dresser and nightstand; rivers of dry wax clung to the wood. The trappings looked expensive—tassels and gold thread—and it was covered in fancy clothes, but he'd expected a headliner for a popular nightclub to have a nicer place. Bigger, at least.

He settled down on her bed because there was nowhere else to sit.

She brought him a tall glass of scotch, the same as her own, and sat beside him. She took off her hat and drank half the glass before coming up for air. "You didn't tell nobody else at the club your name, did you?"

"I may be ugly, darling, but I ain't that stupid," said Augy.

"So, what do you want to know exactly?"

"Let's start off easy. What was Mr. Elmsly to you?"

"He made sure he was everything to me."

"I don't follow."

"When I started working at the Dragon, it was owned by Mr. Li. He was a decent guy, and he treated me and the girls real good. I loved working there back in those days."

Augy furrowed his brow and sat back, waiting for more.

"But Mr. Li was a gambler. Made a lot of silly bets with serious people, and one day he lost everything. The club, his house. They even cut off one of his hands." She finished her scotch. "That's when Mr. Elmsly showed up. The people who owned the club sent him there to look after their investment.

"I didn't give a hoot either way at first." She sighed and leaned back on one hand. "Bread is bread, you know what I'm saying? But it didn't take long to figure out Mr. Elmsly wasn't gonna run things the same."

"Go on," Augy prompted after she'd paused for a good minute.

"He wanted to be my man. Made that real clear from the start. He came into my dressing room every night after my show. He was a looker, sure, but he never jived with me."

"What do you mean?"

"He thought he was so smooth, but there was something lumpy about him. He was real handsy. Raunchy, the way he'd talk to me. Thinking he was turning me on. And the girls started talking about him too. The things he was trying to get them to do. Get them to spend time with VIPs after hours." She rolled her head on her neck. "I put up with it for a while cause I loved my job, but pretty soon, I couldn't take it no more. I told him I was done. I quit."

She went back to the kitchenette and poured another big glass of scotch. She didn't keep talking till she was back on the bed beside him, staring down into the honey-colored liquid. "He came to my apartment that night and beat the hell out of me. He told me he'd kill me before he let me leave."

She stared at something Augy couldn't see, through time.

"He made me do things to him," she said in a low voice, "all covered in blood like I was. And he made me lay still while he did what he wanted to me."

"You don't have to…"

"No. I want you to know. It's time somebody knew." She pressed the back of one hand to her eye, maybe plugging a tear. "Right over there on the floor like a goddamn animal."

He nodded. It was hard to keep looking at her while she talked, imagining the things she said, but he also couldn't bring himself to look away.

"That was three years ago. And that's what it's been like since." She took another long pull of scotch. "And he stopped paying me. He'd buy me perfume or dresses. He'd pay my rent. But I never got any cash in hand. Nothing I could use to get away. He even made me keep my jewelry at the club."

Augy took a deep breath. "What do you know about Countess London?"

Her eyes flinched to meet his. He recognized the expression. It was the same look little Sumika had given him when he said that name. Same as Katya. Each woman wore it differently, but it was unmistakable—like three sizes of the same suit.

"One night, Mr. Elmsly made me go with him to a party up in the mountains. We must've drove fifty miles. I don't know. But we came to this place—this real primo mansion in the middle of nowhere. It was the biggest house I ever saw. Real modern. All angles and glass." She polished off her whiskey. Augy realized he hadn't had a sip, so he finished his off, too. He fetched the bottle from the kitchenette and refilled both their glasses.

"That's the only time I met Mr. Elmsly's associates. There were a lot of white fellas, as you might expect, but what got me was how many Japanese there was."

"Japanese?"

She nodded. "And they were all there with their girls. Girls like me. Showpieces, you know?"

He lit two cigarettes and fit one into her holder before passing it over. "Did you recognize any of them?"

"Nuh-uh." She took a drag, then chewed her bottom lip as the smoke filtered out through her teeth. "But some of the guys there weren't with girls. I mean, they were, but... they were like girls girls. Little kids. I don't know what else to call them... Anyway, as the night went on, things got a bit... I mean... It started out perverted, but it got really..."

Augy groaned and lay back on her bed. The scotch had already gone to his head. He didn't have the cash to drink much anymore. "Don't tell me."

"We were things to them. I guessed quick which guys had dates what had never been there before cause they all looked sick like me, or plain terrified. But some of the other women, they went right along with their fellas. I don't know how to describe—"

"Please don't. I understand."

"You can't," she spat. "Cause you weren't there."

"I'm pretty sure I've seen the aftermath." Augy propped himself up on his elbows to look her in the eye. "It got violent."

Lily nodded, her face reddening. He couldn't be sure if it was from the drink or the story.

"You've been to more than one of those parties, haven't you?" asked Augy. "There was one a few weeks ago?"

Again she nodded, then stood and rushed to open the window. Staring out into the darkness, she gasped in the cool desert air. "At that first party, they took me and some of the others into a back room. There were about twenty of us. Mostly dames, but a couple of fellas, too." She was breathless now, red fingernails digging into her thighs. "They lined us up and made us take our tops off. Mr. Elmsly ripped my dress when I didn't want to. And in came this woman I hadn't seen till then. She was short and old, dressed real simple, and wearing a doctor's mask. But all the guys, they bowed to her and said something in Japanese. And then one handed her... I mean..."

Lily sighed out a heavy breath, then turned to face him. "Come over here, detective."

Augy stood. About two feet separated the bed and the window. She was close enough to smell her—roses and whiskey.

She undid the buttons on her jacket, and then the top ones on her polka-dotted blouse. She shrugged her shirt off one shoulder and turned her back to him.

There it was, burned into her porcelain skin like a garbage truck parked in the Louvre: *Property of Countess London, 12611987.*

As she did up the buttons on her blouse, Augy slumped back on the bed and hung his head between his knees. "Could you take me to that house?"

"He kept me blindfolded both ways."

"Motherfucker."

"Can you tell me now?" She settled beside him. "Who killed Mr. Elmsly?"

"Her name's Katya. She was probably one of the bits of arm candy at that party."

"What's she look like?"

"She's about five-nine, long black hair, light brown eyes. Russian accent. Body like Rita Hayworth."

Lily shook her head. "Why'd she do it?"

"My guess is Elmsly was convenient. She wants to kill all of them."

"I hope she does."

"So do I," said Augy, but he was kicking himself for not agreeing to help Katya the first time she asked. What had it taken for her to run away from her family, abandoning her children to go on this vendetta? How hard must it have been for her to trust him enough even to ask for his help? And what had he done, but reject her and make her wait for days while more people were hurt? He wanted to punch himself in the throat.

It flashed through him to hope she was dead, so she could no longer be tormented. But then he thought of stout-hearted Clemmie and sweet-faced baby Zychik—the bunny rabbit—and he wanted to punch himself in the throat again.

He closed his eyes and pushed his skull against the wall until it throbbed. "Ain't there nothing you can tell me to help me find these bastards?"

"I'm sorry. Mr. Elmsly made sure I was always on the outside."

He opened one eye to peer at her. "Mr. Li still around?"

"He killed himself. At least, that's what we heard down at the club."

Slapping his knees, Augy stood. "Thanks for the drink."

"Where are you going?"

"No offense, darling, but this is starting to smell like a dead end. If you can't give me the name of somebody else what's involved in this circus, I gotta find somebody who can."

She jumped up. "You're gonna leave me?"

"What exactly do you expect from me, Miss?"

"You've gotta help me, Mr. Small. They're sending somebody new to take over the club. They say he'll be coming in tomorrow night. If I have to become a whore for another of these sick creeps..."

She cried bitter tears she'd been holding in for god knows how long. They were those thick painful sorts of tears, hot as blood and twice as salty, that stain the face as well as the soul.

To his surprise, she fell against him and pressed her face into his chest. He wrapped her in his arms and squeezed, trying to still her trembling.

"I'm sorry," he said. "I'm being an insensitive sack of shit."

"If they find out I've been talking to you..." Lily stammered.

"I'll figure out... something. I promise."

He rubbed her back as her makeup melted into his jacket. He didn't have a plan. He didn't have any resources. His body was in a worse state than Ethan Elmsly's Duesenberg. And he was beginning to think he wasn't half as clever as he'd always hoped. He reflected on the movies that had made him want to become a detective in the first place. If Bogie had been on the case, he would've solved it, got the girl, and looked damn good doing it, long before his bones got crushed to paste.

Then again, Ethan Elmsly and his chums made the villains from those flicks look like paper shakers. At this point, unless she turned out to be the devil himself, Augy was going to be disillusioned when he finally found Countess London.

CHAPTER THIRTEEN

If you'd tortured him, Augy never would've been able to explain how he ended up in bed with Lily Wong that night. Scotch was at least half the story; visceral loneliness on both their parts the rest. He hadn't made any kind of move, never would've dreamt of it. And when she first kissed him, he pulled away. Augy was bleary-eyed with booze, but Lily showed no effects. It was obvious she drank at least that much every night. She was looking for something else to numb the pain. He knew it, and she admitted it. And the last thing she needed was him trying to coddle her. So even though he was exhausted and damaged, he sucked it up and gave her every painkiller he had to offer.

Lily Wong lit candles, baring her beauty to him in an easy golden ambiance that could not be mistaken. When he shed his suit, her eyes widened at the sight of him. Augy hadn't been naked with any woman other than Edith since coming back from the war, so he was thankful and incredibly relieved when Lily didn't comment on his scars. She pushed him down on the bed and climbed on top. Then she pressed his hands into the mattress and rode him till he hadn't a drop of liquid left.

As they lay panting, she touched the tattoo on his shoulder. "Is that supposed to be a bomb or something?"

"It's a rutabaga."

"Why?"

"Never mind."

She stroked his chest with the tips of her nails. "When's the last time you got petted properly, baby?" She flicked his erection, which hadn't softened in the least. "You're like a dog just got the cone off his neck."

Augy cracked up so hard his ribs felt like they'd collapse. Lily started laughing too, a lyrical sound he could tell was rarer than an albino alligator. She looked more beautiful at that moment than ever before.

Morning came and he found himself wrapped in her silk sheets, breathing in her vanilla incense, and blinking at uninvited sunshine that peeked through the sheer red curtains. The candles she'd lit last night were still burning, little stubs in clear glass dishes. He was the big spoon, her perfect ass pressed against his groin. His cheek rested on a bed of her smooth black hair. Inhaling its scent, his fingers traced the lines of her.

She made a kittenish whimper and pushed back against him. He hadn't felt so alive with lust since before the war took the man out of him. It almost seemed wrong, given what they'd talked about the night before and what he'd seen and experienced in the last few weeks. But that was what made it right. They were two shattered humans missing huge chunks of their hearts and if for only one night, they fit together and created an illusion of wholeness.

Without changing position, he made love to her once more, slow and lazy as the dawn. She craned her neck to kiss him, her back a perfect rainbow. Her skin craved his touch. He never wanted it to end.

And then it was over. He lay on his back and lit a cigarette. Lily curled under his arm, her face pressed against his gaunt hairless chest. His fractured ribs begged for mercy, but he told them to piss off. The moment was perfect but for their belly-aching, and he wasn't going to give in.

Silence filled the gaps between them, pushing them back into themselves. And Augy asked himself the question which eventually came out of Lily's mouth:

"What happens now, baby?"

Rather than answer, he withdrew to the bathroom. He washed his face, then lingered at the sink a long time, staring into his own chocolate-brown eyes. He wished he were more brash, more confident. But as a dozen possibilities raced through his brain Augy dissected each one and found seven thousand flaws. Nothing was foolproof.

Something unspoken had been nagging at him for a while, and with his head clear in the garish morning light, he gave it voice: he had to go see Sumika. He'd promised to keep her safe. What if he'd already failed her?

There was still the issue of Lily Wong. Knowing what he knew, he couldn't leave her. But he didn't have anywhere to take her. He was rapidly running out of safe houses.

Memories of one of his first cases presented in his brain. It was back when he was still working with a partner before he qualified for his own license. He'd been hired by a rich man called Franklin O'Hara to find a painting that had been stolen from his private gallery: a Georges Braque piece, which to Augy looked like a half-remembered nightmare reflected in a cracked mirror. But the confounded thing was O'Hara's favorite; he'd paid more for it than Augy had for his and Edith's first house. Suffice it to say, Augy found the painting. It had been stolen by O'Hara's own housekeeper. He'd rarely seen a man so grateful; with tears in his eyes, O'Hara had kissed Augy's hands.

And in addition to paying his fee and expenses, O'Hara made a bizarre offer.

"If you're ever looking for a vacation spot," O'Hara had said, "I have a house in Malibu. I would be honored if you and your lovely wife—" Augy had still had one of those at the time "—would be able to make good use of it. You're welcome anytime, and for as long as you like."

Five months he'd been homeless and this was the first he was thinking of this. Sometimes his brain was about as efficient as local government.

When he came out of the bathroom, Lily was standing in front of the mirror wearing a beige knit dress and brushing out her bird's nest.

Augy snatched his jockeys off the floor. "You got a phone, darling?"

Lily gesticulated to her nightstand. "What's up?"

"I think I know a safe place you can go for a while, but there's a girl we gotta pick up first." He grabbed the earpiece and dialed the operator.

"You leave your car down at the club?"

Augy nodded as the operator came on. "Hello? I need the home of Franklin O'Hara. North Hollywood."

"I'll go pick it up," said Lily.

"Connect me," he said to the operator, then looking at Lily, "Give me two minutes. I'll go with you."

"That's a hairbrained idea. If somebody sees us together, there's gonna be trouble."

"Let me go get it alone then."

"There's a few things I gotta pick up at the club."

Augy bit his bottom lip and drew his brows together.

"You look like you ate a basket of lemons," said Lily, turning to pat his cheek. "You worry too much, baby."

"I don't think I worry enough."

Lily pulled his face to her and kissed him so deep he got goosebumps. Then, she grabbed his suit jacket off the floor and pinched the keys. "Where's it parked?"

"In front of the noodle joint. Hunk of junk Studebaker. You can't miss it."

"I'll be back in two shakes of a lamb's tail," she said, then put on her pointed red kitten heels and sashayed out the door.

When Mr. O'Hara came on the line, he recognized Augy's voice and was downright enthusiastic to hear from him. Augy had to make with the small talk for a few minutes—learn about the new nightmarish art jolly old O'Hara had gotten his hands on. The old collector's personality was a bizarre dichotomy—kind and genial, but obsessed with darkness. Augy didn't have the time or motivation to ever understand it.

Finally, he got around to asking about the house and was thrilled to learn that not only did the offer stand, the house hadn't been lived in for a year, and nobody was planning on occupying it anytime soon.

"My wife loved that house," said Mr. O'Hara in his clear keen voice, "but since she passed, I can't bring myself to go there."

"You planning on selling the place?"

"I shouldn't think so. Too many memories. But it would make me happy knowing you and your wife were enjoying it. You're welcome to stay as long as you like."

"Thank you," said Augy. Telling the old man about his divorce would serve no purpose, but he still felt guilty for keeping it quiet.

After hanging up, Augy took a shower. He was used to showerheads being way too short; he had to get down on his knees to wash his hair. When he finished dressing, he checked the time on the ornamental golden clock on Lily's dresser.

She should've been back by now.

He searched for coffee, contented himself with tea, and checked her icebox. Nothing but a bottle of unlabeled brown sauce and a few leftover steamed buns. He ate them cold. The sauce was sweet and salty.

He was washing the plate when an explosion rattled the floor.

Augy threw on his shoes and raced outside. Neighbors milled on their stoops. A cone of black smoke rose to the north. The business district.

With his broken toes, he couldn't run no matter how badly he wanted to. He limped the half-mile from Lily's apartment to the source of the smoke. Sirens filled the air. A smell of burnt rubber.

A crowd was gathered in front of the noodle house. He shoved his way through.

"No. Please god."

The Studebaker was engulfed in flames, red death pouring out every window and from under the hood. The tires too were circles of fire, rubber melting into the asphalt. The black smoke was so thick it was impossible to see through.

He closed his eyes, feet glued to the spot, as firemen doused the blaze. Then they dragged a body out of the driver's seat. It was burnt beyond recognition, melted and still glowing like charcoal. But on its black feet were pointed kitten heels.

Augy walked away. Shoulders bumped him, but he felt nothing. Shouts filled the air, and he heard nothing. He tasted the smoke, and soon it was everywhere.

His mind stumbled. Blackness encircled him.

He was gone.

The blood splattered his face. The guard was under him, his skull blown open. Pink and squishy insides smeared like old paint. Augy was yanked back and beaten, but soon he heard the bark of a commanding officer, and they let up. Augy spoke Japanese. He'd been forced to learn it like all the other internees so that he would be able to obey the guards' orders. But at that moment, he didn't understand a word. The guards shot the three men they'd been beating—the ones Augy had been trying to save. Then they shot the two men who had been standing on either side of him in line—two Taiwanese infantrymen he didn't know from Adam.

Augy screamed and begged them to kill him, but that was too much like mercy. They bagged his head and led him away to the place that now filled his every nightmare.

His own voice echoed: "Please! For the love of god!"

He was lost in Elysian Park by the time his vision cleared. He sat down on a fat root twisting out of the earth and cradled his arms. He shouldn't have let her go. The bomb had been meant for him. There was no doubt about that.

A thousand images of her circled in his skull. The wreath of red around her eyes as she confessed the truth. The quiver of her lips as she begged for his help. Her red tears. Her long black hair pouring over her shoulders in the candlelight. Her rusty laughter. And finally, the corded embers of fire on her black skin, her face a grotesque inhuman mask.

How could he still be alive when she was dead?

Why was he still alive if she was dead, and they were dead, and everyone died except him? He'd killed her, this woman who'd begged for his protection. He'd killed them all.

He should've died when his plane went down in Singapore. If he could go back in time, he'd go to seconds after the machine gun destroyed his wing and let go of the joystick. Why had he worked so hard to land safely? He should've gone down in flames and glory.

Maybe if he'd done that, they'd all still be alive.

Augy began to tremble. No tears came. But his shaking grew so intense he had to sink down to the dirt and lay on his side.

The sun rose high in the sky, bathing the greenery surrounding him in warmth. But he felt so cold he thought his heart would stop beating if his skeleton didn't shake loose first.

Augy vomited, tasting that sweet salty sauce he'd taken from her fridge.

"Please," he whispered. "For the love of God."

CHAPTER FOURTEEN

Augy arrived at the White Dragon about an hour before opening. No customers were in line yet, but the doorman was there readying his podium. Augy waited till he was looking the other way, then walked past to the back alley. He stood beside the door Lily had come through the night before. Not only was it locked, it had no outside handle. But that was what he'd expected. He pressed his back against the brick and waited.

Time slid by. He listened to customers line up out front, chattering as they readied themselves for an exotic night out. Augy was a statue, but his muscles were loose. Ready. His eyes began to sting because he forgot to blink.

He had thirteen bullets.

At last, the door swung open. Augy didn't wait to see if it was some poor kid from the kitchen coming out for a smoke or even one of the girls. He grunted so the body turned towards him, then punched it in the solar plexus. The figure—a mere shadow—fell backward off the stairs onto the concrete. Augy propped open the door with the overstuffed garbage bag, then lifted the person by the scruff of the neck and punched it hard enough to make the head reel back, unconscious. The face came into focus: a kitchen boy after all.

He picked him up and threw him in the dumpster, then wedged the lid closed.

He slipped inside, kicking the garbage bag out into the alley behind him. Gun in hand, Augy edged down the hall. He may not have spoken Cantonese, or Mandarin, or native Taiwanese, but he knew enough to tell the languages apart. The White Dragon was a Cantonese establishment. That was the language Lily Wong had called out when he first knocked on her door, the same that swirled through the hallways now. He passed a noisy kitchen and a large dressing room where he heard the Tam-Tam girls speaking in hushed, frightened tones.

He found what he was looking for: an office with a plaque on it. Embossed in English was the word: Manager.

Augy had to pause for a deep breath, then pressed his ear against the door. The blood was rushing through his ears so loudly it was hard to hear over. Then, at last, came a voice:

"They found Campbell's brat, huh? Sloppy so-and-so. The Countess must be furious... I bet not. Who they sending to take her out? Bowman... ain't he in Frisco?" The voice was gruff and quick, speaking American English. "No, no, no. I told you. Nobody saw her leave with him. He said he was Elmsly's cousin. The doorman saw him go to the car. They let him right in. I know. I know. Well, whaddya expect, huh? These chinks ain't got the sense to pump piss out of a boot. I've got a new girl lined up for the night. There's always a hungry one in the wings." He paused. "Yeah, it's a shame. She had a sweet pussy."

Augy opened the door and stepped inside, gun first. The young man froze in place. He was East Asian, presumably Japanese, wearing a slim-fitting suit with a whiff of facial hair on his chin.

"Say goodbye," said Augy.

"Look, I gotta let you go. Yeah, yeah. No problem. Call you later tonight." He hung up the phone. "Now, calm down, buddy. Don't do anything you might regret."

"Keep your hands where I can see them."

He put them up. "Listen, buddy. There's ten guys out there with guns. If you shoot me, you're gonna end up so full of holes they could use you as a sieve."

Augy stepped up to the desk. He turned the Rolodex around and flipped through some cards. "Did you plant the bomb in my car?"

"You're August Small, huh?" The man smirked and leaned back. "You're not what I expected."

"What's your handle, while we're making nice?"

The man hesitated and his gaze flinched across the room before he settled back into his cocksure smile. "The name's Johnny Chiba." He gestured to a pack of cigarettes on the desk. Augy nodded and the man picked one up and lit it. "Listen, Detective. I think you may have gotten the wrong impression about what's going on here."

"Go ahead, Johnny." Augy rested a hip on the desk. "I got time."

"I assume you're here about the unfortunate thing that happened to Miss Wong. I can assure you, I had nothing to do with it."

"This your first day, huh?"

"Excuse me?"

"Seems you don't know how thin your walls are."

His eyes widened. "All right. You got me."

"Don't I just."

"You gotta understand who's business you've been poking around in."

Again, Chiba looked askance. When Augy turned, Chiba reached for the gun. Augy relinquished it without a fight, but with his left hand, he snatched up a letter opener and stabbed it through Chiba's other hand, pinning it to the desk. Chiba screamed and dropped the gun to grab at the wound.

"You're gonna wanna pipe down." Augy picked up the gun and resumed his seat on the edge of the desk. Chiba reached to yank out the knife, but Augy threatened the gun. "Leave it."

Chiba sat back, breathing hard through clenched teeth. "You can kill me, but it isn't going to change anything."

"Might make me feel better."

"You have no idea who you're dealing with."

"So you keep saying."

"Countess London owns the cops, the mayor, the whole goddamn city! You're a dead man walking."

"Who exactly is Countess London?"

"Fuck you!"

Augy snatched up the letter opener then stabbed it back down. Chiba screamed, his bones folding in pain.

"Who is Countess London?" said Augy.

"I don't know!"

"Come on, you expect me to believe that?" He twisted the knife.

"I swear I don't know!"

"Where is Katya Tyler?"

"Who?"

"Wrong answer." Augy pointed the gun at Chiba's crotch.

"They took her to the Lumbermill!"

Augy opened his mouth to speak, then bit his tongue. He felt like somebody had smacked his chest with a baseball bat. He couldn't have heard right. "What'd you say?"

"The Lumbermill. The address is there." Chiba pointed to the Rolodex with his nose. "It's a warehouse outside Burbank."

"What else is it called?"

"What?"

Augy backhanded him with the gun. "What else is it fucking called?"

"I don't know what you want!"

He leaned over Chiba and gripped the armrests of his chair. In a low voice, Augy said in Japanese, "Was it ever called the Epidemic Prevention and Water Purification Department?"

Chiba's eyes widened. His lip trembled. "How could you possibly know that?"

The doorknob twitched. Augy whipped around and shot the lumbering bouncer in the head the moment his face appeared in the doorway. The bullet left only a tiny red hole but sprayed the doorjamb with gore. Chiba screamed for help. Augy turned and shot him between the legs. Blood and flesh exploded. The sound he made was like a pig being slaughtered. He fell from his chair, but his hand was still pinned to the desk. Augy yanked out the letter opener and stabbed it through the side of his neck.

Augy shoved the Rolodex in his pocket and ducked behind the door as two more men loped into the room. While they gaped at Chiba's body, Augy put his gun to the back of one of their heads and fired. The other turned and raised his weapon. The bullet whizzed past Augy's ear so close he felt the wind and his hearing went tinny. He fired twice into the man's chest.

Chiba's gurgling and choking followed him into the hall. It would take him a few minutes to die. Still too fast.

Augy staggered towards the dressing room and threw open the door. The girls were huddled in the corner, frightened by the shots. He fired once into the ceiling. "Everybody out!"

The girls screamed and scattered.

Eight bullets left.

He turned to see two young guys in suits rush towards him down the hall. The taller one already had his gun drawn, the other was reaching into his jacket. Augy pressed his back against the wall to make himself a narrow target, as the first fired. The bullet skimmed Augy's chest, cutting open his shirt and leaving a perfect line of blood. Augy gripped his gun with both hands. There was no time to aim properly.

The first shot missed. The second buried into the stomach of the short man, and the third the same. The fourth bullet hit the shoulder of the tall man who'd shot him.

Without even repositioning, the man fired again. He was sloppy, frantic. Holding the gun with one hand, he didn't bother to level it. Augy didn't flinch as the bullet zoomed past him. He stomped closer. Two more shots. Two more misses. Augy clocked him across the face with the butt of his pistol. He grabbed the man by his shirt and hit him three more times. Augy forced the barrel of the tall man's own gun into his mouth and pulled the trigger.

He returned to the abandoned dressing room. Were those sirens in the distance, or just burgeoning tinnitus? Either way, the cops would be there any minute. Augy grabbed a blouse and rubbed it between his fingers—a nice cotton-poly blend. He struck a match. Soon the fabric was an inferno. He lit a cigarette off it, then dropped it onto a chair. As he turned to leave, there came a satisfying whoosh.

Augy shoved the gun in his belt as he rushed through the dance hall to the coat check. The heat of the barrel radiated through the fabric of his pants. He put on a fedora and ripped off his blood-spattered jacket. After transferring his money, cigarettes, and the Rolodex into a black trench, he threw it on and buttoned it up to the collar. He smiled, thinking of the thirteen bucks these murderous assholes had stolen from him the other night.

He left the same way he came. The kitchen boy inside the dumpster pounded on the lid, begging for help in Cantonese. Augy figured the dumpster was far enough from the building that it wouldn't catch, but he couldn't be sure. He didn't want to be responsible for the horrific fiery death of an innocent kitchen boy, so against his better judgment, he un-wedged the latch and peered inside.

"Stay put and be quiet or I'll blow your brains out, got it?"

The terrified, garbage-covered kid nodded and bit his lips.

Augy slammed the lid and hurried out to the main road, where pandemonium had ensued. Men and women in their best clothes scattering, showgirls in their underpants screaming. He turned for one last look at the White Dragon and smiled at flames billowing out the back windows.

He pulled the hat over his eyes and rushed through the crowd, then mounted a row of concrete steps that led up to College Street. Several police cruisers passed as he walked. He continued west to Spring Street, where he managed to hail a passing cab.

"Did you see what all the commotion is about?" the driver asked, as Augy settled into the backseat.

"Fire in Chinatown, I think." He put up his collar. "Take me to Union Station."

It was a quick drive. Augy boarded the 6:40 to Burbank. The train was busy with folks headed home late from work. He found a seat near the back but soon gave it up to a silver-haired old woman with arms full of groceries. He held onto the grab bar and gazed out the window as the speedy train took off from the platform.

He felt no remorse for what he'd done, nor did he feel any sense of justice. Lily Wong was still dead, no matter what he did. And that would always be his fault. But two words were echoing through his brain now: the Lumbermill.

It couldn't be true, and yet here it was. Worse than that, it made sense.

A lady wearing a medical mask, that was how Lily had described Countess London. The people under her may have been nothing more than a bunch of high-powered libertines, praying on the poor and disadvantaged to satisfy their own sick lusts, but the Countess herself was more than that. She wasn't simply running a human trafficking ring for profit. And if she called her facilities the Lumbermill, then everything was even worse than Augy had suspected.

CHAPTER FIFTEEN

Just as little things could send him back to the war, sometimes when he tried to analyze terrible things, Augy's brain went into retreat. As he stepped off the train in Burbank and got into a cab bound for Cohen Dale, his mind drifted from the horribleness that surrounded him back in time to when everything was simpler.

He saw his mother working in the garden, her long hair braided down her back under an oversized sunhat, her hands and knees golden brown. Mary sat nearby, reading. Her cheeks the same blush as the roses in the garden. And there was his father—still in his gray suit and cardigan, even on a warm spring day—frowning as his only son bounced a baseball off the side of the house.

Unlike his friends' fathers, when Augy joined the scouts, his father grumbled. When Augy played baseball or went to the movies, his father punished him. He never struck him; he was far too sophisticated to use his hands as anything other than glove holders. Instead, he made Augy read complicated books and write long essays.

By the time he was a teenager, Augy chose the language he used and most of his activities based on how much it might annoy his father. He kept it up with the prosaic books and trashy movies, but it turned out dangerous things worked even better. That's why he joined the wrestling team. That's why he rode a motorcycle. And that's why he dropped out of high school at seventeen to get his pilot's license.

The worst thing Augy ever did to his father was joining the army air force. He was supposed to have gone to Stanford, earned a graduate degree, written a few dry books, and taught a new generation of nosebleeds the unparalleled genius of John Stuart Mill. Putting on a uniform for the US was supposed to make everybody swell with pride, especially your father. But his dad wouldn't look him in the eye as he boarded the bus to San Francisco to get on a steam liner that would take him halfway across the world, maybe never to come back.

When things got bad, Augy sometimes imagined what life would be like if he'd listened to his father. Boring, probably. And better.

He had the cab drop him off down the block from Dr. Larkin's house. Another dollar and a half down the swallow. It was a little after ten, and the small town was pitch dark. Turning the corner, the doctor's collection of gnomes came into view. No cop cars were parked out front. Moretti had promised he'd keep a presence there so long as Sumika was in the house. He feared the worst, but was also a mite relieved. In the last few days, he'd killed eight people, kidnapped two children, and lit a nightclub on fire. Needless to say, he no longer felt comfortable around police.

He came up behind the house. A lattice was nailed to the side below the window where Sumika had been staying, covered with purple clematis in bloom. Augy rubbed his hands together and started to climb. When he peered through the window at the top all he saw was an empty bed.

"Nice to see you've been taking it easy."

Augy started so hard he nearly fell off the lattice. Dr. Larkin stared up at him from the driveway, arms folded, her high-necked nightgown billowing around her legs in the wind.

He descended the lattice to jump down in front of her. "Where's Sumika?"

"Is that her name?" Dr. Larkin lifted one eyebrow. "Come inside."

"Is Sumika still here?"

"Come inside, Mr. Small." It wasn't a request. She opened the wooden screen door to her kitchen, and Augy clomped after her.

She walked to her stove and grabbed the copper kettle, shaking it to see how much water was left. "The girl needs more specialized care than I can provide," she said as she lit the stove with an oversized match. "They took her to Children's Hospital in the city."

"God damn it!" He punched the counter so hard the old porcelain tiles cracked. "When?"

"A few hours ago." She pulled off her glasses, letting them dangle around her neck on a beaded chain. "They told me you were dead."

"Of course they did." He shook out his fist and snarled at the doctor, "Was it Moretti and them?"

"I haven't seen that troop of clowns since you all left here three days ago."

"Other cops then?"

She nodded. "I rode along with them and helped the girl get settled at the hospital. I assure you she's perfectly safe."

"I have to get to her."

"Sit down for a moment."

"They're not going to let her live, do you understand?"

Dr. Larkin grabbed his shoulder. "I believe you, Mr. Small. And I want to help."

He narrowed his eyes, searching her face. A pointed nose, long flat lips, chin like a garden spade, all poised atop a thin sinewy neck. Her face held every imaginable wrinkle—from laughing, concentrating, worrying. He didn't know if it was her serious expression, her take-no-prisoners confidence, or her zero-tolerance for bullshit, but she reminded him of his mom.

He decided to give her the benefit of the doubt.

"You got two minutes."

"When those cops came to get her, I sensed something off." She tapped one stubby finger on the cracked counter. They both watched it. "They didn't want me to come along. And I thought, this little girl is traumatized, both physically and emotionally. And they want to take her away to the hospital in a police cruiser—not an ambulance, mind you. And without any kind of medical personnel present. Why would they do that?"

Augy clenched and unclenched his jaw. "There more?"

"When we got to the hospital, nobody was expecting us. That's when I started to get suspicious. I have an ex-boyfriend who's a doctor there. He's a good man, you can trust me on that. He promised to have somebody with her round the clock and to call me before releasing her, even if it's into police custody or to social services."

The phone conversation he'd overheard Chiba having presented in his mind, tightening his stomach. The girl he'd been talking about—the one some sloppy so-and-so had left alive—he'd said she'd been taken to a hospital.

The only thing standing between Sumika and the man sent to *take care of her* was the drive from San Francisco. About seven hours... six if he laid on the gas. Augy wrinkled his nose at the clock on the wall.

"I want to help, Mr. Small," said Dr. Larkin. "Please, tell me what is going on."

"You wanna help…?" His first instinct was to tell Dr. Larkin to get stuffed, not because he didn't trust her, or from a pigheaded sense of pride, though he had to admit it nipped at him. He didn't want anybody else to get hurt. But he also realized how useful having a doctor around would be. How many more victims might he find along the way? How many more times might he get himself injured?

Not to mention, if Countess London was who he thought she was, then a doctor's perspective would be invaluable.

Augy looked at her again. She may have been over sixty and weighed about ninety pounds soaking wet, but there was something about her that told him she could handle herself. No woman who can't ends up a doctor.

"You got a car?" asked Augy.

Before they left the house, Dr. Larkin provided Augy with more clothes. She'd noticed the blood on his shirt and the fraying cuffs of his trousers, and she said everybody else would, too. This time she gave him a classic 1940s tweed suit in Irish brown. It fit better than the last one, high-waisted pants that stretched down to his ankles, a vest and jacket that practically looked tailored, and a red tie with yellow spots. It was the ugliest tie he'd ever seen, though it was silk, so the doc's idiot ex-boyfriend had obviously paid a pretty penny for it. From the ankle up Augy looked downright respectable, but his shoes were haggard. Since his feet were far too big for the boyfriend's size nines, Dr. Larkin gave Augy some polish and a brush. He shined them as she drove them back to LA in her old Chevy truck. It felt stupid, but Augy was thankful for some menial work to keep his hands busy.

"Somehow you look even worse than you did when you left," she said. "What happened to you, Mr. Small?"

He spat on the leather. "There'll be plenty of time for that once we have Sumika."

"I told you she's perfectly safe."

"Can't this hunk of junk go any faster?"

They arrived at the hospital, a curved building of dull red-orange brick with silver windows. It was almost midnight, so the streetlights were aglow, and every office looked closed.

"Where is she? How do we get in?" asked Augy, rolling down the window to light a cigarette. It was the last one in the pack of Encores he'd bought at the White Dragon. Lily and he had smoked most of them together. Christ, was it only last night?

He crushed the pack and chucked it out the window.

"We'll go through the ER," said Doctor Larkin. "I had them register me as Sumika's primary care physician, so they should let me right in."

"And who am I exactly?"

"As long as you're not you, I don't think there should be any problems."

They walked inside. The odor of plastic, soap, and rot filled his sinuses. The waiting room was abandoned but for one old man in a wheelchair sucking on a tube of oxygen. A middle-aged nurse with vibrant makeup and deep worry lines sat behind a massive wooden desk, behind her a mosaic of multi-colored accordion folders. Augy lingered by the glass doors as Dr. Larkin approached the desk.

Dr. Larkin talked to the nurse for what seemed like an eternity, until at last, she buzzed open a set of heavy metal doors.

The low heels of Dr. Larkin's saddle shoes echoed as they clicked on the tile. They took an elevator to the fourth floor, then continued through twists of hallway.

"She's in room 491," said Dr. Larkin as they turned another corner into a general medical ward. Down the corridor, a large man in a white jumpsuit with a golden nametag leaned against the wall: an orderly. Beside him was a leathery guy in a black overcoat, a distinctive lump under one of his arms. An assault rifle, maybe. Or a shotgun. It sure as hell was no civilian pocket burner, and had no business anywhere near a hospital.

Augy pulled Dr. Larkin back before the men looked up. He took out his Browning HP 9 mm—which seemed even smaller than before. If his count was right, there were six bullets left.

He felt like a jackass for not picking up new heat at the club but decided to let it go. He'd been a bit distracted.

"What in god's name are you doing?" Dr. Larkin hissed, pushing down his gun. "You can't use that thing in here."

He rolled his shoulders. "I don't want to."

"You're not thinking clearly. Let me go talk to them…"

"No."

She grabbed his shoulders and squared him to her. "I know you've been through things these last few days, Mr. Small."

"Stop calling me that. That's my father's name."

"Augy, put the gun away." She was ten inches shorter than him, her eyes dull and ordinary. He couldn't even have said their color. Yet looking at her pupils was like staring down a train tunnel.

"If you shoot that thing off in here, all you're going to accomplish is getting us both arrested, if you don't manage to blow up the damn hospital." Dr. Larkin crouched down and opened her leather bag. She rooted through then pulled out two syringes and a small brown bottle.

"It doesn't matter where you stick them." She filled both syringes with a clear fluid, then handed one to Augy. "If you get even half the drug into them, they will go down."

"Will it kill them?"

She twitched her nose and didn't answer.

Augy took a few deep breaths and stuck the gun back in his belt. "If this doesn't work…"

"That—" she pointed at his gun "—is an acceptable Plan B. Now, follow my lead."

Dr. Larkin put on her glasses and stepped out from around the corner. Augy followed, the syringe gripped behind his back. It was good luck he was so banged up; he looked like he belonged in a hospital.

The two men looked up. The orderly took a wide step to block the door to Room 491. He had the hands of a great ape, but his neck was so thin his head floated over it like a balloon. His giant white face sneered and bobbed.

The one in the black coat tried to force his crusty lips to smile.

"Excuse me, young man," said Dr. Larkin, her voice sounding older than any time before, "I believe my patient is in that room. Would you mind letting me…?"

"It's off-limits."

"That's room 491, right? My patient is a Miss Sumika—"

"What, are you deaf?" the man snapped. "The room's off-limits."

"But I'm her doctor."

He snorted. "She's got a new doctor. A real doctor."

"Has she? Who?"

"None of your goddamn business, that's who."

"Sorry to cause you any trouble…" As Dr. Larkin started to turn to leave, she tripped over one heel and dropped her bag. The contents scattered across the floor. The orderly rolled his eyes. Dr. Larkin bent to one knee, then took out the needle and jammed it into his thigh.

Augy leaped on the man in the coat and got the needle into his neck before he could react. He staggered and fell to the tile. Both men jerked as if from seizures. He didn't wait for them to go still before yanking open the door.

Sumika lay prone on the bed, unconscious. The noxiously sweet smell of ether filled the room, a mask hooked over her nose and mouth. At her side was a surgical tray covered in gleaming instruments—scalpels, tongs, clamps. The floor and bed were covered with thick plastic sheets. A mustached man stood nearby, a rubber apron tied over his street clothes. He had a Liston knife in his hand—a six-inch-long surgical blade used only for amputations.

"Who are you?" the man asked, lifting his thin blond eyebrows.

Augy's vision went red and he lunged.

It might've been a second or an hour before a voice pierced through the blur, "He's dead! He's dead! Augy! We have to go!"

His bones were shaking, blood sluggish as drying concrete. Prickled skin dripping sweat. He blinked through pulsating tunnel vision, eyes stinging and throbbing with his heart. White and pink coalesced into an image. What had once been a face now looked like the dog's dinner.

The strength left his bones and he wobbled on his knees, then fell onto his ass. His jaw trembled as he looked at his hands. They were covered in paste—flesh, blood, even fragments of bone. His own blood where he'd torn the skin on his knuckles. He wiped his eyes on his sleeve. More blood.

He'd blacked out. Again. What had he done?

A hand touched his shoulder. He whipped around and raised a fist, but then he saw those deep pupils. He wasn't sure who the eyes belonged to, but they stopped him dead. He set a fist on the ground to steady himself.

"They're outside." The voice came straight from the eyes. The rest of her was still blurry. "Please. I can't do this without you."

Furious knocking at the door brough him back into the room. He felt the plastic under his fingers coated in blood.

Sumika.

He stumbled towards the hospital bed. Sumika lay comatose. Her straps had been undone, but it was a while yet before she'd regain consciousness. She was still so hurt it was hard to look at her, but nothing was new, except dotted lines across her upper arms and thighs. It came crashing back all at once. The man in the rubber apron. The Liston knife.

The son of a bitch had been seconds from cutting her into quarters.

A sob filled his throat and he didn't try to stop it. He cupped the side of her face, feeling her pulse against his fingers. For once, he'd made it in time.

He looked down at the dead man on the floor. His body was twisted, limbs flailed out like a spider. His skull was flattened.

Augy's fists throbbed. He hadn't used a weapon at all.

It took another few seconds for him to understand what he was supposed to do. Drawing his gun, he picked up Sumika and braced her knees into the crook of his arm so he could still use the gun if necessary.

He turned to the door. "Open it."

Dr. Larkin swallowed hard, then did as he asked. Outside stood two orderlies. One had a key in his hand. Augy pointed the gun at his belly. "Hand over the key, son."

The young man's face flooded with fear. He swallowed audibly and lifted the key. Dr. Larkin snatched it up.

"Go on in." Augy turned the barrel to the other fellow, a bit older, a bit meatier. "You too, sweetheart."

The two men stepped inside Sumika's room and horror filled their faces. Augy decided they weren't a part of this and moved his finger outside the trigger guard.

He kicked the door closed in their faces. As she locked them inside, Augy knelt beside the man in the suit. Resting Sumika against his shoulder, he searched the man's pockets. The gun was an Ithaca Model 37 pump-action military shotgun with a few extra shells. He also found a wallet and a CIA badge. Special Agent 973, Michael Heller.

Augy read the badge over and over. Memorized it.

"Come on," said Dr. Larkin, "we'll go out the fire exit." She did not wait for a response before bolting down the hall.

Sumika made a moan and her eyelids fluttered. In an instant, her whole body tensed. She began to scream before her gaze focused on his face.

"It's all right, angel," he said and hugged her to his chest. "You're all right now."

She put her arms around his neck and began to cry hysterically. He forced himself to stand. His ribs should've been screaming, but for now pure adrenaline lied that she weighed nothing at all.

He lumbered after Dr. Larkin. "Ain't there an alarm?"

"Have you got a better idea?" she shouted, then pushed open the big metal door with the red and white stripes painted on it and slipped inside. The alarm sounded. Augy followed down the narrow concrete steps, illuminated by nothing but one fluorescent bulb per floor.

He was going down the mine shaft, pick slung over his shoulder, resolute to finish one more day of work. To earn one more day of starvation rations. To survive long enough to be rescued.

Bursting into a parking lot, he saw Dr. Larkin already throwing open the door of her truck, parked some thirty yards away. He loped after her, but the engine roared to life and then raced towards him, squealing to a halt mere feet away. Dr. Larkin threw open the passenger-side door, and Augy put Sumika in before climbing in after. His foot was barely off the ground when Dr. Larkin peeled out, leaving a patch of rubber behind them.

Sirens blared in the distance, but the sound was forgotten when Sumika fell against him, clawed at his jacket and cried, "*Kaette kite kureta.*"

You came back.

She said it over and over again until her weeping would allow her to speak no more. Augy's heart cracked open and he clenched her to his blood-sodden chest.

CHAPTER SIXTEEN

Sumika didn't want to let go of him. When they pulled up to the house in Malibu, he had to send Dr. Larkin into the backyard to search for the key Mr. O'Hara had promised would be hidden under a big black rock. Augy carried the girl inside. He sat cross-legged on the kitchen floor with her—the only place he figured wouldn't leave a stain—and rocked her until she fell asleep. Augy buried his face in her hair and let a few of his own tears fall. Not only was it cathartic, he felt closer to her than he had to another human being in years. He realized he didn't want to let go of her any more than she did him.

All the same, when at last she fell unconscious, he carried her into a bedroom. Dr. Larkin helped him wipe the worst of the blood off her, then pulled back the sheets and tucked her in.

"I'll sit with her while you get cleaned up," whispered the doctor, settling into a rocking chair. "I put a garbage bag in the bathroom for your clothes."

Augy nodded and drifted out of the bedroom. Stinging, pulsing eyes took in the house. Five or six bedrooms, a kitchen the size of a small apartment. Floral wallpaper, bright velvet drapes, and gold leaf Versailles furniture towered over him, crushing him. Absent were Mr. O'Hara's beloved paintings, for which Augy was grateful. The last thing he needed was more nightmares.

In a rose-colored bathroom, he stripped out of his blood-saturated suit. He didn't have any other clothes, but these were beyond redemption. He stuffed them into the garbage bag Dr. Larkin had left for him.

He showered until the water ran clear. All sixteen of his punching knuckles were gaping and blistered. He expected them to smart like the devil, but as he ran warm water over the mangled flesh it barely stung. He'd know by tomorrow if the numbness was an aftershock of adrenaline or caused by nerve damage. He hoped for the latter. He longed for deadness, emptiness. An end to the incessant pain of being alive. It came in waves—at moments like this. When everything was so horrific it left him too exhausted to react. But sensations would return. Feelings. They always did.

Once he finished showering, he put on a terry bathrobe and walked back to where Dr. Larkin was passing out in her rocking chair. He tapped her shoulder until she snorted and looked up, then presented his hands.

"I'm gonna get blood all over everything," he said.

"Jesus Christ." She staggered out of her chair, and he followed her into the next room, closing the door all but an inch behind him.

Augy flopped down on the purple and white floral davenport in the sitting room and laid his hands on his knees.

"You are the most reckless man I have ever met." Dr. Larkin pulled some iodine and winds of bandage cloth from her bag. She shook her head and started dressing his wounds. "Thank god, you are. I thought she'd be safe..."

Augy shrugged. On a small table across the room, he spotted a wooden box with a mechanical cigarette roller screwed to the top. "Do us a favor, Doc," he asked, gesturing with his chin. "I mean, another favor."

Dr. Larkin sighed. She tied off the bandages, then slunk across the room and opened the box, pulling out a bag of tobacco and a pack of papers. She rolled a cigarette, tapped it down, lit it and handed it to Augy. He smoked with his left hand while she bandaged up his right. "Some of these could use stitches," she said, "but I don't have any ligatures. I'll go by the medical supply store tomorrow."

"You're a hell of a lady."

She chuckled grimly. "I must be out of my mind..."

"If it weren't for you, that little girl would be dead," said Augy. "Me too, most likely."

Sighing, Dr. Larkin assumed a seat beside him. He offered her the cigarette. She stared at it a moment before snatching it out of his hand and taking a drag. "These things are killing you. Did you know that?"

"Yeah? Well, they got a lot of competition." Augy grabbed back the smoke. The tobacco tasted stale but expensive. "You can't go back home again. I mean ever."

"That's okay. I'm not going to live much longer anyway."

"Come on, Doc. You're not that old."

"Not that, you little whippersnapper." She cackled dryly. "I have breast cancer. I had a double mastectomy last year. I thought we got it, but…"

"How long have you got?"

"Six months. Maybe a year if I let them do every bit of nonsense to me." She snorted. "Not a chance."

"Why not?"

"Have you ever known anybody who's gone through chemotherapy or radiation?"

Augy nodded. "My father."

"Well, then you know already. Besides, I'm an antisocial old spinster. What have I got to stay alive for? Social night down at the church?"

Augy sighed, shook his head, and didn't say anything.

The doctor cleared her throat. "So, you marine corps?"

"USAAF." He passed her the cigarette.

"Ah, that explains it. You can't tell pilots anything. They're even worse than marines. Think the sun shines out your asses."

He chuckled. "You've known a lot of pilots, have you?"

"I've dated a couple. I was a field nurse in the first war."

"Ah, that explains it." He shook his head. "Nurses."

"That was before I realized I was smarter than three-quarters of those jackass doctors and put myself through med school."

"I bet you were smarter than four-quarters of the jackass doctors."

"Oh, Augy Small," she said, handing back the smoke, "you are a charmer."

A few moments of silence passed before he added, "That man in the suit was CIA."

Her eyes boggled. "What?"

"I don't get it. What could the CIA have to do with this? Or is he some rouge son of a bitch?"

She groaned and rubbed her red eyes. "Well, we're not going to figure it out tonight. Let's get some sleep."

"Go on then. The rest of the bedrooms are upstairs, I think."

"What about you?" She had that motherly tone again, which reminded Augy how long it had been since he called his mom.

He pointed his nose towards the room where Sumika lay sleeping. "I want to be here when she wakes up."

Dr. Larkin handed back the cigarette and meandered away. Augy leaned his head against the wall and closed his eyes.

Sunbeams struck his face. The cigarette had burned out, leaving a pile of ash on his white bandages. He grunted and popped his neck, then turned at a tiny cooing sound. Sumika was curled up on the couch next to him. She was still wearing the blood-spattered hospital gown, a crocheted afghan draped over her. Shaking the ash off his hand, he touched her black hair. He repositioned his aching legs and put a throw pillow over his eyes. He searched for sleep, mind wandering between dreams and memories. And he found himself on a rainy Thursday in April of last year.

The night before his wife got remarried Augy bought two large bottles of gin. He wasn't much of a tippler, but that night there was nothing for it but to drink alone, watch TV, and catch up on paperwork. He settled onto the couch in the quaint two-bedroom he and Edith used to share. When they'd first moved in, Edith had planted irises all around the perimeter, and they still grew strong every spring despite Augy's willful neglect.

He'd had a glass full of ice and a few wedges of lime on the table. Bottles of tonic and gin sweated rings into the wood. He wedged a cigarette deep between his middle and ring finger, a pen in the same hand. It was nine pm and Dragnet was starting—*Dum-de-dum-dum*! He was about to pour the first of what would be at least six cocktails when a knock came at the door. He turned up the TV and poured the drink anyway.

Ladies and gentlemen. The story you are about to see is true. The names have been changed to protect the innocent.

The knock came again, louder.

"What ignorant son of a bitch comes over during Dragnet?" He threw down his pen. "If it's a salesman, I swear to Christ..."

He threw open the door. The rain was coming down in inconstant spits, the fog thick on the streets. She was a dot of vibrancy in the gray. Her wet hair hung loosely around her shoulders, cheeks red, and breath heavy. Her green housedress with little white dots was soaked and clung to her.

They stared at each other, the white noise of the rain dulling the awkward silence.

He took a step back. "Do you wanna come in?"

She stepped inside and he turned off the TV. She hurried closer to him. "Bill is a good man."

Augy smirked. "You came here to tell me that?"

"He sends me flowers for no reason. And he calls me practically every day just to say he's thinking about me. He takes me out dancing every weekend if I want."

"Sounds dreamy."

"My family and friends all adore him." Her voice trembled, but she was fighting it. "And he adores me."

"Of course he does, Rutabaga. Why wouldn't he?"

"I never feel horrible when I'm with him."

Augy cleared his throat and looked down at his socks.

"I should love him," she said.

"Don't you?" Augy stepped up close enough to feel her breath on his chest. When he touched her chin, she looked up startled. Her eyes locked on his. Her lips quivered.

"He takes you out," he said with a smile, "but can he actually dance?"

Edith went up on her tiptoes, grabbed Augy's neck and kissed him so hard it hurt. He wrapped his arms around her, lifting her closer, but she broke off the kiss and pressed her forehead against his chest. "Tell me to go."

"No," he whispered.

A second later they were tearing each other's clothes off. Then he had her bent over the couch. Next, she was propped on the kitchen table, her knees slung over his shoulders, grabbing fistfuls of his hair and shouting, "God, I've missed you!"

Finally, he was on top of her in the bed they used to share, kissing her lips, their fingers intertwined, her legs wrapped around his back. Slow, and so intense. He was shaking and she was on the verge of tears, but she begged him not to stop.

It was past midnight when he collapsed breathless beside her, a limp, sweat-drenched heap. Her own skin was dewy and pink, her long hair a tangled mound.

The seconds ticked by, punctuated by gasps for air. He reached for her, but Edith shot up to look at the clock.

"Is that the time?" She scrambled out of bed and yanked on her panties. "I have to go."

Augy grunted and lit a cigarette. "Why?"

"What do you mean why? The wedding's in ten hours."

Pain hit his chest like a bayonet plunging through his ribs. He'd allowed himself to hope, but that was always a mistake. Biting down on his back teeth, he watched her stagger about the bedroom, the moonlight glowing on her skin. "You're still going on with it?"

"Augy..." She pulled on her slip and turned to face him. "Tell me you're happy for me."

"Are you fucking crazy?"

She sat beside him on the bed and reached for his hand. He jerked away. "Are you marrying this schmuck to punish me?"

"That's ridiculous."

"You admit you don't love him."

"That..." She looked out the window and rolled her lips in to bite them both at once, the way she always did when she lied. "I never said that."

Augy scoffed.

She squared her shoulders. "I need a man who will take care of me, all right?"

"I didn't take care of you? Did I leave you homeless? Did I let you go hungry? Did I even once stop you from buying a goddamn hat?" He ashed his cigarette contemptuously. "For that matter, did I make you quit your job so you could stay home and starch my bowtie collection, like certain gerbil-faced podiatrists I could mention?"

"That is not why I quit my job."

"Yes, it is. Mary told me."

"I quit because I wanted to."

"Horseshit. You loved that job. You quit cause jellyfish like Bill are intimidated by a woman who can build a jet engine, instead of recognizing it's goddamn sexy. Because it is."

"All of that is completely beside the point." She clenched her fists, looked down and sighed. "What I need is a man who's capable of thinking of someone other than himself."

"What you want is a dancing monkey."

"You still refuse to get help!"

"Christ, this again." Augy stood and put on his jockeys.

"You're not well, Augy. You're still having night terrors. And Mary told me you had a flashback at her New Year's party..."

He turned on her and shouted, "I am not going to check myself into a laughing academy!"

"That is not what I want! I asked you to go to the VA—"

"Those quacks at the VA couldn't diagnose a dead horse."

"You won't talk to anyone about anything. Not me, or Mary, or Robby…"

"What do you want to talk about, huh?"

"I still don't even know how you got that!" She pointed at his chest. Over the years, the massive T-shaped scar had faded to light purple, almost white. The horizontal cut ran from one armpit to the other, and the vertical cut started a few inches below his clavicle and ran past his navel. He didn't have a navel anymore, just a dent in the thick scar.

"I got it in the war," he growled. "You need a goddamn play by play?"

"You're lying. That ain't from no shrapnel."

"Shows what you know about war." Augy snatched his shirt off the floor. "It doesn't matter."

"It matters to me." Edith had tears in her wide blue-green eyes. "Tell me now. Prove to me you can open up. Tell me right now how you got that scar and I won't marry him."

Augy finished buttoning his shirt and plunked back down on the mattress. Rubbing the stubble on his cheek, he stared at Edith's feet on the carpet. Her manicured toenails. The story was caught in his throat, nowhere near his tongue. Her sobbing ran in waves over his skin. He couldn't stand to look up at it. The pity radiating off her was making him dizzy.

With a sigh, he popped his cigarette between his lips and leaned back on the bed. "You better get going. Can't have bags under your eyes on the big day."

Air hissed out of her nostrils. She didn't look at him as she stomped around to gather the rest of her clothes. Before she left, she turned back. "You are a miserable, arrogant, lonely man. And I feel sorry for you."

"I know that, baby. Don't let the door hit that beautiful ass on your way out."

He could tell she wanted to say more, but she swallowed it and slammed the door behind her.

Augy went into the living room and drank gin from the bottle. Later, he put his foot through the TV.

CHAPTER SEVENTEEN

The next day, Dr. Larkin went out early and returned with coffee and donuts. It cheered Augy to see Sumika eat, even if she remained silent as ever. It was ingenious how she managed it: gripping a fork with one finger, she stabbed the donuts and brought them to her lips. It reassured him that she was going to pull through this.

All the pain caught up with him as he finished breakfast. His hands stung and were stiff with premature rigor mortis, but so long as he kept the bandages on, they would heal. His ribs ached the same as ever, begging for a deep breath that wasn't coming. The novel pain, the insistent and worsening pain, was in his right foot. When he was crushed inside the Duesenberg, all the toes were broken. He'd essentially ignored this fact for the last several days. Every day, it hurt a little more. Now, it was unbearable. The only way to heal a broken foot was to keep off of it, but since that was not an option, he asked Dr. Larkin for a more immediate fix.

When she took off the bandages, she snarled and shook her head. The swelling was such all the contours of the fabric could be read on his black and purple skin.

"No wonder it smarts," he said.

"You need to elevate and ice it."

"No time."

"Thirty minutes now, and twenty minutes every two hours." Dr. Larkin grimaced. "Otherwise, you might lose the confounded thing."

"Drugs?"

"Those, too."

Augy did as he was told, so Dr. Larkin made good with a few anti-inflammatories and one deliciously large shot of morphine. He kept a close watch on the clock, counting down thirty minutes. Hot in his hand was a card from Johnny Chiba's Rolodex: the Lumbermill. There was no address, just a crude, hand-drawn map. But Augy knew Southern California upside down and inside out. He recognized the curve of the canyon, the crinkle of the coastline. Route 156 was even labeled CLVI. Some moron thought they were being clever. The trip wouldn't take an hour.

He wasn't sure what he was going to do. He couldn't storm the place by himself. He needed a plan. The first step was to case the building and see what he was up against.

And buzzing around the back of his brain like a fly was CIA Special Agent 973, Michael Heller. Augy and Dr. Larkin had killed a CIA man. But what was a CIA man doing there in the first place?

While he iced his foot, Sumika coiled on the opposite end of the couch staring at him. When the ice pack started to slip, she repositioned it.

"Thanks, angel," he said before he remembered she didn't speak English. He cleared his throat and continued in Japanese, "I have to leave you again. But I swear, you *will* be safe this time. The cops don't know you're here. Nobody knows. Just me and the Doc."

Looking between her knees, she shook her head.

"I know how it sounds. But a friend of mine has been taken to the Lumbermill. I have to go after her."

Sumika's eyes turned up then. He expected to see recognition, but she looked curious.

"Have you not heard of the Lumbermill?"

She shook her head.

"I heard about it when I was in Tokyo." He licked his teeth. "There was this doctor there. An intern. He was kind of like us. He'd seen too much. And he told me about a place in Manchuria called the Lumbermill. The Japanese, they..."

Augy stopped himself, remembering he was talking to a child. He felt so comfortable with her.

"Where's your family, Sumika?" he said. "Your father and mother, are they...?

Her eyes fell and her shoulders tightened. He knew the answer.

"Were you born in the US?"

She nodded.

"What are you, twelve?" Augy chewed his bottom lip. "Your parents were American citizens, I guess. So, that would mean you were in the camps?"

Again she nodded, so slight it was almost imperceptible.

Chuckling, Augy said in English, "So, that means you speak English, don't it?"

She opened her mouth, then closed it.

"Please, Sumika. Please talk to me. I need to understand what happened to you if I'm gonna be able to stop it happening to someone else."

She didn't move, didn't look up.

"Somewhere," he said, staring at the top of her head, "there's a little girl like you who's about to be taken. Branded. Beaten. Raped. Like you. And maybe, if you talked to me, maybe there's something I could do for that girl. Figure out who she is, why they want her, where to find her. But if you say nothing…" He stopped himself and wiped the crust out of the corners of his lips. He felt like a massive hypocrite. How many times had he been on the other side of this conversation—someone pleading with him, giving a thousand reasons why everything would be better if he just talked.

Eight years he'd been silent. No matter how Edith begged him, threatened him, or eventually abandoned him, he could never talk to her because she didn't live in the same world as him. Her world was a nice place full of sane people, freshly mowed grass, and mailboxes with her name on it. She thought everything would be better if she knew what happened to him as if simply knowing would let her understand. But she could never understand. No matter how she tried to empathize, all she had to offer was pity streaked with horror and revulsion.

He looked at little Sumika—the long vertical cut cleaving her lips in half, the thick bandages wrapped around her fingerless hands. In his mind, he traveled back to the sinkhole, smelled the stink of rotting flesh, felt it squelching under his feet as he fumbled towards her. When he imagined himself in her position—covered in stab wounds, trapped under a dissected body, and staring up at the cold sky with no hope of rescue—he realized it was unfair to ask her to talk about anything.

He had to find the courage to go first.

"I understand how hard it can be to talk about these things," he said. "I don't like to talk either. Not about the past. When I was in Tokyo…" He stopped himself and swallowed hard. His hands were shaking. His tongue stiff. He clenched his fingers into fists and that little bit of pain gave him the push he needed to keep going.

"Maybe I should just show you." Augy sat back and opened the top of his robe to reveal his chest, and the massive purple scar that looked like it belonged on a corpse after an autopsy. She scanned it, then he closed up the robe and folded his arms over his chest.

"I was a POW," he said. "You know what that is?"

She nodded.

"Well, I messed up pretty bad. I lost my temper and I killed one of the guards, so they took me out of the camp and transported me to a hospital." He set aside the ice pack, then stood and limped to the cigarette box across the room. "There were a few other Americans there."

He rolled two cigarettes and licked them closed. Inside the box, he found an opera length holder, which he put one of the cigarettes into before lighting it and handing it to Sumika. She clutched it between her bandages.

"Anyway," he said, taking a few long pulls of smoke, "the Japanese doctors had done a lot of experiments on Chinese to develop weapons, which they were gonna use against the US. But they had to be sure it all worked the same inside us Caucasians. So, they started cutting us up too."

The smoke curdled in his mouth, sucking up what little bits of moisture remained. He crouched down on the floor, watching the twists of white damask on the soft gray carpet. "It happened to three guys right before me. This was near the end of the war, so they were all out of ether. They just strapped them down and cut them open. I saw the bodies after. One, two, three." He slashed his hand across his chest, then vertical down his torso, and finally across his guts. "It was that third one that spilled everything everywhere.

"I never got that one." Augy swallowed hard and sucked on the cigarette for a while before continuing, "They had me on the table and had done the first two cuts when someone ran into the room shouting. I couldn't understand. I was insane with the pain, desperate for them to make that last cut so I could die. But they didn't. They threw a sheet over me and wheeled me into the common room where they kept all the non-ambulatory prisoners.

"I heard a lot of shouting, and then some soldiers came in and started going down the rows of beds, bayonetting everybody through the guts. And when one came to me, I stayed still. He saw all the blood and figured someone must've already stuck me, and passed me over. Then they left. And I lay there slowly bleeding to death for god knows how long before I heard American voices in the hall.

"I was the only survivor." Augy realized there were tears on his cheeks, so he wiped them as discreetly as possible. "The American doctor who eventually sewed me up said it was a miracle I survived." He scoffed, "A miracle…"

"You must hate me," said Sumika in perfect, unaccented American English.

Augy rubbed his eyes hard. He stood and stubbed out his cigarette, then rolled another. His hands were shaking, his fingertips moist with sweat. He ripped three papers before he got one into the rolling machine. After lighting it, he returned to the couch and sat beside Sumika. He grabbed a throw pillow and hugged it to his chest. "Why would you say that?"

"After what they did to you, you must hate all Japanese people."

Staring hard at his lap, Augy shook his head. "What I hate is war. It cages men and turns them all into monsters."

Looking up at her face, he remembered how he'd thrown up in his mouth when he'd first heard about the Japanese internment camps. America was supposed to be better than that. And sure, Tule Lake was no Auschwitz, but the very fact that it existed made him wonder if it ever could've been. If a few battles had gone differently, if the Soviets had buckled, if the Manhattan project had been a failure, if Japanese boots had touched US soil, what might've happened to all those people behind barbed wire in remote locales throughout the American West?

He didn't like to think about it, but that sort of thing had been on his mind more and more. Could American doctors ever have done to someone like Sumika what the Japanese doctors did to him?

He bit down hard on the insides of his cheeks, using the pain to help chase away the nightmarish imaginings threatening to overcome him. Then refocusing on Sumika, he made a weak fist and touched it to her cheek. "I could never hate you, angel."

"My daddy was a soldier like you. He fought in Europe."

"Your dad was in the 442nd Infantry?"

Nodding, Sumika pulled her knees closer to her chest. "He got a Bronze Star. Did you get one of those?"

"Nah..." he laughed and shook his head, wiping his runny nose on the sleeve of the robe. "I got a Purple Heart... briefly."

"Daddy got a Purple Heart. Well, we got it. When he died."

Augy sucked on his cigarette, waiting for her to continue.

"After we got out of the camps, Mama wanted to go back to San Francisco, but our house had been sold. We didn't have any money. Mama was trying to get Daddy's back pay and everything, but things were all jammed up and we were having to wait a long time. And then a man came and offered Mama a job."

"What sort of man?"

"His name was Mr. Moriyama. He was from Japan. He ran some kind of factory and he owned a big apartment complex that we moved into. There were a bunch of different buildings. There was one for Chinese, one for Russians, one for blacks, and one for Japanese, like us.

"We'd been there about a month when Mama got real sick. Her neck got all swollen till it was about as big as her head, and then she got these little purple bumps all over. They came and took her off to a hospital. I didn't see her again after that."

"How old were you?"

"Five." Sumika rested her chin on her knees. "I got put in an orphanage. Me and the Chinese and Russian and black kids from the apartment whose parents had died were all together in one place. But it was only kids from the apartment. Then the men started coming."

The skin around his eyes tightened so hard it hurt. "The men?"

"I was one of the first to get bought. His name was Mr. Campbell, but he made me call him Papa. And he called me doll." Sumika hugged her knees tighter, staring so hard at the wall you'd think it would burst into flames. "He liked to make me cry. And when it got harder to make me cry..."

"Is he the one who did this to you?"

"I got too old," she said.

Blood congealed in his veins. Fingers clenched into fists. His jaw hung slack, twitching for words that weren't coming. He swallowed a breath.

It wasn't his suffering. She owned it, and he had to let her keep it. But that didn't make him any less angry.

The doorbell rang, and Augy shot up from his seat. With an apologetic glance at Sumika, he hurried out of the room into the foyer and peered through the peephole at a tuft of white hair and black-rimmed circular glasses. Augy breathed a sigh of relief. He tightened the belt on the robe. He'd sent Dr. Larkin out to get him some new clothes, but she hadn't come back yet.

He grasped the door handle, but his hand was still shaking. Though he couldn't see himself, he knew his eyes would look puffy, his face pale. He took a deep breath and forced it out.

"Get a grip, Small."

He forced a smile onto his face and opened the door. "Mr. O'Hara. What a pleasant surprise."

The old man's clean-shaven face was good-natured, with deep laugh lines and uneven dimples. He wore a classic three-piece suit and penny loafers so shiny you could see your face in them. In his hand was a large basket filled with fresh groceries. "Goodness, my boy," he said, his smile fading. "What happened to you?"

"One wisecrack too many," said Augy, then watched O'Hara's face twist in horror. "I'm pulling your leg. It was a car crash."

"Oh." He laughed uncomfortably, then patted Augy's chest as he stepped inside. "You had me going there, son. I had no idea you were coming so soon. I wanted to drop by and get the place ready first."

"I got some unexpected time off and the missus—"

"Not a word of it. I hope you two have been enjoying yourselves. Where is your charming other half?"

Augy smiled, hoping he didn't look like he'd spent the morning eating shit and telling lies. "She went for a walk."

"I brought you some essentials," Mr. O'Hara sang, lifting the basket.

"You shouldn't have, sir."

"Nonsense, young man. It's the least I could do. You don't want to spend your time worrying about groceries while there's romance to be had." He was headed for the kitchen, which was still covered in blood from where Augy had sat rocking Sumika the night before.

"Let me take those." Augy stepped in front of him and grabbed the basket. "Can I get you anything? Coffee?"

Augy crossed his fingers, praying the old chin-wagger would be too busy.

"Thank you, son." He took off his hat and settled onto the couch. "Don't mind if I do."

CHAPTER EIGHTEEN

Over and over he tried, but all polite suggestions for the old man to leave parted his white hair as they sailed over his head. Augy chain-smoked and drummed his fingers as he endured no less than three hundred thousand stories about Mr. O'Hara's late wife.

He'd all but forgotten about Dr. Larkin when the front door swung open and she pushed her way inside laden with vinyl garment bags. "I'm really starting to resent being your errand girl," she called, not looking up. "Think you can manage not getting blood all over this one?"

Augy cleared his throat. Turning, she noticed Mr. O'Hara sitting on the divan. Her eyes widened and she sucked her bottom lip deep into her mouth.

"Hi." Augy stood and helped her to set down her bags. "This is Mr. O'Hara, the lovely fellow who's loaning us this house. Mr. O'Hara, I'd like you to meet… my mother."

"Your mother?" she whispered.

He smirked. "Grandmother?"

"Hi, I'm Augy's mother." She extended her hand and approached Mr. O'Hara.

"Oh, it's so nice to meet you." He beamed and covered her hand with both of his. "You must be so proud of your boy."

"He's a lovable little scamp."

"Now, what's all this about blood?" Mr. O'Hara looked discreetly horrified.

Augy laughed. "She's giving me a hard time about the car accident."

"That's right," said Dr. Larkin, her plastic smile extending all the way to her ears. "Augy always drives like a goddamn ape."

"Mother…" Augy laughed through clenched teeth. "Language."

"Oh." She smiled sheepishly. "Sorry."

"I'm so sorry, Mr. O'Hara. I've gotta go pick up Edith now. I was waiting for my Mom to get back with the truck."

Dr. Larkin turned to him with wide eyes. "You're not leaving right now, are you son?"

"Edith's waiting for me." Augy snatched up the garment bag and slung it over his shoulder, then turned to Mr. O'Hara. "You should come have a meal with me and Edith sometime."

"That would be lovely," said Mr. O'Hara. "How's lunch tomorrow?"

"Perfect." Augy's eyes widened painfully. "Well, I'll leave you two kids to get acquainted."

He left the room before Dr. Larkin could protest. Hurrying up the stairs, he cursed his mother for having taught him to be so damn hospitable. Later, he'd have to make yet another awkward phone call.

Dr. Larkin had bought him a double-breasted ready-to-wear sack suit in charcoal gray, with silver-buckle suspenders. The jacket fit well, but the pants were baggy, as pants tended to be. Why were so many clothes made for short, fat people? At least these were long enough. She'd also bought him a gray fedora with a speckled guineafowl feather in the hatband, and some shiny black oxfords. He'd never owned a Brooks Brothers suit. It had always seemed rich for his blood. Still, when he bent to check himself in the bathroom mirror he couldn't help a lopsided smile. All his smiles were coming out lopsided these days.

He stopped off to tell Sumika he was leaving. He promised that they would talk more when he got back, that she would be safe, and nobody knew where she was.

"I swear to Christ," he said, "I will drive off a cliff before I lead anybody back to you."

To his surprise, she gave him a quick hug. She had such delicate arms he hardly felt the embrace on his skin, but it touched him deep in his chest. Tears brimmed in his eyes again, but he managed to get inside the truck before any of them descended. He took out his handkerchief and pretended to blow his nose, then wiped his cheeks.

He hated to admit it to himself, but he was nervous to be behind the wheel again. Every time a car got involved in his life, things turned sour. When all this ended, if it ever ended, he was going to be a public transit kind of guy.

He put the hand-drawn map up on the dash as he turned onto Pacific Coast Highway. He'd never been to Tuna Canyon before, but he knew the surrounding area like an old friend. South of the canyon, not far from Las Tunas Beach was a general aviation field. It was one of several small hubs in Southern California for Delta crop dusters, which is how Augy made a living when he'd first started flying. It was there at Budwood General Airfield, situated on the sandy flattened top of a small sagebrush-covered mountain, that Augy first laid eyes on the redheaded aeronautical engineer who would eventually, if regrettably briefly, become Mrs. Augy Small.

When he thought about Edith wrist-deep in engine oil, her long messy hair tied up in a brown bandana, her denim coveralls cinched at the waist, and a monkey wrench in hand as she popped out from behind his Boeing-Stearman Model 75, he still got butterflies. He remembered her wiping the sweat off her forehead with her arm, leaving a gray streak. And how her perfect little bee-stung lips parted to show the gap between her front teeth. Then she'd smirked and asked how long it had been since he'd changed the oil. It was one of the memories that had kept him alive and kept him wanting to live those three long years in captivity.

In those days, there was a CCC camp in Tuna Canyon, where the unemployed youth of America worked on outdoor projects to help drag the country by its bootstraps out of the Great Depression. He'd heard that when the war started, that camp and all 3000 odd others shut down. After all, the youth of America had Nazis and Japs to kill now and didn't have time to build trails in national parks. Then when Roosevelt signed Executive Order 9066, many of the old CCC camps were converted into internment camps for enemy aliens—Japanese, Germans, and Italians—and then just every Japanese person they could find, even if they were born in the US, and even if, like Sumika's father, they were ready to go to war and die for their country.

He didn't know where the camp was exactly, or what had become of it since '46, but he couldn't help wondering if it had anything to do with the location of Countess London's Lumbermill.

He turned off Pacific Coast Highway, away from the glittering sapphire waves and into the gray canyon. He followed CA 27 to Tuna Canyon Road, and from there, things got a little more complex. He tossed his cigarette out the window and picked up the map. Down Big Rock Motorway, up some unlabeled patch of dirt. The car rattled like jacks in a tin can. When he thought he was about a mile off, he pulled off the road into the brush and parked behind a heap of black boulders. He'd walk the rest of the way.

After only a few minutes he came to a broken fence with a faded sign attached:

No Public Access. Tuna Canyon Detention and Processing Center.

Augy chewed his bottom lip as he stepped over some twists of barbed wire.

In his belt was his pistol, still with two bullets. He'd also brought the Model 37. There were four shells in the chamber and ten more in a fabric holder strapped to the butt of the gun. He'd never fired a shotgun in a combat situation but remembered the fundamentals from his scouting days.

He wasn't here to pick a fight, simply to see what he was up against. So he left the pistol in his belt and the shotgun hanging from a holster concealed inside his jacket and took out his other weapon: the Zeiss Ikon Contax S. He removed the lens cap.

The walk was uneventful, one sagebrush the same as the next. And then a gray building manifested on the horizon. It was several hundred yards off the dirt road, so any vehicle that came up to it would have to have big tires and a solid frame. It looked abandoned at first glance: no cars parked nearby, the windows boarded up. But there was something inexplicably neat about it. All the boards on the windows were the same size, the same color, and grain. And the path of tire tracks leading up to it looked fresh.

Augy circled the structure taking photos, staying hidden in the surrounding brush. He found the entrance on the opposite side of the building—two heavy steel doors with no outside handles. He snapped a photo, then knelt down behind some brush. Zooming in, he scanned the building, but there was nothing to see. He felt confident nobody could see him either.

Why would anybody be looking? Johnny Chiba certainly hadn't told anyone he was coming.

It was deadly quiet, the wind slack. All major roadways too far away to hear even a murmur. He waited, his eyes on those doors. They were large enough to drive a car through. He wondered if the people who worked at this place went home at five o'clock like everybody else.

Hours passed. His mind drifted. The conversation he'd had with Sumika was playing on repeat, tremors rippling across his skin. Soon he found himself back in Tokyo, talking to the young doctor who'd first told him about the Lumbermill. His name was Dr. Katsuki Muto. He was one person Augy would never forget. Not if he finished going crazy. Not if he forgot everything else. Katsuki Muto with the wild eyes would never leave him.

The rooms they used for prisoners at the hospital had all been full when he'd arrived on the Hell Ship from the mine in Hokkaido, so they'd handcuffed him in a dingy utility closet. He'd had six cigarettes on him, and when he'd lit one, a young doctor with a chubby face and short, western-styled hair poked his head in and asked where he'd gotten them. His tone held no anger, just that unmistakable appetite.

Augy told him the truth. When they'd thrown him in front of a machine gun after he'd killed the guard, Augy spat on it and told them to get it over with. The commanding officer had been so impressed by his arrogance and his willingness to die, he'd let him keep his cigarettes and shipped him off to the capital to let them decide what to do with him.

Katsuki Muto asked if he could have one. A veteran of POW camps at this point, Augy gave it. Muto wasn't supposed to ask him for anything. The cigarette represented a tacit agreement that one day, when asked, Muto would scratch Augy's back in return. That was the way these things were supposed to work.

What Augy hadn't known at the time, was that Katsuki Muto was so far gone he'd passed any concept of quid pro quo. His brain had been picked clean like a chicken bone, and he had nothing to offer but fractured memories punctuated by nonsense.

It was late at night and the floor was abandoned. As they smoked, Muto leaned against the wall opposite where Augy sat chained on the floor. "Where were you imprisoned before this?" Muto asked.

"Hokkaido," Augy answered.

"I just came back from assignment in Manchukuo." Dr. Muto had a halting way of speaking, harsh and croaky. Augy had the sense he wasn't speaking to him at all. "There was an outbreak among the staff, so I had to go. Sixteen hundred died, they said. Not enough. Not enough. All of us."

"What are you talking about?" Augy chuckled, but it was a pitiful mask for his discomfort.

"They call the installation the Lumbermill. It's a joke. Can you believe they make jokes?"

"Tell me," said Augy. "I could use a joke."

"How many logs fell today?"

"I don't get it."

"That's what they ask each other, the doctors. Logs. Not even rats, or worms. Logs. Not people." His lips trembled as he sucked on his cigarette. "The Chinese. They aren't people."

"What happens to the Chinese at the Lumbermill?" asked Augy, surprised by the quiver in his own voice. Muto's tremors were infectious, droplets of terror falling from him like the flu.

Muto looked at him then. Augy had never seen such eyes as his. Protruding and twitchy, like an animal caught in a net—hunted and terrified.

"They call it the Epidemic Prevention and Water Purification Department," said Muto. "But there is nothing pure in a thousand miles. The pollution leaks out, the death. They send it out." He slid down the wall till he was crouching. "You should know, you're not the first. Not even the thousandth. I helped them do it. I had to."

"I'm not the first what?"

"I could've said no and stayed behind. But what would I be staying for? I had to help them do it. Didn't I?"

"Help who do what?"

"They took people from the village. All kinds of people. Women and children. Old people. They infected them, then they cut them open. They froze and burned them, then they cut them open. They made the women pregnant, then they cut them open. Some would be cut apart and then sewn back together upside down or inside out. I assisted on an operation where they cut a woman open and took out her stomach, then attached her esophagus to her intestines. They wanted to see how long she would live."

"I don't understand... I..." The air was like ice in his lungs. "Why?"

"To study the inner workings of a living human machine. Really, it's all for you," said Dr. Muto, looking at Augy with a hundred-mile stare that cut through time and space. "For America. To kill you all."

"How did they make them sick?"

"Many ways. They'd inject them, or lock them up with somebody who already had whatever they were trying to give them. They'd force male and female prisoners to have sex to give each other syphilis or gonorrhea. But the fleas were the worst, I think. They filled barrels with fleas and strapped them to airplanes, then dusted them over the villages indiscriminately. Tens of thousands of people were infected. They developed buboes and small purple pustules all over their bodies, then their fingers and toes became necrotic."

"Wait." Augy drew his eyebrows together. "Are you talking about the plague?"

Those wild eyes looked up. Muto nodded. "That's why I had to go. Sixteen hundred of our men died. Not enough. All of us. And all of them. And all of you. Human beings are an infection."

Muto couldn't seem to keep his head still. It twitched hard to one side, then wobbled on his neck before twitching again. "They sent us into the villages in hazmat suits," he continued. "We took the peasants out into the fields and cut them open."

"While they were still alive?" Augy whispered.

Footfalls in the hall and Muto started so hard he dropped his cigarette in his lap. He smacked it out, then rose to his feet. Without a word he started walking away, then paused and looked back at Augy. "They told you they brought you here to give you some vaccinations before sending you to another camp. That's what they told you?"

Augy nodded.

"That's how they get the prisoners to walk into their own vivisections without making a fuss. They don't want any fuss. They want to make sure that our techniques will work the same on you, that your insides are the same as the Chinese. But of course, they are. We're all the same on the inside. Pink and slimy and soft. Even me. Tonight I'll make sure of that."

Augy snapped back to the present at the sound of a jeep easing up the drive; its back and sides covered in black cloth. The driver stopped outside the doors and got out to open them. He was a white guy of medium build and height, dressed in a simple beige uniform, no decoration. A service revolver hung in a loose shoulder holster.

The driver got back into the jeep to rumble through the metal doors and Augy made a quick decision. He darted out from behind the bush and leaped onto the back. He nearly lost his footing but managed to hold tight to the top rail and slipped underneath the fabric into the dark bed.

The truck only drove another few yards before stopping. Augy held his breath and peeked out underneath the fabric at a large parking garage.

The walls of the garage were made of corrugated metal. Several jeeps were parked in neat rows along one wall, a backhoe and a dump truck along the other. The man's footsteps echoed as he walked away from the jeep towards a small door in one wall. When he'd disappeared behind it, Augy took his opportunity to slip out.

He'd walked less than twenty feet before the door creaked open again. The only place to hide was the back of a second fabric-covered jeep.

It stank like the devil—rotted meat and sulfur. He wrinkled his nose against it, and his eyes watered. Echoey footfalls approached, then the driver's side door was yanked open. Moments later the jeep roared to life and was on the move. Augy peeked out to check if the coast was clear, but three men were standing at the center of the garage in a circle, smoking cigarettes.

The metal doors whooshed open, and as quickly as he'd gone in, he was out again. The jeep trundled down the dirt road. Augy lifted the back flap to allow in some sunlight. By the brown stains and unmistakable odor, he could tell the jeep had been used to transport bodies. But, thank Christ, that wasn't the cargo at the moment. A few large metal barrels were strapped to the walls. A logo on the sides read: *Holzklotz Medical Supply*.

He opened one and found it full of medical waste—used needles, broken scalpels, twists of blood-sodden bandages. He slapped it closed.

The radio flipped on—*Kiss of Fire* by Georgia Gibbs. The driver sang along loudly.

The jeep hit a bump and the fabric slipped closed. Something shuffled in the darkness. A figure jumped out from behind one of the barrels and tackled him to the ground. A shiv came flying at his neck.

CHAPTER NINETEEN

Augy caught the wrist and twisted. A woman cried out and headbutted him.

The fabric covering the back of the Jeep flapped in the wind, revealing the contours of a familiar face. But before he could say anything, she punched him twice.

"Katya! Stop! It's me!" he cried.

Her fist was cocked back, ready to strike. "Detective Small?"

"In the flesh." He spat out a mouthful of blood. "Please stop hitting me."

Not lowering her fist, she asked, "Why you here?"

He touched the stitches on his forehead. They'd split and were bleeding again. "I was hoping to rescue you."

"Rescue me?" She chuckled and lowered her fist.

"What the hell are you doing?"

"Escaping. What it look like?"

He was still laying on his back, Katya straddling his chest, when he heard the radio switch off. The jeep rolled to a stop and the engine cut.

"He heard us," whispered Augy.

Katya put a finger on his lips. She lifted the shotgun from the holster hanging from Augy's shoulder. They listened to the crunch of gravel under the man's boots. Augy thought he heard a gun being cocked.

The fabric was thrown open. The man lifted his revolver.

Katya fired first and his head exploded like a ripe zit. His body teetered a little, then fell back.

She lowered the gun and looked back at Augy. "You okay?"

"Peachy." He sat up, pushing her to one side.

"They must've heard that back at the compound," he said, crawling out the back of the jeep. She was close behind. Under the bright cloudless sky, he finally got a good look at her. She was dressed in a shapeless white gown, spattered in blood and filth. Her hair hung flat and oily over her shoulders. There were burn marks on her temples, but otherwise no obvious injuries. She shook out the wrist he'd twisted. No doubt it would swell.

Katya knelt beside the dead man and took his gun, wallet, and keys. She was headed for the driver's side door when Augy stopped her. "I have my truck nearby. Come on."

She nodded and followed him into the desert. It didn't take long to spot the pile of boulders he'd parked behind. They staggered towards it. She kept looking over her shoulder towards the building, though it was hidden beyond the horizon.

They reached the truck, and Augy steered them back onto the road, pushing the wheels as fast as possible. Katya started grunting and breathing hard, sounds that slowly morphed into scream-laughing. She shouted something in Russian and punched the dash.

"I knew I liked you!" She slapped his knee hard. "How you find me?"

"It was an ordeal." He pulled a pack of cigarettes from his pocket and bit one out before offering them to her. She took one but didn't light it.

"We must get my children now," she snapped, her demeanor changing in an instant from giddiness to anxious determination. "They will be at my husband's house. 225 Sycamore..."

"I have them."

"You have them?"

"I have them. Clemmie and Zychik. They're safe."

She burst into tears and folded into her lap, then looked up from under her hands. "He hurt them?"

He shook his head. "They're fine. They miss you."

She lunged over the seat and wrapped her arms around him. "*Bol'shoye spasibo*. How I thank you... I... *Ty khoroshiy chelovek*." She kissed his cheek twice, then sat back and patted his chest. "*Krasavchik*. You are good man."

Augy just smiled. He had nothing to say.

She closed her eyes, taking a moment to catch her breath, then wiped away her tears. "Where are they now?"

"They're with a friend of mine."

She scowled. "What friend? Who is this friend?"

"We can trust her. I've known her a long time."

"Tell me who she is."

He chewed the corner of his lip. "My ex-wife."

"You're married?"

"I was. She divorced me because I'm insane." He shook his head. "I promise you'll see them soon, but we gotta be careful. I don't wanna lead these people to them."

"How soon? What is soon?"

"Soon is soon. They're safer where they are right now." He lit a match and held it out to her. "Smoke your cigarette and try to calm down."

She snarled but leaned towards the flame. She was out of breath and trembling, her eyes darting around the car like a caged animal.

"How the hell did you escape?" he asked, but she waved the question off like a fly.

He desperately wanted to go back to Malibu, get another stab from the doctor's happy needle, and sink into a soft mattress, but they couldn't risk it. Not yet. Even though he watched the rearview all the way down the canyon, it was impossible to know for certain they weren't followed. He and Katya were in the middle of this, and she'd made it clear she could take care of herself, but he was not going to bring any more pain to anybody else. He decided they ought to check into a motel. If they had been followed, he could count on the bastards to make their move that night. And if nothing happened, it was safe to assume nobody knew where they were.

When he told Katya his plan, she didn't respond. He glanced at her eyes in the side-view mirror and recognized the vacant, yet intense, expression. She was miles away.

He drove to a little hotel in downtown Burbank. He knew the city better than the back of his hand, because what half-witted moron memorizes the back of his own hand? Burbank was the aviation capital of California, where he'd first gotten his pilot's license. Edith had been a floor supervisor at Lockheed during the war, so it was in Burbank's own Magnolia Park they'd bought their little two-bedroom bungalow after he got back stateside. The same house that had been foreclosed on not six months ago.

Leaving Katya in the car, he limped into the office of the La Hacienda Hotel and shelled out nine bucks for a double queen. Until now, he hadn't bothered to look in Special Agent 973 Michael Heller's wallet—two hundred and eighty-seven bucks, and a Diner's Club card.

Against all odds, Augy had kept his suit clean, but his face was quite another matter. The guy running the front desk was quick to loan him a first aid kit. In the motel room's bathroom, he wiped away the blood and patched up the giant cut over his left eye. Luckily, his hat hid it well enough for him to go into polite society without frightening too many children.

"You need go buy me clothes," said Katya the moment he stepped out of the bathroom.

All he wanted was to sit down. He had a splitting headache and was so dizzy he feared he might pass out. It was high time he iced his foot. Not to mention he needed to call Dr. Larkin to let her know he wasn't dead.

Augy rubbed the bridge of his broken nose. "No problem."

"Do not buy ugly things."

He threw his hands up in a thoroughly hopeless gesture. "Okay."

Katya wrinkled her upper lip, ducked into the bathroom and bolted the door behind her.

Grumbling, Augy limped down the boulevard to the nearest department store. He had no clue what constituted ugly in Katya's book, no clue about ladies' fashion in general. He recognized a good-looking broad when he saw one, but how much that had to do with clothes was debatable. Thinking back, he realized the two times he'd seen Katya fully dressed she had looked devastating—like a girl in a catalog. This was hardly helpful.

He'd only been standing in the ladies' section looking bewildered for about three minutes when a salesgirl with tight blonde curls and wide swinging hips came to his rescue.

"Can I help you, sir?" she asked, a southern accent.

"I..." He drew the syllable out, unsure what came next. "I have this friend. She needs a dress. A suit. Some clothes. Not ugly."

"Okay," said the salesgirl, smiling through it all. "Can you tell me a little more about her?"

"She's... uh, mid-thirties. Black hair. Gold eyes. Full pouty lips. Hourglass figure. Long legs. Skin like butter. Sooner punch you in the throat than look at you."

The girl chuckled uncomfortably. "What's that, sir?"

"Gorgeous." As Augy's eyes refocused, he was surprised at himself. How could he be thinking about Katya like that at a time like this? After everything that had happened to him, and to her. After what had happened to poor Lily

Wong. His libido should've been permanently out of commission. And yet here it was, rearing its ugly head and obsessing over Katya's every detail. He smashed it down with sheer willpower.

"Anyway." He cleared his throat. "No bright colors. No weird patterns. Something, um…"

"Classic?"

"Classic." He smiled, lopsided out of his numb face. "And nothing too flowy. I think she'd more want one of those skirts that don't—" he mimed a triangle "—but goes more like…" He ran his hands over the hips and legs of an imaginary woman.

"A pencil skirt?"

"Yeah."

"Is she a provocative woman?"

"Does a one-legged duck swim in a circle?"

The salesgirl smiled indulgently. "I think I know what you're after."

Augy stopped at a general store on the way back to get his film developed and to purchase stationery. He slipped the guy an extra ten so his prints would be ready by morning, then he swung through a burger joint. When he came strolling through the door into the motel room, Katya was on the bed in an oversized cotton-terry robe with a towel wrapped around her head.

He tossed down the bags. "Look, I did my best. I got you a suit, a nightgown, undergarments. All that jazz. I'm sorry if it's hideous."

"I would not know what I think if you pick out ladies' clothes *too* well."

He winked, then showed her a paper bag with grease stains at the bottom. "Dinner."

She nodded and riffled through the clothes, then went into the bathroom. Augy sank onto the bed and took off his shoes. The tip of one sock was tinged with pink blood. Dr. Larkin's words rang through his head like a death knell: *you're going to lose the confounded thing.*

She'd been exaggerating. He was almost positive she'd been exaggerating.

He picked up the phone. First, he called the front desk and asked for a bucket of ice, then he called the operator and had her connect him to the house in Malibu. He had to let it ring no less than twenty times before Dr. Larkin picked up.

"Hello?" Her voice was brisk, nervous.

"It's me, Doc," he said. "Everything's fine."

"Christ, Augy..." She sighed with relief. "You're a real son of a bitch, you know that?"

Augy gave a wooden chuckle. "What, you didn't have a nice time with O'Hara?"

"I swear he didn't take a breath for two hours he was talking so much."

"How'd you get rid of him?"

"I told him I had a headache."

"Classic move."

"What move? That chin-wagger could give a corpse a headache."

Katya stepped out of the bathroom in the sleeveless, white satin nightdress the salesgirl had picked out for her. The smooth fabric clung to her upper body and flared out all the way to the floor. Even with her wet flat hair, the bags under her eyes, and the burn marks on her temples, she made it look like evening wear.

"Where are you?" said Dr. Larkin. "When will you be back?"

"I'll be back in the morning," Augy said, then hung up the phone before Dr. Larkin could respond.

Katya slipped under the covers of the bed opposite him, her gaze fixed. "Who you talking to?"

"Doctor Larkin. She's good people. She's back at the safehouse."

"Safehouse..." Katya jutted out her bottom lip in false esteem. She grabbed a paper-wrapped burger from the bag.

Eventually, someone came with ice, which Augy loaded into a towel and draped over his bleeding, blistered, swollen, angry, and neglected foot. Again, he thought fondly on the doctor's friendly syringes.

"This from car crash?" Katya asked.

He groaned and leaned his back against the headboard.

"You save my life then, maybe. And today again, maybe. I am glad you hit me with your car."

"To be fair you did kind of dart out of nowhere." He smirked. "Your head any better?"

"No."

Silence pooled between them, a tinge of awkwardness he probably only imagined. He wanted to ask how she'd escaped and what had happened to her in that place, but the bite of his own memories told him to stay back. If where she'd been was anything like what he imagined, Katya didn't want to talk about it, and he didn't want to hear about it.

Not yet, anyway.

Augy decided to take the opportunity to ask a question that had been burning in his brain for days. "Why'd you come back and find me?"

She scoffed. "You found me."

"No. I mean, after you stole my car. I understand now why you couldn't go to the cops, but you had five grand. Other than one case, I'm hardly prestigious, am I?"

"I tell you already." She waved that dismissive hand again.

"Tell me again."

"You want know?" She pressed her lips together and scoffed. "Fine. Three reasons. One, because of what you do, they already ruin your life and eventually to kill you, so I would not be hurting you much."

"Ah." He chewed his bottom lip.

"Two. You say it was poor girl who come tell you about Hollisters, no? Girl who go to police and they tell her go away?"

"Yeah."

"She pay you, this girl?"

He scrunched up his shoulders. "She offered me eighty bucks, but..."

"You no take it." She smirked, folding her arms over her chest.

"It was everything she had in the world. All she wanted was someone with a white face and a pecker to go ask those bastards where her baby was."

"You say things like this." Katya laughed and pointed at his nose. "This reason two."

"And the third?"

She shrugged. "I like your face."

"You're the first."

"Eh, you are not so ugly. And for a man, all you need is not to be *so* ugly. But your face, there is no lie in it. No American, um... big happy smile like you want to sell me something."

"That's good, I guess."

"My bet is you lousy detective. Too, how you say? Expressive? And lousy soldier. Too sensitive."

He pointed at her. "Hey, I can't vouch for my sleuthing skills lately, but I was a damn good soldier."

She lifted her eyebrows. "Lucky for me I no need detective. Or soldier, even damn good one. I need you."

"Why?"

She sighed and bit her bottom lip. "I have known enough bad men to spot a good one when I meet him."

Augy looked down. "Nobody's ever said anything like that to me."

"No crying, you pussy."

"You're a funny bird, you know that? Real big tickle."

She smiled brilliantly, baring straight white teeth. They were pure Hollywood, probably bought and forced into her mouth by her husband. He wondered what her real teeth had looked like, and how much more charming her smile might've been.

Augy picked up his pistol and pulled out the magazine, dropping it into the drawer of the nightstand before laying the gun on the ground on the other side of the bed. He turned to Katya, who was eyeing him suspiciously. "If you're gonna keep the shotgun loaded, put it somewhere I don't know where."

"Why?"

"Sometimes I sleepwalk."

"You sleep shoot?"

"It's been known to happen."

With one eyebrow at an almost comical height, Katya signaled with her finger for Augy to turn around and stashed the gun.

"We sleep now," she said, curling under the covers. "We have many people to kill tomorrow."

"Don't put the cart before the horse, gorgeous."

"I do not know what this means."

"It means lousy detective or not, I've still got some serious questions for you."

She waved her hand again. "Fine, fine. Sleep first, you ask questions, then we kill people."

Augy repositioned the pillows and lay back in bed. The relief to his back and ribs was instant.

"Goodnight, Katya," he sighed.

She didn't respond. When he glanced over, she was already asleep.

Apart from those rare occasions when he'd black out and wake up somewhere else, Augy was always a light sleeper. Several times that night he was awakened by the trundle of a train, by voices in other rooms, or by a horny cat howling at the moon. It didn't disturb him. He'd look up, identify the source of the sound, then plunge back into sleep. So, when he heard a rustling in the other bed, Augy opened one eye and watched as Katya stood and went into the bathroom. She closed the door and locked it, but no light came on. He heard the bathroom faucet.

He closed his eyes and began to drift off again when he realized the water had been running a long time. Gingerly, he slipped out of bed and limped to the bathroom door. He didn't even have to press his ear against it to hear her crying. The sound was harsh and guttural, controlled hysterics. He imagined her back pressed up against the door, her hand like a vice over her mouth as sobs racked her body.

He wanted to knock, to take her in his arms and hold her until the fit passed.

Augy went back to bed, but there was no sleep. Not for another half hour until Katya emerged from the bathroom and returned to her bed. He had to bite his lip to keep from saying something. Only when he heard her breath become steady was Augy able to fall back asleep.

CHAPTER TWENTY

Being cautious didn't come naturally to him. It was something he'd learned in the Army Air Force, watching one over-confident showoff after another fall to their fiery deaths executing overly risky and aggressive maneuvers. So the saying went: *there are old pilots and there are bold pilots, but there are no old bold pilots.*

He figured the maxim could equally be applied to outlaws, which was, after all, what he was now. The problem was, Augy had been one of those bombastic jackasses playing chicken with planet earth, if not the leader of the pack. He'd gotten lucky. So far.

Who the hell wants to be old anyway?

He called Edith and told her to bring the kids to the place in Malibu. Katya was anxious to get back to them, and Augy was anxious to get back to a large dose of morphine, but he had a feeling once she was reunited with her kids it would be harder to get her alone for an interview. He convinced her to stop for breakfast at a little mom and pop diner across the street from the motel. Old maple syrup grabbed at the fibers of his jacket every time he set his arm down, but the coffee was decent.

Katya had arranged her hair to cover the burn marks on her temples. The clothes he'd bought for her fitted like a glove—a black suit with a silk floral blouse, white gloves, and red Mary-Janes. He swelled with pride to have guessed her size accurately. She looked like pure class, sprinkled with a bit of lurid glitter. When he'd asked if the clothes were ugly, Katya had smirked.

As they waited for their food, Augy stuffed an envelope with the photos he'd taken of the Lumbermill, along with Johnny Chiba's hand-drawn map. He wrote a letter and addressed it to Ed Gundy, a friend he'd made at The Burbank Daily Review back when the Hollisters' case broke. They hadn't spoken in months, but Gundy would remember him. More than that, he was a good reporter: the kind of guy who actually followed leads and didn't eat bullshit for breakfast, no matter how much cash it was wrapped in.

Katya didn't ask what he was doing, and she didn't answer him the first few times he sent out a feeler. He gave up and let her stare at the wall until the food arrived. Only once the plate was half empty did she seem to remember he was there at all.

"What you do in the war?" she asked between assaults on her omelet.

"I was a fighter pilot in the Pacific."

"Rank?"

He popped his neck. "Captain."

"You are drafted?"

"Pilots were all volunteers. I was one of the first in line for the army after Pearl, which was good cause it was a hell of a long line. I had a civilian license, I was an Eagle Scout, and I was in the best shape of my life, so the recruiters were on me like white on rice. I was only in training six weeks before they shipped me out. I was part of the 419th Night Fighter Squadron, 8th Fighter Command, 13th Air Force."

"So many numbers." Katya crossed her eyes. "Decorations?"

"I got an air medal for Midway. Got six confirmed kills. That's the only battle I fought in before I got shot down over Singapore."

She raised one eyebrow. "Why Singapore? Is Japanese before Americans join the war, no? English, they surrender. Humiliating."

He sighed. People asked him about the incident often enough, but it had been a while since he'd answered.

"Me and seven other fighters were there to give cover to four B-29s sent to drop a payload on the main shipping port. I was in my P-38, Scarlet Fever. It was a damn fine plane, but they weren't made for good old-fashioned blighty dogfights, which is what I ended up in that day. A Zero came in high at one o'clock on the bomber. I shot it down easy, but my wingman—Eugene Goldman was his name—he followed too close, and when I fired, the shells from my 50 caliber got sucked into his intake."

Augy set down his fork and leaned back in the seat. "I tried to guide him out over the ocean so he didn't have to bail on the island. Even back then, the Japanese had a reputation for the way they treated POWs. But before we reached the shore, two more Zeros came in low and fired on us. They finished him off. I shot one of them down, and then led the others inland away from the bombers. They did manage to drop the payload, I found out later. Goldman was the only American casualty that day. I was declared MIA. Until the end of the war, everybody thought I was dead. My parents. My sister. My poor wife…"

"Refill?" asked a chubby waitress in a too-tight uniform. Both Augy and Katya pushed out their coffee cups. The sugar and cream sat untouched.

"What happen to you?" Katya prompted.

"Three Dragon Slayers joined the Zero. I made a few passes on the formation, but they took out one of my engines. I didn't have what it took to get back over water. The electrical was shot, and I pancaked it on some dirt road. Other than a few cuts and scrapes I was fine, but as I climbed out the Japs were already there." Augy stabbed a sausage and smiled. "Enough about me. You ready to tell me your story, gorgeous?"

"Is too long. Boring."

"Give me the Readers Digest version."

"The what?"

He mimed an inch with his fingers. "Newspaper edition."

She bit one knuckle, tilting her head from side to side as if trying to roll the words into place. "My family is Russian, but we live in Kiev. When I am nineteen, I go to Moscow for school, and maybe to find husband." Katya finished off her omelet and started to take big forkfuls of hash browns off Augy's plate.

"You want the rest?" he asked, pushing the plate towards her. "I'm done."

"You need eat more. You are too skinny."

"I'm not skinny. I'm wiry."

"You are skinny." She dragged his plate across the table, speared a fried egg and shoved the whole thing in her mouth. "I should like one day to get really fat, like four… five… six hundred pound. No man will ever look at me. And if you stab me, it will be like pricking whale with toothpick, and then I eat you."

"What?"

Katya swallowed loudly. "I remember every day we learn what Germans do…"

"Are we not gonna address what you just said?"

"They take Poland and then France, and everybody think they are coming for Moscow next. The government deny it—they have treaty. *Khrovina*. It was, how you say? Plain as nose?"

Augy chuckled and shook his head. "Apparently we're not gonna talk about it."

"I remember," she continued, shaking a finger in the air, "May Day 1941, only month before three million Germans come into Russia, they have military parade in Moscow. It was to make us feel better. Make us think Russian army so huge, so better than German, they would never invade.

"And then they invaded." Katya dragged Augy's pancakes across the table. "And one town after another, armies is cut down. What is word? Anhilated?"

"Annihilated?"

"Yes. Annihilated. In two weeks half-million Russian are dead, and another million are prisoner. Almost all of those die too, eventually."

"I remember reading about it," said Augy, nodding. "What happened in Russia was worse than what happened in a lot of Europe. And the way the Germans treated the Russian POWs..."

Katya called the waitress over and ordered another round of toast. "We all assume they were head for Moscow, like I say. Millions leave. Our army was destroyed. Stalin had cut its head off killing every person what knew ass from elbow. I remember at that time people in Moscow they shout at government officials in the street. They spit on them. No one would do that before; they be killed."

Katya finished off his pancakes with a bite the size of her fist. "I am like you," she said, still chewing. "I am want defend my country. But I am no pilot, no... how you say, Eagle Scout? I am ordinary woman, and they do not want me. I am try volunteer ten times, but they send me home. Tell me get married, have sons, work in factory, help build defenses. Go away."

Her eyes darkened and her expression flattened as if every muscle in her face had gone numb. "Then the Germans, they do not come to Moscow. They turn south and attack Kiev. Three of my sisters are killed. And my father."

"Jesus." Augy pressed his fingers into his eyes. He was supposed to offer condolences now, to say he was sorry. But those words never helped, and he always hated it when people said them to him. Back in the mine nobody ever commiserated with each other. If you gave a guy sympathy, you'd make him depressed. But if you gave him a hard time or cracked a joke, you might make him smile. Make him forget for a moment. Augy couldn't think of anything like that to say to Katya, so he stared at the sticky table.

"I volunteer again and this time they take me." Her lips didn't move, but a smile filled her eyes. "I learn drive tank and fire machine gun, but I end up on mortar crew. For month I no sleep. I so want Germans to come to Moscow so I can kill some."

The waitress dropped off the toast, and Augy held out his cup for a refill. He'd heard the Russians had armed some of their women and sent them into battle, something he'd always scoffed at as barbaric. But hearing the hunger in Katya's voice when she talked about killing Germans made him dubious. She deserved to defend her country as much as anybody. And he already knew she handled herself in combat at least as well as any other soldier he'd ever known.

"It was October they come," she said, smearing her toast with a pallet of butter. "The panzers on their way to Moscow, they kill everything. And then finally, it started to snow. We waited, all of us, for ground to freeze. For cold to kill their engines. For their fingers to turn black. They have no winter clothes, we find out. No boots. No furs. Hitler was so sure Russia fold like France." She said something in Russian Augy felt sure was half insult, half gloat.

"Stalin called Siberian troops to help defend city, and my unit, we go out with them. I never forget that first day when we run up on them and they could not even fire back. Their little guns were frozen." She showed a predatory smile, made all the more intimidating by those glittering Hollywood teeth. "I cannot tell you how many Germans I kill that day. Forty, maybe? Kill me, I cannot tell you.

"Anyway, that is how I meet my husband."

Augy furrowed his brow. "Tyler?"

"No." She chuckled derisively. "No. My real husband. Fabiyan. Fabi. He was Siberian. We fight together. I am in foxhole when German sneak in behind to cut my throat, and Fabi blow his brains out. This how we meet."

"How romantic."

She shrugged, but her grin told another story. The look on her face and softness in her voice as she talked about this man made a pit form in his stomach that had no business being there. Augy lit another smoke and leaned back in his seat.

"Anyway," she said, "a year later we are married, and I go with Fabi back to Siberia. We are stationed along the border with Manchukuo." Katya stopped herself and grabbed one of Augy's cigarettes. He reached across the table to light it. In her eyes, he thought he saw her brain tripping over jagged edges. He sensed the story was about to take a sharp turn, and he wasn't sure he was ready to go along. It was difficult to explain to himself why he felt so close to Katya after such a short time. But the scars on her skin, and imagining how she'd got them, filled him with such rage his muscles tensed and he wanted to scream.

He called for the check, and they left the diner. Only after they'd driven for about twenty minutes, as he turned south towards Santa Monica, did Katya speak again.

"Rumor come across the border that Japanese in Manchukuo were developing chemical and biological weapons. But it was rumor for long time. Just rumor." She kept her eyes trained out the window as shaggy palm trees and prickly sagebrush sailed by. "And then our spies come back with story about anthrax outbreak in Longjiang. Fabi was sent to find the truth. I would go with him, but I was pregnant."

"You have another kid?"

She nodded, not looking at him. "Fabi never come back. Six months go, nothing. And there are more rumors, worse than ever, coming across the border. You remember I think, the stories about the Japanese in China…"

"Of course. Even before Pearl, the newsreels showed it a lot. Nanking, especially. The Japanese lining up hundreds of civilians and shooting them. Burying them alive. Raping the women over and over until they were dead. I even heard stories of the soldiers throwing Chinese babies up in the air and catching them on their bayonets. It's why we were all so anxious to get over there and kill them once the war started. I don't remember anybody caring about the Nazis in the beginning, but the Japs? They didn't even seem human." Augy ashed his cigarette out the window and chewed on his bottom lip. "The Japanese soldiers, they were brainwashed, ready to throw their lives away or do any horrible thing."

"I think my Fabi was captured by those animals, so I leave my daughter with Fabi's mother, and I go to find my husband. I never find him. And I never see my daughter or Russia again."

Augy didn't say anything but focused on the road like it was a blackboard covered in math equations.

"My daughter would be ten now. Fabi's mother is good woman, and not so old. She will raise her. And maybe my sisters will find her." Katya wiped her nose with her finger. "Who can know?"

"What's her name?"

"Galina. Is for one of my sisters I lose in Kiev."

"Maybe when all this is done," he said, "you can go back and find her."

Finally, she looked at him. Her eyes were wet, but no whisper of a tear was on her cheeks. She smirked and punched his arm. "You come with me, eh detective?"

He chuckled. "Well, I don't speak Russian, but I'll do my best."

"I teach you Russian. Is easy."

"You're gonna teach me Russian?"

"*Ya tebe pokazhu gde raki zimuyut!*" she shouted and then started to laugh.

"*Ya tebe poka*... what? What does that mean?"

"*I will show you where lobsters spend the winter.*"

He chortled. "Why?"

"Is threat if someone no want answer your questions. Like sleeping with fishies."

"Oh. I get it."

"You pull out here."

"Hmm?" He looked at the upcoming exit. "No, there's a few more to go."

"You pull out here." Her voice was solemn as the grave. "I need make stop."

"What kind of stop?"

"This road. Go left at light."

He followed her instructions into the lush canyons of Bel Air, one of the priciest neighborhoods in Southern California. Celebrities, movers, shakers and all-around rich SOBs called these emerald green streets home. Augy had driven by the neighborhood on the highway countless times but had never taken the exit. He had no business in a place like this.

The old Chevy bounced along the pristine streets, sharing road space with shiny Buicks and Bentleys, not to mention enough Cadillacs to make even Harry blush. Augy wiped the corners of his lips and lowered the brim of his hat. "What are we doing here?"

"Turn right on Chantilly."

"Katya..." He felt hot under the collar. Some of the houses here were bigger than aircraft hangers, adorned with marble walkways, gated with wrought iron, and dripping with climbing roses, wisteria, and crested birds of paradise. They came to a fork, and she pointed him left down Chalon Road, where the houses were even more beautiful, if not bigger. At last, she told him to bring the car to a stop in front of an imposing hedge that said *keep out* as emphatically as the Great Wall of China. Across the street two ceramic lions guarded a long driveway of red brick, twisting up behind a partition of flowering trees. The house was hidden.

Katya grabbed the shotgun from where she'd stashed it under the seat and popped open the door.

"Has your head come loose?" Augy reached across and yanked it closed, then punched down the lock.

She turned her eyes to him, those big golden beauties that changed with every breath of air. Now, they were on fire. "This man, he is doctor. Um... brain doctor. Talking doctor." She snapped her fingers a few times, calling the word to her like a dog.

"A psychiatrist?"

"Yes. Psychiatrist." She flashed a smile, then resumed her military stare. "He is close friend to my husband. I go to his house for dinner, cocktails... too many times. His wife, she is horrible woman. And he is worse."

Augy took a long breath, holding it as he said, "Tell me why."

"This is why." She lifted her hair to show him the burn marks on her temples.

He folded his arms on the steering wheel and rested his forehead on top.

"My husband, he ask Dr. Walker to *make me better*. He try erase my brain with electricity. If I no escape when I do, he was to cut through side of my head and..." She pointed at her temple and twirled her finger, the universal sign for crazy.

"They were gonna lobotomize you?"

She didn't nod, staring through him. "He will be home. His office is in back of house."

"This is a bad idea."

"You say you help me, no?" She snatched him by the chin, forcing him to look at her. "Put money where your mouth is, Detective Small. Or are you coward?"

Augy jerked out of her grip. Sighing, he rolled down the window and lit a cigarette. In the side-view mirror, he saw a woman in a red silk kimono and white pumps walking a miniature dog. He'd never seen such an ugly animal: a ball of brown fluff on four fat legs. It looked like its face had been beaten flat with a shovel. Its fleshy ears dragged on the concrete. With every wheeze, the dog seemed to beg, *kill me*. Meanwhile, its owner was busy making sure her hair remained carefully disheveled.

"Does that work on Russian guys?" asked Augy, not taking his gaze from the dejected little dog.

"What work?" asked Katya, shifting.

"That whole *do-exactly-as-I-say-or-you're-a-big-girly-man* schtick of yours. Cause I gotta tell you, it ain't landing." He turned over the engine and put the truck into drive. "I'm a lot of things, gorgeous, but a coward isn't one of them."

"What you doing?"

"I'm not about to commit murder in Bel Air in broad daylight."

"I will do it alone." She seized the handle and pushed open the door.

Augy grabbed the barrel of the shotgun. "I swear to God, don't make me hit you with the car again."

"You threaten me?"

"What about your kids, huh? After everything they've been through, you want to leave them motherless?"

"Do not talk about my kids," she hissed through clenched teeth. "Who you think I do this for?"

Augy rolled his lips together and cracked a knuckle. "I need you to tell me everything you know before we take this transnational Bonnie and Clyde act of ours on the road."

"What does that mean?"

"Don't get me wrong, gorgeous. You're looking for some sweet revenge and there's nothing I'd like better than to serve it to you on a silver plate, but first I need to know exactly where this ends. I mean, are we gonna be going after Eisenhower, or what?"

She flexed her chin and narrowed her eyes, but lowered the shotgun.

He flicked his cigarette out of the window, turned over the engine, and eased back onto the road. "Couple of days ago I went to the hospital to pick up that little girl I told you about. The broken one I fished out the sinkhole, which I haven't forgotten you seem to know all about, by the way. Now, imagine my surprise when I find an honest-to-god Company man guarding the door while one of these doctor types was about to slice the poor thing open."

"Company man?"

"CIA."

She sat back in the seat and rolled her head on her neck. "What you do?"

"I lost my temper." He shook out his knuckles, which had become so stiff it was everything he could do to grip the steering wheel. "Let's start easy," he said, easing the truck back onto the road towards Malibu. "Who is Countess London?"

Katya rolled her shoulders like she had a chill. "I do not know her real name."

"Don't tell me what you don't know. I got plenty of that already."

"She is doctor from Osaka. I know is Osaka. She was at Lumbermill in Manchukuo. One of chief researchers."

"Why do they call her Countess London?"

Katya pushed air out her nose so forcefully it made a noise. "Because when she is girl she marry Englishman and go to England. And she is first—maybe only, I do not know—Japanese woman to go to medical school there and become doctor. The Japanese call her... what is it? *Hankashaka*?"

"*Hankushaku*?"

"Yes."

"Countess."

"Is joke. They take her lightly. At first." She made a noise like an irritated horse. "Give me cigarette. You and your talking will send me to the grave."

He chuckled and passed over his pack. "Did you meet her in Manchukuo?"

"Yes."

"But you were never in Unit 731?"

"Everyone who was ever prisoner at Unit 731 is dead."

"Why are you being so evasive?"

"Because it no matter! What matter is she is here. Now. And she is still working."

"Why is she still working?"

"Because she is evil."

"There's no such thing as evil. There's only humans and the things they do. She's still doing her research, and there's a guy from the CIA making sure it gets done. Do you know what that might mean?"

They pulled up to the house. Edith's car was parked on the curb.

"I am not talking no more," Katya shouted, jumping out of the car so quick you'd think it was full of spiders. "Not until I see my children. Understand?"

"Get in the house before the neighbors hear you."

Katya grumbled, but trotted up the front steps. Once the truck, and more importantly its license plate, were safely hidden away in the garage, he followed her in.

CHAPTER TWENTY-ONE

Katya's voice filled the air, Russian and awash with happy tears. He turned the corner and saw her down on her knees clasping her children to her chest. That unbearably cute little boy was weeping and shivering, while Clemmie had her eyes closed, nuzzling into her mother's hair.

A smile grew on his lips watching her. No matter how he tried, he couldn't seem to fit her in a pigeon hole. In fact, he was fairly certain he didn't understand her at all.

Edith stood in the doorway, holding her elbows, trying to disappear into the wall. She met Augy's eyes and showed an almost imperceptible smile.

He stepped up behind Katya and touched her shoulder. Without looking up, she grabbed his hand and squeezed it tight, a thank you too profound to be spoken. He squeezed back, then let go and stepped past her towards Edith. Nodding for her to follow, he walked into the sitting room. Her heels clicked on the hardwood behind him.

"Call your sister," she said, plunking down on the loveseat.

Augy approached the cigarette roller. "Mary gave you an earful, huh?"

"She is the only person who has always stuck by you and you're treating her like garbage."

He nodded. There was no argument. "Thanks for looking out for the kids."

"I'm glad you found their mom. I shouldn't ask, should I?"

Once he had two cigarettes rolled he walked back to the couch and handed one to Edith. "You're gonna wanna strangle me, but I need one more favor."

She opened her eyes wide. "What?"

He explained about the house, and how in about an hour old man O'Hara was coming over expecting to sit down to lunch with Augy and his charming other half.

"You didn't tell him…?" Edith began, then she rolled her eyes. "What am I saying? Of course, you didn't."

Augy poured two small glasses of gin, then settled onto the couch beside her. "He seems happier thinking I'm part of a loving couple. He's such a sweet old bugger, I don't wanna disappoint him."

"It's all for his sake, huh?"

Augy chewed on his cheek. "At his age, bad news can be hard on the ticker."

"This is ridiculous. Why do you need this house anyway?"

"I'm working a complicated pro bono case, and I need a base of operations."

Edith hesitated, swirling the gin. "Call. Your. Sister."

"All right. I'll call her right after lunch."

"You call her now or you can forget about lunch." She knitted her forehead so two deep lines appeared between her brows; they always did when she was angry, or disappointed, or anxious. Augy sat down beside her and smoothed them with his thumb, the way he used to. She met his eyes and softened a little.

"Fine." He tipped back his glass of gin for a bit of courage, then picked up the phone on the table beside him.

He'd been avoiding calling Mary for days, though every few hours he thought about it. She was less than a year older than him, but in terms of maturity, she could've been his grandmother. She was one of those people who'd been born forty-five years old. A long and storied lecture awaited him, filled with guilt trips and I-told-you-so minefields nine miles long. She had a way of putting things in perspective, telling him all the things he didn't want to hear. Nothing seemed real until he told Mary about it, which might have been at least part of the reason he was ducking her now.

With his eyes never leaving Edith, he dialed.

When Mary picked up the phone, the words that tumbled uncensored from Augy's mouth were, "I know I'm a piece of shit."

"August? Oh my god, is that you?"

"Now before you start in, I can explain."

"Where are you?" She started crying. "I thought you were dead. And you don't even call. Do you hate me so much?"

"Don't be crazy."

"You leave me and Robby thinking you got shot to death by that psychopath Tyler! If Edie hadn't called me…"

"I asked her to call."

"You don't know what's been happening around here. Robby got thrown off the force."

"What? Why?"

"For the Tyler thing. They didn't give him suspension or pay. They took his gun and his badge and told him to get out."

He shouldn't have been surprised, and yet against all logic, he'd still been hoping Special Agent 973 Michael Heller was a one-off. That Tyler had been lying when he shouted that he knew the mayor. But once again, his gut knew the truth his brain couldn't own up to.

Was it only a couple of weeks ago he'd been chasing chickens and finding little girls' dolls for a living?

Mary blew her nose. "I swear a thousand cops have come by asking about you."

"What'd you tell them?"

"The truth. What do you think?"

"What's the truth?"

"I don't know anything. You made damn sure of that, so I figured there had to be a reason." Finally, that old umbrage returned to her voice. "Answer yes or no. Are you on the wrong side of the law right now?"

"Yes, but…"

"I don't wanna know. I'm a terrible liar and I don't wanna get you in trouble."

Relief rushed into his lungs. "Thank you."

"This all has to do with *that woman*, doesn't it?"

"Some of it has."

"Are you shacked up with her?"

He chuckled. "Not that it should matter, but no."

"Do you wanna be?"

"Mary…"

"Just making sure your blood is in your brain where it belongs."

"Yes. Thank you, sister. Just calling to let you know I'm alive."

"What about Robby?"

"What about Robby?"

"You made him lose his job. Aren't you going to do anything about it?"

"I got bigger fish to fry. Besides, what do you expect from me?"

"Let him help out at your agency for a while. I know you don't like working with a partner, but…"

"I got a confession, Mary…" He hesitated to confess in front of Edith, but he couldn't go on with the charade. It didn't seem to matter anymore. "I ain't got no agency. I'm out of work. And homeless. Have been for months."

"You what?"

"I'll call you later. Love you."

"August!"

He hung up and turned to Edith. "Happy?"

"Not remotely."

"There's some groceries in the kitchen. Think you could throw something together?"

The deep lines returned with a vengeance. "Jesus Christ, Augy."

"What? I can't cook. I live on spam and tuna fish, you know that." He bumped his shoulder against hers. "Come on, it'll be like the old days. You charming the pants off my clients. Get them all suspicious how a guy like me ever landed a number like you."

Her nose twitched. "These days they'd be right to be suspicious."

"These days…" He struck a match and held it a few inches from his face so she had to lean in close to light her cigarette. In the mid-morning light, her eyes appeared greener, softer. And her lipstick glowed coral against the golden highlights of her skin. Her hair was parted on one side and curled in soft waves like Lauren Bacall: a red, shimmering sunset over the desert.

After the first time he saw her, it took him six weeks to pluck up the courage to ask her out, and even then he only managed it under false pretenses. He finagled himself a regular job out of Budwood General Airfield, and one day found her sitting on a bench in the maintenance bay eating a triangular sandwich. His stomach did flips as he walked up and asked if she wouldn't mind taking a look at the release lever in his cockpit since it had been giving him some trouble in the air. She complained to be taken away from her lunch but followed him back to the plane to test out the perfectly functional release system. Within a minute she concluded, correctly, that it seemed fine.

"Yeah, it always does on the ground," he said, "but when I get in the air it sticks half the time. I end up having to make three or four passes."

"Leave the plane here overnight. I'll take it up tomorrow morning and see what I can do."

"The thing is, I got a job needs doing today." He took the deepest breath of his life. "Any chance you'd come up with me now?"

His old Stearman 75 Kaydet had space for two, a pilot in front and a student behind. Augy had purchased it for little more than the price of scrap metal, as its previous owner had been too fond of carrying a flask in the cockpit and had subjected the poor biplane to not one, but several, botched landings. Augy had sunk three hundred dollars into fixing it up and installing the dusting rig. It was stone-age tech—pull a lever connected to the lids of two canisters mounted under each wing—so far below Edith's level of expertise, there was no doubt she knew he was trying to be slick. So, when she agreed to go up in the air, his heart had swelled like a teenager whose sweetheart agreed to go with him to the dance.

He didn't remember the exact conversation they'd shouted at each other as the wind buzzed their ears in the open cockpit, only that it had been the best date he ever had. When they got to the field and Augy pulled the release lever, dousing the crops without incident, Edith hadn't even called him on it.

"What are those?" she shouted, pointing at the short, green-tufted crops below.

"I think they're rutabagas."

"They're what now?"

"You don't know what a rutabaga is?" He giggled. "They're like big sweet turnips."

"What's a turnip?"

"Like an evil potato."

"What's a potato?"

He turned in the cockpit to look at her and she was smiling a mile, biting the tip of her tongue. She pushed his shoulder hard enough that he swerved a little.

"Hey! Watch yourself, Rutabaga!"

Within the week Augy and Edith were jacketed. Three months later they were engaged, and two months after that he was in a tux and tall hat in front of god and all his friends swearing to love this woman until he died. He'd never forget how blue her eyes had been that day against the white of her dress and the blush of her cheeks, sparkling with happy tears like cold water on a hot day.

That was December 22nd, 1940. Less than a year later, over 360 Japanese aircraft would launch a surprise attack on Hickam Air Force Base and Pearl Harbor, causing the deaths of 2,403 United States servicemen and women.

"I said is this some kind of game to you?"

"Huh?" Augy looked up, surprised to find himself in the tawny light of an ostentatious sitting room in Malibu. He blinked, remembering why he was there. The ash had grown long on his cigarette, drooping towards the carpet like an old cock. He grabbed the ashtray off the table and tapped it off. "Is what a game?"

"What are you trying to accomplish here?" snapped Edith.

He flubbed his lips. "Accomplish?"

"It's over, Augy. You do realize that, right? I'm married. Happily, I might add."

He scoffed. "To the human equivalent of macaroni and cheese."

She stood and marched out of the room.

Augy was quick behind her. "Edie, wait..."

She yanked open the front door and stepped out onto the porch. "You can make fun of Bill all you want. And I'll be the first to admit he can be a bit square."

"The guy's angles give dice a complex."

"Yeah, fine, Augy. But you know what he has that you don't have? That you will never have again?"

"What?"

"Me."

Augy sneered and rolled his shoulders. "So what if I tell him?"

"Tell him what?"

"Maybe ole Bill wouldn't think the sun shined so bright out your ass if he knew where you were the night before he married you."

"You'd do that to me?" She put her hands over her mouth and breathed through them like a gasmask. "You'd tear apart my marriage over that one mistake?"

"I want you back."

She laughed in his face. "In your twisted imagination if you get my husband to divorce me I'm gonna come crawling back to you?"

"Look, I messed up. Bad. I didn't treat you right, and you're not a gal what's gonna stand for it. I get it. Haven't you punished me enough?"

"This is not about you. This is about me. My life!"

"Edie..." He reached for her hand.

"Don't you touch me!" She yanked away from him so hard and fast she stumbled. "Bill and I, we're gonna have a baby. We've talked about it."

The words cut into his chest like a scalpel. He had to take a second to regroup. "Is that why you aren't drinking? Are you pregnant?"

"I'm not drinking cause I don't like gin."

"What are you talking about? You love gin."

"No, Augy," she said slowly. "I loved you, and you love gin. I prefer sherry. And Bill knows that about me."

"Sherry, huh?" Augy licked his lips. "I can get you sherry. I can get you all the sherry you want."

"You just don't get it."

"I love you. I've loved you from the start. I know you still love me too. I don't care what you say." There were tears in his eyes and he couldn't stop them. He wiped them back with a thumb and forefinger. "You're all I had. You're the only thing that kept me alive."

"What was I supposed to do, huh?" she asked, lowering her eyes and her voice. "Hang around to watch you break our furniture, argue with ghosts, and hide from Screaming Mimis? That's the life you want for the woman you love?"

"Baby..." He reached for her again, but she stepped back. "I'm better now."

"Really? What made you better? You ever go see a doctor?"

Augy grabbed the bridge of his nose and shook his head. "Doctors can't fix what's wrong with me."

"Why not?"

"Because doctors caused what's wrong with me!"

Edith flinched at his outburst, then put back her shoulders. "What does that mean, Augy?"

"Nothing," he mumbled. "It doesn't matter."

"What does that mean?"

The truth was on the tip of his tongue, but when he looked at her face it wouldn't come out. She already pitied him so much. If he told her the truth, she would never see him as a man ever again, just a pathetic whimpering charity case.

"Forget it," he said.

"Fine." She clenched her fists and marched down the steps towards her car. "While we're forgetting things, why don't you go ahead and forget my number?"

"Edie…"

She yanked open the door of her Chrysler. "In fact, why don't you forget you ever knew me?"

"Edie, wait!"

But by the time he got down the steps, she'd revved the engine and reversed out of the driveway so fast it left skids.

"Edie!" he screamed and smashed his glass on the sidewalk. "Edie!"

She didn't look back once. He fell to his knees as her backlights vanished around the corner. And he couldn't stop the tears falling any more than he could stop the tremors rocking his shoulders. Any more than he could stop himself from punching the concrete. He wanted the physical pain back to blur the pain filling him now. The worst pain he'd ever known.

He would never understand why he still saw colors, why he could still taste sweetness, or hear music. What was the point of any of that if what she said was true? She wasn't testing him, wasn't waiting for him. Wasn't hoping he would get himself together and come back for her. All she wanted was to get away from him.

And suddenly he saw her crying. He'd made her cry so many times since he came back from the dead. He didn't remember what he'd done in the minutes before. He didn't remember where he'd been—in the mine, on the ship, with the doctors. But he'd come to and his knuckles were bloody. The walls of the living room were full of holes. Edith was crouched in the corner behind a broken coffee table, hysterical and too frightened to speak. She'd flinched and tried to get away when he approached her. It was the first time he'd seen fear in her eyes when she looked at him. The first time he realized that he was the monster in her dreams.

He hadn't hit her. He had never hit her. But he didn't have to. She looked at him like she thought he might, and he wanted to die all the same.

Hands touched his shoulders and encouraged him to stand. He heard a voice, but he couldn't understand any of the words. It didn't matter.

He let the hands guide him inside.

CHAPTER TWENTY-TWO

"Oh, son. You should've told me." Mr. O'Hara put a glass of wine in front of him and settled into the chair across the kitchen table. Augy couldn't stand to look at the old man's kind gray eyes, so sympathetic. So full of pity. Dr. Larkin, Katya, and the kids were nowhere to be seen. He could at least be grateful for that.

The walls seemed to be breathing, but his lungs weren't. He had to find air. Had to calm down.

Augy glared at the shimmering white wine. He found the taste about as appealing as cat piss, but this was a desperate situation.

He drained the glass.

"Love can be difficult," the old man purred. "I was lucky with my wife, but believe me, I know sometimes you can try your best, do everything right, and it still goes pear-shaped on you."

"I'm done," said Augy, slapping his hands on the table. "If she wants to be with that anthropomorphized TV dinner, that's fine by me. I have wasted enough time and energy and sleepless nights and restless days thinking about this." He laughed at himself and clenched his teeth. "I'm being ridiculous anyway. I can't be with anyone. There's no scenario where my story ends with a white picket fence and fucking mailbox with my name on it. So let her have those things if that's what she wants. Maybe someday, I'll figure out how to be happy for her."

Mr. O'Hara wrinkled his brow. "What are you talking about, son?"

"Mr. O'Hara—" Augy looked up at him, "—I owe you an apology. I haven't been honest with you. Me and Edith have been divorced for years. I wanted your house cause I'm working a case right now where I got a few individuals need a safe spot to stay. And it's not exactly all above board."

O'Hara poured them both more wine. "Can you tell me more or is it strictly on the Q. T, as the kids say? Do they still say that?"

"Not even a little bit." Augy chuckled and shook his head. "You're not upset?"

He reached across the table to tap Augy's hand reassuringly. "It all sounds terribly exciting."

Dr. Larkin appeared in the doorway. Her head was pitched far forward on her slender neck, displaying long tendons as tight as violin strings. Her eyes bulged, the whites so wide they glowed. "There are police cars outside," she said.

Popping up from his seat, Augy rushed to the window and peeked through the drapes. Six cars had lined up by the curb, and two uniforms were striding towards the door.

"How did they find us?" asked the doctor.

Katya strolled into the kitchen, the barrel of the shotgun rested on one shoulder. Her thick eyebrows were cocked all the way up again.

"Not with the kids in the house," Augy groaned.

She pumped the shotgun. "You have better plan?"

"I'll go talk to them," said Mr. O'Hara, standing. "They can't possibly have a warrant, and if they try to get inside without one, my lawyers will descend on them like vultures on festering carrion."

Katya glared at O'Hara. "Who the hell are you?"

Augy glanced through the drapes again; the cops were nearly at the door. Several more waited by their cars, leaning against the hoods with their guns out. It made him sick that he recognized most of them as guys he'd been out for drinks with.

Was it possible the neighbors had called about his little outburst? But that didn't make sense. No way this many cars would've shown up over a simple domestic.

Had one of the neighbors somehow recognized him? Was his face plastered on wanted posters all over town?

One thing he knew for certain.

"This is all my fault."

Excepting the two trotting up the front steps, the uniforms probably didn't know much about the call they'd been sent on. They probably thought they were there to apprehend a single, possibly armed, suspect. Dr. Larkin's truck was tucked in the covered garage. Parked on the curb, Mr. O'Hara's Bentley was now sandwiched between two of LA's finest.

But the cruiser bringing up the rear had a good amount of wiggle room. And the way the cops were standing, all their backs to the street...

It might work.

Augy turned to Katya. "Take the kids and the Doc and load yourselves into the truck."

The doorbell rang and Mr. O'Hara straightened his tie. "I'll handle this, son. Not to worry."

"Stall them as long as you can," said Augy.

"Stall them?" He scoffed. "By the time I'm done with them, they'll be begging for my forgiveness." Looking over his shoulder at Katya and the Doc, he doffed his porkpie hat. "Ladies."

He puffed out his chest and strode from the room. Katya wrinkled her nose. "Strange man."

Augy grabbed her arm and guided her to the far corner of the room, away from the windows. "Lock the door from the house to the garage and barricade it."

Her gaze poured over his face. "What is your plan?"

He rolled his shoulders. "My bet is they don't know you're here, so when I leave, they will follow me. You wait for the commotion to die down, then gun it."

"You try outrun them? You sure you can?"

"Does a neutered dog miss his balls?"

She wrinkled her nose. "Where I find you?"

"At midnight, I'll be waiting where we first met."

Katya nodded. "*Udachi.*"

"What's that mean?"

"It means, do not die."

"You either, gorgeous." He held her gaze for another half-second, as long as he could linger, then slunk out of the room towards the back of the house. He heard Mr. O'Hara arguing with the cops.

Augy slipped out the back, locking the door behind him. The centerpiece of the yard was a large pool styled to look like a Hawaiian lagoon. Bitter chlorine set off the heavy sweet scent of tropical flowers. Quartzite tiles underfoot sparkled in the hot midday sun, as the glint of clear water bit at his eyes.

He sneaked along the edge of the house until he came to a bedroom window. Thanking God she'd picked a room on the ground floor, he knocked out Shave and a Haircut.

"Angel?" he whispered loudly. "Shake a leg."

An eye peeked through the curtains. When Sumika saw him, she struggled with her bandaged hands to crank open the glass half an inch.

"You gotta go to the garage with Doc Larkin," he said before she even had the opportunity to ask.

"Why?"

"Don't argue. You gotta go now. Get down to the garage."

She disappeared, but as he turned away, he saw her struggling with the handle to crank the window wide open.

"What the hell are you doing?"

She swung a leg out onto the ledge. "I'm coming with you."

"No!" he hissed. "You gotta…"

That was as far as he got. The cops were inside the house now, turning the place inside out. Sumika wouldn't be able to get to the garage without being seen, and if Augy didn't make his move soon, Katya and the others would be discovered anyway.

"Fine." He grabbed Sumika by the forearm and helped her out of the window. "Stick to me like glue. You got it?"

Nodding, she clasped the back of his jacket between her palms. With Sumika in tow, Augy sneaked along the perimeter of the house until he came to the tall wooden gate that separated the front yard from the back.

The fence encircled the property. If he went up on his tippy-toes, which was a big ask, he could see the trunk of the nearest police car. The cops were all watching the front door, but even the stupidest cop would notice if the gate swung open and two invalids came limping out.

Augy followed the fence into the banana leaf plants that surrounded the perimeter until he could look over into the neighbor's yard.

Clear.

Without a word, he laced his fingers and put them in front of Sumika like a holster. She looked between his hands and his eyes, then swallowed audibly.

She always looked apprehensive, every moment since the day they met. Sumika had these eyes—wideset, almond eyes that inclined towards her nose. He could never be sure if he was reading them right, or if her face had been painted by nature to stay vigilant.

To his surprise, she didn't hesitate. Bracing herself on his shoulders, she stepped into his hands. He lifted her up and helped her get a knee over the top of the fence. Augy grabbed the fence, planted his left foot on the wood and pushed himself up high enough to swing his right leg over. He landed on the other side and helped Sumika down.

The neighbor's yard had looked empty when he'd first checked, but now a dog the size of a small horse bounded towards them. Sumika stifled a scream and hid behind his back. Augy tensed as the dog shoved its nose in his crotch, covering him with happy slobber.

Augy petted its big floppy ears, then hurried across the emerald green lawn, through a flock of ceramic pink flamingoes, to a gate that led to the driveway.

The dog was desperate to come along. It whined as they sneaked through the gate, then started to bark. Augy tensed, but soon another dog joined in and then another. Before long the neighborhood was a chorus of canine voices.

They bolted along a row of zinnias until he could peer around a corner. The cops still had all their guns pointed at O'Hara's house. He recognized the unmistakable mix of excitement and boredom on all their faces. Their lackadaisical posturing was both good and bad. It meant they weren't hypervigilant. It also meant they were experienced. They were anxious for something interesting to happen, but they also knew true excitement is scarce in the life of the average cop.

He eyed the nearest cruiser: a black and white Ford Deluxe Fordor. No mesh separated the front and back seats. The angle was wrong to see if the keys were in the ignition. It was logical to assume that since the driver was standing not five feet from the vehicle, he wouldn't have bothered to take the keys. If he had, the whole plan was ruined. Augy could hotwire an engine, but not in the five seconds he'd have before they noticed him.

If he were caught, a jail cell would be nothing but a quick stop on the way to his real destination, which might be anything from the electric chair to

Countess London's own torture chamber. He was ready to endure whatever might happen. But Sumika...

He turned to her. "We're gonna make a break for that car," he said, pointing to the cruiser. "I'll go first, then if I wave you on, you run from cover and get in. The moment we're on the road, climb into the backseat, lay down and do not look up until I say, understand?"

She nodded, eyes on the car as she sucked on her upper lip.

"Listen," he leaned down and clutched her shoulders. "If I get caught, hide yourself. At midnight, Doc Larkin and the others will be waiting on the road not far from where I first found you. Try to make your way back to them."

Her eyes widened fearfully and she shook her head.

"Angel, if you're gonna survive, you're gonna have to learn to trust people."

"I trust you," she said.

Augy's chest swelled. He kissed her forehead quickly. "You're a poor judge of character."

Keeping low to the ground, he rushed up behind the car. He paused, waiting for any reaction. Nothing. He tipped his gaze over the window and smiled at the silver chain dangling from the ignition. He waited until a truck passed to pop open the car door, hoping the whoosh of the engine would mask the noise. Again, the cops made no move. Augy waved Sumika on.

Silent and stealthy as a cat, she came to his side. Augy pulled open the door enough for her to slip in, then climbed in after. He kicked the seat all the way back and revved the engine. The cops turned and began to shout. His foot sank like an anvil on the accelerator, and the wheels squealed. Sumika flung herself into the backseat before the first shot rang out.

"You all right, angel?"

"Yeah," came the trembling reply.

Sirens wailed to life and he saw one car after another appear in the rearview mirror. Red and blue filled his vision. He tapped his fingers in succession on the steering wheel and shifted into high gear.

It was a terrible plan. The cars were equally matched, and Augy was comfortable with high speeds, but there ended his list of advantages. The cops could communicate with each other, coordinate an omnidirectional assault, utilize an infinite supply of cars, and every other bit of technology available to them. If he tried to gun it in one direction, they would lay down spikes. But trying to lose them in an intricate pattern of twists and turns had even less chance of success. Augy had lived in LA all his life, but he knew cops. Most drove a hundred miles a night, five nights a week, along the same narrow streets of their beat. If you took them all together, nobody knew a city like cops.

His best hope was to get into heavy traffic where the possibility of civilian casualties would keep them from shooting at him. Augy sped through the next intersection, narrowly avoiding being T-boned by an approaching truck. Up ahead, railroad crossing lights flashed, the barrier lowering. He threw the transmission into overdrive and smashed through the wooden beam like tissue paper. Splinters exploded. The car jumped the track seconds before the train zoomed through, trapping the pursuers behind it.

Augy didn't entertain fantasies of freedom yet. He was in a numbered police cruiser in the fourth biggest city in the country. He was contemplating the possibility of leaping onto the train when he heard it: the unmistakable sound of blades beating air into submission.

He ran his tongue over his teeth and looked up through the windshield at the approaching helicopter. "That was fast."

He popped the clutch and peeled out. Trying to hide in this car was a fool's errand, so after taking inventory of the buttons and switches on the dash, he flipped on the siren. Traffic parted, and he was able to swerve to the other side of the road, run red lights, and drive like a maniac with impunity.

"Attention all units," the radio blared. "High speed pursuit in progress. All available units respond. Suspect is headed southbound on Puerco Canyon Road towards Pacific Coast Highway."

Merging westbound onto the highway, Augy cleared his throat and picked up the radio. "This is Officer Haulass. Suspect is in sight headed eastbound on Pacific Coast towards Corral Canyon."

"Negative. Suspect is headed eastbound on Pacific Coast."

"Suspect is headed northbound up Corral Canyon Road."

"Negative, Haulass. Check your position."

"The suspect just pulled out a machine gun," said Augy. "We're taking heavy fire. He's mowing down civilians. There's blood everywhere. We need backup!"

"Confirm your location, Haulass."

"Officer haul ass?" A crusty, familiar voice came over the radio: Yeltz. "Small, get off this line."

"I will when you stop chasing me."

"You have to give yourself up, kid," he said. "You're gonna get yourself killed."

"All units respond. Marilyn Monroe is buck naked and walking down main street!"

"Change frequency. License KB49175."

Augy had no idea what that meant, so he slammed down the receiver.

Four cruisers sped onto the road as he passed the pier. He kept the speedometer at a healthy seventy-five as he weaved between cars, plaiting a twelve strand knot the cops couldn't follow. Within a few minutes, he was out of sight of the cruisers.

But so long as the helicopter was on his tail, all the fancy driving in the world couldn't save him.

Pushing in the cigarette lighter, Augy snatched the pack of Chesterfields off the dash. He had to stay calm.

The wail of more sirens cut into his skull, and more cars joined him on the freeway. Some were already in front of him, but the Fords were too slow to get to sixty. He left them in his exhaust.

They caught up inch by inch. One got into position for a PIT maneuver— a bump to the left backend that would send him into a spin. Augy swerved in front, forcing the cop to hit his brakes. He had to stay ahead of them. Stay out of sight. Get out of range.

But where the hell was he going?

He passed a sign saying he was twelve miles from the airport and was struck with an idea. He didn't know LAX as well as Burbank, but all airports are basically the same. Given his history, the cops would probably assume he was about to do something incredibly stupid when they realized where he was heading.

He came to a stretch of road with a paved shoulder and took to it flat out. The speedometer climbed a hair above eighty, then maxed out. A cop pulled out to follow him and was gaining when Augy saw rough shoulder coming up. Alongside him were two eighteen-wheelers with a stretch of clear road out in front. He swerved in front of them without easing off the gas. The cop got stuck behind the huge trucks long enough for Augy to lose him around a bend.

The traffic around Venice Beach let him get some more stitches in his knot, and soon he was far enough ahead he couldn't see lights or hear any sirens. But the helicopter was still tight on him, radioing his every movement down to the boys in blue. He flicked off the siren and took the exit towards LAX. He was in sight of the terminal when it finally happened. The vicious sound of the helicopter warped and then began to fade as it turned back.

He'd entered restricted air space and it couldn't follow.

He turned into the first parking lot, careful to follow the speed limit and every posted sign, then drove down a line of cars until he saw a lone old lady trying to load luggage into the back of a black Volkswagen Beetle. He pulled up beside her and killed the engine.

"Excuse me, ma'am," he called, lowering the brim of his hat as he approached. "Let me help you with that."

"Why, thank you, young man," she said, smiling and stepping aside. She had a babushka over her wiry gray hair and yellow bug-eye glasses. "You wouldn't believe how few people will stop to help with a lady's bags these days. I was in New York visiting my daughter, and I swear, God help me, it's the end of the world."

He lifted up her two suitcases and threw them in the trunk. "I hate to do this to you, ma'am, but I need you to give me your keys and get into the backseat."

"You've never met such a rude group of people in all your life. Gloomy little so-and-so's, too, I don't mind telling you. Maybe it's the weather." She popped her lips a couple of times. "What's that you said?"

"Hand over your keys and get into the back seat of the car."

"Now, why would I do that? Am I in some kind of trouble, officer?"

"Oh, I'm not an officer," said Augy, grinning. "And while I do have a gun, I'd prefer not to show it to you, unless you really need to see it."

The old lady's eyes darted. He sensed she was about to suck in a breath to call for help.

Augy took the Browning out of his jacket pocket, holding it close to his body to conceal it from passersby. "Don't make this harder than it has to be."

With another look askance, she relinquished the keys. "You are going to regret running into me," she said. "I will make sure of that. My daughter is married to a very important man."

"Get in the backseat," he said. "You can tell me all about it on the way."

Once the old lady was in, he returned to the cruiser. As Sumika struggled out, he reached over her head to take the M1 Carbine and two fifteen round cartridges mounted to a bracket above the back windshield.

When he got into the Beetle, he passed the gun to Sumika, who looked about as intimidating as a Dresden figurine holding it. Laughing, Augy pulled off his jacket and laid it over the gun.

When the old woman saw Sumika, she gasped. "My god, child. What happened to you?"

Augy turned to the granny. "Give me your glasses."

"My son-in-law works in the district attorney's office in New York City," she contended in a voice which had risen at least an octave in the last minute. "You are in big trouble, young man. I wouldn't want to be in your shoes. No, sir. They must really be heating up."

He snapped impatiently. "Glasses."

"Utterly reprehensible." She passed them over. "What kind of a person—"

"Shut up, please." Augy put on the glasses—a couple of foggy fishbowls— and flipped up the brim of his hat.

He pulled out and joined the line of cars leaving the airport. Sirens blared as cops parked on the curb in front of terminals, no doubt convinced hotheaded old Captain Small was about to attempt a daring escape by air.

Meanwhile, an unremarkable black Beetle containing one old chatterbox, one small girl, and one four-eyed nosebleed left LAX without incident.

CHAPTER TWENTY-THREE

He kept the old woman with them most of the day, worried that if he let her loose she'd alert the cops to what had happened. The presence of the carbine didn't dampen her chattiness in the least. By sunset, Augy and Sumika knew everything about her, her late husband, her daughter, her daughter's husband, her two grandchildren—of whom she even produced a picture—and her Yorkshire terrier, Fifi. Augy had a throbbing headache by the time they dropped her off at a bus stop outside Compton. He told her to wait until the next morning to report the car missing and to tell the cops it had simply been stolen from the parking lot. When she refused, he was forced to remind her of all the personal information he now had on her and her family, and about the massive gun he carried, and his devil-may-care, explosively violent, criminal disposition.

Looking sheepish, she agreed to his terms. He didn't trust her as far as he could spit, but there was nothing else for it.

With her gone, Augy headed straight for Ben's, which was only a mile or so away. Given how nervous Sumika was around, well, humans, he let her wait in the car while he plodded up to the heavily modified Sears home and tapped on the aluminum screen door.

Ben opened the door, half a cigarette hanging out of one side of his mouth, some bizarre twist of metal in one hand and a screwdriver in the other. When he recognized Augy, he snarled.

"Look what the cat dragged in," Ben said, leaning inside the house to set down his project. "You owe me two hundred bucks, motherfucker."

"I need another car."

Ben spat out a laugh. "You got a fat sack on you, I'll give you that. Surprised I didn't hear you come up, dragging that thing around."

Augy narrowed his eyes. "I'm sorry about the car."

"Did you know her? The lady that got…"

Nodding slowly, he looked down at the dirty welcome mat. He stepped aside so Ben could see the Volkswagen. "I can trade you that. It's practically brand new. All I need is something with clean plates that runs."

"Is it hot?"

"Of course, it's hot."

"What happened to you, Small?" Ben shook his head. "You used to be such a Boy Scout."

Augy shrugged. He felt a little guilty for robbing the old lady, but one of the many facts she'd shared about herself was that she had a comprehensive car policy, so she would be reimbursed for the full cash value of the vehicle by her insurance company. And fuck insurance companies, honestly.

"You interested or not?" Augy asked.

Ben went back inside, returning a minute later carrying a huge old-fashioned flashlight, with a square battery underneath. He circled the car a few times checking the tires, the paint, the doors, and under the hood—or the trunk, or whatever you call it on a Volkswagen. When he came strolling back towards Augy, he lit a cigarette. "I'm guessing the girl doesn't come with?" He shuddered. "What happened to her face?"

Augy didn't answer, his heart heavy. Sumika would never be able to escape that question. Those scars would be the first thing everybody judged her on, whether they inspired pity, disgust, or some combination. For the first time, Augy was thankful his scars were under his clothes.

A few minutes later, Augy and Sumika drove off the lot in a rust and hunter green 1938 Hudson 112 coupe. It had an engine that roared like a hurricane, no radio, and the steering was so stiff Augy's arms and chest were burning after only a few minutes. But it had clean plates and a filed off VIN number, and that was what you paid for at a place like Ben's.

They arrived at the meeting spot half an hour before midnight and Augy parked the car alongside the road under some foliage. By the fingernail-clipping moon, it was hard to see his own hand in front of his face. Normally, such complete darkness would've sent his heart racing, but he felt oddly calm. Sumika, on the other hand, was on the verge of convulsions.

"How long do we have to stay here?" she asked. "I don't like it here."

"Me neither."

"We're too close."

Augy bit his lip. "The mansion is right near here, isn't it? Where they give those... parties?"

Sumika nodded, eyes darting.

"We'll be out of here before you know it." He laid a hand on her shoulder. She flinched and looked up. The moonlight hit her face, and he saw tears on her cheeks.

She'd found a shapeless skirt and baggy sweater, which made her look even smaller than she was. Her wounds were healing quicker and cleaner than his, her young skin resting in bed where it ought to be. But it was clear they would never fade to smooth white scars, either. They had been too deep, too brutal. Especially the gash in her lips. Even with Dr. Larkin's careful stitching, they were healing askew. She would never be able to smile without feeling the scar stretch. What made it even harder, was it was so easy to imagine what she had looked like before—innocent and clean, with bright intelligent brown eyes and smiling pink lips. The sight of her filled Augy with so much rage he struggled to stay focused.

A nagging suspicion was chewing at his insides, a heart flu filling him with black phlegm. He couldn't go on ignoring it.

"Do you know Katya Tyler?" he said, then scrutinized her reaction. Her shoulders shrank and her back straightened. Quickly her face turned to his, and he saw terror in her eyes that confirmed what he'd been hoping she would deny.

"How do you know her?" he asked.

Sumika shook her head and looked away.

"Listen, angel. I can't have you going silent on me again. Not about this." He licked his lips, trying to keep his frustration out of his face and away from his tongue. "Did she hurt you?"

She looked up into his eyes, and it sent a chill down his spine. "Not me," she said.

Augy closed his eyes and pressed a hand against his forehead. "Others?"

Sumika nodded, then looked away again. "She took away the dying ones... to..."

"To finish them off," he said. "Like they tried to do to you."

She didn't answer. She didn't need to.

Augy pressed his palm into the side of his face. He couldn't get a deep enough breath and his skin was prickling with needles. He didn't want it to be true. He wanted to deny it, to call Sumika a liar.

"Katya didn't want to hurt anyone." The words tumbled out of his mouth even as he thought them. "She did what she had to do to stay alive."

Sumika shrugged. "How many of them did?"

Augy opened his mouth, but there were no words. He was looking at Sumika, but all he could see was Dr. Katsuki Muto, with the wild eyes.

"Come here, angel," he said, encouraging her to slide across the seat. He put his arm over her skeletal shoulders. Slowly, her breath became more steady, and her face melted against his chest. He grabbed his jacket off the gun on the floor and laid it over her. Soon, she was no longer shaking. When he craned his neck to see her face, he realized she'd fallen asleep.

He smiled and gave her a squeeze, but there was an unexpected pain in his heart. He probably wouldn't ever have any kids of his own. He'd always wanted a family, but Edith never did. He'd been willing to put it aside to be with her. They'd both wanted to travel, to focus on their careers.

When she said she and Bill were trying for a baby, it was like she shoved a dagger in his guts. Now Augy realized it wasn't that she didn't want kids; she just hadn't wanted to have kids with him.

He forced Edith out of his brain, but that left an empty hole to fill with other concerns. Augy had forbidden himself from worrying about Katya and the others until after midnight, but as the clock on the dash flicked to 11:58 his neurosis geared up for a special performance. Before the tension broke the surface, headlights peeked around the bend.

It wasn't the truck, but as the vehicle drew closer, it slowed to a stop behind them. Augy pulled his pistol out of his pocket.

A shadow emerged from the backseat, and then the car took off. He recognized a Yellow Cab as it passed.

The shadow lit a cigarette and sashayed towards the car. High heels and a pencil skirt. He rolled down his window, and she leaned on the sill. Her scent filled his nostrils—no perfume, just her own sweat.

"Hey there, gorgeous," he said, his voice a flatline.

Katya smiled and lifted her eyebrows. "You lived."

"So did you. Any problems?"

She flattened her chin and shook her head. "Piece of cake."

He grunted. "My cake got hit by a train, but we're no worse for wear."

"We?" Katya craned her neck, noticing Sumika for the first time. "This is girl? The doctor worried she was caught."

Augy snuck out from behind Sumika and slipped from the car. He walked around the car and rested his hip on the trunk. Katya followed.

Lighting a cigarette, Augy looked up at the dark sky pinpricked with little white stars between dirty sheepskin clouds. Katya watched him. Waiting.

"I gotta ask you," he said, searching for her eyes. "That night we first met, what were you doing out by the sinkhole?"

Katya pursed her lips. She had such sharp symmetrical features—high cheeks, cleft chin, and a chiseled, almost mannish jaw. The shadows and light played on her as if on a statue. "I think you know."

"That changes things, don't it?"

"Does it?" She rolled her tongue over her front teeth.

"Listen, I understand…"

"Do you?" she scoffed. "Has somebody put a gun in your hand and told you to kill a stranger or kill yourself? And even if you choose yourself, they will kill stranger anyway? Has this happened to you?" Katya widened her eyes as she stared at him and didn't speak again until he looked away. "You cannot understand."

Augy swallowed hard. His brain was still tumbling over dark imaginings and dwelling on the face of a man he barely knew, and whom he was certain was dead now.

"I'll tell you what I do understand," he said. "*He who fights monsters must take great care that he doesn't become one.*"

A car zoomed by not two feet from Katya's back. She didn't flinch. "Fuck Nietzsche."

"Fair enough," Augy shrugged, silently impressed she caught the quote. "My point is there's no way we can possibly know one hundred percent who was acting under duress and who wasn't. What would you have done to stay alive? Or me? Or anybody? Like you said—and you're absolutely right—if you haven't been in that situation, it's impossible to know."

"What you want we do then, huh?" She crossed her arms and cocked a hip. "What is your genius plan where everybody get what they deserve, including me?"

"I don't want anything bad to happen to you."

"Why you care?"

He flicked his cigarette into the road and watched the tracer bounce on the asphalt. "I think it's clear Countess London has been acting with some kind of government sanction. The mayor is in on it, apparently. Some dirty cops. Now what I'm wondering is why in god's name would any member of the government allow this kind of thing to go on?"

"You tell me."

"I have a theory, but I don't like it." He bit the corner of his lips. "Let's prove me wrong."

"How?"

"I say we start with the devil we know. Your husband."

Katya lifted her chin, looking at him straight again.

"He owns a company that manufactures medical supplies, right?" asked Augy. "Holzklotz?

She nodded.

"So, I think it's pretty clear the part he plays in all this. If we can get ahold of records of the orders Countess London has been placing and where they've been going, we'll have a much better idea of the actual size of this operation, not to mention proof. Most importantly, we need to find out who's been paying the bills."

"It will not be easy." She leaned back against the car.

"You know these people better than I do."

Katya shook her head. "I collect names, places, numbers, but without my book..."

"We can't get your book back, gorgeous. Not without involving the cops."

"Then you are right. We go for Frank." She sighed through her nostrils. "I was wanting save him for last, but... *c'est le vie.*"

"How'd you end up with that worthless son of a bitch anyhow?"

"Countess London give me to him. Like present." She chewed on the tip of a nail. "He decide to marry me. I think he think I am going to fall in love with him."

"Was he... I mean..."

"For long time he try, what is word? Make me want him?"

"To woo you?"

"Yes. He buy me jewelry. He take me places. He try talk to me." Her lips furrowed and twitched. "But I hate him. Of course, I hate him. He will not let me leave. He has his goons on me all the time: guns and locks and threats. And he think I would fall in love with him."

"But he is your kids' father, right?"

"The children were accidents." She shook her head as if resisting memories. "What I can say? Man look at me too long, I get pregnant."

"I'll keep that in mind." He kept his eyes down, watching the reflection of the moon in his shiny shoes. "Where are the kids anyway?"

"Your doctor is with them at hotel." Katya smiled. "I like her. She remind me of my baba. Little bit."

"Yeah, I like her too. She's a tough old bird."

"We take girl there?"

"Sumika," he corrected, his voice harsh. "And yeah. I think we'd better. She can't be a part of this."

"We go now. No more wasted time."

She moved to get into the car, but he grabbed her arm. "It's you and me then, right? We're gonna see this thing through to the end, and not involve anybody else. No more innocents get hurt." He put out his hand, asking for a promise.

She clasped it. "Only you and me get hurt."

"You and me, gorgeous."

CHAPTER TWENTY-FOUR

While Katya stood several yards away, smoking and kicking rocks, Augy roused Sumika and told her he was going to drop her off at a safe place with the others.

"Please don't send me away." Her voice trembled. She stared down at her lap, rubbing her bandaged hands together. "I can help."

"I know, angel. But this…"

She looked up at him pleadingly. "Did I do something wrong?"

"God no. I don't want to see you get hurt."

"I'm sorry I'm so ugly."

"What are you talking about?"

"You don't think I'm ugly?"

Trying to resist the stabbing pain in his heart, he closed his eyes. "Of course not."

"I can still be useful," she said. Before he knew what was happening, she'd hiked up her skirt. "I can make you feel good."

"Sumika, stop that!" Horrified, he pushed down her skirt.

She shoved herself far away from him and forced her body against the car door, crying uncontrollably. "I'm sorry!" she shrieked, her voice muffled by tears. "I'm no good for anything anymore."

Augy stared hard at the steering wheel and took a few deep breaths. He'd forgotten how to talk. What Dr. Larkin had said that first night he'd found Sumika flashed through his brain—how the young girl had already had at least one abortion. The full reality of it hit him for the first time. Sumika had been only five years old when she lost her mother and was taken to that so-called orphanage. And then some man had taken her home. Mr. Campbell. He hadn't heard the rest of the story, but he knew how it ended. For the first time, he couldn't help imagining it, and he tasted vomit in the back of his throat.

"I'm not angel anymore, am I?" Sumika whispered through her tears.

He pressed his face into his hands, choking on horror and disgust. Finally, he found the will to look up at her. Her face was bright red, bottom lip thrust out, eyes contorted and streaming tears. Part of him wanted to reach for her, to take her in his arms and rock her like a baby, but he was afraid to touch her.

"You will always be angel," he said, which caused her to cry harder. "You can stay, all right? I want you to stay."

"No, you don't."

"I was being stupid. We can't do this without you."

He gave her some tissues and Sumika climbed into the backseat. He called Katya over and asked her to take the wheel. Augy spent the entire trip staring out the window, watching lines on the road pass. Seething.

Katya guided them to the lavish Brentwood home of her slimy husband. A stone's throw from Bel Air, the houses here were equally large and opulent, and likewise the foliage lush and impervious to drought. Green like money. But the lots were larger, particularly here in Mandeville Canyon. Francis Tyler, for example, had his own private lake, complete with cascading waterfall, a swath of wilderness, two guest houses, servants quarters, a pool, and tennis courts. And those were just the amenities visible from the drive. If the American dream was a successful career, a big house, a beautiful wife, and two-point-five children, then Francis Tyler epitomized it. At least, for the next twenty minutes, he would.

Augy had never spent so much time lurking in such expensive places, and never had he felt like such a failure.

"There is maid," said Katya, checking the chamber of the shotgun for perhaps the eighth time. "And butler. They are not talking much English."

"Will they be in the house?" asked Augy.

"Sometimes Frank make them work all night. We will not hurt them—" she wagged a finger, eyes wide "—but maybe tie them up."

Augy nodded. "And the boss man himself?"

"Will be sleeping or in his office." Katya leaned over him to point out one of the upper windows of the three-story, Tudor-style mansion. "That was our room."

"Will he be armed?"

"His man, Charlie, would always stand guard outside our door while we sleep. If he will be there now, I do not know."

"Is that the good-looking fellow with the cork bullets?"

She nodded. "He use cork on me, but he always have real ammo, too. He was a, uh... how you say? American... not army, but..."

"A marine?"

"Yes."

"That's great. Fantastic."

"If knowing this, you think different of plan..."

"No, no. I'm fine." He picked at his teeth. "You're happy with the shotgun?"

She shrugged. "I take rifle if you want give."

He passed over the carbine. "You still have the revolver?"

"I give to Dr. Larkin." She checked the carbine and shoved the extra cartridges in her suit pocket before handing him the shotgun. "How's your pistol?"

"I got two bullets." He scratched his forehead with the Browning's barrel. In the side-view mirror, he saw Sumika slumped in the backseat staring impassively out the window. He lifted the gun for her to see. "Think you could work this thing?"

She took it, and after some maneuvering, wiggled her one remaining finger through the trigger guard. Holding the gun between her bandages and bracing it against her chest, she nodded.

"Only use it if someone is coming straight for you," he warned.

The little girl nodded and sat back in her seat.

"I will be quick to check office," said Katya, "then meet you."

"Speaking of quick, you sure you're gonna be able to walk in those shoes?"

Glancing at her five-inch-high heels, she smirked. "If I can rumba in them, I can do this."

"You rumba?" asked Augy, chuckling.

"Why you laugh? What, I am Russian so I cannot rumba?"

"No. It's just... I rumba."

She rolled her eyes. "You do not."

"No, really. Me and my ex even did a ballroom competition one time. Got second place."

"I do not believe you."

"You think because I look like a giraffe I must dance like one?"

"Yes, I do. I think that."

"This jive bomber's got solid nervous pegs, mama. I'll prove it to you." He shifted. "Well, not now, obviously."

"Obviously." She shook her head, laughing. "Do you want do this, or you want to talk more?"

He cleared his throat. "Let's get it over with."

"You always want to talk. You are like old woman."

"I am not. Shut up."

She popped the car door and scanned the dark drive. "You sure you can climb up to window with your foot?"

"Hey, if you can manage in heels..." He met her eyes and furrowed his brow. "*Udachi*, gorgeous."

She winked. "See? I am learning you."

Katya darted off to the left and soon was lost in shadows. Augy lingered for another few breaths. He wanted to say something more to Sumika—something wise and comforting.

He had nothing.

Stepping out of the car, he shoved the shotgun in his belt, popped his knuckles and ground his cigarette under his heel. The house looked comatose. Even the porchlight was out. It nagged at his nerves that he should've felt panicky, and still, he didn't. How many years had it been now he trembled every time the lights went out in his own house? And yet here he was, standing on the edge of what might be his own dark death, and he felt nothing.

That was the nature of trauma. It doesn't like loud noises, retreats from its own kind. In silence and calm, it makes its home, filling a soul that should be quiet with its sickness. But in the thick of it, trauma curls up in the corner and goes to sleep. Like an old dog under the table, it gets fat off the scraps even though it doesn't take part in the dinner.

That last thought sent trembles through his bones. Maybe his dreams of the mine, of the operating table, were going to fade away—as he'd prayed they would for years now—only to be replaced with nightmares of fumbling through bodies in a sinkhole. Of poor Sumika and everything he could never do to help her. Memories of shards of skull embedded in his knuckles.

He'd outlived so many more deserving souls. It had all started with Eugene, his wingman. So many men—little boys, really—came home from the war with nightmares of combat. Of watching their comrades blown to smithereens. Army, navy, marines: their nights were filled with gun blasts, gore and blood, screams of dying men.

Augy only had one experience of combat, and it had been an unequivocal victory. Those four days he flew at Midway, he had been unstoppable. He was born of the sky, filled with exhilaration for the moment that left him wanting more. Like all fighter pilots, the only place he felt comfortable was in the air. Every moment on the ground was a wasted one. The cockpit was his true home, where nothing mattered except jet fuel, blue skies, and clear shots.

He hadn't been afraid the morning he left Guam for Singapore. Two nights earlier, he'd prayed to be chosen to fly the mission.

Eugene was eighteen. Smart as a whip and twice as biting; he had this amazing sarcastic sense of humor that sometimes left Augy crying he was laughing so hard. Rolling on the floor, grabbing your ribs, hoping you don't piss yourself kind of laughing. Technically, Eugene was a good pilot, too, but for all the confidence he had in conversation, his fingers always shook on the stick. And who could blame him? Seeing as the US was so desperate for pilots, and Eugene was so smart, so technically good, they pushed him through flight school at a shameful pace. He had less than thirty flight hours under his belt when he was assigned to the Singapore mission. They thought his high IQ would carry him through.

But brains don't count for much in the heat of the moment. Augy had known some real shit-for-brains who made great pilots, and some real geniuses who had no business in the air.

They'd flown in a four-finger formation that day. Standard procedure. Augy, recently promoted to captain, was the flight leader—the middle finger. Eugene was his wingman, defensively positioned on his left. The element leader and his wingman made up the ring finger and pinky. Rudolph Jones and Sammy Williams, two pilots who'd been at Midway. Sammy would die at Iwo Jima in a banzai charge while asleep in his tent. Rudolph was a commercial pilot now. He and Augy got together for lunch once a few years ago. He seemed to have come through fine.

But Eugene, the anxious rookie...

He couldn't even remember the names of all the men he'd watched die at Changi, and later at Hokkaido. All Augy knew is he kept on living, while one man after another—Aussies and Brits, Dutch and Filipino, Chinese and

Koreans, men fitter than himself, stronger both physically and mentally, men who had more to offer a peacetime world than he did—he watched one after another die. And then finally at the hospital in Tokyo, where every single ally soldier died. Fit or not. They all died. Every last one speared through the gut. Except him.

He'd given up asking why. Heaven was empty, and only a madman demands answers from stars. Balls of hydrogen burn with impunity, and they care nothing for human life.

Lily Wong was dead, too. Beautiful Lily, who'd made him laugh like he'd thought he'd never laugh again. Like Eugene made him laugh. She'd burned to death on a pyre built for him. And sure, he killed some people over it. But that didn't make her any less dead. And heaven was still empty, and the moon was just a rock.

He wasn't frightened for himself as he approached the Tyler house and climbed the drainpipe to the third-story bedroom window. He would live. No matter what pain they might inflict on him, he was destined to live. Live to hurt the ones he loved. To lose everything he'd ever worked for. To fail, again and again. To be the tragic, comical figure that goes on living like he doesn't know what's good for him. Like he can't accept that nobody cares anymore.

But Katya had a reason to live. She had two kids to look after, a future that mattered.

And that meant she was probably going to die.

These were the thoughts in Augy's brain as he crept through the open window into Frank Tyler's bedroom. And these are the thoughts that fell out when the light flicked on and three AK-47s pointed at his chest.

Men in suits with robotic expressions stood in a triangle formation facing the window.

"Get out your gun and kick it over here," said one. Augy had no choice but to comply.

Any one of them could've cut him in half with a twitch of their trigger finger, and yet, it wasn't them or their terrifying machinery that drew his attention. For sitting across the room in a highbacked white chair, dressed in a gray Mao suit, her salt and pepper hair pulled back into a severe bun, and her chin resting on top of tented fingers was a woman who commanded attention without ever needing to ask for it.

She was in her sixties, or maybe hard fifties. Her eyes were wedge-shaped, colorless, and shiny as marbles. The upper eyelid hung loosely over the lashes. She had heavy horizontal marks all across her forehead like a musical stave. Her nose was as wide as her lips and flat, barely jutting out farther than her cheekbones. Whether she'd once been beautiful was superfluous. Hers was a face designed for thought and action, not simply to be looked at.

"Is this him?" she asked in Japanese, her voice as sharp as an arctic wind.

"August Small," he returned before any of the gunmen could respond, then added in her own language, "And who could you be but Countess London?"

At last her eyes focused on him, yet no muscle in her body moved. Her face was as a mask that nonetheless blinked and breathed.

She sat back and folded her hands in her lap. "I assume you haven't come alone."

"I'm a lone wolf," he lied.

She didn't respond. She didn't have to because at that very moment shots broke the silence—rifle fire.

The woman looked between two of the gunmen. Without a moment's hesitation, they lowered their guns and left the room. Another three shots rang out in succession. It still sounded like the rifle, not return fire.

Get out Katya, he thought. Get out now.

Augy forced himself not to show concern, returning the interminable gaze of the Countess.

"You will provide the names and contact information of every individual whom you have involved in this ludicrous crusade," she said, her voice as monotone as her face was cold.

"Now why the hell would I do that?"

"Because if you do, I may consider giving you a quicker and less painful death."

Augy reached into his jacket pocket for a cigarette. The remaining gunman tightened his grip on the AK47 and took a step closer. "Hands up."

"Easy, sport." Augy lit the smoke then set the pack and lighter on a nearby table. "That's no toy you're playing with."

"If you refuse to cooperate," the Countess continued, "you will be tortured."

"That's more like it." He stepped closer to take a seat across from her. The gunman lifted his weapon, but she raised a hand to hold him.

Augy plunked down on the sofa.

She leaned back, wrinkling her nose and regarding him like something she found on the bottom of her shoe. "Are you going to cooperate?"

"Given your reputation, I can't help thinking that no matter what I do my death is not going to be quick or painless. So why don't you cut the shit?"

Putting on a pair of frameless reading glasses with circular lenses, she grabbed a file folder off the table. "Captain Augustinius Erasmus Small," she read, "419th Night Fighter Squadron, 8th Fighter Command, 13th Air Force. Self-employed as a private investigator. California license number 547683. Previous employer, Delta Airlines. High school dropout. Most recent address: 890 Hearst Boulevard, Magnolia Park, Burbank California. Son of Richard and Wendy Small. One sister, Mary Wollstonecraft Stern, wife of Harry Stern, mother of two children, Murphy and Carol, ages six and one."

She pulled off the glasses and looked up at him. "Do we understand one another, Mr. Small?"

CHAPTER TWENTY-FIVE

Augy fought to keep control, but he was starting to sweat. In turn, every muscle tensed. His pounding heart sent blood cascading through his veins like Niagara Falls, and his brain was in the barrel swelling with memories.

Shadows at twilight. A bright spotlight overhead. The sound of rubber gloves snapping. Water trickling across the floor, washing the blood into the sewers of Tokyo. He saw the doctor, the white surgical cap on his head like a fez. Eyes cold and gray, deeply set in his bloated face. The rest was hidden behind a medical mask. Behind his shoulder, the twinkle of steel as the nurse lifted the scalpel.

A scream was in Augy's throat, but he forced himself to swallow it. Dread weighed anchor, threatening to sink him deeper into unreality. Away from light and oxygen.

"They don't know nothing," he said.

The Countess folded her lips smugly. "Then so long as you cooperate, they have nothing to fear."

"What do you want me to do?"

"First, tell me who else you've been working with."

"I haven't told anybody anything, except for people who already knew."

"Tsubasa," she said to the gunman, "radio the unit outside Mrs. Stern's house and tell them to go ahead."

"Wait!"

Snarling, she turned on Augy. "I am not going to waste my time asking the same question twice."

Gunfire rang out somewhere in the house, this time from a machine gun. It was answered by rifle fire, and back and forth. And then only machine gun, followed by silence. Both Augy and the last remaining gunman were on edge, looking towards the door, their bodies tense. But Countless London was unflappable.

"It seems they've found your wolfpack," she said, standing with the subdued groan of an old woman. "Katya Tyler, I presume."

Augy nodded. There was no point lying about that.

"That's what that fool Tyler gets for marrying a log," she said to herself. "You expect me to believe you and she are in this alone?"

"We are."

"And what about that doctor? What's her name?"

Augy snarled. "All she knows is there's a lone psycho who cuts apart little children for kicks."

Her eyes narrowed. "Kicks?"

"What do you call it?"

"Science, Mr. Small."

"Science?"

"I wish you could appreciate how many lives my work will go on to save."

"How is letting a bunch of ghouls rape and torture little children going to save lives?"

"It won't," she conceded. "The caprice of some of my associates is a regrettable necessity, which I've no option but to indulge. Males will always insist on their comfort women. But they are not a part of my true work."

"And what exactly do you learn from branding your test subjects?"

She shrugged. "We can hardly be expected to remember their faces. If one escapes they can be found easily."

"Horseshit."

"Excuse me?"

"As if your men are gonna canvas the general population ripping people's shirts off to see who has your fucking mark?" He flicked his cigarette across the room. It bounced off the wallpaper onto the carpet. "Branding your victims is a liability and you know it. You do it for the same reason people like you do everything."

"And why is that?"

"It makes you feel like god."

A twitch in her lips betrayed irritation. "I would hardly expect a high school dropout to be able to understand, let alone appreciate, my work."

"It doesn't make it true. You can cover them with your brand, but you don't own any of those people."

"I could cut it off, and it wouldn't make them any freer." She gazed into his eyes, unblinking. As hot and unrelenting as a midday sun scorching his corneas. He looked away.

"It seems to me you're quite stalwart," she said, "particularly for an American. I should like to test your resolve."

"Fuck does that mean?"

She loomed closer, the barest hint of a smile at the corners of her lips. "You will go freely into the operating theater and lay yourself on my table. And if you cry out or shrink from my blade even once, I will have your sister's entire family brought to the Lumbermill and I will dissect them, one by one, starting with the baby."

"Why? What the fuck is the point?"

"The human body is a complex machine, that unfortunately begins to shut down the moment you open it up to look at its moving gears. Many are needed."

"Japan surrendered. You do realize that?"

"Japan is inconsequential, and hardly the only country willing to finance research into my area of expertise."

"Are you trying to tell me you're working with the authorization of the American government?"

She simpered. "You'd be surprised the lengths to which certain individuals went to make sure my operation took place in this country, and not in say, the Soviet Union."

"I don't believe you."

Sighing, she shook her head. "Patriotism is willful blindness, Mr. Small. I should know."

She put on her coat—plain, shapeless, gray. Everything about her was aggressively simple: her practical hairstyle, her flat work shoes. She wore no jewelry, no makeup, had no distinguishing features. Physically, she was so much a part of the crowd that she blended into the walls if no crowd was available. Yet, for her cultivated averageness, Augy could not tear his eyes from her. He couldn't put his finger on why, other than her face didn't move quite the way human faces do. Like a doll come to life.

"We'll perform your operation in the morning," she said, gathering up her files. "I wouldn't want to leave you waiting in the dark too long. I understand you had enough of that in Hokkaido."

With that, Countess London left, and the man with the big gun ordered Augy to stand. His body obeyed without his mind even being consulted.

"What about Katya?" he asked.

"She's too dangerous to be left alive any longer," the man replied with a shrug.

At first, Augy was upset, but after some thought, he supposed he should like to be shot, too. At that moment, imagining Katya filled with bullet holes made him smile. At least there was some peace there. And no more pain.

He didn't think himself equal to the challenge the so-called Countess had laid before him. In fact, it had entirely failed to sink in.

"What's her real name?" Augy asked.

The gunman shrugged again. He had a big mustache and wide eyes, a disturbingly friendly face. "She doesn't usually take the time to talk to her patients. Or anyone. You should be honored."

"Yeah, I feel honored."

Augy was guided into the hall. For the first time, he noticed the building he was standing in. Tiny triangles all over the carpet. Thick teal drapes. Robins nesting in the wallpaper. Not at all like the prison he'd imagined, but full of color. He looked back at the bedroom door where Katya was forced to share a bed with her so-called husband. There was a bolt on the exterior.

An engine whinnied to life outside, presumably the Countess leaving. It wasn't the hunk of junk they'd come in. Augy trudged down the stairs like he was being led to the guillotine. When he blinked, he saw an operating theater tattooed inside his eyelids. If he made the gunman shoot him, would things still end the same for Mary? Even if Augy somehow managed to lay still and keep himself from screaming while the mad doctor ripped out his insides, would she spare his sister and her family?

Beyond the window, he heard the gentle whoosh of Francis Tyler's private waterfall and felt spiders crawl up his back.

The giggle of the stream as he wandered deeper into the woods, the stars winking in the heavens. Their blue light pouring over the dead bodies of dozens of young girls, freezing them in time and space.

He'd failed to help any of them. He would die knowing there would be dozens more like them. And he'd failed to help them too.

Worst of all, they were going to find Sumika.

His vision blurred. He reached out to steady himself on the railing. The gunman was quick at his back, shoving him. Augy gagged, doubled over, and dry-heaved. If he'd had any food in him it would've come out; instead, yellow bile dripped down his chin. The gunman shoved him, shouting incomprehensibly, but Augy's feet were cemented in place, his bones rusted. A fever was coming on: filling his head with fog, lacerating his muscles, twisting his insides.

Once more the gunman jabbed the barrel of the AK47 hard against his ribs. Pain shot through him like lightning, splitting his nerves and igniting a fire. Reflexively, he whipped around and knocked the gun far aside. A quick burst of rounds cut into the wall. He grabbed the barrel—hot as a frying pan— then kicked the man in the groin. With one hard twist, the gun was his. The man moved to strike, but Augy smashed him across the temple with the butt of the gun. The man reeled back, lost his balance. With one final kick, Augy sent him tumbling down the stairs. When he hit the bottom a loud crack sounded like two four-by-fours being smacked together.

His neck had snapped like deadwood.

Augy stood frozen until the sharp pain in his foot snapped him back to reality.

"Motherfucker!" Grabbing his toes, he sank onto the steps. He must've been out of it to kick a guy with his broken foot.

You're going to lose the confounded thing!

He sucked breaths through his teeth, waiting for the pain to subside. It didn't. Instead, the burn on his palm flared from where he'd grabbed the barrel of the gun.

He wiped some spittle off his chin with his wrist, then pulled himself to his feet. He limped down the stairs, over the pointless bag of flesh that had once been called Tsubasa.

Augy grabbed the receiver off the ornate, gold-plated rotary phone and dialed in a number. After about twenty rings, Harry answered, "Who the hell is this?"

"Harry, let me talk to Mary."

"August?" he hissed. "Didn't I tell you not to bother my wife anymore? It's two o'clock in the goddamn morning!"

"It's an emergency."

"It's always an emergency with you…"

He heard Mary on the other end, groggy and quiet. "Is that my brother?"

"Go back to bed," snapped Harry.

"Let me talk to him," she said.

"No. I'm not putting up with this horse hockey a minute longer." Harry came back on the line, "Now you listen to me, you good for nothing parasite…"

"Harry, you're in danger. You need to take your family and get out of there."

He scoffed. "Excuse me?"

"Just drive. Drive and don't stop. You can't go to the police. You have to trust me."

"Are you drunk?"

"I know it sounds crazy, but you have to listen to me. Get out of there. Now."

A snort of a laugh. "I'm not going anywhere."

"Let me see the phone, Harry," Mary said in background.

"Mary!" Augy shouted. "It's Countess London! She knows you're my sister! You have to…"

The call disconnected. Augy tried the number again, but only got a busy signal. He snatched up the heavy phone and threw it across the room. It crashed into a corner bar and sent shards of glass tinkling across the floor like crystal.

Something creaked in the hallway. A shimmer in the darkness. Augy lifted the gun and gave a three-bullet burst. The body dropped.

Outside, he heard a muffled crash like a bottle breaking, and then silence.

Augy stepped towards the body and kicked the gun away. In the movies, a torso shot is instantly fatal, but in real life, those kinds of wounds usually leave a person bleeding in agony for hours. And a dying man with a gun can be as dangerous as a healthy one. However, Augy soon realized his caution was unnecessary, as the top of the man's head had been blown clean off.

He let out a stale breath, thanking God it hadn't been Katya.

He had to find her.

As he slung the second AK over his shoulder, he picked out the scent of black smoke. Paint and wood. He looked out the window and was greeted by the inconstant warmth of a new fire, steadily growing. A tiny figure rushed away from the flames, dressed in a baggy sweater, her short flat hair shining navy blue in the pale moonlight.

"Sumika?" he wondered aloud.

The fire swelled. Soon, the whole front of the house was engulfed. Hot and dry June winds were like cheerleaders for the flames. In about ten minutes, he figured the whole building would be overwhelmed.

Augy moved vaguely towards where he thought he'd heard the rifle fire: down a long hallway, past what seemed like a thousand doors, through a kitchen with lavish blue and gold cabinets and a brick floor laid in an impractical swirl. By the fireplace were three rocking chairs: one big, one little, and one in between. Even in his daze, he couldn't help imagining Katya, Clemmie, and Zychik sitting there together, passing long evenings popping corn and listening to the big radio in the corner.

How had someone like Katya let herself be a captive of someone like Tyler for so long? And what had made her run away when she did? Once again, there was something important she was leaving out.

Augy shook his head, trying to gain focus. Why did he keep getting distracted? He was in a burning building, and guys with assault rifles were all over hell and half of Georgia, and here he was with the attention span of a circus monkey. Worse than that, he felt so tired. Part of him just wanted to lie down and rest his eyes for a bit. Since the last time he'd slept, he'd had a massive row with his ex-wife, escaped from the police in a high-speed chase, been threatened with vivisection, and killed two men. His foot was throbbing. His ribs were so sore; every breath hurt. And a headache to end headaches was coming on. Would it be so terrible if he lay down on the ground and closed his eyes? Would he even feel the fire as it ate him alive?

Just keep working, he thought. No matter how much it hurts. If you stop working, you'll never get out of this.

The thought forced him to drag one foot in front of the other. His eyes scanned the house, his voice called out for Katya, and the crackle of fire grew to a crescendo.

The heat was bearing down on him now. Oppressive, sweltering heat. The kind of heat that sucks the oxygen right out of your blood. The ceiling gave way, raining down fire like something out of the bible. Augy jumped back, but he didn't see four-by-fours and plaster burning in front of him, blocking his path. He saw an Australian called RV Sullivan, screaming as the flames consumed his clothes and his hair, and eventually every bit of him.

RV had a broken leg. A beam he'd set up had collapsed, and a ton of rock had fallen on top of him. His mistake had set the job back several days, and the Japs were determined he suffer for it. The next morning, RV was sent down the mine to light the lamps before work began. He had to climb with his broken leg down a ladder three stories long, carrying an open barrel of kerosene on his back. Of course, he slipped. Of course, he fell. Of course, the kerosene doused him. And then, of course, one of the guards lit a match and threw it down.

Never before or since had Augy heard a man scream the way RV did. And he went on screaming a lot longer than anybody would've expected. Augy had thrown up that day and doubled over with convulsions until one of the guards punched him in the gut.

He fell to his knees now in front of the flames, dry heaving again. More acidic bile came up.

But here he was. He opened his eyes and saw blackened wood, embers twinkling along the length. And then all he could see was Lily Wong winking at the crowd with chopsticks in her hair. Letting her hair down over naked shoulders. He tasted the salt of her skin.

Gold tinged blackness. Her face unrecognizable. Her eyes burnt out.

He imagined her screaming, the way RV had screamed. He wanted to reach out and touch the fire, let it fill him up as if sharing in their pain would make it any easier.

As if death would make it easier.

"Just keep working, no matter how much it hurts," Augy whispered, forcing himself to his feet. "If you stop working, they win."

CHAPTER TWENTY-SIX

It took fire catching his shirt to shock him back to his senses. He ripped it off and left it burning on the carpet, then sprang into action. He found Katya trapped under a fallen beam. Good-looking Charlie lay dead a few yards away. Her arm was bleeding. Augy braced the burning beam on his naked back, singeing his skin, and lifted it enough for her to slip out. Thirty seconds later, they were both out of the house, and back in the car with Sumika. Augy took to the wheel like a bat out of hell.

They hadn't talked much since then. The mission had been a total snafu. Katya said Frank Tyler got away. Good-looking Charlie had put a slug in her upper arm before she finished him off. The high-velocity round had missed her bone—thank god for those built biceps. The entry wound was no bigger than a pencil eraser, but the exit wound was like a silver dollar. She barely hissed when he cleaned and wrapped the cyclone-shaped gash in the bathroom of a twenty-four-hour Circle K. She would need stitches and a round of antibiotics, but they couldn't risk going to see Doc Larkin and the kids. Not now.

Augy was singed and black with soot, but otherwise unharmed. He wore his blazer over a bare chest, his massive T-shaped scar visible for all to see. But Sumika had already seen it, and Katya didn't say anything.

He'd never felt himself in such kindred company.

They arrived in Cohen Dale a little before three in the morning. They parked a block from Mary's house in the lot of a small Presbyterian church. An illuminated sign out front read in big friendly letters: *'Praise Him with timbral and dancing; Praise Him with stringed instruments and pipe.' Or just join us for Social Nights every Friday@9 and kill two birds with one stone!*

Sumika stayed behind the wheel, the pistol at her side. She didn't have the upper body strength to steer at low speeds, but there was a straightaway leading from the drive, which would let her get up to fifty before she needed to turn. She was sure she could do it, and after what she'd done at Tyler's— that is, using a garden hose to siphon gasoline out of the tank into an empty beer bottle, stuffing it with an old handkerchief she found in the glove compartment, then lighting and hurling her Molotov cocktail from hell through the front window—Augy and Katya were prepared to trust the little girl with a bit more responsibility.

Augy brought the AK47 he'd taken off the guard, but no matter how "fine" Katya insisted she was, she couldn't hold one properly with her wounded arm. And god forbid she had to fire—the kickback would be agony. He finally convinced her to bring the pistol instead. They left the shotgun and carbine in the trunk.

They sneaked along the bushes towards the house. Light shined through the sheer curtains of the kitchen window, and he made out the barest outline of a hand holding a coffee cup.

Katya clicked her tongue, then pointed with her eyes at a dark car parked across the street a few houses down. It didn't seem like anything until he noticed the cherry of a cigarette hanging out of the window.

They circled the block to come out the other end of the street behind the car—a powder-blue Chrysler. They approached, moving through the front lawns of the houses to stay out of the streetlamps. Two men sat in the car. The one in the passenger seat was slumped and had his hat over his eyes; the other flicked his cigarette out of the window. Katya pulled a combat knife from her jacket pocket and handed it to Augy. Then she crouched down behind a blue wisteria tree and fixed her aim, holding the pistol in her good hand and using her knee to steady it.

Augy pulled the knife from its sheath—a six-inch blade, serrated near the hilt, which was wrapped in black leather. He wrinkled his nose at it.

Crouching down low enough to set the tips of his fingers on the asphalt, he shuffled to the car. With crablike steps, he snuck around to the driver's side of the vehicle. He hesitated, breathing deeply.

A voice overcame the faint drone of a police radio inside the cab, "Duke Twelve, do you copy?"

The driver coughed. "Go ahead."

"Ten-eighteen, ten-nineteen. Proceed."

"Is Adam Henry ten-fifteen?"

"Negative, Duke Twelve," said the radio. "Adam and Alice Henry four-five-one at Frank Tom ten-ten."

"Copy, Duke Six. Go ahead."

"One-eight-seven all parties at your location. Over and out."

One-eight-seven, thought Augy. *Murder all parties.*

He waited till he heard the man put down the radio, then without so much as a deep breath to gather his courage, he popped up, snatched the driver by the hair, and slit his throat.

The geyser of blood that spewed out of him was like opening a hydrant. He thrashed and gurgled, arms flailing. Augy jumped back, but the blood splattered off of the dashboard, soaking the arms and the lapels of his jacket.

The other cop started awake and fumbled with the Tommy Gun in his lap. But it was coated in blood and slipped from his hands. Augy opened the driver's side door and lunged at him with the knife. The man blocked, and Augy's knife cut clean through his palm. The man cried out. He grabbed Augy's wrist, trying to twist him to the side. Augy braced his foot against the driver's seat and yanked his knife free, then swung again. The man ducked hard to one side. His machine gun clattered against the dash, the bullets in the massive drum cartridge tinkling like BBs. The cop fumbled with the handle, trying to escape the car. That was his last mistake. Augy brought the knife down into his back three times in succession. The man choked and slumped back in his seat. Augy grabbed the radio and cut the cord. Then he took the keys out of the ignition and threw them into the bushes.

He'd never knifed a man before. He'd shot more than his fair share, but something about using a knife made him feel crooked. He stepped back and closed the door.

The blood on his face felt so warm it almost burned. He shook his drenched hands, speckling the sidewalk.

Katya trotted closer. "You hurt?"

He shook his head, sneering at his hands. "I'm disgusted."

"Come on."

He took off his jacket and used it to wipe the blood off his face and hands, then threw the thing into the car.

They hurried through the back gate, chain-link clanking in the dark, and up to the back door, which was still, unbelievably—infuriatingly—unlocked. He stepped inside.

His sister was seated at the kitchen table in a bulky yellow robe, her hair in a net, eyes wreathed with teary exhaustion. When she saw him, she rushed to throw her arms around his neck. He clasped her to his chest, even lifted her off the ground a little. He'd never come so close to losing her. Now, he understood why she was so mad at him all the time.

"You stupid bastard!" She smacked his chest then took a step back. "What in god's name are you thinking?"

"You have to get out of here," he said.

"What the hell is going on?" Her gaze swept over him as if for the first time and horror filled her eyes. "Is that blood?"

He could only imagine how he looked—shirtless, AK slung over one shoulder, combat knife sticking out his belt, and tinted pink with another man's blood.

Augy bit his bottom lip and gagged at how salty it tasted. "Where's Harry?"

"He went back to bed."

"Get him up. Get the kids up. You need to pack."

"Where are we going?"

"It doesn't matter. Just keep moving. Don't give anybody your real names. And don't stop."

"For how long?" Mary's voice faltered. "I mean, we can't do that forever. What is going on?"

"When it's safe for you to come back, I'll call Mom and tell her I miss you, and I wish you'd come home."

"Augy, you're scaring me."

"You should be scared."

"But what if Harry won't come? He's real sore, and—"

"You have to make him."

"Make him? You know Harry. I can't—"

Augy grabbed her shoulders and squared her to him. "There have been two men stationed outside your house for at least the last few days waiting for the go-ahead to come in here and kill your entire family. Now, those two are dead, but there will be more. Do you understand? You cannot stay here."

She stared into his eyes for a long time before she finally nodded. Augy hugged her again and kissed her hair.

"Come with us," she begged, glaring at Katya. "This isn't your fight."

"It is," he said. "It always has been."

There wasn't anything more to say. Lingering, or worse, explaining, would only make things harder. Augy decided not to give Mary the opportunity to change his mind, and he and Katya left as quickly as they'd come.

The night wasn't over. After what the Countess had threatened to do, Augy couldn't leave things as they were. He had to show her he wasn't about to be intimidated, and no amount of threats were going to change his course. He had to send her a message. He didn't know where to find her, and he wasn't about to undertake the suicide mission that was the Lumbermill. Not yet. He had to settle for the next best thing: the doctor who left those scars on Katya's temples.

Augy took the wheel and guided them back to the highway, back to Bel Air, back to two ceramic lions on either side of a long redbrick driveway.

Sumika stayed in the car. He and Katya walked in silence down the drive, then ducked into a grove of fruit trees, before at last coming upon a ten-foot-high stone wall that separated one property from the next. Augy put out his hands like a stirrup and helped Katya climb to the top of the wall. He then took a running leap and caught the top. She grabbed his arms and helped pull him over, then they both landed on their feet on the other side. Augy groaned at the shock to his ribs, and Katya stumbled.

"Next time," she said, "I want boots."

The back garden was plotted in zigzags. Manicured beds of red and yellow roses grew alongside a pathway of chalk-white flagstones. At the center was a bulky concrete fountain with a rotating sphere of marble at its center. It glimmered in the soft yellow light put off by electric lanterns that ran the length of the path up to the house.

They kept to the grass, past the circular swimming pool and adjacent jacuzzi, up the steps that crisscrossed to the back door. The house itself would've been satisfactory to any multi-millionaire—three stories of white stucco, French windows, and grand balconies, with a Spanish-style tiled roof. They paused outside the ground level French window, and Katya looked back at him.

"What is today?" she asked.

"It's June, I think."

"I mean, is Tuesday, or...?"

He chewed on his lip. "I don't know. Why?"

"If is weekend, there will have been party, maybe. I mean, there may be someone there who does not want to be." She lifted her eyebrows as if to ask if he knew what she meant. He nodded.

"We will go to big bedroom first." She gestured with her chin for him to follow and eased open the unlocked glass door. They stepped into a massive, sparsely decorated living room with low angular furniture, gray in the darkness. He kept his eyes on Katya, on her swollen feet and ankles as she crept from one room to the next, and up an open staircase.

A familiar scent filled his nostrils the second they reached the third floor: vigorous sex, and lots of it. A waft of sweat, semen, and vaginal fluids so thick it clung to the windows in droplets. But there was a fouler tinge to it: urine and feces. The heat of the stench clung to his cold skin like condensation, seeping into him. His mouth filled with water, his stomach begging to come up. He wrinkled his nose against it and kept going.

They advanced to a set of double doors, which were hanging wide open. Augy came up beside Katya. She met his eyes and sighed inaudibly. They both brought up their guns and stepped inside.

Sheets covered the floor smeared with human waste. A naked woman huddled in a cage in one corner, her hair matted with the stuff. She watched them come in but didn't move or attempt to speak. An empty bed stood at the center, its rubber sheets coated in filth.

Augy approached the cage, and the woman scurried back. She was eighteen or so, East Asian, with skin so pale it glowed in the dim light. How long had it been since she'd gone outside? Since she'd seen anything but inside of a cage?

He touched the large lock on the side, noting the size and shape of the keyhole.

Katya clicked at him as if he were a horse, motioning with her eyes back towards the door. With a final glance at the woman in the cage, he followed Katya back down the stairs.

They passed through the big room again, down another corridor. Creeping closer, he heard a man snoring. They came to a door, and Katya pressed her body against the adjacent wall, while Augy eased it open. It squeaked so loudly, he couldn't believe the people inside didn't stir. Or maybe it just sounded loud in the absolute quiet.

A man in his mid-forties with a great bulbous belly was sleeping on his back, his jaw slack, making noises like he was drowning in oatmeal. He had a bushy walrus mustache with wild eyebrows to match. A woman coiled at the edge of the bed, her hair in curlers. She had a mask over her eyes, plugs in her ears, and a bottle of pills on her nightstand. He squinted in the dim light and made out the name of her prescription: glutethimide, a barbiturate. A doctor had once given him the same drug to help with his sleepwalking.

She wouldn't be waking up any time soon.

Augy and Katya walked to opposite sides of the bed and pointed their guns at the man and the woman, respectively. Their eyes met. She nodded, and he flicked on the lamp on the bedside table.

The woman didn't move at all. The man grumbled, choked, and awakened. He started to sit up and smacked his head against the barrel of Augy's gun before he realized what was happening.

"Good morning, Dr. Walker," said Augy, smiling pleasantly. "Please, don't get up."

"What's going on?" Walker stammered in a gruff rasp. "Who are you? How did you get in here?"

"My name's August Small. I believe you know my associate." Walker's eyes drifted across the bed to Katya, and only then did his expression grow to match the situation he was in. "I need to ask you for a couple of favors," Augy continued. "Do you understand?"

"You can't be here..." he said, still staring at Katya.

Katya smiled, said something in Russian, and spat on his face.

"Bitch! I'll have you—"

"Easy now." Augy pushed him hard in the chest with his gun, knocking him against the headboard. "Do you have any antibiotics in the house?"

"What?"

"Oh, I'm sorry." Augy cleared his throat, then repeated in a much louder voice, "Do you have any antibiotics in the house?"

"There's some in the medicine cabinet in the kitchen, but why in god's name—"

"Good. Now, I need you to give me the key to that cage upstairs. You know the one."

The man's eyes darted to his nightstand, then he stiffened his lower lip. Augy followed the gaze. He opened the drawer and pulled out a ring of keys and stashed them in his pants pocket. Straightening, he noticed a little white card on the nightstand behind a sheet of transparent tissue paper. He picked it up and read:

Please join Dr. and Mrs. Marvin Hoffman at their home on June 22nd for the Eighth Annual Barbarossa Masquerade Ball. Cocktails and Light Fare will be served, with Hepatic Delicacies for the gentlemen. White tie attire.

P. S. Only the best and brightest get in. How was copper wire invented?

"How was copper wire invented?" Augy mumbled. He stashed the card in his pocket, then looked back at Walker. "Is that supposed to be some kind of riddle?"

The skin under one eye twitched. "I won't tell you anything."

After examining his face for a moment, Augy sighed and nodded. "I believe you."

He pointed his gun at Walker's forehead and pulled the trigger, sending a three-bullet burst into his bloated walrus face. The bullets made clean holes, but the back of the skull exploded, showering the wall with brains, bone, and blood. Simultaneously, Katya fired into his wife's head.

She never did wake up.

They stepped out of the bedroom, and Katya laid her palm on Augy's arm. When he looked up, she was already staring at his eyes.

"*Bol'shoye spasibo*," she said.

Augy slung his gun over one shoulder. "What's that mean?"

"Thank you."

"Never mind that, gorgeous. How do you say *I'm sorry. I'm a jackass. I should've listened to you all along?*"

"*Ya obozhayu tebya.*"

"*Ya obozhayu tebya*," he said, sounding it out and knowing he was fucking it up.

She grabbed his chin and pecked his lips. "Go get the girl. I meet you at car."

A goofy smile infiltrated his face, but it faded quickly. "Are you sure there aren't any others? I mean, there's a fuckload of keys here."

She shrugged. "I do a quick sweep. Make you happy."

"*Bol'shoye spasibo*," he said with a wink, then hurried upstairs.

When he got back to the room, he tried to hold his breath and hurried to unlock the cage. He threw the gate open, but the woman didn't move.

"It's all right," he said, taking a few steps back, and slouching to look less intimidating. "I'm not gonna hurt you."

She made no move. He repeated himself in Japanese, but that made no difference. He wasn't sure if she didn't understand or if she were frozen in shock.

A double horn blast cut the silence. The signal Sumika was meant to give if she saw any trouble approaching.

His eyes darted from the woman to the door. "I can't account for what might happen if you stay," he said and offered his hand. "Please."

She said something—a high-pitched, frantic, and accusatory voice. He recognized Cantonese, but he didn't speak a word. Not one word.

Two more beeps split the night. He couldn't linger, but neither could he leave. If he threatened her with the gun, she'd probably move. But he wanted her to come on her own.

The only option he saw was reckless, on the verge of senseless. But it was the *only* option.

He unslung the AK47 from his shoulder and set it on the ground in front of the cage.

"Go ahead," he said, taking a step back. "It's yours."

CHAPTER TWENTY-SEVEN

For what seemed like forever she didn't move. Her eyes darted between his face and the gun.

"Augy! We need to go now!" called Katya. It sounded as if she were already outside. In his periphery, he recognized blue and red lights through the window, but they were far off.

The woman dashed forward and snatched up the gun. She pointed it at him, her finger on the trigger, and began to speak. Her voice was choked with tears, savagery in her eyes, face reddened with fury, but all he could see was that finger on the trigger.

Anybody who knows anything about guns knows you keep your finger outside the trigger guard unless you're pointing at something you don't mind shooting. You do this basically because shit happens, and when shit happens with guns, people die.

Then again, she was pointing at something she didn't mind shooting.

He put up his hands and slouched even more. "I hope you can understand me. We can't stay here. If they find you here, you'll end up right back where you started. Come with me. Please."

Her posture softened and her face slumped. The gun went slack in her grip. Her chest heaved with every breath. She downcast her gaze and said something more, her voice low, raspy, and calm. Then she lifted the gun and pointed it at her chin.

"No, no, no, no!" He lunged forward as she pulled the trigger. In an instant, her face split and tore away. A geyser of blood and bone hit the ceiling. She fell limp, smacking against the cage before landing on the ground with a thump.

A scream ripped from his chest. Blood turned to froth, and his vision went red. He punched the wall as hard as he could, breaking bone and plaster. He felt no pain.

A faint gurgle came from the floor. Frozen, he clenched his eyes shut, willing the noise to go away. It came again, and weak thrashing.

His gaze dropped to the destroyed woman. She had no face, nothing but a great bloody mask of nerves and bones. But her arms and legs flailed weakly.

The first tear came, and then he began to cry hysterically. Clenching his teeth, and holding back hyperventilation with the sheer force of will, he reached down and yanked the gun from her hands. How could there still be strength in them?

He put the barrel against her head, but he was crying so hard his hands were shaking. His fingers felt rigid, throbbing. He steadied the gun with both hands and looked away, clenching his eyes closed so hard they ached. A hand grabbed his ankle. He shook it off, but the gun's barrel slipped on the blood. He aimed again, turned his back, and pulled the trigger. Hot blood sprayed his pant leg. Finally, the noise stopped.

He dropped the gun in the puddle of blood and ran out of the room. Down the stairs and through a hall. He had no idea where he was going. Blood stung and burned in his eyes, fire at his back. He had to get out before he suffocated. Everything was red. Had Sumika lit the building on fire again? Smoke was closing in around him. Black smoke and white skin. Such white skin.

He tripped and landed on his hands and knees, and then the tears overcame him. He punched the carpet over and over.

"Harden up," he said, but the voice was like a stranger. "Pull it together."

Guys in the service talked about going numb. How once a person experienced enough horror and dread, their heart shut down, and they didn't feel anything anymore. He'd been waiting for that switch to flip for years now. How much more could this heart take?

All he wanted was to help, but every time he tried, innocent people died. In that moment, he knew he was worse than weak, worse than useless: he was poison.

Somehow, he managed to look up and saw night sky pouring in through the window, roses swaying in a light breeze. The moon shined down pitilessly, brighter than before, on such white skin.

He stood and walked outside. Only after he'd closed the door behind him did he manage a deep inhalation. Crisp desert air. Familiar. He tried to get a cigarette out of his pocket, but he fumbled the pack. He lifted his hands to his eyes. He'd bled through the bandages and was trembling something awful.

Closing his eyes, he forced his lungs to keep working. Then drawing on his last reserves, he bent, picked up the pack of cigarettes, drew one out, and put it between his lips. It took six attempts to light the damn thing. The matches kept shaking out of his hands. In the end, he pushed his left hand hard against the window with the weight of his shoulder, striker in grasp, and lit the match.

After taking a few drags, he followed the center path towards the big stone wall. He didn't have a prayer of scaling it right now, but there was a tiny wrought iron door recessed in the stone, overgrown with periwinkles. He took Walker's keyring from his pocket and struggled to place the key in the lock. His fingers were so numb, so shaky. Even after he had it in the lock, he had to use both hands to turn it. He kicked the door open. It clanked loudly, ripping the periwinkle. He slipped through. He didn't bother to close it behind him, and he left Walker's keys in the lock.

He stumbled through the trees. When his cigarette cherry singed the filter, he lit another off of the butt. He was on his third by the time he reached the road.

The red and blue lights struck his eyes. He'd forgotten about them. Sumika was sitting on the curb in handcuffs as a uniform searched the trunk of the car. Something clicked and Augy's eyes focused. Katya was crouched behind a tall green hedge, her gun leveled at the cop's back. Augy stood right in her sights. She motioned for him to get out of the way, to hide himself before the cop saw him, but he shook his head.

"Is there a problem, officer?" he asked, staggering closer.

"I should say so," the man began, turning. A cowboy mustache twitched, then an age-spotted hand pushed back a black Stetson. "Small?"

"Yeltz? What are you doing here?"

White bushy eyebrows drew together. "What in hell happened to you?"

Augy looked down at himself. He'd forgotten he wasn't wearing a shirt, that there were spatters of blood on his chest and arms, that his pants were soaked in gore, that he was held together with stitches, and that the bandages on his hands were dripping blood. Bringing his cigarette to his lips for another drag, he also remembered how severely he was shaking.

"I'm fine." Augy rubbed the back of his neck. "What's going on here?"

"You look like you crossed no man's land, son. Who's blood is that?"

"Why don't you mind your own business?"

"I beg your pardon?" Yeltz approached.

Augy started back, nearly tripping over his own feet. "Have they given you a new partner yet? I hear Moretti got canned."

"How's about you come on down to the station with me, huh?" said Yeltz, holding his hands up as he took one ginger step closer. "We'll get this all sorted out."

"Hold your fire," he said to the bush, then glanced at Sumika. "Why'd you put that little girl in cuffs?"

"This unlicensed, underaged Jap was loitering in a lights-out neighborhood in the middle of the night in an unregistered vehicle which has two military-grade assault weapons in the trunk."

"She's not a Jap. She's my friend." Augy looked past Yeltz into the cab of his cruiser. It was empty. "I guess they haven't given you a new partner. Transferred you to traffic control, huh?" Augy coughed out a mirthless laugh. "Motherfuckers."

"Small, what you been doing in that there house?"

"Didn't I tell you to mind your own business?" he snapped, then rolled his shoulders and smoked his cigarette for a bit. "I mean, questions like that can get a guy killed."

"Okay." Yeltz narrowed his eyes. "Forget I said anything."

"Don't you recognize that little girl there?"

Yeltz looked back at Sumika. "Can't say as I do."

"She's the one from the sinkhole. The one you and Moretti couldn't find."

"I never saw her. Never went by the site neither."

"You what?"

He lifted his shoulders. "None of us went down there. Top brass assigned a special team."

"Of course, they did." Augy took a step closer, but Yeltz shrank back. Augy recognized the expression on his face more easily than he would his own name. He was scared.

"Listen to me, Yeltz." Augy lit another cigarette off the butt of the last. "The department is filthy. So's the whole damn city. Do you understand what I'm saying?"

"Nah. I mean, yeah. Of course, I do. But how would you know?"

"What have you radioed back to dispatch?"

"Nothing." Yeltz took a step back. "Just an eleven-ninety-six."

"You're gonna forget you saw me. And her. And you're gonna say you made a mistake when you stopped this car."

"I'm afraid I can't do that. You're covered in blood and you need to come down to the station."

"I'm not going nowhere."

"Don't make this hard." Yeltz's hand moved towards his gun.

"Put up your hands," said Katya, emerging from her hiding spot, pistol tight on Yeltz's forehead. "Augy, give me my knife."

"Don't hurt him," said Augy. "He's one of the good ones."

Katya nodded. "Get in the car."

He felt like he ought to argue, but part of him was grateful to have some orders to follow. After relinquishing the knife, Augy slouched to the car, opened the door to the backseat, and crawled inside. He cranked open the window and lit another cigarette, then leaned back in the bench seat and searched for patterns in the fabric on the roof.

A few minutes passed. The voices outside faded. The passenger door opened, and Sumika slipped into the front seat. Augy glanced through the rear windshield and saw Katya ripping the sparkplugs out of Yeltz's engine. The old marshal was in the front seat of his cruiser, his hands tied to the steering wheel with some wire.

Katya fetched a suitcase out of the foliage and threw it in the trunk before settling into the driver's seat, and easing the car down the street.

Nobody said anything for miles. They stopped at some ratty shithole motel not far from the Long Beach pier. Augy had never spent time in the city and didn't know much about it, other than it was where Douglas Aircraft Company had its biggest factory, where they produced the seminal B-17 Flying Fortresses, among others. Augy had been offered a job there after the war but turned it down to start his own detective agency. He hadn't wanted anything to do with planes anymore. Now, he didn't want anything to do with detective agencies either.

After parking in a cracked-up little lot strewn with litter and oil spills, Katya went into the office. Gray paint peeled from weather-beaten boards. The VACANCY sign buzzed, both Cs flickering on and off.

When she came back out, she motioned Augy and Sumika to follow her into a room. All the walls were wood-paneled, the ceiling stained deep yellow by smoke. Two full-size beds were dressed with threadbare orange comforters and a few pancake pillows. Sumika hurried to the window and drew the yellow and orange checkered drapes, as Katya locked, chained, and bolted the door.

Augy made for the bathroom. Three inches of space separated the tub from the toilet, the toilet from the sink. He tossed his cigarette butt in the toilet, stripped off his clothes, and turned the shower to near-scalding. He unwrapped the bandages from both his hands. The joint connecting his pinky to his right hand looked sunken in, absent even. A hard bump had formed on his palm in the same spot, angry red. No doubt he'd dislocated the bone when he punched the wall. He could still move his fingers, but couldn't make a fist. Every beat of his heart brought an excruciating throb to the outer edge of the hand.

He stepped into the shower, unwrapped the thumb-sized bar of glycerin soap, and washed away all the blood—the Countess's goons', Walker's, the woman's, his own. It all washed away, swirls of pink floating down the drain. But he didn't feel cleaner.

When he was done, he put his underwear back on and wrapped his hands in some thin, tattered washcloths. He was amazed to find a bathrobe, though it was made for a much smaller human. Lighting a cigarette, he stepped out.

Sumika had tucked herself into one of the beds, the covers pulled up to her ears, eyes clenched shut. Something told him she wasn't sleeping. Katya sat in a wooden chair near the window, winding more gauze around the wound on her upper arm. Blood had soaked through. It would leave a nasty scar, but so long as it didn't get infected, she'd be all right.

"Did you find antibiotics?" he asked.

She picked up a little orange pill bottle and shook it. On the table beside her were some extra pillows and blankets, and a bucket of ice. "For your foot," she said.

"Thanks." He poured the ice into a towel, grabbed the extra pillows and blankets, and made himself a nest on the floor.

"Take the bed," said Katya.

"It's yours."

Shrugging, she walked into the bathroom and shut the door. It was after eight am now, the hot sun glowing through the thin curtains. It seemed a million years since he'd slept. He leaned back on the floor and waited, but nothing happened. He cracked a window and lit another cigarette. His hands were still shaking. He was starting to wonder if they'd ever stop.

Sometime later—a long time later, in fact—Katya came out of the bathroom. She wore white undershorts and her button-down blouse, which hung a little past her hips. Her long dark hair was braided over one shoulder. She climbed into the empty bed above where Augy lay on his back. He was so busy counting stains on the popcorn ceiling, it took him a minute to realize she was staring at him.

When he met her eyes, she asked in a whisper, "How did she get the gun?"

"Numskull here gave it to her, didn't he?"

Katya sighed, rolled over in bed, and didn't say anything more.

He kept smoking until he ran out of cigarettes. Every time heavy eyelids began to drift closed he startled himself back awake. Eventually, he couldn't fight it anymore.

He fell into the timeless whirl of dreamless sleep. Perhaps it was minutes only before something rustled beside him. He started, but couldn't force himself to move. Someone was next to him, rearranging his blankets. He blinked in the dim light until he recognized Sumika's slight frame and hunched shoulders, sitting back on her heels, hands folded in her lap.

He closed his eyes again and relaxed onto the pillow. "What is it, angel?"

"I'm cold," she said in a trembling whisper.

He splayed an arm and slowly, meekly, she curled up beside him. He wrapped his arm over her and absentmindedly rubbed her shoulder, as she folded her limbs against his side and rested her forehead on his chest. He pulled the blanket up over them before drifting back to sleep.

Sometime later, he felt shifting on his other side, and then a hand stroking his neck. Trying to force his eyes open was impossible. He couldn't remember the last time he'd been so tired. He groaned and rolled his head back and forth, driving his eyelids open on perhaps the tenth try. Meanwhile, the hand continued stroking him from his earlobe down his collarbone and back up again.

Sumika was still curled up at his left side, fast asleep, her bony elbows and kneecaps jabbing him. But another head rested against his other shoulder, her black hair in a French braid. He closed his eyes again, moved his hand to the small of her back and squeezed her closer until her chest and stomach were flush against the side of his body. She nestled deeper into him, and stroked the skin under his collarbone, from his shoulder to the middle of his chest. He sighed and let his head fall back. That little bit of touch made him feel like he could breathe again.

"It was not your fault," Katya whispered. Her palm touched his neck, encouraging him to look at her. He opened his eyes enough to see hers, somehow more golden in the haze. She raised her head and kissed him between the eyes, then rested back on his shoulder. She kept petting his neck and collar until he fell asleep again.

When he awoke many hours later, the inside of the room was warmed by the sunset. The beds lay empty, all three warm bodies huddled together on the floor. He looked first at Sumika, curled into a fetal position at his side, her forehead resting on his robe, touching him just enough to balance. For once, she looked unwary.

Katya had moved aside his robe to press her cheek flush against his skin. The warmth of her body surged through him, the moisture of her breath, her scent. His hand was on her back, clutching her tightly. Katya's arm stretched across his chest and her hand rested on Sumika's elbow. The sight made him smile.

He squeezed them both gently and realized he was no longer trembling. And the feeling that had been growing since they'd first infiltrated Francis Tyler's estate, and maybe even since his plane got shot down all those years ago, was at least momentarily abated.

He didn't feel like a failure. He didn't know what he'd done right, but he must've done something for these two—two of the most extraordinary people he'd ever met—to think he was worth holding onto.

He could only hope they were right.

CHAPTER TWENTY-EIGHT

"There must be ten grand here." Augy steadied himself with one hand on the wall as he gazed at the contents of the suitcase Katya had brought with her from Walker's house. It was filled with loose twenty and fifty-dollar bills, a diamond necklace, a silver watch, some gold bullion, drugs, bandages, and weapons.

Katya smirked. "I think is more like twenty."

He snatched up a roll of tape and secured his injured pinky to his ring finger to immobilize it. "Where the hell did you get it?"

"I tell you, Walker is friend to my... to Tyler." She made a face like she tasted something bitter. "I know where he keep his safe."

"Then why the hell did we spend the night in this shithole?"

She shrugged. "You were in bad shape, and at nice hotels, woman cannot get reservation without man's permission."

"So, it's my fault?"

"Also, this is no money for wasting. We need better car, better equipment, bribe money, all of that."

After biting off the tape, Augy thumbed through the weapons. There were two Colt Government pistols, with four additional magazines, and a Hollister M12 shotgun. Digging into the case, Katya pulled out a knife in a leather sheath and handed it to him.

The sheath had USMC Ka-Bar printed on it in big black letters. Augy grinned, unsnapped the guard and pulled out the shining seven-inch tapered blade. "For me? Why, I do declare."

"You need have one. Is the best, no?"

"Oh, it certainly is, gorgeous. Thank you."

Katya showed a close-lipped smile. He met her eyes and went about his work of memorizing the details of every highlight of gold, amber, and cognac. She sucked on her bottom lip, then opened her mouth to speak, as the door to the bathroom popped open. Steam billowed and Sumika stuck her face out.

"Augy," she said, her voice so tiny it was barely audible. Her anxiety chilled the air.

Katya looked away. She took up one of the Colts and busied herself cleaning it.

"What is it, angel?" he asked, approaching. Sumika opened the door to let him slip inside, then closed and locked it.

A towel was wrapped around her hair and several more over her body in a great mish-mash of wet and cotton that made her look a bit like a sock monkey. Vigilance had returned to her expression.

"What's the matter?" he asked.

She worried her lips a while, then peeled away one towel so he could see her stomach. He hadn't seen her stab wounds since the night he'd found her. There were twenty-nine. Dr. Larkin had counted them off as she cleaned and closed them. The blade which made them had been short and thin, like a penknife. Even so, every blow had missed her major organs and arteries, which was nothing short of a miracle.

He had no medical background, but any idiot can tell the difference between a healthy cut and an infected one. A healthy wound is simple, a red line surrounded by clear skin. Sumika's wounds were anything but simple. The centers were puss-filled, yellow and white. The edges were black, even green in places. And every cut was wreathed in red.

Augy's heart seized in his chest. "Why didn't you say anything?"

She covered herself up and downcast her eyes.

"Just a minute," he said, then stepped out into the main room.

Katya sat cross-legged on one of the beds, counting out the money in staggered rows like a dealer in a casino.

"We have to go see Dr. Larkin."

Katya shook her head without looking up.

"There's something wrong with Sumika. She has an infection."

Leaning carefully over the bed so as not to disturb her rows of money, Katya snatched the bottle of antibiotics from the nightstand and tossed it over her shoulder.

He snatched it out of the air and looked at the label, but still, he shook his head. "We can't risk not taking her to a doctor."

Katya looked up, eyebrows drawn together. "Is that bad?"

"The fact that she can move around at all… She should've been resting all this time." He shook his head. "You could do with some patching up too, frankly."

"I'm fine."

"I've seen guys die from the kind of wound you've got."

She pushed her lips together. "All I need is some vodka to wash it. No problem."

He clenched his teeth, laughing in frustration. "Well, I need some then. My hand is fubared."

"What I do with my children, huh? I have make sure they no see any of this, and they will no see it now."

"We just need to go see the doctor. In and out."

"What if someone follow us?"

"What the fuck do you want me to say?" He stepped closer and continued in a harsh whisper through clenched teeth, "Sumika is covered in stab wounds and they almost all look infected. She'll die if we don't get her to the doctor."

Katya glared at him, her bottom lip twitching. "Is really that bad?"

Augy shuddered.

Sighing, she pushed out her bottom lip and nodded, then resumed to count the money.

He snatched up the first aid stuff and returned to the bathroom. Sumika sat huddled next to the sink, her chin pressed hard against her knees.

"I'm gonna take you to see Doc Larkin." Her eyes widened and she opened her mouth, but he cut her off. "Don't argue. We need to make sure you're healthy. That's the most important thing."

She nodded and looked away, wiping her nose on her forearm.

"I'm gonna clean you up, okay?" he said, showing her the gauze. "Let me see your hands."

For a long moment, she didn't move, gazing through him with those cold suspicious eyes. He knelt in front of her and reached for her wrist, guiding it towards himself. He unwound the bandages slowly, partly to spare her pain, and partly because he didn't want to see what was underneath. He wondered why the bastard had left her the one finger, but he would never ask. If she even knew, maybe someday she'd tell him.

As the layers wound down, the blood increased. Dry and crusty. He had to peel away the bottom layer very carefully as the fabric had adhered to her skin. The place where her fingers should've been was nothing but stitches—clean and uniform. Doctor Larkin had cut away leftover stubs and sewn together lumps of skin, so it protruded past where he'd expected to see. But, thank god, they didn't look infected. In fact, the bleeding had stopped and the swelling had gone down considerably. He rewrapped them in clean bandages, these much thinner.

"You're gonna be okay," he said, tying off the second bandage. Augy opened a tube of triple-antibiotic ointment and set it on the sink. "Let me see the wounds again. I'm gonna rub some of this on. Okay?"

Reluctantly, she peeled aside the towel. He slathered the ointment over her stomach. He knew there were more wounds on her chest, but he hesitated to ask to see them. Kicking himself, he pressed his nails into his palm. "And the others?"

She shook her head, her gaze cast away.

"Sumika, please. You said before you trusted me."

Biting her lip, she looked down at the floor. Then with tears in her eyes, she peeled away the towel from her chest. Augy averted his gaze as much as possible and worked quickly to cover the wounds in the ointment, then he took some gauze and wrapped it around her chest, and down her stomach.

"Okay. That's it," he said as he tied off the gauze and took a step back. "Do you need any help getting dressed?"

She shook her head hard, so Augy left the room.

Twenty minutes later, they were on the road. They stopped at a Winchell's for coffee and donuts, picked up a carton of Encores, then kept on to a Best Western motel in East Pasadena.

The yellow sign with the big crown glowed out front, it's electric buzz louder even than the growl of the car's engine. It was nothing extraordinary, a gold brick building wrapped in metal staircases, although it was miles better than where Augy, Katya, and Sumika had piled up Z's. They were all on the staircase headed towards the room when Augy saw something across the street that gave him pause.

In the play of buttery streetlight and gray shadows, a man staggered down the road, a bottle of wine in hand, talking to himself and kicking imaginary objects. Nothing so strange, except when Augy caught a glimpse of his face, he recognized the smooth pink and white skin, chubby cheeks, a button nose.

"Moretti?" he said to himself. This was his old beat, after all. Augy turned to Sumika and Katya. "You two go ahead. I'll be right up."

"Where are you going?" asked Sumika. She sounded scared.

"Just across the street. Don't worry, angel." He jogged down the metal steps, his feet like drumsticks on the lid of a garbage can. Crossing the street, he whistled and called, "Hey, hooch-hound!"

The man looked up, pushing back the brim of his not-so-fashionably tipped hat. "Smalls?" He squinted, then staggered from standing in one place too long. "Smalls! I thought you were dead."

Moretti threw his arms around Augy and hugged him close. He stank of pee, cheap wine, and too much aftershave.

"It's gonna take more than that," said Augy, patting his friend on the back.

Stumbling, Moretti scanned him. "You look like shit."

"Right back at you, sweetheart. But what are you doing out here? I heard you got canned."

"Canned? Canned..." He farted his lips, then took a long pull of wine. "They pulled down my dungarees and beat me to the tune of *Ave Maria*."

"What reason did they give?"

"Well, Tyler... goddamn son-of-a-mother Tyler... captain of industry Mr. Francis my-farts-don't-stink Tyler, apparently has pockets even deeper than we realized. He keeps the mayor in there, the chief and the new DA, too. I swear to Christ, if District Attorney Esposito were still around, he wouldn't have stood for this. He would've found a way to cut that fat-cat down to size."

"Esposito was one of the good ones," said Augy, thinking of the man who had so devotedly prosecuted the Hollisters' case, and who had died in a car crash not ten days after the conviction. At the time, Augy had thought it was a terrible accident. Now, the truth was obvious.

"This is all your fault, Smalls," said Moretti as if he'd just remembered. He stumbled back to point an accusatory finger. "I told you we shouldn't go down there. I told you it was a hairbrained idea..."

The door of one of the motel rooms opened, and Augy watched as Katya stepped out onto the landing. She held tight to her daughter's hand, her little boy hoisted on her hip with her good arm.

"I'm sorry, Moretti. It had to be done. And it wasn't for nothing," he said, eyes following Katya. "Listen, whatever happened to that book you found in the crash? The one with all the names and addresses?"

"I got it right here." He patted his breast pocket.

"You have it?"

"Yeah, I took it. I ain't gonna let those sons-of-bitches take credit for my work."

"Give it here."

"Go to hell. You know, I oughta turn you in." He jabbed a finger at Augy's face. "If I brought you in, they'd put me back on the force. Probably give me a goddamn metal."

"Don't joke about that."

"Ain't no joke. This whole vigilante act of yours is a no-go as far as I'm concerned. You know what...?" He bent to set the wine bottle on the ground but tipped it over as he straightened back up. "That's exactly what I'm gonna do. You're under arrest."

Augy smirked. "Take it easy, cowboy."

"Don't tell me to take it easy, you superior so-and-so. You think you're such hot shit cause you were a fighter and managed to take down one or two goddamn Jap planes."

"Nine."

"You got shot down on your second goddamn mission, and ain't nobody impressed."

Augy examined his fingernails. "At least I didn't spend the war pushing pencils in Des Moines."

"That's it!" Moretti ripped off his coat and threw it to the ground, then proceeded to roll up his sleeves.

Augy rolled his eyes. "What are you doing?"

"I'm gonna feed you a knuckle sandwich, you gangly son of a bitch."

"Moretti, you're drunk. I'm not gonna fight you..."

A fist connected with his chin. It smarted like a bee sting. Moretti bobbed back and forth like some kind of featherweight champion with an inner ear infection.

Augy touched his bottom lip. Bleeding again. "Why you cheap, dirty little bastard."

Moretti licked his teeth, then swung again, this time wider and with more power. Augy sidestepped and caught him by the elbow. He twisted down hard, rolling Moretti to the ground. Augy came down on top of him, one arm slung across his chest, pinning him to the asphalt.

Augy barely exuded any energy to hold him down, relying on weight and positioning. Moretti thrashed and kicked his legs, but he was like a fish in a net. "Get off me!"

"Are you done?"

"Get the fuck off me!"

Heels clicked on the concrete as Katya jogged closer. "Can you go five minutes without causing fights?"

With a bone-deep sigh, Augy released the hold. "Everything's fine. I'm perfectly calm," he said, standing. "I'll be up in two minutes, gorgeous."

She narrowed her eyes before heading back towards the building.

Augy wiped his lips and lit a cigarette, as Moretti struggled to his feet. "Listen, Moretti, I'm sorry I got you canned. I shouldn't have gotten you involved in this. But I need that book."

"Go fuck yourself, Smalls." He spat on the ground. "The whole department is looking for you. They've found your fingerprints all over the damn city. They're gonna find you, and when they do, you and that commie whore are both gonna be wearing pine overcoats."

Augy stuck his cigarette between his lips and rolled his shoulders. Then, he clocked Moretti in the nose with a southpaw. The pocket-sized ex-cop's feet flew up over his babyface as he hit the ground with a thump. A river of thick blood streamed from his nose. He moaned and flopped on the asphalt, then bit by bit fell unconscious.

Augy yanked the book out of Moretti's jacket pocket. "Sleep it off, you spiteful fuck."

Walking back towards the motel, he saw Katya and her brood huddled on the steps.

Clemmie waved, then hopped up and hurried towards him, her wild black curls bouncing as she came. When he realized she was coming in for a hug, he bent down and caught her in his arms.

"Hi!" she said, showing a smile bright as the sun and twice as natural. "Who was that guy?"

"Erm... just an old friend."

"A friend? Seriously?" Clemmie poked his swollen bottom lip. "I don't think he likes you much."

Augy chuckled and set her down, then looked up at Katya. She was frowning hard. Her little boy was in her lap, his arm slung around her neck. Dressed in striped pajamas, his brown hair hanging in his eyes, his brow was knitted and his lips pursed as he stared at Augy. Even his chin—which had a deep, sculpted cleft like his mom's—was flattened in anger.

"You said you were calm," said Katya.

"I am calm." He handed her the book.

"How did you...?" Grinning, she flipped through the pages. "You said we would never get it."

"I'm wrong sometimes. Not often, but it does happen." He loped past her up the stairs towards the room. Knocking, he glanced down at the parking lot. Moretti still lay prone, twitching a little. Augy tried to ignore the stab of guilt, but it was insistent. Moretti was one of the only friends Augy had left, and he hoped it wasn't ruined forever. He'd never known Moretti resented him so much, or at all. Maybe he was just drunk.

He shouldn't have hit him. He should've let it all roll off. The events of the last few days had left him a bit trigger-happy, as if violence were the ultimate answer to every problem. It was a dangerous way of thinking, but calling Katya a commie whore had been one step too far.

He looked at her and the kids. Everything from the soft voice she used, to how she smiled, to the way she kept finding every opportunity to tousle her kids' hair or hug their shoulders showed what a devoted mother she was. Even as she held them, and whispered tender comforts, he saw she kept wiping away the same tear. She could be so soft sometimes for someone so hard, and the contradiction made her all the more beautiful. And his mind kept drifting back to the night before when she'd lain beside him and covered him in her gentleness.

Locks clicked on the other side of the door and it crawled open.

Dr. Larkin didn't say anything as she let him inside. She had a lot of luggage under the eyes and hard lines around her lips. Smudges covered her delicate half-moon glasses. She was wearing a housecoat and slippers, her long gray hair wound into a bun on top of her head. Her colorless eyes seemed less alive than ever. Even those train-tunnel pupils looked closed for business.

The motel room was strewn with toys, clothes, and dishes. A distinctive lived-in smell wafted through the air—not sweat or food, just the raw whiff of musky humanity.

"Hey, Doc," said Augy. "How you been?"

"Remembering why I never had kids," she grumbled.

Looking over her shoulder, he saw Sumika on one of the beds, knees to her chest, of course. One of her arms was propped on some pillows with a needle in it. An IV bag was hoisted above, hanging from the reading lamp.

"How is she?" asked Augy.

Dr. Larkin worried her bottom lip. "The infection is pretty extensive. I'm administering intravenous antibiotics. She needs rest, and normally I'd recommend hyperbaric oxygen therapy."

"Hyperbaric? You mean like scuba divers use?"

She yawned and nodded. "Scripps Mercy in San Diego has one, though I doubt I could get her in for treatment."

"I'm not going to no hospital," said Sumika in the loudest voice he'd ever heard come out of her. He swelled of pride.

"You're not going to no hospital," he said, taking a seat on the bed beside her. He looked up at the doctor. "It looks like you managed to resupply." He lifted his mangled hands limply. "You mind?"

CHAPTER TWENTY-NINE

Augy insisted they move to a new hotel. Not that he thought Moretti would turn them in. He was probably just drunk, and he'd probably come to his senses. Probably.

Once the bag of antibiotics had drained into Sumika, he packed everybody into the Hudson and took them down the road a few miles to a proper hotel, with a pool for the kids, a full breakfast, and a separate bedroom and en suite for the poor doctor turned governess. Now less irritated, Dr. Larkin got to work sewing up Augy's wounds and was even nice enough to give him a big dose of the good stuff.

She gave Sumika some morphine too, in spite of the girl's protestations. Sumika never complained of pain, though to look at her you'd think she'd be capable of little more than lying on the ground and crying. He'd met some brass-bound personalities over the years, not the least of which were Katya and Dr. Larkin, but Sumika was playing a different ballgame. She had a core hard enough to shame a bowling ball.

But she needed rest, and Dr. Larkin played a bit fast and loose with the drugs when it came to hard-headed patients who didn't know what was good for them. It had crossed Augy's mind that he and Katya could use some R and R themselves, not to mention TLC, but he had an idea, and there was no time to waste. So, while Dr. Larkin stitched up Katya, he wrote Sumika a note, promising to be back for her as soon as humanly possible. She'd be upset, but the only other option was to throw her unconscious body in the back of the car and hope for the best. Even stubborn Sumika would understand why that wasn't an option.

Before he and Katya cut out, Augy took the opportunity to make some phone calls. He was worried about Mary, desperate to know if she'd gotten out of town all right, so after a few minutes on the phone with the operator, Augy was connected to a little rambler home in Tampa, Florida.

A woman answered, "Small residence."

"Hi, Mom."

"August!" she exclaimed in a sing-song voice. "Somebody call an ambulance. Both of my children called me in one day. I must be dying."

"Mary called?"

"Yeah. She said she was bringing the kids out for a visit. Imagine driving all the way across the country with a one-year-old baby. I told her she was out of her mind, but she's insistent. I'm not dying, am I?"

"That's not funny, Mom."

"Well, I don't think so either. Is everything all right with your sister? She sounded a bit uptight. I mean, more so than usual."

"Yeah. She's fine. Just misses you, I guess. When did you hear from Mary?"

"Oh, it was about an hour ago. It seems odd you both calling me when I know it's damn early in the morning out there."

"I don't know. I heard Mary was heading out and I thought..."

"Right..." she sang, then cleared her throat. "You'd tell me if something funny was going on, wouldn't you, August?"

"Mom. You're being paranoid."

"If you say so. Look, I can't talk. The girls are waiting for me."

"No problem. I love you, Mom."

"Forever and ever, baby boy."

Augy pushed down on the disconnect plunger with his finger and bounced the handset in his other hand. He didn't want to call her. He really didn't want to call her. But even though Countess London hadn't mentioned her in particular, he had to make sure she was all right.

"One last time," he said to himself, dialing in the fateful number. "Then never again. Never ever..."

Two rings and the line connected. "Hello?"

It was Bill. Augy opened his mouth, but nothing would come out. He was about to hang up when Bill said, "I can hear you breathing."

Fuck, Augy mouthed. "Hi, Bill. It's August. Can I talk to Edith please?"

"One moment." The phone rumbled as Bill set down the receiver. Augy sat on the bed beside unconscious Sumika and squeezed her hand. He lit a cigarette and had smoked it to the filter by the time a voice came back on the line.

"She doesn't want to talk to you."

"I appreciate that, but this is important."

"I can give her a message."

"Listen, just…" Humiliated, he pushed a fist into his forehead and closed his eyes tight. "All right, Bill. I hate to put this on you, but there are people out there who are trying to get at me, and I'm worried they might be willing to go through Edith to do it."

A beat of silence. "Is that all?"

"Didn't you hear me? You're both in serious danger. You need to pack up and leave town for a while."

"I'll give her the message."

The call disconnected. Augy clenched his fists and swallowed a stream of profanity. He dialed the number again.

"Hello?"

"I don't feel like you're taking this seriously."

"Goodbye, August." Bill hung up again.

Augy twisted his hands around the receiver as if he were wringing its neck. "Fucking weasel."

He dialed again. A busy signal.

Augy slammed down the phone so hard the plastic cracked. Every eye in the room turned. He wanted to throw the phone through the window, but soon the morphine pumping through his system decimated and dispersed his anger, until all that remained was a lingering sense of impotency. He popped a cigarette between his lips and stepped out of the room onto the landing, closing the door behind him. The sun was cresting over the cluttered, synthetic horizon, spraying orange haze across the land. Augy took a deep breath of fresh air, choked on it, and lit his cigarette.

A moment later, the door opened behind him and Dr. Larkin stepped out. "Everything all right, champ?"

"Goddamn, I love morphine," he slurred. The dizziness was already wearing thin, but it was like the sandman was whispering a lullaby in his ear, willing him to close his eyes.

"Are you sure you're going to be able to drive?" asked the Doctor.

"Psh…" Turning to face her, he leaned his back against the railing. "What's hepatic mean?"

She wrinkled her brow. "Pertaining to the liver. Why?"

"I might've known." He smoked a while, narrowing his eyes at the wall and cutting golden bricks into imaginary triangles.

"Why?" said Dr. Larkin again, louder.

He waved off the question. "You got any more of that stuff we used on those goons at the hospital?"

"Why?"

"It was copacetic, and I think I'll soon have the need to quiet some guys down quickly."

"Sorry, sport. No can do. That was epinephrine. It's supposed to be given in small diluted doses. Taking out those two ate a year's supply."

"Well, what do you got?"

"If you're looking for something that will reliably and quickly knock somebody out without killing them, I'm afraid the substance doesn't exist. Anesthesiology wouldn't be its own branch of medicine if things were that simple."

"And what if I ain't too concerned about killing them?"

"You mean you want poison?"

He nodded. "Something potent and fast-acting."

"Give me a break. I'm a small-town doctor, not KGB."

Augy grunted and shook his head.

Half an hour later, Katya and he were on the road headed vaguely towards Hollywood. For most of the drive, her nose was wedged in her little leather book, until finally, she cried, "Aha! Dr. Marvin Hoffman. He is… I do not know how to say in English. *Gastroenterolog*. He work at Lumbermill."

"You got his address?"

She nodded. "Trousdale. I think I am gone to this before. Frank hate parties, but we have to go sometimes."

"Was it one of the ones with the—" he swallowed a lump "—with the kids?"

"No, no. That is thrown by the Countess once a year and has happened already. This is more tame. I would be surprised if Countess come herself, but most others will be there."

Augy lit a cigarette and rolled down the window. Katya closed the book and set it in her lap. She grabbed the smoke out of his hand and put it to her lips. "Who is that man you fight with?"

Augy lit another. "A beat cop I used to work with."

"Why were you fighting?"

"Does it matter?"

He felt her staring at him, those arched eyebrows lifted. Waiting.

"He called you a commie whore."

Katya shrugged and looked out the window. "Is what I am."

"Don't say that. I mean, commie, sure. But who cares? My father was a communist."

"Your father?" she chuckled.

"He was a college professor. It's practically required. He made me read The Communist Manifesto when I was in sixth grade."

"How you like it?"

"It's... short. But that's neither here nor there. You are not—" the word wouldn't form in his mouth "—what Moretti called you."

"What do you call woman given away as a present to a man she hates, then lets him do whatever he want because she thinks will make her life easier?" She sucked on her lips. "I call her a whore."

Augy chewed on his tongue. His mind was still behind a pane of foggy glass, and he was caught off guard. "That is not who you are," he croaked out.

"Is exactly who I am." Her voice was flat, emotionless. When he glanced over, she was staring hard out the window. He watched her eyes in the side-view mirror, yellow and distant, as cold as a wolf moon.

Sighing, he shook his head. "I don't get it, Katya. Why did you stay so long? You could've left sooner—Good-looking Charlie or not. Why?"

"After Manchukuo, I do not care about anything." She grabbed the bridge of her nose, squeezing her eyes closed. "Before she give me to Tyler, Countess London tell me what they do to Fabi when they catch him. He go to spy on Unit 731, the Lumbermill. I do not know what he found, or what he did, or how long before the Japanese find him. But when they find him, they take him in and they do skin graft experiments. You know what is?"

Augy nodded, swallowing the bile rising in his throat.

"I do not know what is, so she tell me. They take skin from one place, put it another. They freeze and burn off skin, try replace it. They take muscles from his back and move them around. She say he lived four weeks like that." Her voice cracked. "Four *weeks*. And I know she is not lying. Why would she lie?"

She pushed her face into her hands and took a few long deep breaths, sniffling on each inhalation. Her knuckles were turning white she was pressing them so hard.

Augy said nothing. There was nothing to say. He pulled to the side of the highway and parked in the shade of a yellow and green acacia tree. The sky above was pure blue, no clouds to be seen. The sunshine warm and vibrant. Another beautiful day.

Snatching her cigarette out of the ashtray, Katya tried to inhale, but it had gone out. Augy rushed to light it. It was all he was good for.

"She would do the same to me. Worse, maybe." She wiped a few undescended tears with the tips of her nails and flicked them out the window. "The war was nearly over when I was captured. When they found out Japan would surrender, they blew up the compound. Every person who was inside was killed."

At last, she turned to face him. Her skin was flush, features twisted as she fought to keep control of a voice on the verge of screaming. "Nobody who did these things... to Fabi, to you..." She reached out two shaking fingers and touched his chest. "Ten thousand people and more. None of them were ever punished."

"That can't be true."

She looked up at his face. "The Countess was not like the others. She did not care about her country or honor or glory or any of that. She only care about her work. So, she took me and a few dozen others, Chinese and Russian, and she bring us here. We are slaves to her, but how you say... like money? Tokens...?"

"Bargaining chips?"

"Yes. I do not know what happen to rest," she continued, turning away. "I am only one left, maybe."

"Okay. I get all that," said Augy. "But why'd you stay so long? Nine years, and then one day you just change your mind and run away?"

"Why do you care?" she asked, her voice low and enervated.

He looked down at his hands. "I want to understand."

"You want understand?" she snapped. "Fine. After I am with Frank one month maybe, I try to escape. They catch me. I think they will kill me, but Frank, he forgive me. Still want to charm me. *Izvrashchenets*. He make me have dinner with him, give me wine that make me dizzy and sick. And I wake up pregnant next day."

"Oh, Katya…"

"I am not to leave another baby. I lost my Galina…" She was crying now and trying so desperately to stop that her body trembled. "But time go by and I cannot stand it anymore. I start to fight back again. So Frank, he take my children away. Say I no can see them. And then I know I have to get us out. All of us, before they turn my daughter into something like what they made me. Before they turn my son into…" She gritted her teeth and looked out at the sky. "I could not take them right away. I could not get to them. And I do not think he will hurt them. Not until I am in the Lumbermill and he says to me he will sell them to his friends if I do not do as he tells me."

Tightening her hands into fists, she turned on him and said through clenched teeth, "You have more questions, Detective?"

He shook his head. Katya popped open the door of the car and hurried away on unsteady legs, around the tree, and up a small hill covered in prickly grass. Closing his eyes, Augy listened to the thrum of passing traffic. That sound was coming from her throat again, the one he'd heard that night in the motel as she tried to hide from him. Harsh and guttural, on the verge of hysterics, and yet defiant. When he looked up, he saw her hand pressed over her mouth, her shoulders trembling.

He got out of the car and approached, each step an eternity. Vitriol pooled in his stomach—for himself, for the world, and all the people in it, excepting so few he could count them on his fingers. He accidentally kicked some gravel, and she turned, such fury on her face that part of him wanted to turn and run. But her cheeks were streaked with red, soaked in thick tears.

"What do you want?" Her empty hands reached forward. She had nothing to give. Her wrists looked so thin, fragile as a broken wing. He knew she didn't want him to see her that way. She wanted to be strong. Indestructible.

He tried to answer, but his voice was trapped in his throat.

"What do you want!" she shrieked.

"I'm sorry." He took a few steps back and turned his eyes to the horizon. More acacia grew in the distance beyond a carpet of sharp brown grass. Power and phone lines stretched across the sapphire sky, cutting it into long isosceles triangles. Two birds sat on the wire less than a foot from one another. One of them was tweeting, making an ass out of itself. The male, no doubt.

"I always do this," he finally said. "I push and I push until nobody wants anything to do with me."

He found the courage to look up at her. She was breathing hard, arms twisted around her chest, staring at him.

"I don't think you're a whore, Katya," he continued. "And I don't think you're weak for anything you've done or anything that's happened to you. But even if you were, I wouldn't care. You're the most…"

He gave a gloomy chuckle. "I'm no good at this kind of thing."

She bit her bottom lip and looked down.

He stepped closer, watching carefully in case she cringed or recoiled, but she was a statue now. With the edge of his thumb, he traced an inch of her jawline, then dropped his hand to his side. "*Ya obozhayu tebya.*"

An unexpected laugh broke her lips, and she covered her mouth with her hand.

Augy furrowed his brow. "I'm starting to think that doesn't mean what I think it means."

"No."

"What does it mean?"

"I will never tell you."

"You're a pain in the ass, you know that?"

She laughed again and punched him in the chest. Hard. His ribs buckled and the air rushed from his lungs. When his vision cleared he was on his knees in the dirt.

"What is wrong?" she asked, kneeling in front of him.

"Ribs. Broken," he squeaked out. He sounded as if someone had closed his scrotum in a book, and he kind of felt that way, too.

"I am sorry," she said between chuckles.

"Oh, you are such a pain in the ass."

"No. I am so sorry." She touched his shoulders comfortingly, but she was still laughing.

He coughed and wheezed. "I'm in serious pain here."

She helped him up and guided him back to the car. He flinched when she reached into his jacket pocket to get his cigarettes, then she lit one and handed it to him. She folded her hands in her lap and watched him, an expression on her face that may as well have been written in Cyrillic for all the sense it made.

"What is it?" he asked.

She leaned across the seat and kissed his temple. Then she shook her head and put back her shoulders. "We go now?"

CHAPTER THIRTY

A tailor, a jeweler, a hatter, a cobbler, three costume shops, six hundred and fifty-four dollars, and four hours later, Augy was finally ready. He was clean-shaven, sprinkled with expensive cologne, and his dishwater blond hair was styled into a short wavy pompadour. In his shopping bags was a black tailcoat, black pleated pants, white waistcoat, wing-collared dress shirt, white bow tie, mother-of-pearl studs, mother-of-pearl cufflinks, patent leather pumps, white leather gloves, platinum pocket watch, and one hand-painted, black, white, and gold checkered, long pointy-nosed, *medico della peste* mask. Never in his life had Augy spent so much time or money on clothes. His ex-wife's wedding dress had cost a fraction of what he'd dropped on this pile of nonsense, and he'd bitched about that for weeks. It crossed his mind that he could return it all come morning, but then he remembered what had happened to the last several suits he'd owned.

He had to keep reminding himself that the money was stolen. He'd been broke for so long it caused him physical pain to shell out eighty-nine dollars for a pair of cufflinks when a nickel got you a dozen plastic buttons that did the job just as well.

Of course, that wasn't the only obscene sum he'd dropped that day. Before he even began shopping, he'd had to make a little detour. So, after dropping Katya off on Melrose, he headed downtown towards Little Tokyo.

Most of the Japanese Americans in Little Tokyo were the children or grandchildren of immigrants. In spite of the contempt they'd endured from the government and Americans in general, most were still out for their own piece of the American Dream. Given what little he'd learned of Sumika's circumstances, he would've bet money the Countess would've viewed most of the residents of Little Tokyo as race traitors.

He had the cab drop him off at a restaurant called Sakana, where he'd once helped the owner get out of a jam with some unsavory characters involved in illegal food importation. He could only hope old Ueba hadn't cleaned up his act.

Approaching, Augy saw a flyer in the window with a black and white picture of some big-eared doofus and written in both English and Japanese: *For Confidential Services, Private Investigator August Small. Free Consultations.*

He ripped it off and shoved it in his pocket as he stepped inside. Conversations stopped and every eye turned to him—the only white man in a mile. Showing a closed-lipped smile, he bowed. "*Sumimasen.*"

"*Irasshaimase!*" the man behind the counter called out the traditional greeting, but didn't look up. He was busy splitting a fish in half with a massive cleaver and tearing out its guts. He wore a leather apron and had a white band tied around his bald head. A pencil mustache clung to his upper lip.

"*Ueba-san!*" called Augy, stepping up to the counter.

Lifting his eyes, the cook smiled, then bowed twice in quick succession. He wiped fish guts on his apron and shook Augy's outstretched hand. "Mr. Small," he said in Japanese. "Good to see you. What can I get for you?"

"Do you have fugu?"

"Fugu?" He pushed his chin back forcing a lump of fat to poke forward on his throat. "You don't want fugu. Who told you about fugu?"

"Do you have any or not?" Augy showed Ueba a few hundred-dollar bills in his jacket pocket.

The old cook's eyes widened. He stepped out from behind the counter, touched Augy's shoulder, and led him towards the back of the restaurant. "You can't get fugu here," he said in English, perhaps hoping the other patrons would be less likely to understand.

"What happened to you, Ueba? I remember a chef once told me he could get anything if the price was right. Shark fins, whale eggs, sea turtle, walrus penis."

"Yes, yes, but…"

"And you're saying you can't get me a couple of little pufferfish? Not even for four hundred dollars?" Augy took out the money again and shook it.

Ueba shifted. His face was flat, but his eyes were following the gentle dance of Benjamin Franklin. "I might know one person who can get it."

"I need it tonight."

"Tonight?" He laughed and shook his head. "You're crazy. I could never get it that quickly."

"Not even for six hundred dollars?"

Ueba leaned in close, assaulting Augy with his fishy breath. "How many do you need?"

"I don't need the whole fish. Just the poisonous bits."

His face contorted like somebody had stomped on his foot and he was trying to hold in a scream. "How dare you come in here and ask me for that?"

"I don't mean to disrespect your place of business. Cards on the table, you're the most important person in my life right now." He pulled out one more bill. "Can you help me?"

Ueba's face relaxed, and he folded his arms. He stared at Augy for a good long time, then leaned in close again and whispered, "Why not use arsenic? It's a lot cheaper."

"Irony, my friend. Worth every penny." A lightbulb switched on, and Augy snapped his fingers. "A penny."

"What?"

"I think I just figured out how copper wire was invented." He looked down and shook his head. "Fucking Nazis."

They made the arrangements, and Augy gave him half the money—three-fifty before and three-fifty after delivery to the agreed place, an Italian restaurant on Melrose and Vista.

Augy got back to Hollywood around two in the afternoon, then commenced his marathon shopping. For the last two hours, he'd been sat on the patio of *Tutto e Troppo*, sipping gin and tonics, eating antipasto and *cacio e pepe*. He smoked through a deck of Encores waiting for both his delivery and Katya, who apparently needed even more than eight hours to put together an evening look. He wasn't stupid enough to complain. It was sunset, and while the invitation hadn't specified a time, he couldn't imagine such a soiree would begin before dark. Sitting down and doing nothing was pure luxury, let alone the amenities of a fancy downtown eatery. He couldn't remember the last time he'd had real food.

With his battered foot resting on a chair under the tablecloth, Augy ordered another gin and tonic. The waiter gave him a snot-nosed expression again, but he didn't care. He didn't drink wine or beer or whiskey. It wasn't just that he was picky. Guys who served in the Pacific for any real amount of time, especially marines and infantry, and even more so POWs, invariably caught malaria. And once you catch malaria it never goes away. As often as every three or four months some guys would relapse into fevers, chills, hallucinations, nausea, and muscle pain. The treatment for malaria was quinine, which was also the ingredient that gave tonic water its distinctive taste. Augy liked to keep a bit of quinine in his system at all times, often without the addition of gin. Maybe his method was nonsense. A doctor had even told him once that the amount of quinine in commercially produced tonic water was insufficient to have any effect on malaria. But unlike most guys you heard about, Augy had never had a malarial relapse since returning to the states. Doctor's orders be damned; you don't mess with success. Besides, he liked the flavor.

Sighing at an orange-red sky, he picked an ice cube out of his glass and ran it over his forehead. Late June was when the temperature tended to ramp up, and being in the sun without so much as an awning was making him sweat. Of course, Los Angeles never really got hot. Not hot like the equator. Not hot like the jungle. Not hot like the cockpit of a P-38. Those closed-up tin-cans got so ungodly hot it wasn't unusual for pilots to fly in nothing but their skivvies and helmets. Which was precisely what Augy had been wearing the day his plane got shot down. The Japanese soldiers had laughed at him when he came rolling out of the cockpit mostly naked. And they'd made him stay like that the next several days.

First, they took him to a POW camp in eastern Singapore called Changi, which was where he caught malaria. It was a converted British barracks, located next to an infamous prison where the Japanese had detained several thousand Chinese and Malay civilians. The massive camp held 50,000 POWs, mainly Brits and Australians. As the headquarters of the Kempeitai, the Japanese military police, most POWs at least passed through Changi to be interrogated before being sent along to their final destinations.

The Aussies gave him a tin of fish and some rice noodles, as well as some pants and a bottom bunk. Augy warmed up to the idea of spending the rest of the war with them, but six days later, he and two thousand others were crammed into the hold of an unmarked cargo ship bound for Hokkaido.

There was little food or water, and even less air. That was the hottest he'd ever been, with four inches of personal space and human heat and humidity all around him. At that point, Augy was better fed and healthier than a lot of the guys, even though he was in the throes of his first-ever malarial episode and his tibia had been broken during the interrogation. Cabin fever was putting it mildly. By a week in, a quarter of the guys had become delirious. Another week later, dysentery broke out. Everybody had the shits and no way to wipe themselves. Two hundred were dead by the time the ship landed in Hokkaido. The Japanese hadn't bothered to remove the swollen corpses either, not even when they exploded from the heat.

"Are you finished, sir?" the waiter asked.

Augy returned to the present and wrinkled his nose at the plate of antipasto. The smell of the ship was in his nostrils—feces, noxious vapors, rotting meat. The well-appointed plate of cheeses and meats looked like vomit. He covered his mouth and waved it away.

Just then, a Japanese man in a double-breasted suit and fedora stepped onto the patio, garnering many disapproving glares from the exclusively white patrons. He walked to Augy, put his briefcase on the ground, and set his pack of cigarettes on the table. He made a ridiculous face for the sake of the peanut gallery—exaggerated squint and bared teeth—then said loud enough for people nearby to hear, "So sorry. Do you know the way to the train station?"

Augy set his pack of cigarettes on the table. "It's three more blocks south. You can't miss it."

"Thank you. Thank you so much." The man bowed, picked up his briefcase and some cigarettes, then scurried away.

Diners grumbled as he left, and Augy showed a face as if to say, *Oh, I know*. They were all so focused on what the man looked like none of them had noticed what he'd done.

Augy put the pack of cigarettes in his jacket pocket.

The smell of the food was making him sick and dizzy. He was starting to wonder if everything had gone all right for Katya when a black Cadillac Sixty Special rolled up and beeped the horn. The back window lowered and someone clicked their tongue. He'd come to recognize and respond to that click almost without thinking, but when he looked up he barely recognized the woman gazing back.

Her hair was platinum blonde, cut shoulder length, and pinned into salon perfect curls that framed her face. Gold, diamond, and sapphire cornucopias were pinned to each ear. Her makeup was heavy—porcelain white skin, long eyelashes, and deep red lips.

"K-Katya?" He staggered closer. "You look… different."

She wrinkled her nose. "What?"

"Nothing. Just, your hair. You changed it."

"Is wig."

"Oh, thank god," he breathed.

With a dry chuckle in her throat, she sneered and looked him up and down. "You are not ready."

"I just gotta change." He showed his shopping bags with a biddable grin.

"You going to dress in fucking bathroom? This is white tie."

The smile tightened. "Give me five minutes."

"Hurry." With contempt, the dark window rolled up.

Biddable through and through, he did as he was told. Once he'd put on all the Ritz, he stooped to check himself in the mirror. The fresh shave made his long rectangular face appear marginally more civilized. His nose didn't look too bad, even though Katya had broken it just the other day. It had already been broken so many times, it squiggled down his face like a drop of rain on a windshield. One more bump was a fart in a swimming pool. His bottom lip was puffy from Moretti's bee sting, but it didn't look bad if he smiled. The circle under his one eye had faded to hazy yellow. The worst of it was still that massive diagonal cut on his forehead, stitched and re-stitched till it was distended. The mask would cover it. If only he could find a mask that covered his chimp ears, he'd be in business.

He hurried out to the car. The driver's window was rolled down and when he glanced in, expecting to see a stranger, he staggered at the familiar face under the chauffeur's cap.

"Sumika?" He leaned down on the windowsill. She was wearing a men's chauffeur uniform: black riding boots, knickerbockers, a mandarin-collar jacket with T-bib and shield buttons, leather driving gloves. "What are you doing here?"

"Katya came back and got me," she said. "Is that okay?"

"That depends. How are you feeling?"

"I'm better. Dr. Larkin said it was okay."

"In that case, it's brilliant.'

She smiled and nodded, then pulled the cap down over her eyes. Laughing, Augy opened the back door and climbed inside. The car was cherry—fawn leather interior, silver handles. Even the ashtrays sparkled. But it was just an expensive frame.

The dress was royal blue satin, backless and sleeveless, held up by magic. A full-length skirt fell unsupported over superlative legs, clinging and shimmering. A white lace and gemstone armband covered the bullet hole in her bicep.

Pursing her lips, Katya leaned over and adjusted his tie. "You clean up nice."

"No." Augy shook his head and furrowed his brow. "This will never do."

"What is problem now?"

"Do you have to be the most beautiful woman there? You couldn't tone it down a little?"

She rolled her eyes. "Do not flirt."

"I'm not flirting. I'm complaining."

"Please." She frowned hard, but her eyes were laughing. "I can tell when a man is crazy about me."

"I figured you'd assume we all are."

Even under all that makeup, her natural blush showed through. He tried to suppress it, but an honest-to-god giggle filled his throat. "I know this is supposed to be all business," he said, "but you have to dance with me tonight."

Biting her thumb, she shook her head.

"Come on. I got all dolled up."

"I do not like these things." When she turned back, all the amusement had drained from her face, her pupils wary pinpoints. Vertical lines appeared on either side of her mouth, and frown lines between her brows. Even through flawless makeup, fear showed her age more clearly than would sunlight.

"Chin up, gorgeous. After tonight, you never have to see any of these people again. I promise." Augy patted the cigarettes in his jacket pocket. "Now, let's go crash a party."

CHAPTER THIRTY-ONE

As they pulled up to the valet station, they donned their masks. Katya wore one made of gold lace and rhinestones that encircled both her eyes and continued down one side of her face to curl around her chin, with a spray of white and blue feathers up top. Her golden eyes, long lashes, and crimson lips were still visible, but it obscured her Mona Lisa nose, Elizabeth Taylor eyebrows, and Ava Gardner chin.

Augy told Sumika to wait around the corner and to keep her eyes peeled. Watching the car leave, he said to Katya, "Why did you go back for her?"

"We need driver, and she seem to want job." She bit her bottom lip, then added in a soft, unsteady voice, "Anyway, I think she need woman in her life, maybe."

Tears welled in his eyes, but he fought them back. "Thank you."

Wrinkling the skin around her eyes, Katya smiled and slipped her arm in his. Together they approached the side of the house, where a doorman dressed in a white tuxedo waited to greet them. Lights glimmered in the back garden; music and laughter drifted on the temperate night air.

"Don't hate me for this," Augy whispered, then smiled at the maître d'.

"Good evening, sir and madam." The man had a mellow German accent, slicked-back blond hair, and a tight smile. He wore a simple white mask over his eyes. "*Willkommen.* May I see your invitation, please."

Augy produced it. The man held it up to a light, confirming the presence of a watermark, then he set it down on a pile of identical cards and said, "How was copper wire invented?"

Augy forced himself to smile to hide the sinking sensation in his gut. "Two Jews were fighting over a penny."

"Very good, sir," the maître d' laughed, though of course, he'd heard the punchline several dozen times already. "Would you care to contribute to the host's joke book?"

The man indicated a large leather-bound guest book on his podium. Augy narrowed his eyes at it. Since half the fun of a masquerade ball is guessing one another's identities, instead of their names guests were writing horrible anti-Semitic jokes.

The maître d' held up a pen expectantly.

"Would you look at that, my dear. Isn't that fun?" he said to Katya through gritted teeth, then he took the pen and tapped it on the paper for a while. "I'm no good at this kind of thing."

"Is this your first time to the masquerade, sir?"

Augy nodded.

"This is a cherished tradition of the Hoffmans," the maître d' gushed. "At the end of the night, the book will be read out with the microphone."

"Does anybody read them before that?"

"No, sir. Neither I nor any other staff read them to maintain the anonymity of the authors."

"Well, in that case..." He scrawled something. The maître d' closed the book and thanked him, then handed Katya her dance card and waved them on.

As they walked towards an open-air ballroom, Katya eyed him suspiciously. "What you write?"

"What sits naked in a meadow and eats grass?"

"A cow?"

"No. A German in 1946."

She choked on a laugh and elbowed him in the gut. "You are going to get us killed."

They followed a red carpet to a huge wooden dancefloor that had been erected over the grass. It boasted as much square footage as the adjacent house. Ropes of golden lights were wound around trees and strung over the dancefloor, glittering like massive stars. Cut white and purple flowers framed the area. Round tables were situated around the perimeter, each with a centerpiece of long-stemmed white roses. Out on the floor, attendees in their Viennese best danced the waltz. They were largely white, with a minority Japanese. The men all wore the same prescribed uniform, their only distinguishing features their cufflinks, pocket watches, and masks. White was a popular color for women's dresses, with pink a close second.

Waiters made the rounds with champagne and canapes. He zeroed in on one with an empty tray and followed the man's trek up the back steps of the house towards where he assumed the kitchen had to be. Augy patted the pack of cigarettes in his jacket pocket. Three were stuffed with small glass vials of toxin. The other seventeen were real. He badly wanted to smoke one, but didn't dare.

At the edge of the dancefloor, a long white tent had been set up, decorated with flowers and more lights. Augy took a step closer, searching for shadows within, but it stood empty.

He realized Katya had let go of his arm. When he looked back she was frozen in place a few yards behind him, her attention locked on something across the crowded dancehall. Following her gaze, he found a blond man with a perfect square jawline and eyes so blue they shined like sapphires. Though he was wearing a mask, that chin was unmistakable.

Francis Tyler.

The band finished their number and dancers changed positions. Some rose from their tables and made for the floor, while others headed for the perimeter in search of refreshment. In the shifting crowd, he lost sight of Katya.

Augy took a glass of champagne from a passing waiter, just to have something to do with his hands. He smiled and nodded at people as they passed, wondering how many of them he might recognize if they hadn't been wearing masks. Was the chief of police here? The mayor?

Turning again, he saw that a tall, broad-shouldered man with chalky skin and a prominent Adam's apple had Katya in a social lasso. Augy had never seen such a forced smile as the one on her face. The man grabbed Katya's hand and lifted it to eye level to look at the dance card she had hanging from her wrist. She tried to pull away politely, but he tightened his grip. Katya's other hand clenched into a fist.

Augy threw back the champagne in one gulp and headed over.

"Your card's empty," the man said in a syrupy voice. "What do you say, doll face?"

"Sorry, boss." Augy stepped up beside Katya and pulled her wrist away from the interloper. "This dance is mine."

The man bristled and put out his thick bottom lip. "I don't see your name on the card."

"It's right there."

The man leaned in closer and Augy tweaked his nose.

"Ain't that a bite?"

Taking Katya by the hand, he led her away. She shot her suiter an apologetic gaze, but Augy tasted her relief through her skin.

It was imperative she not speak to anyone. They'd tried it out in the car, but her fake American accent was an affront to the language. And anybody who'd ever met her was likely to recognize her contralto Russian drawl. More importantly, he could tell the thought of any of these men putting their hands on her, even for a casual dance, made her feel like her dress was filling with land crabs. And not that it mattered much, but that same thought made Augy feel like somebody had strapped him to a tree and was about to use him for bayonet practice.

Two violins and a piano set the mood while a singer with bright white victory rolls and a polka-dotted dress took to the stage. Augy stepped up behind Katya. He took one hand gently and guided her arm out to the side, resting his other hand on her waist. She was breathing fast, her pulse like a bee's wings. He recognized the way her eyes were darting, the hard grip of her fingers on his, the tremor in her stance. She was on the verge of a panic attack.

Leaning close to her ear, he whispered words he'd always wanted to hear when he felt like the walls were closing in, but which nobody had ever said to him: "You don't have to stay here. We can leave right now."

She leaned back against his shoulder and looked into his eyes. She was close to tears, her red lips quivering. "We stay till the job's done," she said.

"You gonna be all right?"

She sighed and closed her eyes. "Promise you will not let me go."

"Not for every diamond-encrusted Rolex in this shithole." With a palm on her diaphragm, he leaned her weight against his chest and took slow measured breaths, silently encouraging her to do the same.

He could feel eyes on them, not the least of which belonged to the gentleman Katya had rejected. Augy was so tall, and she was so beautiful.

The band began in earnest—*Little Things Mean a Lot* by Kitty Kallen—and the singer started in with a crackling, juvenile alto.

"This is music?" he whispered to Katya, as they swayed lazily to the four-four rhythm. "I mean, if I wanted to listen to teenagers daydream…"

She snorted and took a real breath. "You are crotchety old man."

"Wanna hear something sad?" He spun her around to face him, then laying one hand on the small of her back began to lead her in a slow foxtrot. "I've been living in a car so long, listening to the radio by myself day and night, I know every word to this stupid song."

He slid his hand higher up her back and dipped her, watching the curve of her neck as she relaxed into the movement. When he pulled her back up, he spun her under his arm, then pulled her in so her own arm crossed her body and she was nestled in the crook of his, their shoulders touching.

"*Give me your arm as we cross the street.*" He sang into her ear. "*Call me at six on the dot.*"

She looked up at him. "*A line a day when you're far away. Little things mean a lot.*"

"Oh my goodness." He spun her again. "You're a goof too."

"I love top forty. Is problem?"

"Um… you're in your thirties."

"So?"

"So you should know better."

At last, a giggle chased away the lingering fear in her eyes. "You make me laugh."

"That's amazing."

"You have no idea."

They danced the rest of the song without speaking. He'd scarcely danced with anybody except Edith and he'd expected it to take some getting used to. Edith was a talented dancer, but she was always so concerned with technique and doing everything just so—she wouldn't let him lead. He tried to do it the way she told him. He even took private lessons to learn how to lead better and help her gain some confidence in him. But even though his dance instructor—a thousand-year-old Austrian woman with skin like tissue paper and legs of concrete—regularly praised him, he was never good enough for Edith. The ballroom became another battlefield until one night as they danced the Viennese waltz, he tried to change direction and she tugged his shoulder so hard it tripped them both.

He'd yanked away from her and shouted, "You wanna lead? Fine. I don't need this!"

The band stopped. Everyone stared. Augy lit a cigarette and marched to the bar where he planted his ass for the rest of the night. Edith had been humiliated. They argued all the way home. It was the last time they ever danced together.

Now that his rose-colored glasses had been torn off his face and buried six thousand miles beneath the surface of the earth, he realized he and Edith had argued a lot. In fact, it was their favorite pastime, even before the war. It was just after the war, it stopped being fun or sexy. She never trusted his judgment, so he fought tooth and nail against her every suggestion, even if he knew she was right.

How had he ever convinced himself they belonged together?

As they spun deftly across the floor, Katya leaned into his shoulders, closed her eyes, and followed his intentions with her body. Once or twice he tried a move, and she didn't quite attend, or she did a creative twirl or shimmy, but he adapted effortlessly. They'd known one another such a short time, and yet this woman—who felt so on edge with life—was at ease in his arms. And it crossed his mind that his arms had been empty all his life until this moment.

Gazing down at her face, his heart itched to take flight, but was grounded by a crushing sense of responsibility. He couldn't fail her. Not her, or her kids, or Sumika. But especially not her. He would see them through this if it killed him.

The music stopped, and the dancers parted to applaud.

"You really can dance," said Katya, her eyes still closed. She seemed dazed, a sleepy smile on her lips. He drew her closer and traced her jawline with the tips of two fingers, then grasped the back of her neck. They were both breathing audibly. She looked at his lips, then into his eyes.

"Kiss me," he said.

Her gaze focused. With the barest hint of a smile, Katya took his bottom lip between her teeth and tugged. Not a kiss, a challenge.

He suppressed a throaty moan, and ran one hand over her hips, coming to rest on her ass. "I've never known a body like yours. Is all of you so tight?"

"Yes." She pressed her forehead against his. "You have no ass."

He chuckled. "I know. It's a drag."

"But you have stomach, chest, shoulders." She pushed her palm against his abs. "You are hard and sharp."

"Please kiss me," he breathed. "I'm about to go crazy."

She moistened her bottom lip. Her eyes drifted closed as he moved closer.

Just then, the band started up; an unmistakable introduction raked his nerves, clawing the softness from his skin. Every muscle in his body constricted. The blood drained from his face. He turned wide eyes to the stage as the inept songstress began in her grating, childlike voice:

"You won't admit you love me
And so, how am I ever to know?
You always tell me
Perhaps, perhaps, perhaps."

"What is wrong?" said Katya.

"I think I'm gonna be sick."

Putting a hand on his shoulder, she led him off the floor. Dizzy and nauseous, he had to keep his eyes on his feet to keep from falling over. She led him to a small table at the back and helped him sit down. She put a glass of water in his hand and he tried to drink it, but it turned to ash in his mouth.

"A million times I ask you
And then I ask you over again
You only answer
Perhaps, perhaps, perhaps."

"I need a cigarette," he said. Laying a hand on the table, he watched it quiver so hard the silverware joined in. He put his hands in his lap and shook his head hard a few times. He was so cold, and yet burning, as if someone had force-fed him a bucket of dry ice.

Black filled his senses. A moonless night. Shining black eyes. A cascade of black hair. And red lightning blazing across black skin in waves. Her blackened face, expressionless. Inhuman.

"Here." She gave him a cigarette, sat down in front of him, and struck a match. The slim cylinder shook in his fingers.

After a few drags, he was able to lean back in his seat and close his eyes. A deep breath. He was not going to lose himself. Not tonight. Not here. Not now.

The song would end soon. It had never gone on so long before.

"What is wrong?" Katya asked again.

He forced himself to laugh. "I'm fine. It's just this song."

"You do not like Desi Arnez?"

"No. No, I don't." He cleared his throat. "It... reminds me of someone."

"Your ex-wife?"

He shook his head. "She led me to the man who led me to you, at the... at the place."

"She is dead." Katya sat back in her chair and looked at the floor.

"It was my fault."

"I do not think so."

"It was," he snapped. "There's no two ways about it. I should've died that day, not her."

"For what is worth, I am glad you are alive."

He fought the urge to tear off the suffocating mask. At last, the final notes of that god-awful song played and then fell to silence. Katya grabbed his hand, intertwining her fingers with his, and he took a deep breath, drawing energy from her as if from an outlet.

He looked up, searching for her eyes, but over her shoulder, the stiff-backed maître d' was coming out of the tent. Before the man closed the flap, Augy saw a long table set with gold-rimmed placemats and aperitif glasses.

He pointed towards the kitchen door with his nose. "It's now or never, gorgeous."

Fixing her lips into a frown, she nodded. He stood and started through the crowd. The band started up again—*Fever* by Peggy Lee. The party-goers snapped to the music and took to the floor for a bit of jive.

Augy circled around the dancefloor, headed vaguely for the house. It was good luck so many men were wearing top hats, which made it easier for him to pretend he wasn't so tall. If only Katya were homelier, they might've been downright inconspicuous.

Trying to push Lily Wong out of his mind was an impossible task, but allowing his guilt to overtake his good sense served no one. He pushed it down deep into the pit of his stomach to transform into an ulcer, with all the rest. No way he'd make it past forty with all that disease churning in his guts. The thought didn't depress him, as maybe it should have, but gave him the courage to do what needed to be done.

He'd never been good at making plans. All his life Augy had trusted in his cancerous guts to lead him, for his bumpy nose to point him in the right direction. At least this time, he had an outline.

He scanned the sides of the house for a second door or an opened window, but then he noticed a waiter standing off to the side by himself, enjoying a smoke break.

Augy turned to Katya. "You're my lookout."

She nodded, turned back towards the band, and swayed to the music.

Augy approached the young man, who stood just around the edge of the house so he could scarcely be seen from the garden. Flattening his hand, Augy rushed up behind him. He slid one arm around his neck, bracing the man's Adam's apple against his elbow, then grabbed onto his own bicep and put his other hand on the back of the man's head. Not so much as a squeak escaped his throat. Augy pushed back his shoulders, applying the rear naked choke with full force. The man struggled, but for only a few seconds. Augy counted off fifteen before he felt the waiter go limp in his arms, but he applied the choke for another five seconds afterward to make certain.

Augy dragged the body towards the house, behind a crop of lilac bushes, and laid it down in the dirt. He had between ten and twenty seconds before the waiter would start to wake up. He yanked off his jacket and mask and threw them on the ground. Then he took the waiter's coat, mask, and tie, and donned them. The waiter began to groan and mumble. Augy undressed him down to his socks and skivvies, then hogtied him with the legs of his own pants. He gagged him with his shirtsleeve. The waiter's drowsy eyes opened.

Augy ducked out of his line of sight. "Listen, son, there are two things you can do to make sure that you get out of this ordeal alive. Are you listening?"

The waiter nodded fervently, which caused his hogtied frame to sway from side to side.

"The first is don't struggle, don't try to escape, and don't make any noise until you hear sirens. You got me?"

Again, the body rocked in agreement.

"The second is to find yourself a different employer."

Standing, Augy ran his fingers through his hair, buttoned his jacket, straightened his posture, and headed back towards the party. As he passed Katya, he winked and whispered, "Two minutes."

He didn't wait to see her nod. He jogged up the steps into the house, following another waiter down the hall directly into the kitchen.

It was busy with noise and heat—plates clanking, chefs shouting, steam wafting above. Augy went to the waiter's station and began to load a silver tray with salmon mouse canapes. Once all the other waiters had gone back outside, and he was alone in his corner of the kitchen, Augy stalked deeper inside, his eyes scanning the countertops.

Finally, he saw a collection of about one hundred gold-rimmed appetizer plates set in neat rows. On each plate was a sprig of mint, a dab of shimmering yellow sauce, and one half-ounce portion of brown-red, raw liver.

Augy took the pack of cigarettes from his pocket and removed the vials of toxin. He was about to sprinkle the first plate when a man in a chef's uniform came from around the corner and shouted, "They aren't ready to go out yet! Get back to your station!"

Augy nodded and was about to walk away when a voice cut through the cacophony—ear-splittingly shrill. "Fire! Fire!"

The chef stiffened like a scared meerkat. He and Augy both started towards the sound, but the chef strong-armed his way past. Augy rushed back to the table and uncapped one of the vials of toxin. He worked quickly, dashing each portion of liver with the clear, sweet-smelling liquid before moving onto the next. He was about three-quarters of the way finished when he heard grumbling staffers returning to the kitchen. Working at breakneck speed, Augy finished dousing the remaining plates, then shoved the vials in his pants pocket and ducked away from the table.

From behind a screen of hanging pots and pans, Augy watched as the chef inspected and wiped a few of the plates. He snapped his fingers, and a flock of waiters came and loaded up the plates onto large serving platters and took them out of the kitchen.

Smiling, Augy stood and was about to leave when somebody whistled loudly from behind. "Hey, new guy! Get your ass in gear."

He hesitated, then walked back into the kitchen, picked up a tray of liver, and followed the procession. Outside, the dancefloor was empty, the band playing a mellow classical medley. The ladies were seated at the little round tables enjoying what looked like chocolate cakes. All the men were absent, but he could hear their voices inside the tent.

Augy stepped inside. A man wearing a mask that covered his whole face was standing at the head of the table giving a speech. The mask was hideous— a pink phallic nose, rosy cheeks, a pointed goatee, and laughing expression. Augy figured this was the party's host, Dr. Marvin Hoffman.

Augy and the other waiters served the plates, and the man continued, "This evening, gentlemen, we have a special treat for all of you. Provided for us by the brightest ray that shines from The Land of the Rising Sun, the incomparable Countess London..."

The men grunted a collective, "Here, here."

"For your delectation, tonight we invite you to partake of the liver of a Bolshevik."

CHAPTER THIRTY-TWO

Frank Tyler was among the diners, Augy realized with glee. That shovel-shaped superman chin, those glossy baby blues.

Following the lead of the other waiters, Augy took up a bottle of sweet red vermouth and commenced to fill the diner's aperitif glasses as Dr. Hoffman continued, "Fyodor Sokolov was a lieutenant in the Red Army during and after the German invasion in 1941, the thirteenth anniversary of which we celebrate tonight. He was a commander at the prisoner of war camp Zelendolsk on the Volga River, where he gained a reputation for running one of the most brutal operations in all of Russia. 3500 men went into his camp in late 1941. Half a year later, only 500 Germans were left alive. Sokolov and his men neglected to feed or clothe the prisoners, or provide them with any water. They let them die deliberately, starved entire barracks just to cut costs. He forced the prisoners to bury their own dead along the river, but soon there were so many, they were burying new bodies inside the decomposing remains of old ones.

"The beatings rarely came as a punishment," Hoffman continued. "They came with no rhyme or reason. There were several nationalities in the army that invaded Russia—Romanians, Yugoslavians, Poles. Sokolov forced the prisoners to line up and compelled each of them to say something, and when a word of German was spoken, he would break their teeth with a truncheon."

Hoffman's description of the camp was all too familiar, and Augy didn't doubt its validity. He suffered a twinge of sympathy until he remembered the so-called delicacy of which these men were about to partake.

Dr. Hoffman leaned over a chair and squeezed its back until it creaked. "In Russia, good Aryan soldiers were beaten, starved, humiliated, and forced to perform slave labor. It has been eight years since the official surrender of Nazi

Germany, and many soldiers are still captives in Russia, in the hands of men like Fyodor Sokolov."

Captivated by the speech and lost in his own thoughts, Augy spilled a drop of vermouth on the white tablecloth. The man whose glass he was filling chided him in German, but Augy didn't speak any German, so he moved onto the next glass without offering the man anything more than an apologetic smile.

"We are honored tonight by the presence of Lieutenant Gerhard Schäfer," Hoffman continued, "who spent nearly seven years, from 1943 until 1950, in Zelendolsk and other Russian POW camps. Lt. Schäfer, would you please stand?"

The man who got up from the table had translucent skin and corn nut teeth. His simple black eye mask concealed virtually nothing of his countenance. He lifted one stiff arm in that unmistakable salute and cried, "*Heil Hitler!*"

"*Seig Heil!*" came the programmed reply. Everyone stood and performed the salute—white and Japanese, foreign and American. Even the waiters passed their bottles of wine into their left hands, stood up straight, and extended the stiff arm. Augy was trying so hard to keep himself in the moment he'd fallen out of it. By the time he realized he ought to join the anachronistic *Sieg Heil*, the moment had passed. Most of the diners hadn't noticed and turned their eye to Lt. Schäfer, waiting for him to begin his story of woe. But one man—a sharp-eyed blond with a hawkish nose and skin of upholstery leather—locked his eyes on Augy and sneered.

The bottle of vermouth was empty and every diner had been served, so Augy made a quick exit. Before the tent flap closed, he saw the sharp-eyed man rise from his seat.

"Where're you going, Campbell?" someone said.

The women were still at their tables eating and chatting. Katya was not among them.

Augy made a beeline across the dancefloor towards the house. He'd been on his feet most of the last twenty hours. He'd managed to suppress it on the dancefloor, but now the pain was such that he couldn't walk quickly without limping. Somehow, he managed to lope up the stairs into the house before the man stepped out of the tent. Augy pressed himself against a wall in the foyer and peeked out of the window. The sharp-eyed man scanned the party.

Sneering, he stepped towards a table of women. They spoke for a while until one of the women pointed towards the house.

Augy hurried out of the foyer and down the hall. He came to a bathroom and locked himself inside. He needed to leave, but he couldn't do that until he'd confirmed it with his own eyes. Climbing over the toilet, he peeked through the wooden blinds towards the tent. He reached for a cigarette and had almost lit it before he remembered. He crushed the pack and threw it away.

He watched the movements of looming silhouettes in the backlit tent. After a few moments, everyone took their seats. Hands lifted tiny glasses in a toast. Then, at last, the men lifted forks to their mouths.

Augy smiled. There was no going back for them now.

Augy had first learned about fugu in Japan. Not all the guards in Hokkaido were cold-blooded monsters. Sure, they thought Augy, as a white man and an American—the worst breed of white man—was a racially inferior carbuncle. But people are people, and even in such abominable circumstances, some people just want to connect.

Private Suguro was one such person. Nineteen years old and stick-thin with fishbowl brown eyes and a wispy mustache, he regularly had the nightshift standing outside the barracks where Augy and one hundred and fifty of his fellow slave laborers slept. Or rather where Augy sweated through his sheets and tossed and turned, in spite of bone-deep exhaustion. He'd never had any problem with the dark before that first thirty-day long excursion into the center of the earth to shake hands with the devil, during which forty-five of his fellow prisoners had died of asphyxiation, exhaustion, starvation, accidents, and savage beatings. The terror came quickly and overtook him, so Augy found himself seeking out the light of Suguro's lantern night after night.

It started as small talk. Where you from? How'd you end up a soldier? Read any good books lately? On the fourth night, Augy had asked about Suguro's family. With a conspiratorial smile, the soldier had produced a photo of identical twin teenage girls on a beach in white one-piece swimming suits, smiling at the camera, their short hair in curls, their makeup impeccable. He'd explained the one on the left was his sweetheart, Akari. Augy still remembered the girl's name because she was, unequivocally, Suguro's favorite topic of conversation. Augy had happily listened to every anecdote and asked all the right questions; Suguro shared his cigarettes.

Food was their second favorite topic. They were both hungry. Augy found out the rations the guards got were scarcely more than what they gave the prisoners. Augy waxed poetic about Mexican food—enchiladas and tacos, mole and pozole, tamales and guacamole. Suguro had given him a crash course in yakitori, ramen, and okonomiyaki. And finally, he told him about the one food the Emperor was forbidden by law to eat.

"Yeah, yeah. I know what a pufferfish is," said Augy, rolling cigarettes for the pair of them. Suguro had been impressed how his rollies never had humps. "They have some at the aquarium in San Diego. Little bastards swell up like balloons when you tap on the glass."

"They're poisonous."

"No kidding?"

"One fish is enough to kill thirty people. The female tiger puffer during mating season has enough poison to kill twice that just in her ovaries."

"And ya'll eat them?" Augy whistled. "Say what you will, but you Japs do not shy from the grim reaper. Kick him in the cock every chance you get."

Suguro laughed and struck a match. They were sat on the steps outside the barracks, a brick and bamboo hovel stuck in a muddy quagmire in what had once been a lush forest. Barbed wire encircled the area, but only four guards were stationed along the perimeter. It would've been easy enough to escape, but there wasn't much point. A six-foot-three white man had about as much chance of blending into the local population as he had of turning into a fish. Two Brits had gone for it anyhow not long after Augy first came to the mine. Within a week they were apprehended and returned to camp. They were stood in front of a machine gun, which Augy had expected. What he hadn't expected was for the guards to pick out ten more random POWs and put them to the gun, too.

Escape was worse than suicide. It was murder.

It would've been nothing to distract Suguro and make a break for it, but that was the furthest thing from Augy's mind. All he wanted was a cigarette. And over the months, he'd come to enjoy the young man's company.

"Fugu is a delicacy," Suguro continued. "It's very expensive, too. I've only had it once. I tell you, it is a flavor you never forget. You have to leave a trace of poison to get the full effect, but one-tenth of a drop too much, and you will go the way of all flesh."

"So what happens exactly if you get too much? You just fall over dead?"

"You'll wish you had. It only takes about five minutes before you realize something is wrong. It starts with a tingling sensation in the mouth that travels down the throat. Then you get dizzy and start to vomit. Next, your muscles seize up and you lose the ability to move. But you remain conscious the entire time, as the poison eats your nervous system. Eventually, you suffocate."

"And you find that appetizing, do you?"

Suguro wiggled his eyebrows. "You've never tasted it."

Augy wanted to see what happened to the cannibals inside the tent, especially Frank Tyler. He wanted to witness the expression on his face when he realized something was wrong. He wanted to watch him vomit and fall over. He wanted to see the light go out in his eyes.

His gaze swept the ballroom, but Katya was nowhere to be seen. He didn't know how she'd gotten into the house to scream fire and give him the distraction he'd so needed, or how she'd gotten out again, if she'd gotten out again. They'd agreed that once the deed was done, they'd meet back at the car. He hoped she'd already gone.

He couldn't believe there wasn't any security for such a prestigious, and thoroughly illegal, soiree. Many of the attendees were veterans, so maybe they figured they could handle anything that came up. Either that, or they'd all grown so comfortable in the bosom of their police friends, they didn't worry much about consequences, legal or otherwise.

He knew they'd eaten the liver, but something in his gut wouldn't let him leave it at that. Had Tyler eaten his portion yet? Had he swallowed all of it?

It was wrong. Reckless. Stupid, even. But he had to see it with his own eyes. He couldn't stop thinking about what Tyler had done. Buying Katya from the Countess, forcing her into the role of his loving wife, tormenting his own children to keep her in line. Assuming the man was dead would never be enough. He had to watch it happen.

The sharp-eyed man was nowhere on the dancefloor. He must be in the house, searching room by room for the waiter who'd stupidly neglected to heil Hitler with everybody else.

"Campbell..." Augy whispered, his sluggish memory catching up. It was the name Sumika had given of the man who'd purchased her from the orphanage when she was five years old. The man who'd kept her in his home until she grew too old to amuse him anymore. Then he'd taken her to the Countess's annual party and disposed of her like an old piece of furniture, ripping her body to pieces before throwing it onto a garbage heap.

Augy sneaked out of the bathroom. Making his way down the hall towards the door, he passed a waiter and relieved him of his tray of champagne glasses.

"What's the big idea?" the man protested.

"Chef has a special job for you," Augy replied. "Asked for you on the double. I'll take care of this."

The waiter nodded and hurried inside. Augy held the tray up near his face, using it as a shield as he scurried towards the tent as fast as his gimpy foot would carry him. When he got to the tent, he circled around back into the relative safety of the shrubs.

He grinned at the sound of panicked voices and glass smashing on the floor.

Augy got down on his knees to peek under the fabric. Bodies covered the floor, racked with violent convulsions, vomiting on themselves and on one another. Many of the men had ripped off their masks.

What do you know? Tyler did know the mayor, after all.

And there was old mister shovel-face himself—pawing at his bulging neck, his blue eyes bugging out as he gasped for oxygen like a fish in the bottom of a boat.

Augy grinned and was about to make his exit when the bush rustled behind him. He tried to turn, but something heavy smashed into his skull. His vision flashed white. Blood filled his mouth, his senses. Laid out on his back, blurry eyes searched the gray. The outline of a hawkish nose. He moved for his gun, but a boot came down on his face. Swirling light. A sensation of falling. Another blow. Then nothing.

CHAPTER THIRTY-THREE

Flashes of dull light. Movement. Blood thrumming in his ears. His tongue felt swollen. Voices floated over his head, two men. Unintelligible. He realized they were holding onto his arms, dragging his limp body. A rush of fear and his eyes snapped open. A long hallway stretched before him as if in a fisheye lens. A line of buzzing lights on the ceiling, iron doors along the walls. A woman in white with a nurse's cap stepped out of their way. She had a needle in her hand.

"Where am I?" he tried to say.

They passed through a door. He smelled fire and gasoline long before he felt the heat. He tried to struggle, but his brain was detached from his body. Even twitching his fingers took a herculean effort.

The men pulled his shirt and jacket off one arm, and Augy saw enough of their faces to realize one of them was Campbell. They pushed him face-first against a wall and secured his wrists into leather cuffs dangling from the ceiling. He groaned at the excruciating strain. Planting his feet, he locked his knees and leaned his weight against the warm tile.

The room wobbled like a mirage in the heat. The high-pitched ringing in his ears grew louder. On one wall was a small buoy-shaped incinerator made of concrete and black metal. The grate was open and a long pole shoved inside. It had a delicate handle of swirled metal like an Italian rapier.

A door creaked. He strained to look behind him, but it was hopeless.

"Hello again, Mr. Small."

Her feet were silent as she stepped up to the incinerator and removed her branding iron. Augy thrashed, but the two men held him steady. The hot iron touched his shoulder. Skin bubbled and hissed. He clenched his teeth to stifle a scream, but a bestial growl radiated through his chest.

She held the iron in place for what seemed like forever. He pushed his forehead hard against the tile, forcing himself to breathe through the pain. He was so dizzy. When at last she removed the iron, his feet slipped out. The men unbuckled the straps and let him fall in a heap to the ground.

Balancing on his knuckles, he turned to look at that face. The gray skin, the colorless eyes, the hard parallel lines. Her flat lips furrowed, then curled into a sneer.

"You were right," she said, tossing the branding iron back into the incinerator. "I do feel like god."

The fever was in his throat as well as his brain. He chuckled dryly and shook his head. "That's how I felt after poisoning a hundred of your men."

Campbell punched him in the face. His body collapsed. Those damn stitches broke open again and a spurt of blood cascaded into his eyes. Campbell yanked him up by his neck. Augy spat blood all over his face.

"I'll break your fucking legs!" cried Campbell.

"You will do no such thing," said the Countess. Campbell folded like a cheap camera. He dropped Augy and slinked towards the corner, a naughty child. The Countess never even looked at him.

"Tetrodotoxin," she said. "Was that supposed to be a joke?"

Augy wiped the blood from his eyes and bared pink teeth. "You're the joke."

"I think perhaps I was wrong. You do need more time in the dark." Turning on a heel, she headed towards the door. "Take him to the pit."

The moment she'd left, Campbell straightened and loomed closer, cracking his knuckles. Augy smirked and said, "That would make you Papa Campbell, wouldn't it?"

The hawkish features deformed; piercing black eyes widened and lips pursed.

"Sumika wanted me to tell you, she's counting the days till she sees you again." Augy began to laugh, but Campbell punched him in the head again. Everything went black.

Augy awoke with a scream stuck in his throat. He coughed and shuddered. Rolling onto his hands and knees, he hacked on bile and blood. The smell of plastic, iron, and rubbing alcohol filled his lungs. He choked, an empty stomach growling as he vomited nothing but air.

Under his fingers were tiles coated in cold slime. He couldn't see his own hand an inch from his face. Silence, save his own breath—quicker and shallower with each inhalation

His heart pounded in his ears, blood swelling in his fingertips. Complete blackness pressed on his lungs like a millstone. His ribs cracked under the weight, lungs filling with water. There was no air in this room.

He sprang to his feet. Pain coated his body, but he barely felt it. Putting out his hands he rushed in one direction, but in a few steps, he touched the wall. More slime. More tile. He heard a choked sob, his own voice half a mile away.

With one trembling hand on the wall, he walked the perimeter of the room. At most a ten-by-ten foot square. At last, he found a door—the cold touch of iron. No handle. Not so much as a keyhole.

He heard someone crying. Pushing his back against the door, he buried his face in his hands. His mouth felt so dry, tongue coated in sand. How long had it been since he'd had a drink of water? The sand poured down his windpipe, filling his chest. Coughing, he tried to wet his mouth with saliva but nothing would come. His tongue was swelling. He wiped his lips over and over, even wiped his tongue trying to scrape off the sand. Nothing helped.

"Let me out, please. For the love of God," came a man's voice, weak and trembling.

"No." He smacked the back of his head against the door. "No. I won't."

She knew. She knew all about him. About Hokkaido. She even knew about the dark. That's why he was here, why he wasn't dead yet. Would she leave him in here until he died, or was she softening him up? Would his last breath be taken in crushing darkness or under the garish lights of an operating room?

"Please, I can't breathe," said a voice, the very sound of insanity. "You have to let me out."

A club connected with his stomach. The air shot out of his mouth, wrapped in blood. He pissed his pants. He hit the ground. The guard hit him again and again, as he cried and struggled. It was like a heart attack: a vise tightening around his chest and stomach, crushing his organs. The pain radiated to his brain, limbs, face, and even beyond into that unnamable something that makes flesh human. Intense, inexplicable pain stole his breath, stilled his blood, choked off his tongue.

At last, the beating ended. His ribs were fractured, his leg broken, his shoulder dislocated. Coal dust filled his eyes and mouth, mingling with blood to make a choking black sludge. Like the darkness itself, it filled his entire body.

"Please," he choked out. "Just kill me."

The guard laughed and spat on him.

"Stop! Stop it!" he screamed, but his voice was muffled. It was absorbed by the gloom unheard. He grabbed his hair and pulled, trying to force back what he knew were just memories.

The crying grew louder, more miserable. And a voice kept saying, "No, no, no, no, no..."

"Get up," came the guard's voice, and a boot jabbed him in the gut. When he looked up, he saw the faint flicker of a lantern illuminating the man's face. He wanted to rise to the light, but his body wouldn't move. His bones were made of marble and he lacked the strength to lift them. Hands clasped around his throat, choking the life out of him.

"No, no, no, no..."

"Get up."

The foot connected with his face, breaking his nose. He lost consciousness then. A small mercy. He crashed into black water. Peace and silence soaked into his skin. Death was closer than ever before.

On the horizon, he saw a rush of silver bubbles and a face. Luminous and yet colorless, like the ocean under starlight. Hadn't it once shimmered in shades of red and blue? He saw her eyes brimming with tears, holding her handkerchief to her cheek as he boarded the boat that would take him to the other side of the world.

He'd promised he'd come back to her.

When his vision cleared, he somehow managed to stand. The guard grabbed his pickaxe and thrust it into his arms. And Augy knew he had to keep living, to keep working, to get back to her.

But there was no getting out this time. There was no work to be done. No army was fighting to liberate him. He couldn't be used as a bargaining chip. All his enemies wanted was for him to suffer as much as possible before they cut him apart.

"Don't," said a trembling voice he barely recognized. He realized he was the one crying, doubled over on the cold tile floor, weeping into his hands.

He'd forgotten time, where he was and where he had been. He'd even forgotten what mattered now, and the meaning he'd lost long ago. Every breath he didn't take sent him further back. He had to keep his mind in the moment. He had to find composure.

"Breathe!"

Over and over, the darkness rushed him. Emptiness like cancer in his heart. Too late. His life was over. He'd given everything he had to give.

"Breathe…"

He prayed Katya had made it out. As long as she kept living, and Sumika kept living, his death could have meaning. Maybe they would even remember him and everything he tried to do, rather than his crushing failures. They were worth so much more than him.

At last, it was his turn to die so somebody else could live.

He saw her face before him in full color: eyes of gold and cognac, dark hair, and full lips. Her earthy sweetness filled his senses, her weight resting on his chest.

He should've kissed her when he had the chance.

"Breathe."

The voice sounded calmer this time, no longer shouting at him from a thousand miles away, but nestled in his own throat. At last, he sucked in a gasp of foul air.

He was alone in the dark. Trapped. But there is always one way out. No matter what they did to him, sooner or later he would die. The neurons that made his personality would cease to fire. His relentlessly thrumming heart would go silent. The cold would cover his flesh, and his blood would stop its tireless uphill flow.

Closing his eyes changed nothing. They burned and ached, and the darkness was the same. Infinite, immutable, dumbfounding. But he closed them anyway. He sat up, resting his back against the wall and laid a hand on his chest. He tried to ignore the hammer of his heart and took slow, deep breaths, filling his lungs to the brim before releasing. He counted his inhalations. Two seconds. Four.

He felt nails digging into his knee. He brought his hand to rest in his lap.

Six seconds.

It was too late for him. His mind had been cracked open and left bleeding years ago. Still, he refused to let her break him so easily. It was going to take more than a little darkness.

The guard was a phantom. The crushing pain in his chest a memory. He'd leave the screaming and the begging in the past too, where it belonged.

For all he knew, she was right outside the door listening. Or perhaps his reactions were being recorded for the sake of what she called *science*. He would not give her, or any of them, the satisfaction of listening to his screams. He would swallow them all, fuel the cancer in his gut. What did that matter anymore?

Seven seconds.

CHAPTER THIRTY-FOUR

Time had never been his friend. While most people had at least the illusion of a linear progression of moments, Augy spent the last decade rebounding between past and present, blocked off from even dreams of the future. Now his surroundings matched his insides. Time was meaningless in such darkness. The sun and moon ceased to exist, all natural rhythms forgotten. He couldn't retreat into memories, he couldn't live in the present, and there was no future.

Sleep was his only respite. He was so exhausted. It seemed weeks since he'd slept. It was freezing in the room, but they'd left him in the clothes he'd been wearing—thick wool pants and jacket, starched shirt, leather gloves. So in spite of the cold, he was able to find sleep curled up on the slick tile. In dreams, there was color and light. Even nightmares were a welcomed relief from the melancholy, the wearisomeness of his own company.

When he was awake, he would push hard on his eyes and watch the bursts of color that appeared, neon fireworks in the darkness. Employing his encyclopedic knowledge of both popular and R & B music, Augy sang the hours away. Patti Page, Jo Stafford, Frankie Laine. Dinah Washington, Fats Waller, Etta James. He had a serviceable singing voice at the start, but as time wore on, it began to crack and fray.

He was so thirsty. The cold, hunger, pain, and despair all took a backseat to his thirst. He'd learned in the service that the average person can survive about one hundred hours without water, more in such cool temperatures. No doubt that's what would kill him. Four or five days was not such a long time to wait.

He'd taken off his waistcoat and wadded it up in one corner so he could piss on it and avoid getting urine all over the rest of the cell. As time went on, he never used it. When he touched his own skin, it was beginning to shrivel. If he stood he'd feel faint, and he slept more and more. His organs were beginning to shut down. His blood was turning to sludge, and the toxins were building up in his liver and kidneys, with no way to void them. Death was so close. Every time he closed his eyes he hoped it would be the last, but time after time he awoke in the darkness.

He guessed it was the third or fourth day when he was startled awake by a heavy iron whoosh. Light blazed forth. He shrank from it; it burned his corneas. At first, he thought he was dreaming. Only the smell of the cell convinced him otherwise—the plastic and urine. His own rotting body.

Squinting, he examined a square of pure white no bigger than a piece of paper. The blue tiles of his cell shimmered in the light. A hand pushed a sweaty jug of water through the opening, followed by a small bowl of what looked like rice and seaweed.

Augy crawled towards the light. He snatched one of the chopsticks from the bowl and thrust it towards the opening as it slammed closed. The Judas gate hit the tip of the chopstick, preventing it from latching. A sliver of light remained. Holding his breath, he waited, listened, and prayed the person hadn't noticed. The dull creak of a metal cart—the first noise he'd heard in days other than his own voice. Footfalls. The rattle of chains. A door creaked open then slammed shut. Silence.

He waited for the space of one hundred breaths, then carefully lifted the chopstick and got his fingers under the gate. It weighed thirty pounds or so, but he barely had the strength to push it. He used one of the chopsticks to prop it open and set up the other to jam it should it slam shut, then sat back and basked in the buzzing electric light.

The water glistening in the jug was more beautiful than a spray of stars on a moonless desert night. Every instinct in his lizard brain told him to lunge for it, drink it all, and save his own life. But he didn't move. He was so close to the end. That water was nothing more than a promise of more days trapped in darkness. More suffering.

He bent to the Judas gate and pressed his cheek against the floor to look out. Twists of pipes and wires covered the concrete walls. To his right stretched a hallway lined with steel doors, each with a heavy iron bar holding it closed. A clipboard hung beside each door on a rusty nail. He could only assume those were the *patients* charts and wondered what might be written on his.

To the left, he saw a stainless steel door with a keyed lock. It had to be the way out.

Sitting up, he peeled off the gloves and looked at his own hands in the light. Still wrapped in long twists of sodden bandages. The tips of his fingers were dimpled as if he'd sat in the tub too long, his skin so white it glowed. Did skin forget the sun so quickly?

Unbidden memories of the woman in the cage filled him. Moonbeams on her face, what could've been beautiful if only a little sunlight touched it. He flinched, trying to force back the image of that face peeling away, leaving behind oddments of brains and bones. At the time, he hadn't understood why she did it. He was offering her an escape from her suffering, but she couldn't bring herself to accept it. She so belonged to misery only death promised relief.

He used to think he understood the depths of human suffering, but there was further to sink. He'd never truly experienced hopelessness. Even at the hospital in Tokyo, the dread of pain was so hot and acute, it overrode the dull, moist throb of hopelessness. Now, gazing at the pitcher of water, it all made sense. Now, he knew.

If their places had been switched, would he have seen the gun as a way out, as she did?

He looked at the water.

The human capacity for cruelty never ceased to astound him. No matter how many horrible stories he heard or unspeakable things he witnessed, it seemed it could always get worse.

"Human beings are an infection," said Dr. Katsuki Muto.

Augy looked up. The young doctor leaned against the wall opposite him, smoking a cigarette. His wild eyes sparkled in the dim light, like the water in the jug. He handed a cigarette to Augy.

"You're right." Augy tilted his head against the wall, inhaling the familiar taste. "I never thought you were. Even with everything that happened. War is hell. I know that. But I guess I always believed that once it was over, and we all got back to ordinary civilian life, things would be different. People would be different. Better. There had already been so much death."

"Not enough. All of us. And all of them. And all of you."

"Why? Why does it have to be like this? Why did she have to keep it going?"

"She told you why," said Katsuki Muto, looming closer. "You just don't want to believe it."

"She told me individuals in the US government fought hard to have this happen in our country, but why would anybody subject their own people to this?"

"The Chinese, they aren't people."

Augy scoffed and shook his head. "Or the blacks or the Jews or the Russians. Or anybody who's poor, for that matter. They aren't people either, are they?"

"You ask your own government." He shrugged. "They aren't the same as us, are they? You and me, we didn't have to be a part of this. In our own ways, we both chose it. People like Sumika... like the rest of the poor bastards in this place. They never had a choice."

Augy pushed a fist against his forehead. "You think that makes it easier for me to die like this? For you to die, the way you did..."

"It was easy enough." When Augy looked up again, Muto's face had changed. A pink bullet hole pulsed in his temple, black blood dripping down the side of his neck.

"They made a deal, didn't they?" The words turned to ash in Augy's mouth. "Like the Germans did for their weapons technology. The US let them off easy—the people who did these things in Manchuria. They let them off, because they wanted the information. They wanted to know everything the Japanese learned opening up the human machine and observing its moving parts."

"Special Agent 973 Michael Heller," said Muto, nodding slowly. "And others like him, working hard to make sure the Countess and those in her employ get every bit of support they need."

"They wanted her to keep working, The Countess."

"But unlike offering immunity to doctors still in Japan," said Muto, "they couldn't afford to outright support this sort of operation happening within their own borders. At least not financially. The government couldn't leave a paper trail."

Using the wall as support, Augy stood and began to pace on wobbling legs. "They helped connect her to private enterprise, private donors. Men like Frank Tyler who were willing to accept human beings as compensation."

"People like the Hollisters and Mr. Moriyama who could procure logs for her, for a fee."

"Christ." Augy thumped the back of his head on the door. "How could I be so blind?"

"Patriotism is willful blindness, Mr. Small."

Augy started at the sound of this new voice. Holding a breath, he turned. Katsuki Muto was gone and Countess London stood in his place. She wore scrubs and a rubber apron. On her head was a white surgical cap. A medical mask dangled from one ear. Her wedge-shaped eyes glowed like a cat's in the dim light. She took a measured step towards him. He scurried back, pressing himself into one corner.

"It's all in the name of science," she said. "Do you know how many lives my work is going to save?"

"You're supposed to be a doctor. How can you justify killing people the way you do?"

"People die every day, Mr. Small. They die of things like cancer and heart disease, ailments that could be prevented if only doctors understood them better."

What little strength he had drained from his legs. He barely caught himself before fainting, slowly taking one knee, and then the other. She approached gingerly. Such a small woman—less than five feet tall—and yet, she filled the room.

"You never went to see your father as he lay dying in the hospital."

The emotions crashed against him like a tsunami. He buried his face into his hands, weeping phantom tears. "I couldn't. After... after everything."

"You'd only been back home a few weeks, and you couldn't bear to be in that place." She sighed, folding her hands in front of her. The rubber gloves squeaked. "He died of stomach cancer. And there was nothing the doctors could do."

"I should've gone to see him..."

"There was nothing the doctors could do, because they didn't understand the inner workings of the human machine. He died like thousands die every day, of preventable causes. And it's because nothing was learned from his death. His death had no meaning."

"Shut up. Stop talking."

"*If there is meaning in life at all, then there must be a meaning in suffering... Without suffering and death, human life cannot be complete.*"

"How dare you..." Rage coursed into his veins, tightening his fists and jaw.

"My patients' deaths have meaning. Your father would've understood that." She stepped closer and laid her froglike hand on his shoulder. It sent a shock of lightning through his bones, forcing his heart into arrhythmic palpitations. "Don't you want your death to have meaning, Mr. Small?"

"Get your hand off me."

"Drink the water."

"Get your hand off me!" He slapped her wrist away, then lunged. His fingers wrapped around her throat. She thrashed and grabbed his hands, like iron claws on her slight neck. Forcing her down on the ground, he straddled her chest, throwing his weight into the choke. Short legs kicked. Gray skin paled and turned blue. Her eyes boggled and rolled back.

He became aware of cold tiles under his touch. With a deep breath, he scrutinized his empty cell. His own sobs echoed as he crawled to the glistening water.

"I will kill you, Countess London." He lifted the pitcher, smooth glass under rough, shaking hands. "And it won't mean a goddamn thing."

CHAPTER THIRTY-FIVE

He ate the food and drank the water, then slept for an indeterminate period of time. Augy felt almost human again. The light energized him, chasing away debilitating shadows, and for the first time, he allowed himself to entertain fantasies of escape.

He made splinters of the wooden chopsticks and used them to jam the latch on the Judas gate so it wouldn't lock in place, even if it closed all the way. The gate opened vertically to a ninety-degree angle, blocking all attempts to reach the heavy door bar. Pressing himself hard against the slimy floor, he was able to twist one arm up and finger the hinges on the gate. Long rusty bolts held each. He tried to grip the head of one bolt to yank it free, but after several attempts only succeeded in tattering his nails.

"Motherfuck!" he hissed as one nail ripped down into the bed. Chewing it off, he took stock of his options. He needed something hard, thin, and metal to pry loose the bolt. The edges of his belt buckle were far too thick. He had nothing else.

"Except..."

Crawling on his hands and knees, he searched the floor for his sock suspenders, as he'd discarded the uncomfortable things after day one. He found them lying near enough the crumpled waistcoat, they were crusty with piss. Each comprised a circle of elastic webbing, a clasp, and two clips on tight hinges. He opened one of the clips. One half had short teeth for grabbing fabric, but the other side was a smooth ledge.

He pressed an arm through the Judas gate. It took twenty minutes to clasp the end of the bolt with the clip, then he wrapped it with the elastic to prevent it slipping. Applying as much force as possible, he tried to work the bolt out by twisting it from side to side. His first attempt failed, and the clip slid off. He repositioned and tried again. And again. It wasn't until the eighth try that the bolt budged in the least, but after that, he was able to yank it far enough out to clasp it with his fingers and pull it free.

The gate shifted, putting more weight on the second hinge. He propped it up using the empty water jug. He examined the clip of the suspenders. Other than some scuffs on the finish, it was still in shipshape. These were quality stainless steel construction, and for the first time, Augy was grateful he hadn't skimped on his party clothes.

He got to work on the second bolt, which was tighter after the removal of the first. His injured hands were stiff and filled with pins and needles. He had to keep shaking them out to maintain any strength. It took an hour at least before the bolt moved, and every subsequent millimeter was just as hard-fought. Five or six hours passed by the time he had the bolt out far enough to grasp it in his palm and yank it free.

The gate fell to the ground with a clunk, shattering the water jug. Augy grabbed the ten by six hunk of iron and pulled it into his cell.

By looking at the door across the hall, he guessed where the bar was that held his cell door closed. With the Judas gate out of the way, he could reach up through the hole. And if he stretched himself to the point where the skin under his arm was so tight it felt like it might rip, he could touch it with the tip of his middle finger.

Even with the boost of food and water, he was still nine-tenths dead and shaking wretchedly. He took a moment to rest his arms and roll his shoulders.

How long would it be before the person with the squeaky cart came back? He wasn't the only prisoner down here. Any moment someone may come, see the damage, and what may be his only chance of escape would be devastated.

Grasping the small iron door in one hand, he threaded his arm through the hole. He could barely lift it, let alone keep it steady. He lacked the strength to try at this over and over. If he dropped the door and it landed out of reach, there was no going back.

Closing his eyes, he took one deep breath and then another. He counted the length of his inhalations. One second. Three. Five.

A low-pitched wail filled his throat as he pushed with all his might. His abs and ribs screamed in pain. His arm shivered. Muscles puffed with air. He fumbled the iron gate. It crashed to the ground with a clang, splitting the tile. A second hunk of cold iron landed on top of it.

Augy fell back panting, his vision blurry with starbursts. With one trembling hand, he pushed on the door. It creaked but didn't move. He rolled over and pushed both his feet against it.

Light spilled over him as it inched open. The air in the hallway was like nitrous oxide. He began to laugh hysterically, and it took several minutes for him to gain enough control over himself to roll to his hands and knees and find his feet.

A line of bulbs buzzed in cages along a ceiling so low he had to slouch beneath it. He grabbed the clipboard that hung on the wall beside his cell door. It was written in English, and he understood now why Countess London branded her victims in English, too. Many of her operators were not Japanese or even Germans, but so-called red-blooded Americans.

He read:

Patient 94150960. Admitted 3:45 AM, 6/23/1954.

Height 190.5cm. Weight: 74kg. Overall health: adequate.

Treating physician: Dr. London.

Treatment plan: No rations for 80 hours, then rations once daily. Special diet: 2 cups rice, ¼ cup stewed seaweed, 3 pickles. Scheduled operation date and time, 7/15/1954, 10:00 am, OT. Do not sedate.

ATTENTION: Unit Zero designation, priority case. Patient is not to be moved, treated, administered, socialized, or disposed of without the express written consent of Dr. London.

Augy scoffed. "She sure knows how to make a guy feel special."

Replacing the clipboard, he walked to the exit door for a closer look. It was solid steel, with no peephole, no handle, no exposed hinges. Nothing but a slit of a keyhole too tiny to peep through. He had about as much chance of picking it as a blind drunk with palsy. He'd have to wait for the squeaky cart and try to brain whoever was steering before they got the better of him.

It occurred to him to open the other cells, yet he hesitated. The woman in the cage filled his senses. He lacked the strength, resources, and mental fortitude to handle another such situation. But he also couldn't leave a human being in similar circumstances to those he'd endured for the past three-plus days. He decided to read the charts.

Eight rooms lined the hall, including his own: B-01, B-02, etc. Five of the charts were blank. He read the sixth:

Patient 94167022. Admitted 9/4/1947.

Height 156 cm. Weight: 69.3kg. Overall health: good.

Treating physician: Dr. Walker.

Treatment plan: Continuing 1947 solitary confinement/sensory deprivation study, 8419. Rations once daily. Quarterly physical performed under sedation by acting nurse. Collect recordings and clean cell.

Shuddering, he replaced the chart. Seven years in solitary confinement. Augy had been ready to kill himself after a few days.

He laid his fingers on the door bar and chewed his bottom lip. Every instinct told him not to open it. This person had to be too far gone to be trusted.

Besides, every time he tried to help, people died.

Getting down on his knees, he inhaled deeply and opened the latch on the Judas gate.

A wall of stench hit like a septic tank layered with old gym socks. Augy covered his mouth and nose to keep from gagging. One flickering lightbulb illuminated the cell. The floor and walls were smeared with human waste. In the far corner, a mass of hair and naked brown flesh rocked back and forth, slapping their knees over and over to some unheard, arrhythmic music. Pink sockets filled the space where eyes should've been, with lumps of scar tissue where ears had been taken off.

Augy closed the gate. There was nothing he could do.

For the first time, he wondered if the operation the Countess had him scheduled for would kill him, or if she would mutilate him, then sit back and watch the results.

He shuddered away from the thought. When he entertained such paralyzing ideas, the fog of hopelessness crept back into his psyche, obscuring every reason he had to stay strong.

Standing, he walked to the last door and lifted the chart:

Patient 14150776. Admitted 5:40 PM, 6/24/1954.

Height 173cm. Weight: 67kg. Overall health: excellent.

Treating physician: Dr. London.

Treatment plan: Do not treat. Double rations twice daily. Provide chamber pot and empty daily. Patient is an addendum to Unit Zero Patient 94150960. Bathe and bring to OT at 10:20 am, 7/15/1954.

"Addendum?" he wondered aloud.

It wasn't Katya. He had her number memorized: 13851677, the number that had started all of this. And Sumika didn't fit the physical description.

Augy knelt to peer through the gate. The cell stank like bleach and burnt plastic. Pale blue tiles glowed dully in fluorescent light. The sound of sniffling and hastened breath. A woman.

"Hello?" he called.

A harsh inhalation. "Who's there?"

He recognized the voice instantly. His heart sank. "Edith?"

"Augy?" Shoes squeaked on the tile as she scrambled into view. All he saw was a flash of pale leg. He was about to stand to lift the door bar when he heard a chain brush against the steel exit door.

"Stay quiet," he said, and let the gate slam shut before she had a chance to argue. He rushed back to his own cell and swept the broken glass back through the open door before closing it, replacing the door bar, and laying the broken gate in front of the hole. A key scraped in the lock. He hurried towards the door and pressed himself into a corner so when it opened, he would be hidden behind it. He took off his belt and wrapped one end around his knuckles.

The door creaked then whooshed open. Those same squeaky wheels inched inside. The back of a ruddy head appeared. A nurse's hat.

She wheeled the cart farther in. He sensed she was about to turn to shut the door, so he shouldered it closed and lunged. He wrapped the belt around her neck and twisted the ends together. She didn't even get the chance to scream.

When she fell unconscious, he released the pressure and let her limp body crash to the ground. Putting his belt back on, he looked her up and down. He didn't see a face, only what might be useful. He took the chain of keys from around her wrist, then riffled through her pockets. When he came upon the familiar rectangle, his throat swelled with a snicker.

Standing back, he lit a cigarette, then stashed the lighter in his pocket. He thought to take her clothes, but she was too short and skinny for them to be any good, so he dragged her by the arms into one of the empty cells and locked her in. A mere twenty seconds of strangulation probably wouldn't be enough to kill her, not that he cared either way.

Darting back to Edith's cell, he threw open the door. She rushed into his arms, sobbing uncontrollably. Again and again, she tried to speak, but her words were little more than screeches. He hugged her close and petted her matted hair. He so wanted to tell her everything would be all right, but the lie wouldn't form in his throat.

"What's going on, Augy?" she asked, clawing at the fibers of his shirt and pressing her cheek hard against him. "What is this place?"

"I'm so sorry. It's all my fault." He held her tighter, setting his chin on top of her head. "I should've come to your house. I should've made you leave."

"What are you talking about?"

"Didn't Bill say anything?"

"Say anything about what?"

Taking her hands, he stepped back to look at her. Bright red circles hung from bloodshot eyes. The rest of her skin was ashy and faded. She'd been chewing her lips so much they were chapped and bloody. The red housedress with little white polka dots drooped from her frame, wrinkled and wet with cold sweat. She still had a string of pearls around her neck and a tiny diamond on her finger.

"What happened?" he said. "How did you end up here?"

"I... I don't know. I was at home..." She sniffled hard. Her voice was still so weak, so quavering it was difficult to understand. "Bill had just left for work. I was about to go weed the garden, and... a salesman came to the door. I mean, I thought that's what he was. I let him in to use the restroom and he..." Tears overtook her and she pressed herself against him again.

Stroking her back, his fingers caught on a shred of loose fabric over her shoulder blade. When he pulled aside her hair he saw the angry mark staring up at him: *Property of Countess London, 14150776.*

The weight of it was like a knife to his heart. His chest deflated.

"This woman tied me to a wall," Edith stammered, "and she... she..."

"Shh. I know."

She grabbed his hand, pressed it against her cheek and nuzzled into it. "You came to rescue me."

Her tears tickled as they ran down his fingers. He shook his head slowly. "We have to escape."

Her gaze swept his face as if seeing the sorry state of him for the first time. "Who are these people?"

"I promise, once we're out of here, I will answer any question you want. But there is no time right now."

"You tell me now." She was shaking so hard, edging towards hyperventilation with every shallow breath. Snot coated her upper lip, no matter how much she sniffled. "What do they want with you?"

He clenched his teeth, a low-pitched growl in his throat. "They want to destroy me, okay? I've caused them a lot of trouble and killed a lot of their people."

"Is that all they want? There isn't anything you could give them?"

Grabbing her shoulders, he looked into her eyes, mossy green in the artificial light. She was shaking violently, breath so shallow it was next to useless.

"Listen to me," he said. "I'm gonna do everything I can to get us out of here. But you need to get control of yourself."

"I can't. How am I supposed to..."

"Breathe with me."

"Augy, I can't..."

"You gotta trust me, baby. Close your eyes. Breathe in."

It took what seemed like forever, but finally, she managed to take a deep breath. He held her hands tight, breathing with her. After several minutes she stopped crying, but there was nothing to be done for her tremors.

"All right. Come on." Still holding her hand, he stepped up to the food cart. On it sat his bowl of rice with seaweed and his pitcher of water. Beside it were three more bowls filled with soup made of root vegetables and hunks of unidentifiable meat. After serving raw human liver to a table of hungry Nazis, Augy didn't think he wanted to eat meat ever again. So, he grabbed the rice and shoveled it in.

"I thought you hated rice," said Edith.

He smirked. "I'm warming up to it."

CHAPTER THIRTY-SIX

Another concrete hallway illuminated by flickering bulbs. The dull roar of machinery shook rusty pipes, the whir of electronics muffled by the narrow corridor. The stink of bleach and rotting meat.

It seemed empty.

Across the hall was a heavy wooden door with a soot-stained brass sign: BOILER ROOM. Another door beside it: GENERATOR. The hall went on ten feet in each direction before turning.

Edith held tight to his arm, her shivers transferring into him, fueling his dread. "I think we should go that way," she said, pointing right.

"Why?"

"It's the way they brought me down. It's probably the way out."

He was about to follow her directions when he noticed another brass sign: STORE ROOM. He led Edith towards it.

Augy tried the handle: locked. One of the keys on his wrist did the trick, and the flimsy wooden door swung inward with a shrill whine. He reached inside and groped the wall for a light switch.

Lines of bulbs buzzed to life, illuminating rows of metal shelving. His shoes echoed as he stepped inside.

Edith tugged on his arm. "What are you doing?"

"Keep watch," he said, pulling himself free of her clutch.

"Augy..." she hissed, but stayed by the door, chewing her poor lips, wringing her waxen hands.

It seemed a typical hospital warehouse filled with wooden crates and boxes made of clean white cardboard, many of which had Holzklotz emblazoned on them in thick black letters. He found boxes of protective equipment, IV tubes, catheters, saline bags, and bandages. He kept searching until he came upon the surgical equipment. There were no scalpels or bone saws, but a box labeled *straight Iris scissors* provided what he wanted—long and sharp. He took three pairs.

As he pushed the box back into place, a small glass bottle fell off the shelf and shattered. The smell of ethanol filled the air. Augy reached to the back of the shelf and found two more identical bottles, each containing 250ml. He took them both.

"Someone's coming," Edith hissed, closing the door. Augy hurried to her and flicked off the light. He motioned her to move back and press herself against the wall, as he readied the scissors. Through a tiny window in the door, crisscrossed with wire, he spied a cart wheeling down the hall towards them. A huge barrel-chested man with black caterpillar eyebrows, wearing a white jumpsuit and a surgical mask, whistled the tune to Nat King Cole's *Mona Lisa* as he pushed a cart the size of a small car down the hall. A black cloth covered the load. A human foot hung off the edge so near the floor its unkempt toenails scraped.

The man turned a corner, but his whistles continued to echo. Augy waited for the space of ten breaths.

He and Edith hurried in the opposite direction and around another corner. The hum and whoosh he'd first heard were loudest here. On the far wall were elevator doors and a stairwell.

He tried to pull Edith towards the stairs, but she yanked out of his grasp. "You want to just run up the stairs? They'll see us."

"You have a better idea?"

She huffed, shifting her weight restlessly. "Do you still have people on the outside? Somebody that might be coming for us...?"

"Nobody is coming for us."

"You knew about this place and you didn't tell nobody? Didn't go to the police?"

He sighed so deep his lungs dropped an inch. "You remember my friend down at the Review, Gundy? I sent him a package, but that ain't gonna help us now. We have to get ourselves out. Now come on."

Their feet clanged on perforated metal as he dragged her up the stairwell. Sun peeked through the boarded-up windows. The brick walls were painted bright white and the yellow linoleum shined underfoot. They were on the ground floor now. A swinging plastic door to the immediate right burped out smells of sweaty food and dish soap, the clank of pots and pans. Voices shouted over one another in Japanese. Augy and Edith hurried past.

"I think it's this way," she said, yanking at his elbow.

Doors lined the right side of the hall, supply rooms, and offices. The voices in the kitchen grew fainter, but Augy kept checking over his shoulder. Turning a corner, he saw a door labeled: GARAGE. He breathed a sigh of relief and was about to dive through when another sign across the hall caught his eye.

"Records..." he whispered and moved closer.

"What're you doing?"

"I have to go in there."

"Are you crazy?"

He reached for the doorknob, but Edith snatched his wrist. "Please. They'll catch us."

"I need evidence."

"What about the stuff you gave to Gundy?"

"It's not enough."

"Is this worth getting us both killed over?"

"I may never have another opportunity like this."

He yanked free of her grasp and opened the door. Inside was cold and quiet as a grave. His shoes echoed as he stepped in. Shelves lined every wall, stacked to the ceiling with accordion folders, file boxes, pathology samples, and loose papers. A repurposed surgical table lingered at the back, flanked by iron folding chairs.

His fingers skimmed pink and yellow pages as he walked the perimeter. Many of the labels were nine-digit numbers, all starting with either a nine or a one. Patient files: men and women. He hadn't figured out what the other numbers meant.

He paused at a collection of ring binders labeled: *Catalog of Internal Activities*. Corresponding dates ranged from November 1946 to the present. He picked up the most recent volume and laid it open on the table.

"You're going to read it now?" Edith rasped, pulling on her own hair and dancing nervously in place.

The binder was an index of documents in the archive. It listed the experiment, which doctor was in charge—Walker, London, and half a dozen others—how many *logs* had been involved, and the outcome. The names of the studies were things like: *Occurrence of blindness, joint and blood infection in infants born to mothers with active Gonorrhea; and, Men with cutaneous anthrax significantly more likely to develop meningitis if exposed to Streptococcus pneumoniae; and even, Survival rate of sixty-four percent at atmospheric pressure 460lb/in².*

He'd expected as much, but still, his stomach roiled and his hands clenched into fists. The detached clinical tone was almost too much to swallow. He knew the mothers with active gonorrhea were not only forcibly given gonorrhea, they were forcibly impregnated. Men were exposed first to anthrax and then to Streptococcus. And based on the ratio, he guessed at least one hundred people had been locked in pressure chambers until forty-six of them were dead.

Over a hundred studies were detailed in 1954's catalog, and it was only June. He found logs of patient numbers as well as admittance, and what they laughingly called discharge, dates. Edith's number was the newest entry, scrawled in pencil, and his before that. Katya's number wasn't there. He read the page three times to make sure.

Balling up a fist and pressing it into one eye, he laughed, even as a tear streamed down. His first real tear in days.

She'd gotten out. There was still a chance.

At the back of the binder, he found a map of the building, color-coded to show which cells, and therefore which inmates, were treated by which doctors. The second floor was little more than rows of cells, each only five foot by four. There was also a natal unit and four operating rooms.

Augy ran a finger over the word *natal*. This was where the Hollisters' fosters had ended up. Not merely suffocated so their custodians could collect money, but sold, dissected, and desecrated in the name of science.

The third floor included laboratories: a weapons' testing area, pressure chambers, ovens, freezers, and six quarantine areas: leprosy, smallpox, typhus, tuberculosis, bubonic plague, and anthrax.

Counting squares on the map, he did the figures in his head. Assuming each cell contained but one soul and the quarantine areas no more than twenty, some four hundred and fifty individuals were imprisoned here at any given time. People from the lower classes, no doubt. Hobos, prostitutes, immigrants, ex-cons. People the police didn't file missing person reports over, or at least, they didn't follow up on them.

They aren't people, said Katsuki Muto.

The taste of burning hair filled his throat. He remembered something his father used to say—or rather, something Mary Wollstonecraft had said, which had so inspired Professor Small that he'd named his daughter for her.

"It is justice, not charity, that is wanting in the world."

"What?" whispered Edith, hazarding a step closer. "What does that mean?"

Shaking his head, he looked up at her. "I can't just open the doors and let them out. Even the ones who aren't in quarantine need help I don't have the resources to give."

"What are you talking about?"

"The victims of Unit 731 died like worms in Manchuria and not one of them ever got retribution. Most of the men who did it aren't here. They're back in Japan living ordinary lives—pillars of the fucking community.

"I can't do anything about them," he continued, closing the binder, "but I can do something about this. And I don't care if it makes me a monster. I want the abyss to look back."

"Augy, you're scaring me."

"I never wanted you to see any of this... to be a part of this world." Stuffing the binder under his arm, he stepped nearer to her. "I lost you because I didn't want you to know."

Meeting his gaze, she reached one tremulous finger towards his chest. When he nodded, her eyes welled with tears and she buried her face in her hands.

"I knew all along," she said in an unsteady whisper. "I knew... something..."

"I wanted to protect you. To protect myself from your pity. But I'm no good at protecting people or helping them. I'm poison. The only thing I can do right is inflict myself on people who deserve it."

"That is not true. You saved those kids and their mother. And what you did for that little girl you found..."

"I was just in the right place at the right time." Augy stifled his next words and licked his lips. "How do you know about Sumika?"

"What?"

"I never told you about her. How do you know about her?"

She rolled her lips in and bit them both at once. "Mary told me."

"You're lying."

"Why would I lie about that?" She stepped behind one of the metal chairs and white-knuckled the back.

"She got to you, didn't she?"

"Who did?"

"Fuck!" He smacked the chair away. It crashed into a shelf, creating a blizzard of paper. Edith flinched and retreated until her back was against the wall.

"I knew this was too easy. Sticking your cell right next to mine. Leaving me my fucking belt." He laughed insanely. "She wants to see how stalwart I am."

"You're crazy."

"What did she tell you, huh? How did she turn you against me?"

"I don't know what you're talking about."

He advanced on her. Before she could dodge, he grabbed her by the shoulders and shook. "You answer me, goddamn it!"

"She promised she'd let you live!" Edith shrieked. "She said she'd let us go."

It was as if someone had stabbed syringes through his ribcage and sucked all the air out of his lungs. As he watched red tears streak her face and listened to her frantic gasps, all the strength left him. His grip loosened. She fell to her knees, crying hysterically.

"Oh, Edith…" He slouched away on rubbery legs and covered his eyes. "Why did you believe her?"

The door crept open, and a shadow entered. "So, Mr. Small," it said. "Did you find what you were looking for?"

CHAPTER THIRTY-SEVEN

He could've picked her voice out in a crowd of ten thousand. And she always looked the same. A gray Mao suit and white shoes. That flat nose and deep marionette lines. Loose skin hanging over her eyes. A thin-lipped, superior sneer.

And why shouldn't she look superior? She was untouchable. Or at least, she was so confident she was untouchable none of her cronies had followed her in.

They couldn't be far.

"So, what did we find out?" the Countess asked, approaching Edith. It was the first time he'd heard her speak English. She sounded British. Perfectly posh.

"Edith, don't say anything..." Augy said. The defeated tone of his own voice surprised him. He realized he wasn't telling her, or even asking. He was begging.

The Countess approached, a Type 14 Nambu 8mm in her grip. The gun had been the standard-issue sidearm for Japanese soldiers during the war. It wasn't the first time he'd had that distinctive slender barrel pointed between his eyes. "Get down on your knees."

He did as he was told, and the Countess turned her choler on Edith. "You have three seconds to tell me everything. Three."

"She's going to kill both of us either way," said Augy. He tried to meet Edith's eyes, but she looked away.

"Two."

"Nothing you can say will change anything."

The Countess pulled back the knurled cocking knob. "One!"

"Wait!" Edith scurried closer, her arm extended. "Please, don't hurt him."

"Talk."

"Edith, don't…" His voice was weak, dank.

Edith bit her lips so hard they turned white and rubbed her arms as if for warmth. He'd never seen those lines between her brows so deep. "He told a reporter called Gundy. He works for the Burbank Daily Review."

The Countess pressed the gun against Augy's forehead. "And where did he get the poison?"

"I didn't get a chance to ask, but…"

"She's not going to shoot me," he said.

Edith met his eyes, tears rolling down her cheeks. "Years ago, he worked a case for a restaurant owner in Little Tokyo who was importing rare foods illegally. It had to be him. The restaurant's called Sakana."

The Countess smiled and angled her head to one side. "And the girl, Sumika. Where is she?"

"He wouldn't say."

Augy looked at the floor. His eyes were burning, a dull throb in his chest where his heart should've been. A cord snapped in his brain and he tumbled listless through emotion and memory, forgetting even to fight back. Nothing in the past could be worse than his present.

He found himself in a cramped wooden room back in Changi, sitting in a rusty folding chair, staring across a card table at a mild-mannered man in a smart uniform with rimless glasses poised at the tip of an aquiline nose. The interrogation hadn't been as terrible as Augy had expected. He was given coffee and cigarettes, then asked about seven billion questions, many of which didn't seem like they could have any relevance. Where was his hometown? Had he gone to college? Was he married? Did he have children? Did he have a civilian pilot's license before joining the army? Did he volunteer or was he conscripted? How did he feel about the non-American allied forces?

Augy told them his name, his rank, and his army serial number. Then he folded his arms and zipped his lips. The interrogation continued another fifteen hours, but he never said anything more. When the pencil pusher finally gave up, a different man came in with a baseball bat. He bruised his ribs, broke the tibia in his left leg and fractured his clavicle. As Augy lay in a bloody coil on the floor, the man in glasses resumed his seat, folded his hands in his lap, and asked, "Is there anything you'd like to tell me now?"

Augy looked up and smiled, blood in his teeth. "My name is Captain August Small, 52-873-0196. And you can go fuck yourself."

His eyes focused on the present, on the Countess. He wasn't sure if he'd been speaking out loud, but suddenly things seemed different. Augy rolled his shoulders. "Why aren't you asking about Katya?"

Her lips twitched. He'd seen the expression before. She tried to cover it up by wrinkling the corners of her lips—what might be called a smile on another face—but it was too late.

"She's gone, Mr. Small," she said.

"Gone where?"

"Nowhere you can follow."

"I'll follow her. You watch me." He showed the Countess a wolfish smile and grabbed the barrel of the gun. Pressing it hard against his forehead, he planted one foot then the other on the ground and stood.

"Let go," she ordered.

"No problem." Releasing the barrel, he took a step back. He pulled open his jacket enough for her to see the cigarettes in his pocket. "Do you mind if I…"

Pursing her lips, she nodded.

"Damn decent of you." He bit a smoke out of the pack. Lighting it, he glanced over at Edith, who was down on her knees in the corner, staring at him like monkeys were climbing out his ears.

He turned back to the Countess. "Something tells me that hidden under all that loathing, you have a modicum of respect for me."

The Countess shrugged. "I find you curious."

"How did I earn that honor?"

"For instance, I wonder where a high school dropout learned a word like modicum."

"There's more to people than numbers." He lit his cigarette and took a long deep drag. "Some of us are educated against our very will."

"I assume you're talking about your father."

"You really did do your homework."

She narrowed her eyes in confusion. "Does that mean you *choose* to sound like an illiterate hooligan?"

"You're damn right I do." He wiggled his eyebrows. "From what I hear someone spent a lot of money on your education. A fancy college in Old Blighty, no less."

Her eyebrows lifted.

"I'll be dead soon," he said. "Why not satisfy my curiosity?"

She hesitated, breathing audibly through her nose. "University College London."

"Now, that had to be tough. A foreign woman trying to make her way into that white boys club. That is something I think anybody can respect, even if you do happen to be one of the most twisted, evil, malicious bags of putridness ever vomited out by humanity." He began to pace a small radius. "So, why'd you go back to Japan?"

She didn't answer, but her grip on the gun had slackened.

"Given you're a *hikokumin*," said Augy, "I doubt it had anything to do with helping the Emperor win his war against the bestial American imperialists."

"I wasn't always unpatriotic," she said. "And I do find you bestial."

"Right back at you, princess." He laughed behind his curtain of smoke. "But you married one of us, didn't you?"

She flinched. "My husband was a neurologist from Alderley Edge in Cheshire. I would hardly lump him in with the likes of you."

"But he was a white guy."

"So what if he was?"

"Eye scum, nose scum. Scum is scum, ain't it?"

"What exactly is the point of this little interview?" she asked, switching back to Japanese.

"See if you've got a goat to get at, and where you keep it." He shrugged. "I mean, this right here..." He put up his hands to indicate the volumes lining the walls. "This is goddamn impressive. Though I doubt it compares to all the info the US got off you Japs after the war."

Her chin flattened. "The research I have conducted in the last eight years dwarfs what Shiro Ishi was able to accomplish."

"Really? Even with all his funding and resources? With the full faith and support of the Empire of Great Japan?" He scoffed. "I mean, the information he provided was enough to save the lives of hundreds of you so-called scientists who otherwise would've been put to the ax by war crimes tribunals."

"All the resources in the world cannot compensate for a lack of vision. No one on that project understood the gravity of the work we were doing, except me."

"Think I touched a nerve there."

"Ishi's focus was narrow," she continued through gritted teeth. "He only appreciated the military applications of the data we accumulated. Whereas my work is comprehensive."

"Comprehensive?"

"Since the beginning of history, physicians have been trying to understand the inner workings of the human body, and until only a hundred and fifty years ago they had failed in every important regard. The Hippocratic humoral theory was responsible for at least as many deaths as bubonic plague. Physicians prescribed poison thinking it was medicine, bled patients dry, encouraged them to smear their wounds with feces, burned their scalps with hot irons, and far worse. Anatomical models of human beings were based on animals, and so wildly inaccurate, their use in surgery caused more damage than if the surgeon had literally taken a stab in the dark. Physicians refused to get their hands dirty and spent their lives in libraries interoperating theological doctrines and prognosticating over vials of piss. Only since the Renaissance have doctors even been willing to dissect the bodies of the dead to improve their understanding."

Augy smiled and leaned forward on the table. She wasn't talking to him anymore, just talking to hear herself talk. He shot a glance at Edith, who was shrinking into the corner trying to disappear. He almost hoped she'd be successful.

"In the nineteenth century," the Countess continued, "medicine improved by leaps and bounds, with the discovery of things such as germ theory, genetics, and massive advances in technologies and procedures. But only in the last fifteen years have doctors been able to look inside the human body while it is still living. The blood still pumping, the neurons still firing. Like any living system, anatomy can only truly be understood if it is observed while still alive. Men like Shiro Ishi, Eduard Wirths, and Aribert Heim did more for medicine in less than ten years than their predecessors were able to accomplish in a thousand. And while the Allies were intelligent enough to recognize the value of their work, their misguided Christian belief in the sanctity of even the most inferior and déclassé human life caused them to feel beholden to put an end to the experiments."

"Thank god for the good old US of A, huh?"

She chuckled privately. "Those who desire dominance always see the value of people like me. The Soviets offered more money, but I knew they would also interfere more. Here, I have the freedom to pursue my true vision."

"Too bad you have to waste your time indulging all these freaks to get the money you need."

She nodded and pressed her lips together. "Securing funding is always the most disagreeable part of my line of work. And while I admit your stunt with the tetrodotoxin has set me back, soon I shall have the technique and the expertise to treat any injury, and to cure virtually any disease. I will be able to extend the lives of those who are worthy, and efficiently end the lives of those who are not. Then stage two of my operation can begin in earnest."

"Stage two?" he prompted.

"A breeding program, Mr. Small. To create the superior human using sound scientific principal, and free of the pseudoscience of racial purity. This will be *true* eugenics. The healthiest, strongest, and most intelligent people from around the entire world co-mingling their superior DNA to create a new breed of human. Not caucasoid, negroid, or mongoloid. A population of multi-racial genetically superior superhumans. I've already selected thirty-five hundred individuals for the program."

Augy stroked his burgeoning beard. "I don't imagine they're all volunteers."

"The means of their procurement is as varied as their genomes. Your beloved Katya was meant to be a part of the alpha test group," she said, her lip twitching again when she said Katya's name, "until Francis Tyler decided he wanted her for his own, and his genetics are passable at best. Now, she's too old."

"I thought you said she was gone."

She turned her eyes on Augy. They sparked with lightning. "You would've been a good candidate. What with your height, virility, tenacity, and impressive tolerance for physical pain…"

He fanned his face. "Oh, do go on."

"If it weren't for your psychoneurosis. Then again, it's important to maintain a degree of psychopathy within a population. They have a tendency to creativity. Then still again, there is your father's stomach cancer to consider…" She took a few steps towards Edith, glowering down at her. "She was an ideal candidate. Confirmed IQ in the 130s, I believe. Tall, healthy, very beautiful. No significant family history of either physical or mental disease. However, it seems she too is too old. My stud has had no success in producing a viable pregnancy."

"What is she saying?" asked Edith in a trembling whisper, but Augy didn't answer. He couldn't let himself get distracted.

"I wish I could live long enough to see the long-term results of it all." The Countess sighed, staring in wonder at the shelves as if boggled by her own genius. "Perhaps in the future, new physicians will swear an oath in my name, instead of that Greek imbecile."

"Huh…" Augy drummed his fingers on the desk, his tongue in his cheek. Rising from his chair, he followed her gaze around the files. "Your life's work is in this room, isn't it?"

With another sigh, she gave the barest hint of a nod.

"Fascinating." He ripped a bottle of ethanol from his jacket and smashed it against a shelf. The Countess screamed as he flicked his cigarette.

CHAPTER THIRTY-EIGHT

A wall of fire erupted. The Countess threw down the gun and lunged for the burning papers. Shrieking for help, she ripped files from the shelf and hurled them across the room to safety. Augy smashed a second bottle and the flames whooshed higher. He snatched up the gun as the door burst open. He fired at the Countess, but his hands were shaking. The bullet slammed into an accordion folder half an inch above her head. She was so absorbed trying to rescue her work from the conflagration, she didn't flinch.

Augy aimed and pulled the trigger a second time, but the damn cocking knob jammed. He slammed it into place with his palm, but too late. One man hooked his arm behind his back and twisted the gun out of his hand as another plunged a long needle into his neck.

Before the man could depress the syringe's plunger, something smashed into his face. Edith stood above him, a folded metal chair in her hands. Augy reached his free arm back and pushed down on his own wrist to loosen the man's hold on his arm. He stomped back on his foot, then twisted and elbowed him in the face. The man stumbled and Edith smacked him in the back with the chair so hard it bent. Augy yanked the syringe out of his neck and flipped it over in his hand. It was still full.

In the scuffle, the Countess was escorted from the room. He could still hear her screaming, "Put out the fire! Save the research!"

Augy snatched the gun off the ground as two men rushed into the room, one armed with an AK47 and the other with a fire extinguisher. Augy fired one round into the armed man's chest, but when he tried for a second, the cocking knob jammed again.

"Cheap piece of shit." He threw the gun at the man's face, hitting him square between the eyes. The man fell, letting off a stream of continuous fire.

Augy flipped the table and yanked Edith behind it, but too late. She screamed, and blood burst from her thigh.

The man with the fire extinguisher had put out the blaze and was standing right in the line of fire. His chest exploded.

The man with the AK struggled to his feet. Augy leaped over the table on top of him, stabbed him in the neck with the syringe, and pushed down the plunger. In seconds, the man's pupils widened and his grip on the gun loosened. Augy yanked it out of his hands. The man pawed for him like a weak kitten. Augy fired a short burst into his skull.

The *Internal Activities* binder laid on the ground beside the fresh corpse, splattered with blood. Augy picked it up and shoved it down the front of his shirt.

Boots pounded the hall, closer and closer. With adrenaline pumping up flattened muscles, he slung the gun over his shoulder and rushed to Edith. At least two bullets had gone into her thigh. She still had the energy to scream and thrash, which he hoped meant the bullets missed her femoral artery. She said something, but it didn't register.

"You're gonna be okay," he said. Kneeling, he slung her arm over his neck and hoisted her onto his shoulders in a fireman's carry. She felt so much heavier than he ever remembered. His fractured ribs screamed for mercy, but once again he dismissed their cry. No matter how much it hurt, they would carry him through. They'd come this far.

The garage door was across the hall. He dashed for it, glancing at a small group of armed men rushing towards them. Campbell was at its head.

"Stop where you are!" Campbell called, then fired twice. Augy flung open the door and stumbled through.

The clang of the door slamming behind him broke open the silence. The parking lot made up half the square footage of the main floor, but it was largely empty. Corrugated metal composed the walls, illuminated by a scant few strips of yellow fluorescents.

Based on the feeble response to his escape attempt, he knew this place was not a proper military installation. The Countess didn't need guns and soldiers to keep her patients in place; she relied on fear, drugs, and isolation. Most importantly, nobody was supposed to know the Lumbermill even existed. Campbell seemed to be the only real fighting man in the whole place.

Maybe Augy had already killed the others.

His steps echoed as he dashed down a row of trucks. His vertebrae felt as steady as a stack of coins in an earthquake. He had to set Edith down.

He ducked behind one of the jeeps and laid her on the concrete. "Stay quiet," he said, slinging the AK off of his shoulder.

"Are you gonna leave me?"

He shook his head and put a finger to her lips.

The door creaked open then clanged shut. Footsteps echoed. The gun shook in his hands.

He edged out along the jeep and peeked around the back. At the far end of the lot, he saw the door—the only door out—outlined by golden sunlight. Two men in white jumpsuits had positioned themselves in front of it, guns in hand. He recognized one as the furry-faced behemoth he'd seen wheeling the cart of corpses through the basement.

Steadying the barrel of the AK on the bumper, he aimed for those caterpillar eyebrows.

He was about to squeeze the trigger when he hesitated. From the outside, the door had looked thick and solid. Now, he realized it was just a few thin sheets of steel. He wouldn't even have to get up much speed.

Shouldering the gun, he sneaked back around the side and popped open the driver's side door of the jeep. The sound echoed through the parking lot, but they could no more triangulate him than he could them. He hefted Edith inside. Her leg wound scraped the upholstery, and she screamed.

Thanking god for his wayward youth, he ducked under the dash and yanked the metal panel off the steering column. He pulled the sock suspender out of his pocket and used the clip to strip the wires. He was going to start wearing those things every day after this. They were almost as good as any Swiss Army knife he'd ever owned.

The engine roared to life, and he revved the gas a few times with his hand before settling into the driver's seat.

A shot cut the air, and the front windshield exploded. Edith screamed and covered her head with her hands as glass showered down. Augy threw his weight into breaking the steering lock, then punched the gas. The truck squealed and smoked. More lead pummeled the side panels. The driver's side window shattered. A slug bit into his neck, a glancing ricochet off the dash. He tightened all his muscles and closed his eyes.

"Hold on, Rutabaga!"

Smashing through the door was thunder. Scraping metal tore at his nerves, broken glass raining brimstone from above.

He blinked in the sunlight. Edith's body twisted in pain on top of his. The truck had turned on its side. Above them, the bluest sky he'd ever seen showed through the passenger-side window. Flames licked through the hole where the windshield should've been. It was another few seconds before he realized the engine was on fire.

Shaking away blurry vision, spikey nerves, and the unrelenting urge to sleep, he dragged himself and Edith over the flames onto the hot sand. He had to get up. Fight or run. But all he could do was lie on his back and cough. His head throbbed, pounding heart somehow stealing the blood from his limbs. He tried for a deep breath, but his ribs were collapsing.

A figure appeared over him, silhouetted against the sun. A halo of blond hair and a long hooked nose. He lifted his gun.

Augy tried to sit up, but a heavy boot stomped his chest. Injured ribs collapsed further. He coughed out blood.

Campbell cocked the gun and fired.

CHAPTER THIRTY-NINE

Augy clenched his eyes shut and froze. He'd been flirting with death so long, they'd rounded first and second. It seemed only natural to go all the way. A thousand memories surged at once, together with a continuum of emotion that ran the gamut from ecstasy to despair, ease to dread, and pure love to total apathy.

"He'll be here," said his wife, squeezing his hand. Her deflated lips and wrinkled brow told a story she refused to. And when he looked at his daughter weeping quietly into her hands, he knew: Augustinius wasn't coming.

He'd delayed taking opioids as long as he could. Corporeal things had never meant much to him. The prospect of losing a leg, becoming paralyzed, even going blind or deaf didn't frighten him. But losing his capacity for thought was worse than mere death. He'd delayed the process as long as possible.

The doctors said he'd had cancer over a year before it was diagnosed. It had started as heartburn. He'd stopped eating bacon and spicy foods, and it had abated, but only for a few months. Next came the abdominal pains, like a constant severe case of constipation that nothing could relieve. When he started losing weight, he knew something was wrong. Now, the cancer had spread to his intestines. After three rounds of radiation therapy, three courses of chemo, and four surgeries to remove excruciating bowel obstructions, the pain had become too much. Yesterday, he'd accepted the drugs and today he would die. He'd made up his mind.

"Mary..." he said, reaching for his daughter's hand. She quickened to his side, grasping his pale, vascular fingers in her firm plump palm. "I want you to tell Augustinius something for me."

"He'll be here, Richard," said his wife, but there was no time for her well-meaning fictions now.

"I want you to remind him, 'If there is a meaning in life at all, then there must be a meaning in suffering. Suffering is an ineradicable part of life, even as fate and death. Without suffering and death, human life cannot be complete'."

Mary wiped her nose and smiled. "Viktor Frankl…"

"You always were the clever one," he said, chuckling. "Make sure you tell your brother that. I think he needs to remember that. Especially now."

"I will, Daddy."

"Please don't talk like this," said his wife.

He squeezed her hand and looked into her chocolate-colored eyes one last time. Then as easily as turning off a switch, he let go.

Another shot cut the air, and another. Augy was shocked back into place and time, to his own brain. It wasn't a memory he'd just had, but a dream. A fantasy.

It had felt so real.

And he realized his father's death didn't have to mean anything. Life was where meaning was.

A fourth blast cut the air. Augy grabbed his torso. His shirt was spattered in blood, but none of it was his.

Campbell dropped the gun. Staggering, he clenched his stomach. Blood drained between his fingers. He turned sluggishly and fell to his knees. Two more shots burrowed into his flesh.

A figure approached, a Browning HP 9 mm strapped to their right hand. Short and slender, dressed in black riding boots, knickerbockers, and leather driving gloves, a balaclava concealed their face.

"Do you not recognize me, papa?" said the masked figure. It was a girl's voice. Leather straps lashed the pistol to her hand. A single finger moved on the trigger.

She took measured steps towards Campbell until the gun was pressed against his forehead. "You left me one finger so I could wipe away my tears."

"Baby doll…?" His shattered face turned up. "Please."

"You've gotten too old, papa."

The final shot rang out. The thud of Campbell's body hitting sand filled the emptiness and echoed on and out until it was nothing.

Augy staggered to his feet and approached. Jupiterian gravity yanked on his legs. She turned to him, black eyes shimmering under the balaclava like jewels yet to be mined.

"Sumika…" he breathed. "What are you doing here?"

"I came to rescue you."

"Rescue me?" He chuckled. "How did you find me?"

"I saw them drag you out of the party with your head in a bag, so I followed them up here. I've been trying to figure out a way to get you out…" She folded her arms together and bent her neck. "Are you mad?"

"Are you crazy?" Augy threw his arms around her, lifted her off the ground, and kissed her temple. Fat tears of joy fell from him unchecked, saturating her balaclava.

"You're crying," she said, scanning his face. "I thought only girls cry."

Setting her down, he cupped her cheeks and looked into her eyes. "I'm proud to do anything girls do."

She embraced him again, her arms stronger than ever before.

"There's more coming," he said. "We have to get out of here. Now."

"Follow me."

Augy ran back to Edith. Her eyes were only half open, and she was mumbling to herself in a hushed, strange voice. He'd seen others in the same state—delirious from blood loss and shock. Some pulled through. Most didn't.

Dragging her over his shoulders, he hobbled after Sumika towards a car she had parked beyond the horizon, just as more men with guns appeared in the door. Sumika took the driver's seat and turned the ignition as Augy threw Edith into the back then dove in after. The car peeled out, leaving a plume of dust in their wake.

"Edith," he said, slapping her face lightly. "Stay with me."

"Augy…?" Her voice was so soft, hazy.

"I'm here."

"I should've listened to you. This is all my fault…"

"Shh."

"It's all been my fault." Tears glistened in her eyes. She choked and trembled. "All of it. Always."

"No, it wasn't. Stop it."

"I love you, Augy," she said, her eyes so blue. "I never stopped loving you. Not for one second."

He bit his lip and tightened his grip on her hand. "You're gonna be all right."

They drove in silence down Big Rock Motorway onto Tuna Canyon Road. Edith passed out on CA 27, but her pulse was strong. Only when they came out of the wilderness onto Pacific Coast Highway, in view of glorious sapphire waves kissed by perfect Southern California sunlight, could Augy breathe again.

"Where's Katya?" he asked.

"She wasn't in there with you?"

"No."

"Are you sure?"

He thought back to the expression on the Countess's face when he asked about Katya. That stoic twitch of irritation. Katya was alive somewhere, irritating her. But that didn't mean she was safe.

"She's not in there," he said.

"Who's that lady?"

"Her name's Edith. We have to get her to Dr. Larkin."

Sumika nodded and followed the signs towards Pasadena. She'd used her teeth to undue the straps holding the gun to her left hand so she could work the stick. The leather gloves helped her grip the wheel of the limousine. Guns and ammo were piled in the front seat, vainly concealed by a transparent bedsheet.

He'd thought he'd never see sunshine again. It hurt his eyes, but he couldn't close them. Even when he blinked a wave of darkness threatened to blot out the light and leech the blood out of his heart. How would he ever sleep again? He felt so tired.

"How long was I in there?" he asked.

"Nearly five days."

"Have you gone back to see the doctor since then?"

She shook her head. Sumika's gaze followed him in the rearview mirror, but he said nothing more.

The phone call he'd made from Dr. Larkin's hotel room went around in his head. How long it had taken Bill to ask a simple question. The son of a bitch hadn't even said anything to Edith.

Augy felt like such a fool. He'd hated Bill on principal from the moment he met him. He'd focused so much on belittling him and trying to make himself appear better by comparison, he'd never wondered much about the man himself. Bill had always seemed so white bread, so desperately dull, so safe and mediocre. Augy spent so much time wondering what Edith could possibly see in such a man, he never bothered to notice how strange it, in fact, was for any human to be so willfully ordinary.

Thinking back, Augy realized it was after the Hollisters affair began and his face started showing up in the papers that Edith met Bill. He'd never imagined the two misfortunes were connected.

Katya was right. He was a lousy detective.

The moment they pulled up to the motel and he saw the yellow crime scene tape over the door, he knew what had happened.

There wasn't a cop in sight. The incident must have happened several nights ago.

Augy climbed out of the car, then thumbed through the weapons on the front seat till he found a handgun—the service revolver he'd taken off the guy at the Lumbermill when he'd first found Katya. Four bullets.

Jamming the gun in his belt, he ripped off his tuxedo jacket, tucked in his shirt, and rolled up the sleeves. Glimpsing his reflection in the side-view, he looked like he'd been through a meat grinder. That deep cut on his forehead was infected now—yellow pus clinging to split stitches. His broken nose was swollen, lips split and lavender-colored, and black flesh swelling over his left eye. Blood oozed from his neck where the bullet had grazed him. No doubt he smelled only slightly better than a porta-john at a construction site, but he slicked back his hair and tried to stand up straight. Put-together from far away was the best he could hope for, like a Seurat painting.

"Give me five minutes," he said.

Sumika checked the clock on the dash before nodding, then cast an eye into the backseat. "She gonna be okay?"

He looked back at Edith. Her pale skin, her dazed eyes.

"Five minutes," he said.

Augy jogged up the steps to the room. The door had been forced. The cops had installed a simple padlock to hold it closed. It crossed his mind to kick the door down before he realized the economy hasp the cops had used had exposed screws. He used the sock suspender to unscrew them. Forty seconds later, he was in.

Children's toys littered the floor. Dr. Larkin's robe hung from a hook on the bathroom door. A chair laid on one side near the far wall. Someone had thrown it. The bedding was rumpled. He found not a spot of blood—no definitive evidence that whatever struggle had taken place had turned violent, or how everything had ended.

He drifted into Dr. Larkin's room. Yellow tape covered the small back window, which had been smashed out. A few words were scrawled on the wall in black marker. The handwriting was so awful he could barely make it out:

What have I got to stay alive for?

Augy hurried down the stairs. Climbing into the front seat with Sumika, he said, "Come on. Let's go."

"Where?"

"South I-5. We have to take Edith to the hospital."

"After what happened to me?" She shook her head hard. "No. I won't."

"She'll die if she doesn't get help soon." He searched frantically through the pockets of his jacket until he found the cigarettes. "We don't have any choice."

Sumika stared daggers at him, but she put the car into gear. Within minutes they were at the emergency terminal of St. Vincent's Hospital in the heart of downtown. He carried Edith inside, and when the nurse at the desk saw the state of her, she called for a gurney. Questions were already being hurled around. Questions he couldn't answer.

"She's allergic to aspirin," he told one of the nurses, cutting off whatever she was saying. "Her blood type is A-negative. She was shot by an AK47 assault rifle about half an hour ago."

The woman wrote down what he said, then pushed her red cat-eye glasses higher up her fleshy nose. "Are you the husband?"

He shook his head. He studied Edith until she was pushed through the swinging double doors. She looked so fragile, so small.

Without another word, he drifted through the exit door. The nurse called after him, telling him that he couldn't leave. But he couldn't stay.

When he came out onto the sidewalk he was surprised to see Sumika. She'd taken off the balaclava and her hair hung around her face like wet straw. She lifted her finger, dangling the car keys. "I'll stay with her."

Augy narrowed his eyes. "What?"

"I can't leave an innocent person alone in there," she said, gazing past him through the rotating doors. "Not somebody those people have any reason to hurt."

"Are you sure?"

She encouraged him to open his hand and set in the keys, but he shook his head. "You can't. She's got bullet holes in her. They're gonna call the police and…"

"You care about that woman, right?"

Augy took a deep breath. "Yeah."

"Then somebody has to watch out for her. I won't let anybody see me, and the moment I think she's safe, I'll get her out of here." Sumika took a step closer. "Don't you trust me?"

The question was like a knife twisting in his guts. "With my life."

"Then trust me with hers, and with mine."

He looked at the keys in his hand, then closed his eyes and nodded. Sumika hopped up and threw her arms around his shoulders. He couldn't believe how light she felt.

"Where do I find you?" he said.

"I'm at the Hotel Plum in Little Tokyo."

"Please be careful." He squeezed her one last time before setting her down.

"I will," she said. "You keep the guns. The money's in the trunk. Now, go find our friends."

Augy walked away. He thought he ought to tell Sumika something to tell Edith, but there was nothing in his brain. Nothing simple anyway. He'd been waiting years for her to tell him that she'd made a mistake, that she still loved him, had never stopped loving him. Now, it felt empty.

In the dark of the Lumbermill, as he searched for a reason to stay alive, to stay sane, there was only one face in his mind's eye, one name on his lips. He had two things left to do before he died. One was to kill Countess London. The other was to see Katya one last time. To tell her.

He stopped at the first phone booth he came across, but as he shut the gray accordion doors he realized he didn't have a dime. He had twenties and hundreds, but not a dime. A Woolworths across the street beckoned, and he realized he ought to get some food and essentials before diving back into the abyss.

A bell chimed as he swung the door open and everybody in the shop looked up. He may as well have been on fire for the way they stared. A frizzy-haired boy in a red cowboy shirt stood nearest him, frozen in mid-sip of his Lime Ricky. "Geez, Mister," he said. "What happened to you?"

"I didn't look both ways before I crossed the street," said Augy.

The boy's broad-shouldered mother pulled her son behind her apron and gave Augy a look like he was a ravenous bear about to strike.

Every eye followed as he picked up a shopping basket. First, he went to the men's clothing section to grab tube socks, underwear, a button-down, and pants and a jacket made of dungaree. Next, he grabbed a flashlight, a pair of binoculars, a bottle of aspirin, some rubbing alcohol, and a box of butterfly closures. As he approached the lunch counter, the kid in the paper hat started wiping down the ice cream machine.

Augy knew he looked a mess, but he hadn't expected people to be so damn intimidated.

He whistled and slapped two twenties on the counter. "Can you ring this up, and get me two grilled cheese, fries, and an extra-large chocolate malt, please?"

The kid nodded, his red bottom lip sticking out so far it cast a shadow. Augy peered around the shop until his eyes fell on the teenage girl on the stool next to him. Blonde hair in a high-top ponytail, fuzzy sweater, black poodle skirt. A freckled boy in a letterman jacket stood by the postcards a few feet behind her. He kept reaching shyly for her arm, but she sipped her root beer float and cast an eyeball at Augy.

"Nice shiner," she said. "You in a rumble?"

"Peggy Sue," the freckled boy hissed. Augy turned to him, but he pretended to be looking at postcards.

"I'm on a real trip for biscuits, I'll tell you that." Augy lit a cigarette and nodded to the boy. "Yours?"

"He's a goof," said the girl.

"You're on the beam. Watch my food."

She winked. "Sure thing, big daddy."

Augy went into the bathroom. Peeling off those disgusting threads was pure bliss. He washed his wounds, irrigated them with the alcohol, and fixed up the cut on his head with the butterflies. He used some paper towels to take a quick hobo shower and pulled on the dungarees. Last, he washed the sock suspenders and put them back on.

You never know.

When he came back out, the store was deserted. The kid in the hat was cleaning glasses like he might find the answer at the bottom of one. The girl was still at the counter, still sipping her soda. Her poor boyfriend had retreated outside but kept peeking through the window.

Augy's basket of food was on the counter beside his change. The handwritten bill sat underneath it. Such clean script, like a typewriter. Why was it waiters and tellers have such neat handwriting while your average doctor could scarcely compete with a preschooler?

The chicken scratches he'd found at the motel presented in his brain, and it all made sense.

Smiling, he pocketed the coins and left the bills. "Mind if I take this to go?"

The kid jolted so hard he dropped his sponge. "Yes. I mean, no. I mean, go ahead. Please."

"Thanks for your help, Peggy Sue," Augy said to the girl as he picked up his food. "I gotta hit the pavement."

She showed a toothy smile. "See you later, alligator."

Turning to leave, Augy saw the boy in the window again, freckles red with fury and skin shock-white as he bounced on his sneakers. It was like watching a heart break right before his eyes.

Sighing, he turned back to Peggy Sue and said, "You know, goofs make the best boyfriends."

She grinned, looking past him out the window. Augy made his exit. When he stepped out, the boy ducked behind a newspaper kiosk. Augy couldn't help smirking at the headline: *102 Found Dead in Trousdale. Poison suspected.*

Sighing, he closed his eyes and tilted his face up towards the sun. The light warmed his skin, but the boy's eyes were crawling over him.

"Real spitfire you've got there," said Augy. "That's the kind of girl can shatter your heart into a million pieces without even trying."

The boy peeked out from his hiding spot. "Are you talking to me?"

"Airplanes."

"What?"

"Some guys might say hotrods or motorcycles, but for my money, ain't nothing like taking a girl on a date at 8,000 feet. Especially a girl like that."

The kid's lip wobbled, but he squeaked out, "Go to hell."

"You're gonna go far, kid." Augy took a big bite of his sandwich and walked back to the phonebooth. The dime slipped down the slot with a satisfying clink.

"Operator, I need the office of Ed Gundy at the Burbank Daily Review, and be quick about it."

CHAPTER FORTY

The red flag on the mailbox had been fixed with packing tape. Augy snapped it off again as he passed.

It was early evening now, though still hot, dry, and windy as a convection oven. He limped down the driveway towards the side door. Augy knew his way around this house. He knew where the blind spot was from the front window. He knew where the spare key was hidden among the orange poppies. He knew how to open the screen door so it wouldn't squeak. He even knew Bill watched The Lone Ranger every Thursday night at 7:30 on ABC and didn't like to be disturbed.

Adultery has its perks, even the emotional kind.

A trumpet blasting out the first notes of the William Tell Overture drowned out his footsteps as he entered the kitchen. The counter was covered in empty bottles. A block of yellow cheese sat on the naked table sweating in the heat. He peeked into the living room. Bill was parked in his green Lay-Z-Boy, a cigar in one hand, a beer in the other, ready to join the daring and resourceful masked rider of the plains on yet another fight for law and order in the early West.

The hypocrisy was mind-boggling.

Augy sneaked up behind him and pointed the gun at the back of his head. "Hey there, stud muffin."

"August?" Bill craned his neck around, then fell out of his chair when he saw the gun. It was the closest thing to a real emotion Augy had ever seen him exhibit. "What are you doing here?"

"Why don't you sit back down, Bill? Take a load off."

"I've been trying to get ahold of you," said Bill, resuming his seat, as well as his sneer. Augy found him unprepossessing at the best of times, with his huge forehead, thin upper lip, and beady blue eyes. But since the last time he'd seen him, Bill had morphed from a mere hamster-faced goon into a genuine gargoyle.

"Somebody kidnapped Edie," Bill dared to say. "You need to speak to the police."

Augy walked to the TV and flicked it off. "I don't think so."

"You're a real piece of work, you know that?" Bill scoffed. "Edie has been kidnapped, and you're here trying to pick a fight with me. I've taken a lot of guff off you this last year, but I've had about as much as I can stand."

"For a wet-blanket of a podiatrist, you seem awfully comfortable with a gun in your face."

Bill's expression hardened. "You aren't the only one who's seen action."

"Is that so? See, now Edith told me you were 4-F on account of you've had diabetes since you were a kid."

Bill's eyes widened, while his pupils shrank.

"Look at the face on you." Augy indulged in a cackle and picked a bit of French fry out of his teeth. "You didn't realize we talked so much, did you?"

"I'd like you to leave now."

"Oh, Billy boy." Augy shook his head. "It's always a gas talking to you. I'm having a real nice time.

"Now, let's see," he continued, tapping a finger on his chin. "If you got diabetes as a kid, then it's the kind you get from genes, not the kind you get from eating too much cake. And yet the Countess told me you were a stud, which goes to show how fucking whacky she is.

"Sit. Down. Bill."

Augy cocked the gun. Bill lowered back into the chair. "She may be whacky, but she ain't stupid," Augy continued. "If you had diabetes, she'd sooner throw you in a woodchipper than use you as a stud. So you ain't 4-F. That begs the question, what are you? You said you saw action, and goddamn if I don't believe it."

The skin under Bill's left eye twitched, and a large blue vein in his forehead began to pulse. "What are you getting at?"

"Your last name is Kowalski. Polish, am I right? Now, I think that really is your last name, but I don't think anybody called you Bill before a few years ago."

"I won't tell you anything."

Augy lifted his eyebrows. "Oh, I think you will."

"Why should I? You've already decided to kill me."

"Not necessarily." Augy cocked his head and showed a crooked smile. "As much as I personally dislike you, you never did anything to hurt Edith, far as I know. And you didn't do anything to hurt those kids I left with you neither. You didn't turn them over to the Countess when you had a chance. Now, why is that?"

"Go to hell."

"People keep saying that to me as if I haven't already been." Augy scratched his temple with the barrel of the gun. "I know you know what happened to Edith, but I'm not entirely convinced you wanted to turn her over to them. In fact, based on all the empty beer bottles around this place and those big ugly circles around your eyes, I think you're kind of upset about it."

Bill swallowed hard, his gaze darting around the room.

"Did you see action in Poland?" asked Augy in a quiet voice. "Did they make you a part of the Final Solution?"

Bill wrinkled his nose and pursed his lips as he stared at the wall. For perhaps the first time he looked like a real human being.

"There's something special about you, isn't there?" Augy approached and knelt in front of the chair to look up at his face. Bill kept his furious eyes on the blank TV. "They think you're special. Genetically superior in some way. I don't care how. It's all bullshit anyway. But because of what they think you are and who I am, they sent you here, didn't they? To spy on me through the person they knew I loved most. To hurt me through her."

"I don't give a damn about you..." he spat, but then he bit his tongue and looked away.

"But you fucked up, didn't you, Bill? You fell in love with Edith."

Bill's hands were like claws on the armrests. He didn't move.

"Of course you fell in love with her. Who wouldn't?" Augy shrugged. "She deserves a good man. Better than you."

"Better than you," snapped Bill.

Augy flattened his chin and nodded. "Me and Edith ain't right for each other. Never were. She figured that out a long time ago, though she didn't wanna accept it. And I wasn't much help."

"She'll never love me the way she loves you," said Bill, his voice a dirge.

Augy ran a hand over his face and chuckled. "This is fucking ridiculous."

"You can say that again."

"What matters is Edith is alive, no thanks to you. And she has every reason to hate your guts, though she doesn't know it yet."

Bill furrowed his brow and looked at his lap, eyes shiny with unshed tears. Augy felt a foreign twinge looking at him. It couldn't be sympathy.

"Maybe there's something you could do to redeem yourself," Augy said.

"To her?"

"If you help me, I might give you the opportunity to tell her the truth yourself, and if she never wants to speak to you again, so be it."

Bill closed his eyes and shook his head hard. "She'd never forgive me. Not after what I've done."

"You may be surprised. I mean, she put up with me a hell of a long time. And I am one ornery, self-centered son of a bitch."

With a knitted brow, Bill looked up at Augy's face. "What do you want from me?"

"I'm missing a couple of kids, and their mother."

"You're talking about the Tylers."

Augy nodded slowly. "Do you know where they are?"

"They told me you'd come here."

"If they knew where I'd be, why ain't they here waiting for me?"

"The Countess expects you to come back to the Lumbermill willingly. And she's made it clear she wants to kill you herself. In fact, it's a death sentence should anybody take that pleasure away from her."

"I'm fucking flattered," he said, jutting out his bottom lip. "Is that where the kids are?"

"I'm supposed to tell you it is."

"But?" Augy prompted.

Bill looked at his lap and sighed. "You really got Edith out of there?"

Augy nodded.

Bill licked his bottom lip, eyes darting. "The Lumbermill is basically unmanned after what you did at the masquerade. She had all her research moved after you lit so much of it on fire. And since both you and Katya managed to escape at different times and in different ways, my guess is she's keeping her leverage in what she thinks is a safer place."

"Your guess?"

"They're not at the Lumbermill."

"So, where are they?"

"You know."

An image of the sinkhole filled Augy's eyes—a tableau of mutilated bodies in the moonlight. He shook it away. "The mansion…"

Bill's gaze drifted upward, his expression written in some dead language. Wraithlike eyes, gray skin. "They gave me something to give to you."

His voice was a blast chiller. Augy didn't want to ask. "What?"

"You don't want it."

"What is it?"

Bill stood and Augy trailed him into the kitchen. Bill opened the icebox and took out a pastel pink, square Tupperware container. Again he said, "You don't want it."

"For Christ's sake, just give it to me." He yanked it out of Bill's limp grasp and popped the seal. His fingers stiffened. He glanced up, but Bill was squinting at the floor.

Tightening the muscles in his core and shoulders, Augy peeked inside.

His heart solidified, and his tongue turned to ash. "No…"

"I told you you didn't want it."

"You son of a bitch!" Augy lunged for his throat and slammed his back hard against the wall.

With expert speed, Bill grabbed his arm and twisted it behind his back, pushing Augy into a deep hunch. He shoved his elbow hard against the back of his neck, immobilizing him.

Augy didn't fight back. His lips were hard, teeth clenched, drooling like a wild animal. A sob caught in his lungs, wouldn't come out, just horrid wrenching breaths as if his stomach were about to flip inside out. "How long were you gonna let me keep on talking?" he said, his voice a parched whisper.

Bill let go. Augy stumbled, catching himself on his hands and knees before his face hit the linoleum. He squeezed the Tupperware as if it had breath to choke out.

Steps echoed as Bill walked to the kitchen table and protective plastic squeaked as he sat. "They found the kids because of me."

"What?" Augy looked up, snarling.

"My phones are tapped. When you called from the hotel to warn us about all this, I made sure to keep the line open long enough for them to trace the call."

"You lying sack of shit," he said through tears and snot.

"When Katya found out the Countess had taken her kids to the mansion, she went after them. They knew she was coming, of course."

"Is she alive?"

"You can't save her. You can't save any of them."

"Is she alive!" he screamed. Staggering to his feet, Augy rushed to the table and slammed his hands down in front of Bill.

Calmly, Bill met his eyes. "The Countess is waiting to kill her in front of you."

Augy picked up the table and threw it across the room. It smashed into the cupboard, sending dishes crashing to the floor in broken heaps. Bill sat stiff-backed and frozen, his eyes flat as glass. Augy turned from him towards the door.

"You love her, don't you?" called Bill.

Augy stopped in his tracks and cocked his head.

"And she loves you?"

"That doesn't matter."

Bill's breath quickened, but he didn't move. "It doesn't matter if the woman you're about to sacrifice your life for loves you back?"

"Is that why you let them take Edith?" He sneered over his shoulder. "You're pathetic."

"What was I supposed to do?"

"Fight back, you fucking coward."

"And end up like you?"

Augy marched back to Bill. He gripped the armrests of his chair until the wood creaked, and leaned in close to his face. "What do you think I am?"

Bill scoffed. "A tenderized sack of meat. A raving lunatic. A divorced, unemployed, homeless loser."

"Maybe," said Augy, "but I'm not a victim. Until that monster actually cuts my heart out, I will never stop attacking. I will fight with every drop of sweat and every ounce of blood, and with my last breath I will tell her to go fuck herself."

Augy cracked his neck and straightened his spine. "You may outlive me, Bill, but many years from now as you lay dying in a comfortable bed surrounded by people who can never really know you, you will remember you're there because you're a malingering invertebrate, and you don't deserve love."

Augy snatched the Tupperware off the floor and stomped towards the door. He ripped it off the hinges. Jogging up the drive towards his car, the contents of the container shifted and the acidic tears of rage returned to his eyes.

"You can cover them with your brand," he'd said to the Countess on their first meeting, *"but you don't own any of those people."*

"I could cut it off as well and it wouldn't make them any freer." She'd gazed into his eyes then, and he'd known what it meant to look into the abyss. At the time, he couldn't endure it.

Inside the plastic container, raw and swimming in blood, was a circular patch of skin the size of his palm. And burned into it in inch-high figures were those hideous words *Property of Countess London* and a number.

Katya's number.

CHAPTER FORTY-ONE

Augy drove to Cohen Dale at breakneck speed, darting in and out of traffic like the devil himself were chasing him. Before going to the mansion, there was one thing he had to check on.

What have I got to stay alive for? Those words had been scribbled in black marker on the wall of the kids' motel room. They hadn't made sense until he realized such terrible handwriting could only belong to one kind of person.

"I'm an antisocial old spinster," Dr. Larkin had joked. *"What have I got to stay alive for? Social night down at the church?"*

He squealed to a stop in front of the small Presbyterian church and jogged up to the sign advertising social nights every Friday at nine o'clock. He wasn't sure what he was looking for, but as he ran his fingers along the cracks of the illuminated sign, he found it. Half of a paper drinking straw folded off at both ends. Inside he found a roll of paper with a phone number written on it.

Augy loped up the stairs of the church and tried the handle. The door swung open. A young woman in a blue and white housedress with a bandana tied over her mousy hair was mopping the hallway. She looked up like a deer in the headlights as he entered.

"Can I use your phone?" he said. "It's an emergency."

"Sure thing..." she stammered. "It's..."

He followed her pointed finger into the office, picked up the receiver, and dialed in the number. Three rings later a mercifully familiar voice answered, "Hello?"

"Doc."

"Augy," she breathed. "Oh, thank Christ. Are you all right?"

"Not even a little bit."

"Listen, someone took the kids. I was out getting groceries and when I came back…"

"I know."

Her words came so quick they squished together. "I'm so sorry. I never should've left them alone. I just wanted a little break. This is all my fault."

"Where are you?"

"I'm in Cohen Dale. Can you come get me?"

He shook his head. The woman appeared in the doorway, her lips puckered. He cupped the phone with his hand and turned his back. "I have to go after Katya and the kids."

"They got Katya, too? Goddamn it. Come get me."

"You don't get it…"

"Oh, I get it." She inhaled harshly. "You. Need. Me. Why else are you calling?"

Augy sighed and pinched the bridge of his nose. "Give me the address."

Less than a block away he found her, standing in front of a bungalow with a white picket fence, her leather bag clasped in her hands. It looked filled to the bursting.

She climbed in, her eyes pouring over his new wounds. "What happened to you?"

He didn't answer. Even before she'd closed the door he had the car in gear.

"I got some supplies." She rooted through her bag and took out an aluminum case about the size of a trade paperback. Opening the lid revealed eight identical syringes, which had been filled and capped.

"What are they?"

She winked. "Copesetic."

She twisted her long gray hair into a bun and secured it with a pencil, then dove back into the bag. "Here." She held out a glass capsule no bigger than a pea.

"What the hell is that?"

"Potassium cyanide."

"What am I supposed to do, chuck it at her?"

"It's for you," she said somberly. "In case you get captured. I have one, too, and three more. Just in case."

"Jesus. That's grim."

"It's better than the alternative," she said with a shrug. "Keep it in your cheek. If you accidentally swallow it, it will pass through your system. But if you get caught, bite it open. You'll be dead in five minutes."

"Give me the other three," he said, and she did. Grimacing, he tucked one in the pocket of his gums, then wrapped the others in his handkerchief and stuffed them in his jacket pocket. "I thought you said you were just a small-town doctor. How the hell did you get these?"

"I have an ex-boyfriend who's a chemist."

"You seem to have a lot of ex-boyfriends."

She grinned. "I never like to completely cut them loose."

Ten minutes later, he pulled the car onto the shoulder and cut the engine. Stepping out, he lit a cigarette and gazed at the skid marks on the road he'd made that first night he crashed into Katya. It felt like a lifetime ago.

He'd checked the address cards he'd gotten off Johnny Chiba, but nothing fit. The only way he knew to get to the mansion was by backtracking from the sinkhole. The sun had started its descent over the hills, but it was one of those gray sunsets. The kind where the sun boils away without fanfare, leaving dull red mist in its wake. At least he was smart enough to bring a flashlight this time.

He also took along the pistol, the AK47, the Ithaca Model 37, and the M1 carbine. The pistol had three bullets. There was one magazine for the AK. The Ithaca was fully loaded with seven additional shells in the strap. The carbine had half of a 30-round cartridge. He shoved the pistol in his sock suspender and slung the AK over his shoulder. The other two he brought along in a duffle bag.

The underbrush had overgrown any evidence of Katya's mad dash to freedom, and the forest bed was clothed in a new layer of leaves. Nature recovers effortlessly from trauma. He shouldered the doctor's massive bag and led the way into the forest. The thorny bushes nipped at their clothes. It didn't bother him so much in his dungarees, but Dr. Larkin, in her clamdiggers and short-sleeve blouse, kept cursing.

After trekking half an hour, the click and whistle of bats started in, followed by the rhythmic trill of crickets, and the dull timber of frogs—exactly as it had been that first night. He was able to hold off the memories, but emotion burst through his mental blocks as if they were made of tissue paper.

His hands grew clammy and the flashlight quavered in his grasp. He tasted old blood, felt it coat his face and hands. The squish of dead flesh beneath him.

The stream announced itself with giggles and idle gossip. Pleasant and pointless. Augy sat down to remove his shoes.

"Is this really the time for a dip?" Dr. Larkin huffed.

"We need to follow the river." Augy looked back at her. Her face was crimson, legs unsteady, chest heaving with every breath.

"Are you all right?" he asked.

She plunked beside him on the boulder and rummaged through her bag until she found a canteen. "You remember that whole thing about me dying?"

He nodded.

"Well, it makes physical exercise a bit of a pain." She took a long gulp of water, then wiped her mouth on her sleeve.

"Go back. Please."

"No, no." She bent to untie her shoes. "If you can manage in the state you're in, I'll be fine."

"But I'm a whippersnapper, remember?"

"Hardly. What are you, almost forty?"

Augy sighed like an old exhausted horse. "Where'd you learn math?"

"How much farther is it?"

"I've never actually been there." He shrugged and lit a cigarette. His last cigarette. Crushing the pack, he tossed it into the stream. It landed a foot from where he'd thrown his empty pack that first night. The old one was still there, saturated with mud. A dragonfly perched atop it.

Dr. Larkin clung to his jacket as they made their way over slippery river stones, never mind he already felt as if he'd fall over with the load he was carrying, and his injured foot, and his cracked ribs, and vision obscured by his swollen left eye. Augy was coming to appreciate he really did have an impressive tolerance for physical pain. If only he could get better at avoiding it.

They came to the waterfall, cheery and sparkly in the starlight. Augy stepped onto the shore and put on his shoes. He helped Dr. Larkin with hers, and led her up the steep incline, through the thorny bushes and cactus grass. He would've warned her what they were about to see, except he hadn't smelled the sickly sweet putridness of dead flesh baking in the sun. And as they crested the pile of boulders, he understood why.

The sinkhole had been filled in. Just another pile of jagged rocks in the craggy mountains now. The tracks of an excavator were obvious.

The cops had never come down here to look for the sinkhole. The guys upstairs were responsible for this. He could only hope some of them had been at that party.

As they continued along the path, he choked on a grim reality. Several identical rock piles dotted this section of the woods. Following in the direction they led, he counted. Three at first, then four more. He tried to stop his brain from doing the math, but it went ahead without him. Eight sinkholes—one for each year the Countess had been in California. One for each of her parties. And each was filled with a dozen bodies or more, meaning about a hundred anonymous souls were trapped inside the mountain being crushed into oil.

This would've been Sumika's grave, too. If Katya hadn't run away. If Augy hadn't hit her with his car. If she hadn't come back to ask for his help, and if he hadn't refused.

He didn't say anything to Dr. Larkin, but she was a smart lady. She knew about the sinkhole. So, when she grabbed his arm with both hands and said, "We're going to stop her," he knew what she meant.

And then he smelled it. The stink of decomposing flesh. Scanning the horizon, he caught sight of a small excavator truck, lonely in the moonlight, its engine cold. A pile of dirt lay beside it, a deep hole in the front. Augy didn't need to look to know what was inside.

Had the Countess thrown an impromptu soiree to boost morale after what happened at Dr. Hoffman's masquerade? Augy had to force himself not to think about it or risk tumbling into a bottomless pit of shame.

Passing the excavator, he peered into the cab. The key was in the ignition. He let it be.

Not unlike the Lumbermill, the mansion seemed to be protected mainly by secrecy, isolation, and the assumption that nobody who could change anything would give a damn. They'd come across no electric fences, no armed guards. When he popped his head through a break in the trees and saw the lonely, rectangular building lifted on stilts above a rugged canyon, he knew the Countess's list of allies and subordinates was growing thin. Perhaps, he should've been cheered by this, but he wasn't. However beweaponed he may have been, he was only one man. One deeply damaged, *not-nearly-as-clever-as-he-should-have-been*, psychoneurotic man. And Dr. Larkin, though brilliant, resourceful, and bold, was only a terminal sexagenarian. If the Countess were at ten percent efficiency, she still had the upper hand.

But there was no going back. One last dance with death, and then a wallflower forever.

The house was the kind of thing you'd see on the cover of Architectural Digest. A rectangular box fashioned of glass as clean as a monomaniac's asshole floating above a sharp canyon. It was intersected by two long balconies, which stretched unsupported over the chasm, daring gravity to have at. The ground floor comprised a parking garage and what appeared to be a garden area, which was open to the elements. What might've been called the main floor was propped up on stilts above. Wildness flanked geometry, creating an incongruity oddly appropriate of the Countess. Science, supported by capricious passion.

He wondered if there were a basement. Most LA homes didn't have one, for whatever reason. The Countess used her house for entertaining investors and suppliers, plying them with the one thing their money couldn't always buy—young and bound flesh. She had to keep them somewhere, and it was hard to imagine she would suffer *logs* to be housed on the same floor with her, even temporarily.

No, there had to be a basement.

"I hate modern architecture," groaned Dr. Larkin.

A laugh bubbled up his throat like a belch. "Of all the things to bitch about."

He brought the binoculars to his eyes. A motorbike was parked in the garage, alongside only one car—a Bentley R-Type Continental in ocean gray. The windows of the building were mainly dark, black roller shades drawn over the walls of glass. But one room at the far corner of the house was verdant with soft light. Much of the view was obscured by lush greenery, but he discerned the outline of chairs and side tables. On the wall was a massive painting. He turned the wheel on the binoculars to bring it into focus. A renaissance style oil canvas—dark colors, lush fabrics, pale skin. The subject was an old woman, her yellow face furled with deep wrinkles. She was in the process of cutting off a young man's head, one hand holding his hair as the other wielded the knife. His blood had a life of its own, soaking her hands and apron, spraying towards the viewer, his face twisted in horror. A younger woman stood over the murderess's shoulder, scrutinizing the scene like a student.

A screen of smoke rose in front of the painting. He followed it down to a highbacked chair facing away from the window. A hand overhung the armrest, small, delicate, nimble-fingered. He knew those hands. The way the thumb pulled back like the legs of a paratrooper on a jump, the sharp angles of the fingers like the limbs of a naked tree in winter. Those were trained hands. Surgeon's hands. A cigarette was stuck in the fold between the middle and ring fingers—the way you smoke so you can type or write at the same time.

It made him sick to think he sometimes held his cigarette the same way she did. To have anything in common with her.

"How the hell am I supposed to get up there?" said the doctor.

"You don't need to."

She groaned. "How the hell are you going to get up there? And even if you do, how are you going to get them out?"

He shrugged and showed her his patent-pending, Augy Small shit-eating grin. "I've never driven a Bentley before."

"If you aren't back out here in half an hour, I am coming after you."

"Half an hour?"

"That's how long I figure it'll take me to get up there."

Augy smiled indulgently. "Doc..."

"And I don't want to hear any damn arguments. I'm already a dead woman walking. If anybody is going to do something brash and stupid, it's going to be me."

"You are one stubborn old bird," he snorted.

She hugged him, her skinny limbs like wires around his back. "Be careful."

"Not really my MO, Doc."

"Well, change your MO, you dumb son of a bitch."

"Tomorrow," he said. "I promise."

Augy tossed the duffle bag over one shoulder and jogged up the hill towards the mansion. The easiest way in was through the driveway, so there was a good chance it would be guarded. He sneaked around the back. When he saw window wells peeking up from under the ground floor, he knew he'd been right about the basement. But when he used the binoculars to get a closer look, he saw they were all covered with iron grates. Six in all, they only ran under one half of the house.

The open area on the ground floor contained a large L-shaped pool with a wet bar, a narrow outdoor dining table, and what looked like a lounge, with a stage and mic-stand, surrounded by dozens of circular tables and wicker chairs. A heavy wall of glass—which he assumed was bulletproof—separated the patio from the parking area, and from a key-operated elevator, which was the only way up to the main floor. The two balconies stretched out like planks of a pirate ship over the deep, jagged canyon, one right on top of the other. There were no railings.

The sliding glass doors leading inside from the top floor balcony were open.

Seeing as he wasn't a monkey or a kung fu master, this information seemed irrelevant at first. Even if he did manage to steal across the lounge and dining area out onto the lower balcony without being seen, the upper balcony was another twelve feet straight up. Then he saw a dessert cart poised at the edge of the space, not far from the head of the long slender dining table. Made of solid steel, it looked to be about five and a half feet tall.

It was an insane idea. One false move and he and the wheeled cart would go plummeting into the ravine with nothing but screams to mark their departure. Even if he did manage to scale the balcony, but knocked the cart off, it's plaintive clank as it bounced down into hell would wake every living being in a ten-mile radius. On the other hand, the door was open.

Augy kicked himself for never learning how to pick a lock. He blamed the Boy Scouts. They taught him how to paddle a canoe up white water rapids, how to identify every species of bird in Southern California from fifty yards, and how to cook a damn porcupine with a magnifying glass, but they never imagined any cornfed American boy might accidentally lock himself out of his apartment? Disgraceful.

He took a few deep breaths and rubbed some warmth into his stiff hands. He was about to make a mad dash for the cart when the door of the upper balcony whooshed open. Augy cursed silently and ducked into the bushes. A figure's shoes ticked as they sauntered out towards the edge. Augy craned his neck, using the binoculars to try to see their face, but the angle was all wrong. All he saw were white work shoes and a gray Mao suit.

His heart leaped into his throat, threatening to throttle his brain. There she was—alone, exposed, with a perfect corpse disposal apparatus yawning beneath her. Gingerly, he drew the AK from his shoulder and leveled the shot. A few bullets in the torso would do the job. It would be so easy. His finger caressed the trigger.

CHAPTER FORTY-TWO

Eight mass graves. Four hundred and fifty cells. Eight years. No, more than that. Fourteen years. Maybe as many as twenty. And thousands of people. Tens of thousands. Tortured for weeks, months, years. And he was going to repay this with a few seconds? It didn't add up.

If he'd believed in hell, the equation would be different. If sinners got their comeuppance in eternity—skewered by devils, floating in rivers of flaming shit, and all that horrific poetry—execution would seem a fitting punishment. After the bullets plunged into her, and she screamed her last scream, drew her last breath, and that cold heart pumped its final load of blood, the real punishment would begin.

But that was a medieval fantasy. When you don't believe in God, you can't see death as a punishment. It's an inevitable part of the journey every living thing must make—good or evil, just or unjust, human or animal. It didn't matter. Yes, it would stop her. If he squeezed the trigger, she would never hurt another soul. But hell would remain just as empty as heaven.

"It is justice that is lacking in the world," he whispered, and there was no justice in simply killing her, no taste of vengeance. He knew death well. Death was always with him, waiting in the hall. How many times had he begged for its merciful embrace? How often had he been ready to leap into those comforting arms, bury himself in them, and let the world be forgotten?

Augy lowered the gun. It was too kind. Too egalitarian. She had to suffer, and she needed to know she was suffering because of him. Because of Katya. And Sumika. And Lily. And every single person who had ever born her mark, dead or alive. Granted, he lacked the stomach to do to her what she truly deserved, but he would find a way to repay dread for dread, horror for horror, and dark for dark.

If only he knew what she was afraid of.

The memory of her scream when he lit her research on fire warmed his body from the inside out like hot chocolate on a winter's day.

He knew exactly what she was afraid of.

She lingered for what seemed like an eternity, sipping a tall glass of red wine. He forgot to blink watching her. Silver lightning flickered at the corners of his eyes. She was so stiff. She didn't need railings on her balconies because she was a creature incapable of leaning. Her body was a corpse that didn't know it was dead yet.

He heard her sigh. He was that close.

She walked back inside, closing the balcony door behind her. The outdoor lights switched off. Augy closed his eyes, which scorched even more than leaving them open, and stood immobile for the space of fifty breaths. The shrill pulse of crickets tore at his underbelly, but it gave him an idea. Once he felt confident the Countess was not going to return to her perch, Augy circled around to the grate-covered windows at the back of the house. The basement. He realized now that if the basement were simply a holding area for *logs*, there would be no windows. She liked to create a controlled environment for her prisoners. No, these had to belong to other types of people—people she considered to be human, even of the lowliest sort: servants quarters.

However, there were only windows under one side of the house, leaving plenty of space for a prison. It was his best bet.

After stashing the bag in the bush, he snatched up a long piece of deadwood. Crouching by the window at the corner, he slipped the stick between the bars and scraped on the glass, working the angle until that nails-on-a-chalkboard screech sounded. He kept it up five minutes, scratching a few seconds, then waiting, and so on. A random inconstant pattern like the wind or an animal might make, but enough to be maddening.

At last, an echoic metal click sounded. Augy took his stick and dashed into the foliage. Peering between the spines of a wild rose, he saw a hatch open in the ground right beside the house. He hadn't noticed it in the dark. The stream of light burrowed into the night, followed by a man with the physique of a bodybuilder. He only stood five and a half feet tall but was double Augy's weight in pure muscle. He was dressed in pajama pants and boots, his chest bare. He rested the flashlight on top of a .45 hand cannon. He made his way towards the window to investigate the irritating sound.

Augy fingered the Ka-Bar in his pocket. After the blood geyser that happened last time he used a knife, he wasn't keen. But he couldn't use the gun either. This needed to be done quietly. He uncapped one of the doctor's syringes and put it between his teeth.

He tossed the stick he'd used to scrape on the window. It rustled a bush nearby and landed with a light thud. The flashlight turned along with the barrel of the gun. The man crept forward.

The bodybuilder passed within a foot. Augy popped up from his hiding spot and clapped him on both ears as hard as he could. The man staggered and started to fall. Augy stabbed the syringe into his neck and pushed down on the plunger. Almost instantly he began to seize, then fell to the ground.

Augy kicked the gun and flashlight out of his hands. He stood over him, watching listlessly until he stopped twitching. Augy picked up the flashlight and clicked it off, then stashed the revolver in his duffle bag.

Shouldering the bag of weapons, he climbed down the hatch into a concrete hallway. Doors lined the left-hand side, numbered from one to six. The door to number one was open half an inch—no doubt the home of the bodybuilder. Augy pushed it open and peered inside.

The apartment was illuminated by the soft light of a small table lamp. White walls with wood panel accents, stout-legged furniture, an open kitchen. A book lay open on the couch beside a plush throw. He picked it up and read the title: *The Thin Man*.

Augy's skin prickled. He didn't like to think of the people he killed doing ordinary things like reading novels. Especially not Dashiell Hammett novels.

His stomach turned, his greasy meal from earlier threatening to add color to the décor.

Throwing down the book, he searched the apartment for anything useful. Save a small collection of guns in the hall closet, the apartment was so normal it might've belonged to anyone. As he left he found the keys hanging on a hook by the door.

The hall continued another ten yards, past doors to five more apartments. Near the corner was the seventh door, but this was different. Pure steel, bolted by two keyed locks, and a padlock with a number wheel. The keys he found worked, but something told him the combination wouldn't be written down anywhere, even if he searched every square inch of the mansion. He'd have to get it out of someone's head.

He touched the final lock, and it bit at him like electricity. She was in there. He knew she was. But there was no choice. He had to go on.

He continued past a bend to the elevator, one of those open kinds with the decorative grate in front. Elevators are noisy, but an exhaustive search turned up no stairwell. It seemed odd, but then again, why would the Countess adhere to California building codes?

Rather than pressing the call button, Augy wedged the grate open and looked into the shaft. The elevator car was on the top floor. The shaft was fashioned of crisscrossing steel girders, the horizontal ones spaced about four feet apart and inches wide.

His broken foot, cracked ribs, and dislocated pinky were all in agreement, but they weren't in charge. His brain told him that calling the elevator would garner unwanted attention, and his heart assured him he could make the climb. It was only two floors, after all.

Leaving aside the duffle bag, he shoved the pistol back in his sock and tightened the strap on the AK. Cracking nine of his knuckles, he grabbed the first beam and started to climb. When he reached the car, he edged his way around the perimeter of the shaft until he was over the counterweight. He was able to squeeze his thin frame in the space beside the car. For the first time, being gangly was the thing that saved him. He was able to grip the top of the car with his long arms, then wriggle up like a lizard on a window. Once he was on top of the car, he opened the hatch and lowered himself in. The elevator car had doors on both sides. After catching his breath, he chose one at random, inched open the grate, and stepped out into a shadowy, empty room.

By what little light permeated the solar shades, Augy could see forms but no colors. The large space was set up like the lounge of a fancy hotel. A long curved wet bar transected the room, metal chairs docked along it like the legs of a centipede. Couches, chairs, and coffee tables shaped like painter's palettes filled the rest of the space. It smelled like a public bathroom—musty and stale. Lily Wong's description of the party she'd been forced to attend filled his mind. It was easy for him to imagine the Countess's gaggle of sadists in this room, sipping cocktails and eating canapes, exchanging their horrific anecdotes.

Since he didn't know where the Countess was now, he decided to first make his way towards where she had been: the room with the gothic painting and greenery. He followed a hall past what seemed to be a small ballroom, complete with a row of ultra-modern starburst chandeliers and a grand piano. Passing a formal dining area, he came to the room in the corner. Its door was opposite the elevator car; if only he'd chosen the other way.

He creaked open the door and shined his flashlight inside. What may have once been a spacious library was stacked floor to ceiling with file boxes, a veritable labyrinth of paper. All the research from the Lumbermill's archives had been brought here. Some of it was badly singed. The spot by the window in front of the painting was the only open area in the whole room: a chair and a peace lily shoved up in a corner. A glass ashtray sat on the floor with three cigarette stubs in it. Encores.

Surveying all the paper, the Zippo in his pocket felt like a bottle rocket about to pop, but Augy clenched a fist and shook his head. It wasn't time yet; she had to see it happen.

Augy turned to leave and a blast cut the air. He didn't feel it at first. Like when a baby gets pricked with a needle, they don't cry right away. Their brain has never experienced the sensation so it takes them a few seconds to process. That's what it was like. The shot echoed in his ears and reverberated down his skeleton. He saw the figure at the end of the hall—a gray suit and pinched lips. That uncanny smile.

The pain hit all at once. He stumbled.

CHAPTER FORTY-THREE

"Americans always seem to think being bold is an admirable quality," she said, stalking closer in her silent, sensible shoes until her gun was a mere foot from his head. Augy was on his hands and knees, gasping for every breath. The pain was like a blister, not unlike when she pressed that branding iron against his shoulder blade, burrowing in deeper and deeper with every beat of his heart.

"I'm afraid that's all Hollywood, Mr. Small. In the real world, it's not the good who die young. It's the bold." She chuckled dryly. "Though I suppose that's part of the point for someone like you."

"Why did you come here?" she asked. "I thought my present would finally inspire you to do as you were told."

He touched his side, expecting his hand to come up covered in blood, but the skin wasn't broken. Then he saw the cork bullet lying on the carpet not a yard away. It didn't change the agony he was in, but he probably wouldn't die from it.

Of course he wasn't going to die from it. She didn't want to kill him quickly any more than he did her.

He tried to speak, but his mouth filled with blood. He spat it on the ground.

"You're getting blood all over my carpet," she said, taking a step closer. "Normally, I'd be upset, but there's something about *your* blood. I don't think I'll even have it washed out. No. I'd like to watch it get crispy and brown over the coming months so I can be constantly reminded what's happening to the rest of you."

She crouched down in front of him. He sat back on his haunches and forced himself to meet her eyes. He wouldn't look away this time.

The edges of her lips tilted upward. She reached forward and touched the corner of his mouth, gathering his blood on one fingertip. Her tongue darted out to taste it. She closed her eyes and breathed an almost inaudible sigh. "You are a rare specimen, Mr. Small," she said, opening her eyes to meet his. "Like a prize stallion that's gone feral. It's a shame you're so irretrievably stupid."

The rumble of an elevator sounded at his back, followed by a cheerful ding. He could only watch the boots step out, listen to the rattle of guns.

"Take him to the vault," said the Countess, rising to her feet. "Let him see his beloved. I'll get scrubbed up and we can begin the surgeries. I think I'd like to start with the little boy."

There was no point in trying to beg or struggle. They stripped away all his weapons, including his lighter, his sock suspenders, and his belt. As they dragged him onto the elevator, he kept locked eye contact with the Countess, until at last, she looked away.

Why hadn't he just pulled the trigger? Or at least lit the damn fire? His father was wrong, always. About everything. There was no meaning in suffering and no justice in the world. By hesitating, by waiting for something better, Augy had killed himself and everyone else.

The elevator screeched open on the bottom floor, and they dragged him by his arms down the concrete hall through the door with all the locks. The inside was immaculate, two identical rows of small glass cells. They were all empty, except two. In one he saw Clemmie and Zychik, curled up together on the floor asleep, sharing body heat. And in the other was Katya. One side of her face was deep purple from bruises. She was wearing high-waisted pants and boots, but no shirt, just a white bra stained pink with blood. He caught a glimpse of her shoulder blade, the muscles pulsating red and black where her skin had once been.

She scrambled to her feet when she saw him. Screaming, she pounded on the glass, but he couldn't hear anything. It was soundproof.

The men opened the cell beside hers and shoved him in, then all four left, closing and locking the main door behind them. Katya rushed to the glass and pressed her hands against it. Her lips mouthed his name.

Augy crawled closer. The hot burning pain from the shot had transformed into a dull ache as if he'd been hit by a bat. It was more manageable. He rose to his knees and laid his hand against hers. "I'm sorry," he said, the bite of tears stinging his eyes. "I'm so sorry."

Her body drooped. She leaned her forehead against the glass, slowly melting into the floor as if someone were turning up the gravity.

"I wanted to save you," he said, even though she couldn't hear him, wasn't even looking at him. "I wish I were strong enough, or smart enough. But I always fuck it up. I am a miserable, arrogant, lonely man who has achieved nothing with his life. Who has nothing. Who believes in nothing." He touched the glass where her hair pooled against it, pretending he could feel its softness. "But I could've believed in you."

He set the top of his head against the glass and ran his tongue over the cyanide capsule tucked in his gums. The Countess wasn't going to let him touch Katya or the kids. And if he couldn't give them a merciful death, then he wasn't going to take one. Whatever the Countess did to him now, he had coming. Every. Last. Cut.

He spat the capsule out.

In his peripheral vision he saw the door creak open, and a figure slipped inside. He didn't bother to look up. What was there to see except another brainwashed crony, another man without compassion?

The door to his cell swung open, and a cold draft encircled him.

"You said you'd keep fighting with your last drop of blood," droned an emotionless voice. "Well, I still see blood."

Augy looked up. He saw a cardigan, an overstuffed pocket protector, that gerbil face. "Bill...?" he said, his chest swelling with hope. "What are you doing here? Why would you come to save me?"

"I'm not here for you, you self-important son of a bitch," Bill spat. "I'm here for Edith. You think she'd ever forgive me if I let you die?" He took a Colt Government from his belt and offered him the handle. "Get up, August. You have work to do."

Augy took the gun into his shaky hand, as one of the Countess's bodyguard's burst through the door. Bill shot him through the chest, but more followed. Augy was struggling to find his feet when a blinding, deafening volley sounded, and the front of Bill's head exploded.

His stiff body smacked the floor, eyes still open, searching. When they found Augy, his lips moved, but no sound came out.

Augy nodded. He understood.

Katya pounded on the glass, screaming to be let out.

The guard fired. Augy ducked behind the glass. Bobbing out, he shot twice, the gun shaky in his hands. The first missed, the second was glancing. Augy ducked behind the glass and counted backward from twenty-one by threes. He leveled the gun and pulled the trigger once more.

It clicked, empty.

"Motherfucker!" He threw it down and barreled towards the other man. Sliding like he was coming into home plate, he hit his ankles, downing him. Augy wrapped his spindly, awkward limbs around him and squeezed like a boa constrictor. He got his fingers on the gun and thrashed it from side to side. Augy headbutted him. The man fumbled the weapon. Augy slipped his finger through the trigger guard and lowered the barrel. When it touched skin, he fired three shots.

Augy uncoiled himself and looked down. He'd shot the man in the stomach. The gurgle from his throat was pure aural torture. Augy shot him between the eyes, and the room fell quiet.

He staggered to Katya's cell and opened the lock. She rushed past him to her children's cell and ripped open the lock. Falling to her knees, she embraced them. Her voice was so thick with emotion, he couldn't tell for sure which language she was speaking.

The quaking, sobbing children clung to their mother like a falling man to a branch. Katya lifted baby Zychik onto her hip, clinging to Clemmie with her other hand.

"*Bol'shoye spasibo*," she said, the sharp angles of her lips softening. The way she was looking at him, he almost felt her touch on his face.

Augy stepped out in front. He held the gun up near his face—a Smith and Wesson Model 29. Before they left the cellblock, he looked back at Bill. His face was frozen, perfectly pressed clothes soaking in a pool of blood.

"I won't tell her," Augy promised.

He did a quick check of the hall, then stepped out. Three men lay on the concrete. Two seemed dead, a third was twitching. The first two had bullet holes in them—Bill's victims. But the twitching one had a syringe stuck in his neck. In his hand was a lock of long gray hair, bloody at one end.

"Doc...?" Augy breathed.

An engine revved. Muffled, but close.

Augy loped down the hall towards the elevator. Pressing the call button, he threw open the grate and tumbled inside. Katya and the kids were close behind.

They reached the ground floor in time for them to see a Bentley disappear around a bend in the road. Augy threw open the grate into the garage, stumbling towards the only vehicle left—a BMW R68 motorcycle. He hadn't ridden a bike since high school, but there was no time for insecurity. He climbed on and revved the engine. Before he peeled out, he looked back at Katya. Her head was cocked to one side, her usually rigid body curved to support the weight of the boy on her hip. She looked so fragile for someone so strong.

"I'm in love with you," he said. Her golden eyes sparkled like midnight on New Year's. She gave an almost imperceptible nod.

"Burn the house down." Augy gunned the bike onto the drive. His hips slid back on the seat, back flattening, as the house disappeared behind him. The taste of the Bentley's smoke hung in the air.

The twisted mountain road kept his speed down. He whipped around corners as fast as he dared, his knees inches from the asphalt. Hot under him, the bike had a mind of its own. Every time the wheels skidded, he worried it would throw him.

He hit a sharp incline and the bike took flight. When it hit earth again, the impact shot excruciating pain through his entire body. He white-knuckled through until he saw the car on the horizon, fishtailing around a tight bend. Countess London had a lot of skills, but driving wasn't one of them. He laid on the gas. The sound of the engine engulfed him like armor. Faster. Closer. Almost.

No hesitation this time.

He came up alongside her and looked into the cab. Her frantic darting eyes, the way she chewed her bottom lip—it was all so delicious! He laughed like the raving lunatic he was, drew his gun, and fired at the front tire. He'd emptied the rest of the bullets before that brilliant pop sounded—a noise that filled up the night and his empty soul. Brakes squealed. Tires slid. The car fishtailed, then careened into the forest. The front bumper slammed into a thick tree, crumpling the hood like tissue paper.

Augy screeched the bike to a halt. He jumped off, letting the machine fall on its side in the middle of the road.

As he staggered nearer, the driver's side door popped open, and she darted into the woods. He jogged after her, growling and hissing. She stumbled over a branch, and he fell on her like a wild dog on a rabbit. She was no match for him in physical strength, no matter how wounded he was.

"Get off me!" she screamed, trying to fight back.

He wrapped his fingers around her throat and squeezed. But by the motorcycle's headlights, he saw it, lonely in the dim light. He let go.

Augy stood and dragged her by her hair up the hill towards the excavator. "The bold die young, you say. Maybe. But you seem to have forgotten something, Countess. This *is* fucking Hollywood!"

He threw her down into the hole. On top of the bodies she'd created. The filth. The death. The pollution.

"Let me out!" she shrieked and tried to crawl up the side, but it was slick with blood, and she stumbled. She fell face-first against a gaping putrid wound in the chest of a body.

The Countess gagged and pushed herself up, just as Augy picked up the scent of smoke. Looking over his shoulder, he saw the unmistakable glow of fire up on the hill. When he turned back, he saw that same fire reflected in those wedge-shaped eyes, growing wider, filling with ice and fury.

"No!" she screamed, making her best attempt yet to climb out. He put his boot on her face and pushed her back down.

"You can't do this!" she screamed. "You're putting medical science back by a century!"

"I don't know nothing about that," he said.

"Please." Her voice brimmed with something so similar to emotion, it sent a thrill up his spine. "I understand you have to kill me. Measured by your crude moral compass, what I have done is inexcusable. But please try to understand how many lives the information I've collected will save. I've killed thousands to get it, but millions will benefit for generations to come. Kill me if you must, but please spare my research!"

He crouched beside the hole to look at her straight and lowered his voice. "No one will ever know you were here. Your life had no meaning. Everything you did. You killed all those people, and nobody will remember you."

"You can't do this. The future is—"

"The future doesn't need you." Standing, he turned his back on her. He climbed into the excavator and turned the ignition. The engine roared to life, and the boom creaked as he gathered a scoop-full of dirt. Whirring back, he threatened it over her head.

"You can kill me and you can burn my research," she whispered coldly, "but it won't change anything. The structures are there, and others will follow me. The Lumbermill is still there. And you can't—"

"I suppose you missed the nightly news, eh?" he said, leaning out of the cab to look at her. "A friend of mine, Ed Gundy? You remember hearing about him. Well, I gave him that binder of yours, and he did an expose on it tonight. I doubt if the US government will be so keen on funding your brand of research after that."

Her eyes widened, and he was done talking. He let the dirt fall on her until her voice went silent. He layered stones on top of it until she couldn't have gotten out unless she had superpowers.

He prayed she didn't.

Augy felt nothing, no sense of justice or accomplishment. In seconds, the pain was creeping back in, deeper and deeper, more intense. He got the bike up and drove back towards the glow of the house. By the time he reached it, he was so dizzy he could hardly stand.

Red fire and black smoke poured out of every window. As he dismounted the bike, a man raced out of the blaze towards him, engulfed in flames. Augy shrank back, bracing for impact, but a gunshot sounded, and the man went down.

Katya lowered the pistol to her side, a silhouette before the fire. He saw the kids huddled behind her a couple of yards off. A skeletal figure was with them, strings of gray hair all around her face.

He staggered towards Katya and she towards him. When they met, he saw the fire reflected in her eyes. His lips parted, but no words would come.

She reached for him. Her hands touched his cheeks, drawing him closer. "Augy..." she said, and he sensed she was about to kiss him.

Sudden despair swelled in his chest and he stepped back. "Oh, gorgeous. This'll never work."

She lifted a brow and scanned his face. "What will no work?"

"You're too beautiful. I'll kill myself when you leave me."

"When?"

"That's right. When. I don't know if I mentioned, but I'm insane, and it ain't likely I'm gonna get better..."

"Augy..." She touched his chin and brought his lips to within inches of hers. *"Ya obozhayu tebya."*

Closing his eyes, he pressed his forehead against hers and whispered, "Are you finally gonna tell me what that means?"

"I adore you."

He kissed her, and it was everything. Butterflies, softness, sweetness, passion. Her lips were water to a desiccated man, fire to a hypothermic body. When his lips touched hers, he remembered that being alive didn't have to be painful. There was pleasure yet to be tasted: a beautiful world filled with experiences, smells, colors, feelings, and music. Every bit of pain he'd ever experienced was a curve in a massive labyrinth leading up to this moment. And he never wanted to dance with death ever again.

A sharp cry roused him from a dreamless sleep. She groaned and shifted beside him, but he touched her hip.

"I got him, gorgeous," he said. "Go back to sleep."

Rolling out of bed, he yanked boxers over his naked ass. The crib was a step away, pressed into a tiny closet. Parisian apartments weren't designed for such big families.

"Come on, monkey bone." Augy scooped up the wailing three-month-old and rested him against his shoulder. He didn't understand how the boy's twin sister managed to sleep through it, night after night. The boy woke up screaming every hour or so, but the girl kept snoozing, her little butt pushed up in the air, chubby cheek pressed against the mattress. Augy wondered if his son had screamed so much in the womb that his poor sister had no choice but to learn how to tune him out.

He had a feeling once his son figured out how to talk, he wouldn't shut up until the day he died. Augy couldn't wait to hear what he had to say.

He closed the door gently, bouncing the baby and patting his butt. By the time he got to the kitchen, the boy wasn't wailing anymore, just whimpering for his milk. Augy put the kettle on. The clock on the wall read four AM.

He sat down at the table to wait for the water—the longest four minutes of his day. Shuffling arose from down the hall, and a pale face appeared out of the darkness. She plopped down at the table with an undead sort of grumble. The red around her eyes had spread to the rest of her face and down her neck. Even her finger looked exhausted. The poor sensitive thing got less sleep than any of them. Every time one of the babies so much as coughed, she awoke in a panic.

"Does he really need to eat so often?" groaned Sumika.

"Yeah, he does." Augy grinned. "But just for another little while. We'll all be sleeping through the night again before you know it."

"Fat chance. You've never heard how Galina snores."

He chuckled. She'd grown so argumentative and moody in the last year, almost like a real teenager. Galina was a good influence on her.

He handed her the baby so he could pour warm water into a glass bottle and spoon in the powdered formula. The boy almost stopped squirming once he was in her arms. The baby loved Sumika more than any other human, except his mother, of course. The whole thing made Augy crack up because Sumika always looked at him like he stank. Which, to be fair, he did.

"Try to get some more sleep, angel," Augy said, taking the baby back. "I wish you'd use the earplugs."

The boy ate frantically, then passed out in Augy's arms like a boned fish. Augy lifted one limp leg and dropped it a few times, giggling. He kissed the baby and took him to his crib. There was no point in trying to get back to sleep. He had to be on a five-thirty bus to *Aéroport de Paris-Orly* to make his six-fifty flight to Lisbon. He'd be away from home for the next four days.

Augy knelt at his wife's bedside and touched her soft black hair. They'd waited to have sex until after they were married—eight months of cuddling, kissing, stroking, and talking—all as they trekked through the Soviet Union looking for the scattered members of her family. Being with Katya, learning everything about her, telling her secrets he thought he'd never tell anyone, and helping her remember how to find pleasure in her own body, had been the most intimate, sensual experience of his life. It hadn't been easy, and of course, it was ongoing. It still happened at times when they were making love, he'd touch her in a way that reminded her of something awful, and she'd withdraw or start crying. But she trusted him enough to tell him what was going on, or at least let him hold her until the feeling subsided. He tried not to pressure her to talk about her past. And when he had nightmares or flashbacks, and became a different person in a different time and place, she was there to help fight his demons. She was never afraid.

Their wedding had taken place two days after arriving in Paris. She was pregnant half an hour later.

Closing his eyes, he kissed her forehead and whispered, "I love you."

Katya moaned softly and reached for him. "Come back to bed."

"I gotta get to work."

Her eyes opened, white stars in the dim light. "I miss you."

"I miss you too, gorgeous."

"Do not forget to eat."

He kissed her, then grabbed his pressed uniform from a hook on the door and drifted out. He hated being away from his family for any amount of time, but flying was the only skill he had, and they needed money. Legitimate money, even if it was earned with a forged license under an assumed identity.

He donned his uniform, then put some ham and cheese in what was left of yesterday's baguette. As he waited for his coffee to heat up, he noticed an unopened letter from his sister on the countertop. They exchanged letters once a week, sometimes more. Augy tore the envelope and read the news. Murphy had won the spelling bee. Harry had bought a brand new De Ville. And what do you know, Edith had gotten her job back at Lockheed. He smiled and set down the letter, then stepped out onto the stoop for a cigarette.

The air was still cool, fresh from midnight rain. His fellow insomniac was already out there, drinking her lukewarm milky tea. He brushed some dead leaves off the concrete and sat down beside her.

"*Bonjour, mon ami*," she rasped.

"*Bonjour, Doc*," Augy returned. His French had come a long way in twelve months. "*Comment vas-tu?*"

"I'm fine. Up with *la luna* again, I see." She had a floral silk scarf wrapped around her head. She'd already lived a year longer than anybody expected, but the treatment was hard on her. She'd lost thirty pounds, and her skin was so sensitive she could only stand to wear fine silk. Augy was happy to provide anything she wanted. She deserved the best.

He lit his cigarette.

Dr. Larkin wrinkled her nose. "Aren't you ever going to give up that filthy habit?" She plucked a cigarette out of his pack and stuck it between her lips. "They're killing you."

"Yeah, yeah." He lit her smoke. "Toke up, hypocrite."

"*You* have a family to take care of."

"So do you."

She smiled and wrapped her shawl more tightly about her slight shoulders.

Augy glared at the smoldering cylinder in his hand. "Are you sure they're killing me? I mean, how quickly?"

"You won't make sixty."

He chuckled and took a drag. "Who the hell wants to be sixty?"

"Might not make fifty."

Sighing, he looked at the cigarette again.

"They're beautiful," she said, "your children."

"Very beautiful."

"All six of them."

"Six? Fuck me, that's right. Six."

"Where're you off to today then, *Capitaine*?" she asked.

"Lisbon."

Dr. Larkin made a noise like someone had farted on her omelet.

"Not a fan?" Augy chuckled.

"I hear it's a hellhole."

"Yeah, well…" Augy crushed out the cigarette and put on his cap. "I've been worse places."

Laya V. Smith is a dedicated history nerd and WWII buff, with a degree in the subject from the University of Utah. She lives in Salt Lake City with her husband, two children, and one beefy Labrador. *The Lumbermill* is her debut novel. To find out more about Laya, please visit layavsmith.com.

NOTE FROM THE AUTHOR

Word-of-mouth is crucial for any author to succeed. If you enjoyed *The Lumbermill*, please leave a review online—anywhere you are able. Even if it's just a sentence or two. It would make all the difference and would be very much appreciated.

Thanks!
Laya

Thank you so much for reading one of our **Noir Fiction** novels.
If you enjoyed the experience, please check out our recommendation
title for your next great read!

Twist of Fate – A Jack West Novel by Deanna King

"...reads like a good Netflix crime series."

–Samantha Calimbahin, *Panther City Media Group*

View other Black Rose Writing titles at
www.blackrosewriting.com/books and use promo code
PRINT to receive a **20% discount** when purchasing.

9 781684 335282